THE
SLEEP
OF
REASON

THE *STRANGERS AND BROTHERS* NOVEL-SEQUENCE BY C. P. SNOW

STRANGERS AND BROTHERS

THE CONSCIENCE OF THE RICH

TIME OF HOPE

THE LIGHT AND THE DARK

THE MASTERS

THE NEW MEN

HOMECOMING

THE AFFAIR

CORRIDORS OF POWER

THE SLEEP OF REASON

C. P. SNOW is also the author of *THE SEARCH*

VARIETY OF MEN

THE TWO CULTURES AND THE SCIENTIFIC REVOLUTION

SCIENCE AND GOVERNMENT

THE
SLEEP
OF
REASON

C. P. SNOW

NEW YORK

CHARLES SCRIBNER'S SONS

El sueño de la razón produce monstruos.

The sleep of reason brings forth monsters.

This is Goya's title for one of his *Caprichos*, inscribed on the etching itself.

CONTENTS

THE
SLEEP
OF
REASON

I
TRICKS OF TIME

VISIT TO
A GRANDFATHER

That afternoon I had been walking with my son in what for me were familiar streets, streets of the town where I was born. I had taken him there only once before, when he was an infant. Now he was nearly fifteen, and we spoke the same language. I was taunting him because he had seen the "pretty England" and nothing of the rest, until that afternoon he had never seen a provincial town like this. He grinned. Whose fault was that? he said.

And yet the town was not so unpretty: shops glittered and shone, well-dressed women walked the pavements, fresh-skinned girls in their spring frocks: cars jarred and halted, bumper to stern, hoods dazzling in a burst of sunshine. Once I had heard a fellow citizen called Sawbridge saying, with equal disapproval of the United States and his native town, that you could put the place down in the middle of America and no one would know the difference. It was nearly accurate, not quite. You could still, if you knew your way about, trace some of the streets of the old market town: narrow harsh streets with homely names, like Pocklington's Walk, along which I had gone to work forty years before, craving not to be unknown, craving to get out of here. That I did not explain to my son Charles, who was discreetly puzzled as to why we were wandering through a quarter which, to any unbeglamoured eye, was somber and quite unusually lacking in romance.

However, when we returned to one of the bright shopping streets, and someone greeted me by name, he did ask, after we had passed on: "What does that feel like?"

Probably it had not been an acquaintance from the past; this was 1963, and I had left the town for good in the late 'twenties: probably it was what Charles was used to, a result of photographs or the mass media. But he was perceptive, he guessed that being picked out in this place might pluck a nerve. Nevertheless, he was surprised by my reply.

"To tell you the honest truth," I said, "it makes me want to hide."

He glanced at me sidelong with dark searching eyes. He knew that, as a rule, I was not self-conscious and was used to the public life. He did not understand it. But if he didn't understand it, neither did I. I couldn't have explained what I had just said. It seemed perverse and out of character. Yet it was quite true.

Charles thought of pressing me, then decided against. The clock on the town hall said a quarter to four; it was time for us to make our way to my father's house, or, to be more exact, my father's room. Charles had seen his grandfather only once, on his one other visit to the town, when he was three years old. To anyone outside, that must have sounded as though we had been heartless, not only without instinctive ties but without responsibility. After all, I had been lucky, my wife and family lived a privileged life. How could I bear neglecting the old man? In fact, my father had his own views. He seemed, and was, the most affable and gentle of human beings. But he just wanted to be left alone, to get on with his own mysterious concerns, whatever they were and if they existed. My brother Martin had tried to persuade him to live with them in Cambridge: I had wanted to have him in London. Not a bit of it. With simple passive resistance, he refused to move. He would not even take money. I had made more than enough, but he would not accept a penny, except for a

bottle of port at Christmas. With his old-age pension and the
rent from his lodger, he had, he said, quite enough for his
needs.

He was, I thought, the most self-sufficient man I had come
across. He was amiably and genuinely uninterested in his
grandchildren. Even that afternoon, I had had to force him
to let Charles and me come to tea. I was having to pay visits
to the town every three months or so, on a piece of minor
duty. This particular visit coincided with Charles being at
home on holiday. So I had brought him up for the day, and
had insisted that my father invite us. After all, he was in his
late eighties: I had my share of piety (from which my father
seemed singularly free), and it might be Charles's last chance
to talk to him.

We took the bus out to the suburbs, on what in my childhood would have been the old tram route. Red brick, the jail,
the gasworks, less change here than in the middle of the
town. And when we got off and walked into the back streets,
there was less change still: the doctor's house, the cluster of
shops, the chapel, the terraced houses up the rise. Not that I
was stirred by memory: I had seen it too recently for that.
Instead, I looked up at the clouds, low on the southwest
wind, breathed in the soft spring air, and said:

"I like this Atlantic weather."

"Meteorological fiend," said my son, with a friendly gibing
smile. He had developed the theory that I, the child of cities,
could not resist an obsessive interest in climatic phenomena:
and that this was not shared by all who heard the results,
including himself. It was the kind of sarcastic banter that
came easily to him. I answered in kind, pointing out that
at least one person had shared my meteorological enthusiasm,
and that was one of the few men whom I actively detested.

He was smiling, as we went past the two-storey terrace,
front doors opening onto the pavement. It was no use preparing him for what he was going to meet: he would certainly

find my father odd, possibly a strain, but that he would have to take. At the end of the row we came to a pair of larger houses, joined together: I pointed to the nearer one, and told him that was where I was born. It was dilapidated, but, to judge from the television aerials on the roof, inhabited by a couple of families. On the strip of earth inside the railings— which my mother used to call the front garden—the laburnum tree had become a blackened stump.

With a concentrated gaze, Charles studied the front-room window, the peeling paint, the carved inscription between the houses, *Albert Villas 1860,* and said nothing at all. Then he asked:

"Could we go in, do you think?"

"I don't think so, do you?"

"Perhaps they wouldn't like it."

The next house along the road had been built in the same period, but was larger and stood on its own. In my childhood it had belonged to my Aunt Milly's husband: he had been a building contractor in a small way, and they were less poor than we were, and had often (offending my mother's pride) been obliged to support us. When my mother died, by this time nearly forty years before, my father had gone to live with Aunt Milly, who was his sister. There he had stayed. Aunt Milly's husband died, then she herself. They were childless, and, though she had willed their savings to various temperance societies, the house had come to my father. He had promptly let it off, keeping one room for himself: and there he had lived for the last twenty years.

I led the way to that single room—down an entry, through a gate, into a yard paved with flagstones. The architecture of Aunt Milly's house, like that of my mother's, was bizarre, as though space didn't matter and the more levels the better, so that there was a one-storey range, with a twenty-foot-high chimney, floors at yard-level: while five steps up was a French window, opening straight into my father's room, which led into the main body of the house. Behind the French window one could see a glow on the ceiling, fluctuating, not very bright although the afternoon was dark, which must come from my father's fire.

"There he is, I expect," I said to Charles.

We went up the steps, and I rapped on the window. (There was a much quicker and more orthodox method of entry through the front door, but my father did not like being a trouble to his lodger.) Shuffle of steps. Rattle of handles. The two sides of the window opened and, in between them, facing us, my father stood.

"Well, I declare," he said.

His first action was to peer up at Charles, making tunnels with his fingers over his spectacles as though sighting some far distant object.

"I shall want a telescope to look at him," my father said.

I was six feet, and Charles, at fifteen, was only an inch or two shorter. My father was a little man. In my childhood he had claimed to five feet four; but now, with extreme old age, he had shrunk an inch or more. Standing there, old wide trousers flopping on his boots, his head seemed to come no higher than our chests.

"I want a telescope, that's what I do." He went on clowning. He had always clowned, as far back as I could remember; he had been cheerful in his clowning then, just as he was now.

After we had sat down in the crowded little room—Charles on a chair on one side of the fireplace, my father on the other, me on the sofa where he slept at night—he was still talking about telescopes, but in a different vein.

"You know, Lewis, I've always thought I should like one."

I asked him why: I knew that tone by heart.

"Well, you never know what you might find out."

He had daydreamed all his life. Just for an instant he was the supreme astronomer, discovering—at an advanced age and to his own mild surprise—new secrets of the universe. Or perhaps overturning established conceptions, an activity for which he had always had a secret fancy. All through my boyhood he had read travel books, often the same book over and over again: then he was the fearless single-handed explorer, going where no white man had ever trodden—he had a special feeling that the Amazonian jungle was the place for him. I had discovered, on my last visit, that he still borrowed travel-books from the library at the corner of the road. As he sat in his chair, I could see a dozen or so books on the shelf behind him: they seemed the only books in the room, the only ones he possessed or had borrowed. How many of those were about travel? Or what other sort of daydreams did he have?

"You never know what you might find out," he chortled. "But I expect I should find out something wrong!"

He went on chortling with satisfaction. He hadn't spoken out of self-pity, or at least, if he had, it was a singular kind of self-pity, which consisted of referring to himself as though he were the most ludicrous of jokes.

He was, as usual, happy. Sitting beneath the mantelpiece, on which stood a marble clock flanked by photographs, some of the choral society of which he had been secretary so long, together with one of my mother, he did not look his age. His hair was white, but he had lost none of it: his great drooping moustache still, amid the white, kept a touch of ginger: the lenses of his spectacles, which he could not manage to put on straight, had not been changed since middle age. His pop eyes remained innocently amused. By some genetic fluke, he had missed the deep blue irises which were dominant in the family: his father had had them and all the rest of us: Charles's, as he watched my father vigilantly across the fireplace, in that light looked not indigo but black. My father's had not faded, but were very light, which made him appear more innocent. Sitting down, he also appeared bigger than he was, since his legs were short and his head out of proportion large.

A kettle was boiling on the hob between them. My father had so far paid no attention to Charles, except once or twice to address him, with impersonal cheerfulness, by my Christian name or my brother Martin's. Charles, on the other hand, was paying complete attention to him. Charles had met a lot of people, some formidable, many what the world called successful: but his grandfather was different from any. This was a test, not only of instinctual ties, but also of insight. At the same time, Charles, I had no doubt, was listening to my father's soft midland accent, of which Charles could hear the vestigial overtones in me.

"Well, young man," said my father, abandoning nomenclature as he spoke to Charles, "I expect you're ready for your tea, aren't you? I know I am."

Politely Charles admitted that he was.

"I'm always ready for my tea," said my father. "If I can't do anything else, then I can always get rid of my tea."

He hooted with obscure gratification, and sang a few bars of a song I didn't know, in a voice still disconcertingly strong. Efficiently, neat-fingeredly, like a man used to looking after himself, he made the tea.

"One, two, three spoonfuls—and one for the pot," he chanted. He shuffled round the room, and produced the tea things. He produced also a large plate of cakes, jam tarts, custard tarts, éclairs, marzipan. "I always say," my father remarked, "there's nothing like something sweet to your tea."

I did not agree, but Charles did. He might be perceptive beyond his years, but he had a healthy fifteen-year-old appetite: and so, while I drank a cup of tea and smoked a cigarette, the grandfather and grandson, with over seventy years between them, sat on opposite sides of the fireplace—in silence, except for appreciative lip-noises under the moustache—eating cakes. Not just one cake each, but two, three, four, half a dozen.

When they had finished the plateful, my father sighed with content and turned mild eyes on me.

"You made a mistake there, Lewis. They went down all right, confound me if they didn't."

Then he seemed to feel that some concession was called for.

"Still," he said, "you've got on well, I must say that."

He had, I was sure, only the haziest notion of my life. He may have realized that I had played some part in affairs: he ought to have known that I was no longer poor, for I had told him so. Certainly he had never read a word I had written. Charles, still vigilant, was wearing a surreptitious smile. Unlike my father, Charles knew a good deal about what had happened to me, the rough as well as the smooth. He knew that, since I left the official life, some attacks had followed me, one or two predictable, and one based upon a queer invention. Charles did not, as some sons would, imagine that I was invulnerable: on the contrary, he believed that this last situation he would have handled better himself.

"I often wish," my father continued, "that your mother had lived to see how you've got on."

Yes, I did too. Yes, I thought, she would have revelled in a lot of it—the title, the money, the well-known name. Yet, like Charles—though without the sophistication—she would have known it all, once again the rough as well as the smooth. Anyone who raised a voice against me, she, that fierce and passionate woman, would have wanted to claw, not as a figure of speech but in stark flesh, with her own nails.

"That's how I like to think of her, you know," my father said, pointing to the mantelpiece. "Not as she was at the end."

I got up, took the photograph down, and showed it to Charles. It was a hand-tinted photograph, taken somewhere round 1912, when they were a little better off than ever after, and when I was seven years old. She was wearing a dress with leg-of-mutton sleeves: her black hair and high coloring stood out, so did her aquiline beak of a nose. She looked both handsome, which she could be, and proud, which she always was, sometimes satanically so. As I remarked to Charles, it wasn't a bad picture.

What my father had said might have sounded sentimental, like a gentle old man lamenting the past and the only woman, the only happiness, he had ever known. On the contrary. My father was as little sentimental as a man could reasonably be. The truth was different. What he had said was a plain statement. That was how, when he thought of her at all—he lived in the present and their marriage was a long time ago—he preferred to think of her. But it had been an ill-tuned marriage: for her, much worse than that. He had been the "wrong man," she used to confide in me, and in my childhood I took this to mean that he was ineffectual, too amiable for the world's struggle, unable to give her the grandeur that somehow she thought should be hers by right. Later I thought, remembering what I had submerged, that there was more to it. I could recall bitter words over a maid (yes, on something like £250 a year before the First World War she kept a maid): I guessed, though I should never know for certain, that under his mild and beaming aspect there was a disconcerting ardor, which came as a surprise, though a pleasant one, to himself. As their marriage got worse, he had, when I was quite young, found his own consolations. Since she died, it had puzzled me that he had not married again. Yet again I guessed that in a cheerful covert fashion he had found what he wanted: and that, on a good many nights, he had returned to his little room raising his robust baritone with a satisfaction, as though singing meaninglessly to himself, which as a child I did not begin to understand.

Charles was still looking at the photograph. My father made an attempt to address him by name, gave it up, but nevertheless spoke to him:

"She always used to tell me, 'Bertie, don't be such a donkey! Don't be such a donkey!' Milly used to do the same. They always used to say I was a donkey!"

The reminiscence seemed to fill him with extreme pleasure. Charles looked up, and felt called upon to smile. But he gave me a side glance, as though for once he was somewhat at a loss.

The clock on the mantelpiece, in measured strokes, struck five.

"Solemn-toned clock," said my father with approval. "Solemn-toned clock." That was a ritual phrase which I must have heard hundreds, perhaps thousands, of times. When she was hopeful, and her hopes though precarious were inextinguishable, it used to make my mother smile: but in a crisis it made her break out in jangled nerves, in disappointment at all the hopes frustrated. That evening, however, the sound of the clock set my father going: now he was really on his own: so far as he had any self-esteem, here it was. For the clock had been presented to him after a period of service as secretary to a male-voice choir: and he had been secretary to similar choirs ever since, for nearly sixty years in all. This had been the theme of his existence, outside himself, and he proposed to talk about it. Which, with amiable pattering persistence, he duly did. It was all still going on. Not so flourishing as in the past. What with television—he had refused to let us buy him a set, though there was a sound radio in the corner of the room—people weren't so willing to give up the time as in the old days. Still, some were keen. There had been changes. Male-voice choirs weren't so popular, so he had brought in women. (That I had known; it had been the one political exertion of my father's life; it took me back for an instant to my speculations of a few moments before.) He had managed to keep a group of twenty or so together. Nowadays they met for rehearsal each Sunday after service at St. Mary's, one of the churches in town.

It was a quiet little obsession, but it gave him all the enjoyment of an obsession. I didn't want to cut him short, but at last he flagged slightly. I could ask a question. Wasn't St. Mary's a longish journey for him? It must be all of three miles.

"Oh," he said, "I get a bus that takes me near enough."

"But coming back late at night?"

"Well, one of our members, Mr. Rattenbury"—I wondered if Charles noticed that "Mr." which my father had applied to each of his male acquaintances all his life—"he usually gives me a lift."

"But if you don't get a lift?"

"Then I just have to toddle home on my own two pins."

He rose from his chair, and exemplified—without complaint, in fact with hilarity—very short steps on very short legs.

"Isn't that a bit much?" At his age, that was an understatement, but I couldn't say any more. Even at this, his face was clouded, and I wasn't going to spoil his pleasure.

"It's a bit slippy in winter, you know. But I get here. I shouldn't be here now if I didn't, should I?"

That struck him as the most clinching of retorts. He was delighted with it. It set him off chanting loudly: "Anyway— the — summer — is — coming — anyway — the — spring — is — here."

Then he seemed to feel that he had certain responsibilities for Charles which he had not discharged. He had given him cakes. Was that enough? My father looked puzzled: then suddenly his face shone with preternatural worldliness.

"Young man," he said, "I want to give you a piece of advice."

Charles leaned gravely towards him.

"I expect," the old man said, "your father gives you some money now and then, doesn't he?"

Charles misunderstood, and was a shade embarrassed. "I'm quite all right for money, thank you very much, sir."

"Of course you are! Of course you are! I'm going to give you a piece of advice that I gave your father a long time ago." Now I myself remembered: he had the memory for detail long past that I had seen before in the very old. "I always tell people," he said, as though he were daydreaming again, this time of himself as the successful financier, deferred to by less-experienced men. "I always tell people that you never ought to go about without a few pound notes sewn in a place where you're never going to lose it. I told your father a long time ago, and I hope he listened to me, that he ought to have five of his pound notes sewn into the seat of his trousers. Mind you, five pounds doesn't go as far now as it did then. If I were you, I should get someone to sew fifteen or twenty pounds into the seat of your trousers. I expect you can lay your hands on twenty pound notes, can't you? Well, you do what I tell you. You never know when they'll come in useful. You just think of me when you find they've got you out of a tight corner."

Charles, his face controlled, promised that he would.

My father exuded content. Charles and I stretched our legs, getting ready to go. When we were putting on our coats, opening the French window so that the evening air struck cold into the stuffy, odorous little room, I told my father that I would drop in during my next visit to the town.

"Oh, don't put yourself out for me, Lewis," he said, as though he quite liked my company but even more preferred not to be disturbed. With his beaming innocent smile he waved us out.

Charles and I didn't speak until we had emerged from the entry back into the road. There was a light, I noticed, two houses along, in what had been our old "front room."

It had been raining, the sky was bright again. Charles gave me a curious smile.

"Life goes on," he said.

I took him the longer way round to the bus stop, past the branch library, past the red-brick church (1900-ish, pitch-pine, and stained-glass windows, scene both of splendors and miseries for my mother), down the hill to the main road. From the grass in the garden-patches there came a fresh, anxiety-lifting, rainwashed smell. We were each of us silent, not uncomfortably so but still touched by the afternoon.

After a time, Charles said:

"It wasn't exactly what I expected."

"You mean, he wasn't?"

"No, I didn't mean that, quite."

I asked him another question, but he shook his head. He was preoccupied, just as I had been in the middle of the town, and this time it was he who did not want to be pressed.

On the top of the bus, on the way to the railway station, he made one reference to my father's practical advice, smiled, and that was all. We chatted on the station, waiting for his train: he was going home alone, since I had an appointment in the town next day. As we were chatting, quite casually, the station's red brick glaring at us, the sulphurous smoke swirling past, just for once that day, memory, direct memory, gave me its jab. I was standing in that station, years before, going to London, nerves tingling, full of hope.

The train was coming in. Charles's education had been different from mine, but he was no more inhibited than I was, and we hugged each other in the Russian fashion as we said goodbye.

TWO

A YOUNG WOMAN
IN LOVE

After leaving my son, I took a taxi to the Vice-Chancellor's Residence. In my youth, there wouldn't have been such a place or such a person: but in the 'fifties, the old College of Art and Technology, where I had once attended George Passant's lectures, had been transmogrified into one of the newest crop of universities. In fact, it was for that reason that I made my periodical visits to the town. The new university had adopted—out of an obstinacy that derived entirely from its Head—something like a Scottish constitution, with a small executive court, consisting of academics, local dignitaries, and a representative elected by the students: since I could, by a certain amount of stately chicanery, be regarded as an old member, they had elected me. I was happy to go there. For years I had been free of official business: this was no tax at all, it did not distract me from my work: occasionally, as in those for the next day, the termly agenda contained a point of interest. But I was happy really because I had reached a stage when the springs of my life were making their own resonances clear, which I could hear, sometimes insistently, not only with my family but with people I had known.

In the April evening, the taxi chugged along in the stream of outbound traffic, past the hedges and gardens of the prosperous suburb, the gravel drives, the comfortable bourgeois houses, the lighted windows. These were houses I had walked by as a boy: but to this day I had not often been inside. I

16

knew much poorer houses, like my father's, where I had been
an hour before: and, because of the way things had gone, I
had spent some time in recent years in grander ones. But
somehow that specific sector had eluded me, and with it a
slice of this comfortable, affluent town.

Was that why, as I stood outside the Residence and saw the
bright drawing room, blinds not drawn, standard-light by the
window, I felt a pang, as though I were an outsider? It
seemed so for an instant: and yet, in cold blood, I should
have known it was not true. I was still capable of walking
down any street, seeing a lighted window, and feeling that
same pang, which was made up of curiosity, envy, and desire:
in that sense, one doesn't age: one can still envy a hearth-glow,
even if one is returning to a happy home: it isn't a social
chance, but something a good deal deeper, that can at untam-
able moments make one feel forever youthful, and, as far as
that goes, forever in the street outside.

I went in, and became, as though a switch had been
turned, at home. Vicky Shaw greeted me. Yes, my bag had
been taken upstairs. Her father was, as usual, working late. I
was to come and have a drink.

Sitting in an armchair in the drawing room (which was
not at all magical, soft-cushioned but with tepid pictures on
the walls), I looked at her. Since her mother died, Vicky had
been acting as hostess for her father, although she had just
qualified as a doctor and had a job at the infirmary. She
was just twenty-four, not handsome, her face a shade too
equine to be pretty, and yet comely: long, slight: fair hair
swept back and knotted. I was very fond of her. She did not
make me feel—as on those visits, despite the time-switch
on the drive outside, I sometimes did—that I was an aging
man with a public face. And also, she had the special radi-
ance, and the special vulnerability, of a young woman for
the first time openly in love.

I expected to hear something of that. But she was direct

and often astringent; there was business to get through first. She was a devoted daughter, but she thought that her father, as a Vice-Chancellor, was a bit of an ass. His enemies were trying to ease him out—that she knew as well as I did. He was giving them opportunities. Tomorrow's case would be used against him, unless I could work on him. She didn't have to tell me about it: I had heard from the appellants themselves. A couple of young men had been found bedding a girl each in a room in one of the hostels. The Disciplinary Committee, which meant in effect Arnold Shaw himself, had next day sent all four down for good. They had appealed to the Court.

"He may get away with it there," Vicky said, "but that won't be the end of it."

Once again, both of us knew. He put people off. They said that he was a shellback, with no sympathy for the young.

"Of course," she said, "he was wrong anyway. He ought to have told them to go and do it somewhere else. But he couldn't say that, you know."

I found it impossible to keep back a vestigial grin. Arnold Shaw could bring himself to say that about as easily as John Calvin in one of his less-libertarian moods.

"Why in God's name, though," she said, "didn't he play it cool?"

Did she have to ask me? I replied.

Reluctantly, she smiled. She knew, better than anyone, that he was incorruptible: rigid: what he believed, he believed. If everyone else in the country were converted to sexual freedom, he would stay outside the swim: and be certain that he was right.

She put more whisky into my tumbler. She said:

"And yet, you know, he was a very good father to me. Even when I was little. He was always very kind."

"I shouldn't have thought you were difficult to bring up," I told her.

She shook her head. "No. I wasn't all that disciplined." She broke off: "Anyway, do your best with him tonight."

I said she mustn't bank on anything I could do. With a frown, she replied: "He's as obstinate as a pig."

There was nothing else useful to say. So, businesslike, she cut off short, and told me who was coming to dinner. It was a small party. The Hargraves, the Gearys—yes, I had met Hargrave on the Court, I knew the Gearys well—and Leonard Getliffe. As she mentioned the last name, I glanced at her. She had the delicate skin common among her own kind of blonde, and she had flushed down to the neckline.

Leonard Getliffe was the eldest son of my friend Francis, whom I had met almost as soon as I first went to London from this town: ever since, our lives had interweaved. But their connection with the university was no credit to me, only to Arnold Shaw. Since Francis gave up being an influence in Whitehall, at the time of Quaife's failure and mine, his scientific work had gone better than in his youth, his reputation had grown. And, though probably not as a consequence, he had recently been made a life peer. So Arnold Shaw, whose academic standards were as rigorous as his moral ones (and who, incidentally, was by no means averse to titles), had schemed for him to be the second Chancellor of the university: and for once Arnold had brought something off. He had brought something else off too, more valuable to the place: for he had persuaded Leonard, before he was thirty, to take a professorship. Leonard was, in the jargon of the day, a real flier. He was more gifted than his father: he was, so David Rubin and the others said, one of the best theoretical physicists going. All he needed was a bit of luck, they said, talking of luck exactly as people did in more precarious fields: then they would be tipping him for a Nobel prize. He might be more gifted than his father, but he was just as high-principled. He could do his theoretical work anywhere; why not try to help a new university? So, when

Arnold Shaw invited him, he had without fuss left Trinity and come.

Vicky was blushing. She met my glance, and her eyes were blue, candid, and distressed. It might have seemed that she was pining for him. In fact, the opposite was true. He was eaten up with love for her. It had happened a year before, almost as soon as they met, perhaps on the first day. He was begging her to marry him. Her father passionately wanted the marriage: the Getliffes would have welcomed it. All their children were married by now, except Leonard, their eldest and their particular star. The only person who didn't want the marriage was Vicky herself. She couldn't respond. She was a kind girl, but she couldn't see any way to be kind. Sometimes, when she saw him, she felt—there was no repressing it—plain irritated. Often she felt guilty. People told her this was someone of a quality she would never meet again: they told her she was interfering with his work. She knew it. For a while it had been flattering, but that wore off. Once, when I had been staying in the Residence, she had broken out:

"It's not fair! I look at myself in the glass. What have I got to produce this sort of passion? No, it's ridiculous."

She had little conceit. She could have done with more, I thought. She wanted to shrug the responsibility off, and couldn't. She was honest, and in some ways prosaic. But she didn't seem prosaic when she talked about the man she loved.

She had fallen in love herself—but after she had met Leonard Getliffe. The man she loved could scarcely have been more different from Leonard. I knew him, I knew him better than she did, or at least in a different fashion, for he was my nephew, Martin's son.

She wanted to tell me. Yes, she had seen Pat last week. In London. They had gone to ————. She brought out the name of a Soho restaurant as though it were embossed, just as she brought out the name of Pat. We had all done it, I thought:

the facts, the names of love are special facts, special names: it made the air bright, even to hear. But it also made the air uneasy.

After all, I was looking at him with an uncle's eyes, not with those of an adoring young woman. I thought he was an engaging youth, but I had been astonished when she became enraptured. To begin with, he was only twenty, four years younger than she was. True, he was precocious, and she probably the reverse. Yet I had seen my brother, a steady-natured man, but also a possessive father, trying to cope with that precocity. It had taught my brother what fatherhood could mean. Pat's name wasn't even Pat. He had been christened after me, but had renamed himself when he was an adolescent. He had rebelled against his first school, and been lucky to survive a second. Martin had managed to get him a place at our Cambridge college: he had given up after a year and gone to London to paint. How he managed to get support out of Martin or anyone else, I didn't know: but I thought there weren't many means that he would consider inappropriate. Had he any talent? Here for once Vicky, in the midst of her delight, became half-lucid. "I do hope," she said, "that he's as good as he wants to be. Sometimes I worry because he might get bored with it."

Then she asked me favors: could they come and see us at our London flat? Could I bring him down to the university sometime? She was innocent and shameless: yet anyone would have said that she was one of the stablest of young women, and it would have been true. That was why it was a liberation to abandon herself like this. If he arrived that moment, I was thinking, she would be proud to throw her arms round his neck.

I asked for another drink. With a shake of her head, coming back to other people's earth, she poured me a small one.

"Go slow on that," she said, tapping the glass, talking to

"Nothing contentious tonight," said Arnold Shaw, rubbing it in. "We're going to enjoy ourselves."

That was one of the inapposite remarks, I thought, as we went in to dinner, and I sat on Vicky's right hand. For Denis Geary, at any rate, despite his good manners, the night had become pointless. For his wife also: she spoke in a soft midland voice like my father's but was as firm as her husband. As dinner began, at my end of the table I had to exert myself to keep any sort of conversation going. And yet the meal was superb. Arnold Shaw indulged himself in food and drink; in the Residence both were better than at any private house I knew, out of comparison better than at great houses such as Basset. Dinner that night was as good as ever: borsch, whitebait, tournedos Rossini: while Arnold Shaw was jumping up and down, going round the table with decanters, buttling. There was plenty of buttling to be done: he loved wine, and was more knowledgeable about it than any of my old Cambridge colleagues: wine-drinking of that quality didn't happen nowadays among my friends.

The food and drink ought to have acted as a social lubricant. But they didn't. To most of the party they were an embarrassment. The Hargraves were rich, but they went in for austerely simple living. The Gearys weren't at all austere but didn't understand fine wine or the wine badinage that Shaw insisted on exchanging with me. I was a light eater, though out of politeness I was doing my best. Leonard was gulping down the drink, hoping to see Vicky before the night was over. As so often, Arnold Shaw could not put a foot right.

In fact, he was proceeding, I could hear down the table, to put two feet wrong. He at least was enjoying his meal, and even more his wine: he was not a heavy drinker, I had never seen him drunk, but alcohol made him combative. He was choosing the occasion to parade himself as an extreme reactionary; in particular, an extreme reactionary about education. He flourished his views, vigorous and bantam-bright, in front of the Gearys, who in the terms of that period believed the exact opposite, and the Hargraves, who spent their money on benefactions. "You're all wrong about education," he was saying. "Quite wrong. Education isn't social welfare. You're quite wrong about universities. A university isn't anything like what you think. Or it oughtn't to be." He went on, with a kind of ferocious jocularity, temper not far beneath the surface, making himself clear. A university was a place of learning. No more, no less. The senior members existed to add to knowledge. If they couldn't do that, they shouldn't be there. Some of them had to teach. The students existed only to be taught. They came to learn. They weren't there for social therapy. They weren't there to be made useful to the state: that was someone else's job. Very few people could either add to knowledge, or even acquire it. If they couldn't, get rid of them. He wanted fewer university students, not more. Fewer and better. This university ought to be half of its present size.

I heard Hargrave, who didn't speak often, say that he couldn't agree. I heard Denis Geary arguing patiently, and turned my head away. I met Vicky's frown, troubled and cross: I tried to distract her, but she was on edge, like someone conducting an intolerable interview, waiting to call time.

For myself, I couldn't intervene: Shaw thought that I was not stupid, but misguided, perhaps deliberately so, and that provoked him more. I let my thoughts drift, wondering why, when I was young, I hadn't known Denis Geary better. He was a good man, and his character had worn well: he had become more interesting than many who had once, for me, outshone him. But, of course, one doesn't in youth really choose one's friends: it is only later, perhaps too late, that one wishes, with something like the obverse of nostalgia, that it had been possible to choose.

The men alone, the port, more of the political testimony of
Arnold Shaw. But, despite the luxurious meals, parties at the
Residence had a knack of finishing early. All the guests had
left, with suitable expressions of reluctance, by 10:45.

Tires ground on the gravel, and Arnold returned to the
drawing room, lips pursed in triumph.

"I call that a good party," he proclaimed to Vicky and me,
challenging us to deny it. Then he said to Vicky, affectionate,
reproachful: "But I must say, you might have kept young
Getliffe behind a bit—"

I had to save her. I said:

"Look, Arnold, I do rather want a word with you."

"About what?"

"You know about what, don't you?"

He glared at me with hot angry eyes. He decided that there
was nothing for it, and said with increasing irascibility that
we had better go to his study.

Before I had sat down, beside the reading lamp in front of
the scholar's bookshelves, ladder close by, he said:

"I warn you, it's no use."

"Listen to me for a minute."

"It's no use."

"I'm thinking of you," I said.

"I don't want anyone to think of me."

What I had just told him happened to be true. I was not
exerting myself, and not crossing wills, entirely—or even
mainly—for Vicky's sake. I should have been hard put to it to
define my feeling for him, but it contained strata both of
respect and affection. Whether he believed that or not, I
didn't know: he was not used to being liked: if someone did
appear to like him, it affected him with something between
exasperation and surprise.

He poured out whiskies for us both, but became more ugly-
tempered still. It was the kind of temper that is infectious,
and I had to make myself keep my own. I told him that
tomorrow's meeting wasn't just a matter of form: if he

pressed for the Court to confirm his verdict, then he would certainly get a majority: some would vote against, certainly Geary, probably Leonard Getliffe and two or three of the younger academics. I should, I said in a matter-of-fact tone, vote against it myself.

"Vote against anything you like," he snapped.

"I shall," I said.

He would get a clear majority. But didn't he realize that most of the people voting for him nevertheless thought he had been too severe?

"That's neither here nor there."

"It is, you know," I said.

I tried another tactic. He must admit, I said, that most of the people we knew—probably most people in the whole society—didn't really regard fornication as a serious offense. In secret they didn't regard it as an offense at all.

"So much the worse for them," he said.

How could he be so positive? I was getting rougher. Most people couldn't find any moral sanction for such an attitude. I couldn't. Where did he get his?

"That's my business."

"Not if it affects us all."

"I'm not going to talk about my moral sanctions. I'm not going to talk about fornication in general." His cheeks had gone puce. "We're talking about a university, which you seem to have forgotten. We're talking about a university which I'm in charge of. While I'm in charge of it, I'm not going to allow promiscuous fornication. I don't see that that needs explaining. It gets in the way of everything a university stands for. Once you turn a blind eye, you'd make nonsense of the place before you could look round."

Then I used my last resource. I said that I too was concerned for the university: and that he was valuable to it. He would never get any credit for that. But he had a single-minded passion for academic merit. As a Vice-Chancellor he couldn't do some things, but he could do one superlatively:

that is, he was a connoiseur of academic promise with as great
accuracy as he was a connoiseur of wine. It wasn't an accident
that this obscure university had put in a bid for Leonard
Getliffe. And Leonard Getliffe, though much the best of his
collection, was not the only one. He had backed his judgment, appointed three full professors in their twenties and
thirties: so that the university was both better staffed, and
more adventurously staffed, than any of its class.

I hadn't been flattering him. That was the fact. For the
first time I had touched him. The smoldering rage dropped
down for an instant, and he said:

"Well, I've got hold of some good men." He said it hum-
bly.

If he left the place, no one else would have the same gift, I
said. And it was possible that he would have to leave. You
couldn't fight all your opponents on all fronts. He was making opponents of people who needn't be: they thought that
he wasn't living in the climate of his time: he gave them
some excuse.

"I've no use for the climate of my time. To hell with it,"
he said.

All I wanted him to do—I was being patient—was to make
some compromise. The slightest compromise. Even just by
permitting the four students to withdraw, as though of their
own free will.

"I'll compromise when I can," he said. "Not when I
can't."

I told him as straight and hard as I was able, that if ever
there was an occasion to offer a token compromise, then tomorrow was the time. With an angry pout, eyes flat and fixed,
he shook his head.

I had had enough, and sat back, silent. Then he said, not so
much in a conciliatory manner but as though he wanted me
to understand:

"I'll tell you this. You say they may want to get rid of me.

That's their business. They won't find it so easy as they think. But if I decide that I'm doing the place more harm than good, then I shall go next day."

He had spoken in a brisk tone, his anger quite subsided, rather as though he were stating his plans for his summer holiday. In precisely the same tone, he added:

"I shall decide. And I shan't ask anyone else."

Even more briskly, he said goodnight, and at something like a trot went out of the room and upstairs. I noticed that the lights were still on in the drawing room, and there I found Vicky waiting up.

"Any change?" she asked.

"None," I said.

She swore. "He's hopeless."

Then she, who usually was considerate, who noticed one's physical state, went on as though I were neither jaded nor tired. Couldn't I still do something tomorrow? I was used to this kind of business: couldn't I find a way to smooth things over?

I'd try, of course, I said. But in real conflicts, technique never counted; when people clashed head on it was no use being tactful. I let myself say that, discouraging her because she was nagging at me, and I needed just to go to bed.

She seemed selfishly, or even morbidly, preoccupied about her father. But it was not truly so. No, she was compensating to herself because she did not want to think of him at all. She was dutiful, she could not shrug off what a daughter ought to feel and do. It was another kind of love, however, which was possessing her. She wanted to guard her father's well-being, she wanted to get her conscience clear—so that she could forget it all and lose herself, as though on the edge of sleep, in thoughts of happiness.

THREE

MEETING

Meetings. To twist an old statement, all happy meetings are like one another: every unhappy meeting is unhappy in its own fashion. But was that true? I had been to plenty of unhappy meetings in my time. Whether they were trivial or secret or (by the world's standards) important, they all had a family resemblance. So had the Court meeting that Wednesday morning.

It began uncomfortably quiet, the good-mornings muted in the long room. The room was both extravagantly long and as light as though we were sitting in the open air, since one side was all window, looking southwards on to an arenalike court. The unrelieved lightness of the room—I had thought, on occasions before this one—drew people apart, not together. It was like the whole range of the university buildings, handsome, stark, functional, slapped down at prodigious expense in the fields, four miles outside the town. The Victorian buildings of the old college, where I had first listened to George Passant, had been abandoned, turned over to offices in one of the streets where my son and I had walked the previous afternoon. No dark rooms now: no makeshifts: now, the wide campus, the steel, concrete, and glass, the stretches of window, at the same time bare, luxurious, unshadowed, costly.

Arnold sat at the end of the table, behind him on the wall—incongruous in the midst of the architectural sheen—a colored plaque of the university arms. There were ten people on each side, Hargrave, who had some honorific title in the university, on the Vice-Chancellor's right, Geary two or three places down, looking at ease and interested. I sat on Arnold Shaw's left, and on my side sat Leonard Getliffe and several other academics, most of them under forty. The rest of the Court were older, hearty middle-aged local politicians and businessmen, four or five well-dressed strong-built women.

Item Number 3 on the agenda read, with the simple eloquence of official documents, *Appeal by Four Students Against Decision of Disciplinary Committee*. The first two items were routine, and Arnold Shaw, who was a brisk decisive chairman, wiped them off. Then he said, in the same unexpansive fashion, not encouraging comment or setting people free to talk, that they all knew the background of the next piece of business: he had circulated a memorandum: the students had appealed to the Court, as was their constitutional right: they had now asked to appear before the Court in person. Whether they had this right as well was open to question: there was no ruling and no precedent. But Sir Lewis Eliot, as the students' representative on the Court, had presented an official request from the student body—that the four students should be given the privilege. He, Arnold Shaw, had with some dubiety granted it. As to the case itself, the facts were not in dispute. There was nothing to be said about them. We had better let the students in straight away.

Better for them if they had not come, I had thought all along. I had tried to persuade them, for I had interviewed the four of them more than once. But the young man Pateman, who was the strongest character among them, was also a good deal of a sea-lawyer: there were other sea-lawyers among the union leaders: they were insisting on appearance before the Court as an inalienable right. I found it distinctly tiresome. So far as the four had any chance at all, they would worsen it

if they came and argued: I knew the impression they would
make: I knew also that one of the girls had already lost her
nerve.

As Arnold Shaw had said, picking up the official phrase,
the facts were not in dispute. They could hardly have been
less in dispute. About 3:00 A.M. on a winter morning (actually it happened early in March) the assistant warden of one
of the women's hostels had gone into a sitting room. It was
pure coincidence that she should have done so; she was having a sleepless night, and thought she remembered seeing a
magazine there. She had switched on the light; on the sofa lay
one naked pair, on an improvised bed another. What conversation then took place didn't seem to be put on record. The
assistant warden (who was both sensible and embarrassed)
knew both girls, they were members of the hostel and had
their own room upstairs. Presumably she found out the men's
names at once: at any rate, next day she had no option but to
report them. It was as simple as that.

We had better have the students in straight away, Arnold
Shaw was saying. He pressed a bell, told the attendant to
bring Miss Bolt.

Myra Bolt came in. She was a big girl, pretty in a heavy-
featured, actressish way: at close quarters she rolled her eyes
and one noticed that her skin was large-pored. She was quite
self-possessed that morning. I had not yet seen her otherwise:
it wasn't she whose nerve had snapped. She was hearty and
loud-voiced, and her parents were much better off than those
of most of the students. Her father was a stockbroker who had
a country house in Sussex. It was easy to imagine her, a little
younger, taking riding lessons and being eager to have a roll
in the bushes with the groom. She hadn't exactly boasted or
confided, but let me know that something of that kind had
duly taken place. At this time, she was twenty, in her second
year, academically not much good.

The table was bad for interviewing, far too long, the candidate (or, that morning, the appellant) much too far away.

Arnold Shaw, though a good chairman, was a bad interviewer. He just snapped out questions, his mind channeled as
though he were wearing blinkers. That morning he was not
only a bad interviewer but a hostile one, and he wasn't going
to pretend otherwise.

"Miss Bolt," he said. "We understand that you have representations to make to the Court. What are they?"

Myra Bolt wasn't overawed, but she wasn't specially used
to formal speeches. I had told them the kind of questions to
expect, but not that one, not as the first.

"Well—" she began inconclusively.

I thought that I had to step in. She wasn't a favorite of
mine: there was only one of the four whom I was really fond
of, and it wasn't she. But it was my job to see they got a
hearing. I said, "Vice-Chancellor, I wonder if I can help the
Court a little, and Miss Bolt? Perhaps I could take her
through what the students wish to say?"

How often had I seen others start a clash like that, voices
smoothed down by official use? Arnold Shaw glanced at me
with aggressive eyes—but he couldn't have stopped me easily.
He seemed to like having an adversary, me in particular. He
nodded, and projected my name.

I began by one or two innocuous questions: how long had
she been living in the hostel? How well did she know the
other girl, Joyce Darby? Not all that well, said Myra: just to
have coffee with, or go out with for a drink. I had two objec-
tives: I wanted to domesticate the whole business, to make
them look more acceptable, so that they might express some
sort of regret (which I knew that two of them at least, Myra
among them, weren't inclined to do). Then I wanted them
to make a responsible case about their careers: what would
happen to them if they were thrown out of this university,
and so couldn't get into another? The more professional it all
sounded, the easier for them—and, I had hoped until the
night before, the easier for Arnold Shaw.

How had they ever got into it? They didn't usually have

this kind of party, did they? I was speaking casually. Myra answered: no, there'd never been anything like it before. She added:

"I suppose we all got carried away. You know how it is."

"Had you been drinking?"

"A bit. I must say, it was a bit off."

That was mollifying. But she was preoccupied—as she had been when I talked to her—by the fact of the two couples in the same room, what in her language they called an orgy.

"If David and I had gone off in my car that evening, and the other two in somebody else's, then I don't suppose we should have heard another word about it."

That was less mollifying. Across the table, nearer to Myra, one of the women members of the Court broke in. She had a beaky profile, fine blue eyes, and a high voice. She said, in a sharp, sisterly, kindly tone:

"You didn't think you were doing anything wrong?"

"That depends on how you look at it, doesn't it?"

"But how do you look at it?"

"Well," said Myra, "I'm sorry other people get dragged in. That wasn't so good."

The woman member nodded. "But what about you?"

"What about me?"

"I mean, do you think you've done anything wrong?"

Myra answered, more lucidly than usual: "I don't think there's anything wrong in making love, if you're not hurting anybody else." She went on: "I agree with Mrs. What-do-you-call-her, wasn't she an actress, that it doesn't matter what people do so long as they don't stop the traffic."

It was like her, in her bumbling fashion, to get the reference wrong. Some of the Court wondered, however, where she had picked it up. Probably from one of their student advisers, trying to rehearse them.

But, bumbling or not, when Denis Geary asked her about the consequences of the punishment, she did her best. Denis was playing in with me: he was experienced, he knew the tone of the people round this table much better than I did: he didn't sound indulgent or even compassionate: but what did the punishment mean? To herself, she said, nothing but a headache. She could live at home or get a job with one of her father's friends (what she meant was that she would find someone, probably someone quite unlike her student fancies, to marry within a year or two). But to the others, who wanted careers, it meant they couldn't have them. Unless some other university would take them in. But they were being expelled in squalid circumstances: would another institution look at them? David Llewellyn, for instance (he had been Myra's partner: she didn't pretend to love him, but she spoke up for him)—he wanted to be a scientist. What chance would he have now?

"Has any member of the Court anything further to ask Miss Bolt?" Arnold Shaw looked implacably round the table. "Have you anything further you wish to say, Miss Bolt? Thank you."

With the next girl, I had one aim and only one, which was to get her out of the room with the least possible strain. She wasn't in a fit state to be interviewed. That she showed, paradoxically helping me, by beginning to cry as soon as Arnold Shaw asked his first formal question. "Miss Darby, we understand—" She was a delicate-looking girl, actually a year older than Myra, but looking much younger. She appeared drab and mousey, but dress her up, make her happy, and she would have her own kind of charm. She came from a poor family in industrial Lancashire, a family which had been severe with her already. She was a bright student, expected to get a First, and that, together with her tears, made Shaw gentler with her. All she said was: "I was over-influenced. That's as much as I can tell you."

It was not gallant. In secret (it sounded hard, but I had seen more of her than the others had) I thought that she was not only frightened, which was natural enough, but self-regarding and abnormally vain.

She spoke in a tiny voice. Quite gently, Shaw told her to speak up. She couldn't. Whether she was crying or not, she wouldn't have been able to. Anyone used to interviewing would have known that there are some people who can't. Anyone used to interviewing would also have known that—despite all superstitions to the contrary—the over-confident always get a little less good treatment than they deserve, and girls like this a little more.

Someone asked her, who had influenced her? She said: "The rest of them." She wouldn't, to do her justice, put special blame on Dick Pateman, her own lover. One of the academics who had taught her asked her what, if she continued with her degree work, she hoped to do? She wanted to go on to a Ph.D. What on? Henry James. She began to cry again, as though she felt herself shut out from great expectations, and Arnold Shaw was in a hurry to ask the dismissive questions.

It had done harm: it might have been worse. David Llewellyn, though he was as nervous as she was, gave a good performance. This was the one I liked, a small neat youth, sensitive and clever. When one compared him and Myra, there was no realistic doubt about who had done the seducing. Probably she was his first woman (they had been sleeping together some months before the party), and I expected that he was proud of it and boasted to his friends. But how he got led into the "orgy" I couldn't understand, any more than if it had been myself at the same age. When I had asked him, he looked lost, and said:

"Collective hysteria. It can't have been anything else."

After his name was announced, people round the table may have been surprised to hear him talk in a sub-cockney accent. His parents, I had discovered, kept a small shop in Southend. Of the four of them, only Pateman lived with his family in the town. But then, the great majority of the university's students came from all over the country, to be put up in the new hostels: just as the local young men and women traveled to other parts of the country to be put up in identical hostels elsewhere. It might have seemed odd, but not to anyone acclimatized to the English faith in residential education.

Llewellyn did well, without help from me or Geary. He was ready to apologize for what had happened: it had given trouble, it had stirred up a scandal. The circumstances were bad. So far as they were concerned, he had no defense. The party was inexcusable. He was nervous but precise. No one pressed him. If they had, he would have been honest. His private sexual behavior was his own affair. On that he and Myra had made a compact: and their student political adviser was backing them. But Lewellyn didn't require any backing. He was ambitious, and shaking for his future. He had his own code of belief, though. An attempt by Shaw or one of the others to make him deny it would have got nowhere.

However, that didn't happen. Leonard Getliffe, not preoccupied as on the night before, asked him some questions about his physics course: Leonard, sharp-witted, was talking like a master of his job, but without any condescension at all: the answers sounded sharp-witted also.

In the silence, after he had left and we were waiting for Pateman, someone said:

"I must say, that seems a pity."

Across the table, Leonard Getliffe said: "He has talent."

For the next quarter of an hour, Dick Pateman sat at one end of the table arguing with the Vice-Chancellor and the others. Pateman's head was thrown back, whether he was listening or speaking: he had staring light eyes in deep orbits, a diagonal profile, and a voice with no give in it. Less than any of the others, he did not want to make human contact: with his contemporaries, this gave him a kind of power; he seemed to them uninfluenceable, waiting only for them to be influenced. It was the kind of temperament which wasn't necessarily linked with ability—he was not clever, he ought to have been finishing his degree but had been dropped back a year—but which is sometimes dangerous and not often negligible. It did not seem negligible at the table that morning—though his logic-chopping and attempts at legalism were stirring up Arnold Shaw's contempt, which Pateman met by a contempt, chilly and internal, of his own.

On the surface it might have sounded like a trade-union boss negotiating with an employer. On one side stood the student body, Pateman was grating away (I had anticipated this, tried to stop it, could only sit by): on the other "the authorities." It was necessary for matters of discipline to be settled by the two sides in combination.

"Nonsense," said Arnold Shaw.

Shaw's temper was seething. The young man seemed to have no temper. He went on:

"If that's the attitude the authorities take up, then the students will have to join forces with students of other universities—"

"Let them," said Arnold Shaw.

So it went on. The authorities had no right to impose their own laws unilaterally on the students, said Pateman. The students had their own rights.

"In that sense," said Shaw, "you have none at all."

Pateman said that they were free citizens. They paid their fees. They were prepared to collaborate in drafting laws for the university, and would abide by them. They accepted that the authorities had their own rights about examinations. Everything else should be settled by mutual consent. Or, alternatively, the students should simply be subject to the laws of the land. In the present case, there was no suggestion that anything had been done contrary to the laws of the land.

"Look here," said Denis Geary, "this isn't very profitable."

"I was speaking for the students—"

"You'd better speak for yourselves. You've behaved like damned fools, and messy damned fools, and you know it. You'd better give us one good reason why we should be spending our time here this morning—"

Young Pateman gave something like a smile. He must have realized, since Geary was well-known in the town, that there was one of their best hopes: he didn't mind, he was enough of a politician to be easy with rough words.

"I don't take back the students' case," he began, and Geary broke in:

"Drop that."

"I should have thought the practical thing you've got to consider this morning," Pateman went on, in precisely the same ungiving tone, "is whether you want to ruin us."

"Ruin's a big word," said Geary.

"What else do you think you're doing?"

The Vice-Chancellor was interrupting, but Denis Geary had his own authority and went on:

"I want to know one thing. How much do you feel responsible?"

"What do you mean, responsible?"

"If it hadn't been for you, would this have happened?"

"I don't know about that."

"You're the oldest of this group, aren't you?"

"Joyce is older than I am. So is David."

"Never mind about calendar age. You're a grown man, aren't you?"

He was young enough to be softened, for an instant. Geary asked:

"Do you think it's a good idea to get hold of youngsters like this—"

"It depends on the cooperation I get."

The answer was brash. Geary used more force:

"But you ought to feel responsible, oughtn't you?"

"I don't know about that." Pateman was repeating himself.

"You do feel responsible, though, don't you?"

There was a long pause. Pateman said, slowly, his voice more grating still: "I don't want to see anyone ruined."

Geary glanced at me, a partner's glance. That was the most he could extract. I touched the Vice-Chancellor's sleeve. He didn't want to let Pateman go, but he acquiesced.

Coffee was brought in. It was about a quarter-past eleven, and we had started at ten. *Motion:* that the Court confirms the decision of the Disciplinary Committee.

In the unconfined hygienic room the air was tight. Not, so far, with anger: remarks were quiet: there was curiosity, unease, something else. I heard, or thought I heard, someone whispering about *the university premises.* Arnold Shaw stared down the table. He wasn't pleased to have lost his leadership during the hearings: he was asserting it now.

"There is a motion before the Court," he said. "Before I put it, I should like to hear whether anyone wishes to discuss it."

Pause. One of the academics spoke up: "Some of us are wondering, I think, Vice-Chancellor, whether it isn't possible to make distinctions between these students—"

Shaw sat, high-colored, without answering. Others were doing that. It was a line some were eager for. Surely one of the girls had been dominated. Didn't she deserve different treatment (I noticed that the handsome blue-eyed woman, though she sat silent, had her own view of Joyce Darby)? No one had any use for Pateman. There was a great deal of talk, scrappy, some of it merciful. Someone said: " 'Whosoever shall cause one of my little ones—' " and trailed off. I caught the word "degenerates." It was left for Leonard Getliffe to make a special case.

"I should like the Court to give consideration to young Llewellyn. I can speak for the physics department. He's worth saving. I said before, he has talent. He's certainly the best student I've taught here. I don't know about the general position. I mean, I can't reach absolute conclusions about student behavior. I should say, in terms of character as I understand it, he is a decent young man."

Leonard was speaking politely but without concessions. On his clever conceptualizer's face, there was a half-smile, a mannerism which some found irritating. It meant nothing. He spoke like a man sure of himself. Underneath the fine nerves, he was more virile than most. If Vicky had been an older woman, she would have been bound to perceive it. Yet it had quite escaped her. I wondered if, free that morning from his obsessive love, he had time to be bitter because it was weakening his manhood, just as, younger than he was, but in this same town, and for the identical cause, I had been bitter myself.

I wondered also if he felt envy for the culprits. Envy because, instead of being prisoners of love, they took sex as though it didn't matter. Or because they just took sex as it came. At various places round the table, through the curious unease, through both the mercifulness and the disapproval, there had been those stabs of envy.

He went on:

"There is another point. I admit that it's a slightly more abstract one. The more people the university sends down, the less penalty it really is. That is, the importance of the gesture is inversely proportional to the number involved. If you send the whole university down, no one will care. If you send one person down, then that is a genuine penalty."

He had spoiled his case, I thought irritably. That was what the theoreticians called cat-humor. Why didn't they keep it for their seminars?

One of his colleagues, more worldly than he was, thought the same. "Never mind that," he said. "Vice-Chancellor, going back to Professor Getliffe's first point, there does seem to be some feeling for discretionary treatment on behalf of two of the students. We should like to ask, rather strongly, whether that isn't possible?"

Shaw had been quiet, like a discreet chairman letting the discussion run. Now he looked round, took his time, and said:

"No. I have to tell the Court it is not possible."

There were noises of disappointment, but he was in control.

"No. The Court must face the position. This is all or nothing. If you ask me for the reason, I give it you in one word. Justice."

Denis Geary said that justice could be unjust, but for once he was overweighted.

"No," said Arnold Shaw. "It would be wrong to distinguish between these four. Morally wrong. There are no respectable grounds for doing so. Age. Some people might think that a respectable ground, though I should beg to differ. In any case, the students whom some members want to favor are the two oldest. Academic ability. We are not judging a matter of academic ability. We are judging a matter of university discipline and moral behavior. No one wants to deprive the university of able students. We haven't got enough. But you can't make a special dispensation for the able when they've committed exactly the same offense. Personally, I am sorry that Pateman ever became a student here —but to dismiss him and let others stay, who are precisely as guilty on the facts, simply because they might get better classes in their degrees—well, I could have no part in it. I'm surprised that anyone could find it morally defensible. Finally, influence. It's easy to think we know who is responsible. We don't. We can have our suspicions—but suspicions aren't a basis for just action. Anyone who is certain he knows what happens between two people is taking too much on himself. In this case, it would be utterly unjustified to go *behind the facts.* I repeat, I for one could have no part in it."

Quiet. It was time to turn the argument. I said, perhaps I might put another point of view. "Do," said Arnold Shaw, firm and beady-eyed.

I was deliberately cool. I didn't want to get entangled in the legalities of the case, I remarked. So far as they went, the Vice-Chancellor's statement was unanswerable. And everyone round the table understood the position in which the Disciplinary Committee had found themselves. All that any of us wished to say was, weren't we making too heavy weather of it? The Committee had been obliged to take action: that was accepted. But wasn't the penalty, now we had had time to realize the repercussions, too severe? Send the students down for the rest of the academic year, and no one would have asked a question. But were we really intending to cut them off from finishing their university education anywhere? It wouldn't have happened at other institutions or American colleges that I knew. Wouldn't it be fairly easy for the Committee to have another look, just as an act of grace?

Arnold Shaw turned half-left towards me: "Sir Lewis, you've just said that this wouldn't have happened at other institutions?"

"Yes," I replied, "I did say that."

"You were a don yourself once, weren't you?"

That was a rhetorical question.

"Might I ask," said Arnold Shaw, "what would have happened at your own college if undergraduates had behaved like this?"

I answered that I couldn't recall a case.

"The question," he persisted, "seems to me a fair one."

Sometimes, I said, I had known blind eyes turned.

"The question," Arnold Shaw went on, "still seems to me a fair one. In your own college. Two of your undergraduates and two women. Or in a room in Newnham. What about it?"

He had won that point, I was thinking to myself. I had to remember a time when Roy Calvert nearly missed a fellowship because he was suspected, as a matter of gossip, not of proof, of keeping a mistress.

"I grant you that," I said with reluctance. "Yes, they'd have been got rid of."

Then I recovered myself. "But I want to remind you that that was getting on for thirty years ago. The climate of opinion has changed since then." I was trying to work on the meeting. "So far as I can gather the sense of this Court today, the general feeling, is very different from what it would have been thirty years ago. Or even ten."

Some murmurs of support. One or two noes I was right, though. The tone that morning had been calmer and more relaxed than in our youth most of us could have imagined.

"I've told you before, I don't believe in climates of opinion," said Shaw. "That seems to me a dangerous phrase. But even if opinions have changed, are you maintaining that moral values have changed too?"

I had had too much practice at committees to be drawn. Arnold Shaw wore a curving, sharp-edged smile, enjoying the debate, confident that he had had the better of it. So he had. But, with some, he was doing himself harm. They wanted a bit of give-and-take, not his brand of dialectic.

I was having to make my next, and final, move. I looked across at Denis Geary, the only useful ally there, wishing that we could confer. I was trying to think of two opposite aims at once, which was a handicap in any kind of politics. On the one hand, I didn't want Shaw to do himself more harm (about that Geary would have been indifferent): if we pressed it to a vote, the Vice-Chancellor would get his support, but—as I had told him flatly the night before—it would be remembered against him. On the other hand, I wasn't ready to surrender. For the students' sake? For the sake of the old-Adam-ego, for after all I was fighting a case? That didn't matter. Someone was saying, and this time the words were clear: "If only it hadn't happened *on the university premises.*"

I had been reflecting only for moments. There wasn't time to delay. But I found myself infected by a subterranean amusement. Arnold Shaw had made me think back to my college in the 'thirties: and, hearing that single comment, I was thinking back again. A college meeting. Report of a pyromaniac. He had set fire to his sitting room once before, and that was thought to be accidental. Now he had done it again. One of the senior fellows, our aesthete, old Eustace Pilbrow, raised his voice. The young man must be got out of college at once. That day. But he must be found (since Pilbrow was a kind man) *a very good set of lodgings in the town.*

"Vice-Chancellor," I said, returning to the occasion, "I have a simple proposition to make."

"Yes?"

"I suggest we take no formal action at all. Let's leave it over till the next meeting of the Court"—which was due to take place two months ahead, in June.

"With respect, I don't see the force of that." Shaw's lips were pouting.

"There is a little force in it." I explained that, to me, and I thought to some others, the formality and the procedures were not important. We should be content if we could save some chance for the students' careers. Given two months, Leonard Getliffe could talk to his physicist-colleagues in other universities: come clean about the events: some department might be willing to take Llewellyn in. And so with the others. Many of us had contacts. Then, if and when they were placed elsewhere, the Court would be happy, or wouldn't worry further about its own disciplinary step.

"Not satisfactory," said Arnold Shaw, but Geary broke in:

"Vice-Chancellor, in the circumstances nothing is going to be satisfactory. But I must say, I've never heard of a compromise which made things so easy for the powers-that-be. You're not being voted against, you're just asked to wait a minute."

"It's not even rational."

"Vice-Chancellor," Geary was speaking heavily, "it will be difficult for me, and I know I'm speaking for others, if you can't accept this."

Hargrave coughed. Under his white hair with its middle parting, his face, often quietly worried, looked more so. He was more distressed by the hearing than anyone there. He rarely spoke on the Court, but now he forced himself.

"It's usually right to wait, if one is not hurting anyone."

"You've listened to those four this morning," said Shaw.

Hargrave kneaded his temples, like one with a migraine, and then said with surprising firmness,

"But if we wait a little, we shan't hurt anyone, shall we?"

Even then, I doubted whether Shaw was going to budge. At last he shook his head.

"I don't like it," he said. "But if you want me to put your motion"— he turned to me—"to the Court, I'm willing to do so. As for myself, I shall abstain."

With bad grace, he sat in the chair while the hands went up. Only three against. There was a susurration of whispers, even giggles, as people stirred, ready to leave.

It wasn't even a rational compromise, Arnold Shaw had complained. But then he was expecting too much. I had twice heard an elder statesman of science announce, with the crystalline satisfaction of someone producing a self-evident truth, that sensible men usually reached sensible conclusions. I had seen my brother cock an eyebrow, in recognition of that astonishing remark. I had myself reported it, dead pan, to others—who promptly came to the conclusion that I believed it myself.

It was not even a rational compromise. I packed up my

papers, quite pleased with the morning's work. Others were talking, glad to have put it behind them. They were used, as people were in a society like ours, highly articulated, but so articulated that most lives touched only by chance, to hearing names, even to meeting persons in the flesh, once, twice, then not again. To most of the Board, the four we had interviewed were strangers, flickering in and out. Myra Bolt, David Llewellyn—they had swum into each other's consciousness that morning, like someone sitting next to one in an aircraft, talking of where he had come from and where he was going to. To people round the table, the names they had heard weren't likely often to recur. That seemed entirely normal to them, just as it so often seemed to me.

FOUR

A SIMPLE HOME

Yet for me, later that day, one of the names flickered, not out, but in again. I had arranged to spend another night at the Residence, in order to have my ritual drink with George Passant, and was sitting alone in the drawing room after tea. Vicky had not returned from the hospital, and Arnold Shaw had gone to his vice-chancellarial office for another of his compulsive paper-clearing spells.

I was called to the telephone. This was Dick Pateman, a voice said, lighter and more smooth than it sounded face to face: he was anxious to see me. He knew about the result, or rather the non-result? Yes, he had been told: he was anxious to see me. Well, I accepted that, it was all in the job. In any case, I couldn't stay with him long. Where, I asked? At the Residence? Not much to my surprise, he said no. Would I come to his own home? I asked for the address, and thought I remembered the road, or could find it.

Getting off the bus at the Park gates, I looked down into the town. There was a dip, and then a rise into the evening haze: lights were coming out, below the blur of roofs. On the left, down the New Walk, I used to go to Martineau's house. I must have looked down, at that density of lights and roofs, many times in those days: not with a Rastignac passion that I was going to take the town, any more than I had felt it looking down at London roofs (that was too nineteenth century for us), but with some sort of pang, made up of curiosity and, perhaps, a vague, even a sentimental, yearning.

I had been over-confident about my local knowledge, and it took me some time to identify the road. This was a part of the town which in the last century had been a suburb, but was so no longer; it certainly wasn't a slum, for those had gone. It was nothing in particular: a criss-cross of tidy streets, two-storeyed houses, part working-class, part the fringe of the lower middle. I asked my way, but no one seemed clear. So far as I could remember, I had never set foot in those particular back streets: even in one's native town, one's routes were marked out, sharp and defined, like the maps of underground railways.

At last I saw the street-sign: on both sides stood terraced houses, the same period, the same red brick, as those my son and I had passed on the way to my father's room. At the end of the road some West Indians were talking on the pavement. That would have been a novelty years before. So would the sight of cars, at least three, waiting outside houses, including the house I was searching for. The window of the front room gave on the pavement: as in the window of the Residence the night before, a light was shining behind the curtains.

When I rang the bell, Dick Patemen opened the door. His greeting was off-hand, but I scarcely noticed that, since I was puzzled by the smell that wafted out, or one component of it. I was used to the musty smell of small old houses, I had known them all my childhood, and that was present here— but there was also something different in kind, not repulsive but discomforting, which I couldn't place.

Behind the closed door of the front room, pop music was sounding: but Dick Pateman took me to the next, and only other, door. This would be (I knew it all by heart) the living room or kitchen. As I went in, Dick Pateman was saying: "This is my father and mother."

That I hadn't bargained on. The room was cluttered, and for an instant my only impression was of the idiosyncratic smell, much stronger. I was shaking hands with a man whose head was thrown back, his hand stretched out, in a gesture one sometimes sees displayed by grandiose personages.

My eyes became clearer. Mr. Pateman was taller than his son, with high square shoulders and a heavily muscled, athletic body. His grip on my hand was powerful, and his forearms filled his sleeves. His light-blue eyes met mine unblinkingly, rather as though he had been taught that, to make a good impression, it was necessary to look your man straight in the eye. He had sandy hair, pale eyebrows, and a sandy moustache. Under the moustache two teeth protruded a little, his underlip pressed in, with the suggestion of a slight, condescending smile.

"I've never met you," he said, "but I've heard a great deal about you."

I said that he was not to believe it. Mr. Pateman, humorlessly, without any softening, said that he did.

Then I shook hands with Mrs. Pateman, a tiny little woman, a foot shorter than her husband or son, wrinkled and dark-skinned. She gave me a quick, worried, confiding smile.

As we sat down, I didn't know why I had been enticed like this, how much the parents knew, nor how to talk to them.

The room was crammed with heavy nineteenth-century furniture. There was a bookcase with a glass window in the far corner, and a piano on the other side. A loose slack fire was smoldering in the grate, and the air was chilly. On the table, upon a white openwork cloth spread upon another cloth of dark-green plush with bobbled fringe, stood a teapot, some crockery, and what looked like the preparations for a "high tea," though—by the standards of my mother's friends —a meager one. Everything was clean: and yet, about the whole room, there hung a curiously dusty air, less like the grime of neglect than like some permanent twilight.

Mrs. Pateman asked whether she could help me to some food. When I answered her and said no, her husband smiled, as though I were proving satisfactory.

He himself was eating tinned salmon. He said, "Well, we're giving them something to think about, I'm glad to say."

I was still at a disadvantage. This was obviously a reference to the morning's meeting, and he seemed as invulnerable as his son. If he had been a softer man, worried or even inconsolable because his son's future was in danger, I should have been more at home. I should have been more at home with Mrs. Pateman, who was watching the two of them with shrewd puzzled anxiety. But, in the presence of the father, it wasn't in the least like that.

"The best we can do now"—I was feeling my way, speaking to Dick Pateman—"is to try and get you fixed up elsewhere. As soon as we can."

"That's not very satisfactory," said Dick Pateman.

"No," said Mr. Pateman.

"It's a bad second best," said Dick—as though he were arguing with me at the end of the long table.

"Some of us," said Mr. Pateman, "aren't prepared to see our children get the second best."

I didn't want to show impatience, though it was displeasingly near. Above all, I didn't want to give pain, certainly not to Mrs. Pateman. I couldn't speak frankly. With an effort, I said:

"You've got to regard this as nothing more or less than a friendly talk. I can't do much. I might be able to give you a little advice, simply because I know the rules of this game, but that's all."

Mr. Pateman faced me with a set cunning look, which declared that he was not to be taken in. He assumed that I was a man of influence, he had an unqualified faith in what he called "pulling strings." The more I disclaimed being able to act, the more convinced he was of my Machiavellian power.

Dick argued, so did his father.

I was becoming certain that he didn't know much, nothing like the full story. Not that Dick had deceived him. He didn't want to know, he didn't even want to hear. He was positive that he was right. Obviously his son was being badly used: which meant, and this was how he translated it, that he himself was being badly used. He was a churchgoer, he pointed out to me, assuming, with an air of pitying superiority, that I wasn't. With a family in distress, I should have expected to feel protective, even though I hadn't asked to be there, even though I didn't like them. But Mr. Pateman made that impossible. By some extraordinary feat of character or moral legerdemain, he took it for granted that all I had to do was my simple duty. So far as there was any pity flowing, he was pitying me.

It was a long time since I had met a man so self-righteous. And yet his son was self-righteous too. That was what had exacerbated the Court, that billiard-ball impregnability in circumstances where self-righteousness didn't appear to be called for. With a prepotent father like that, some sons would have been worn down. Not this one. There did not seem any tenderness, or even much communication, between them. They treated each other like equal powers, each censorious, each knowing that he was right.

The person I was curious about was Mrs. Pateman, not bullied, but excluded from the talk. What could it be like to live here?

Mr. Pateman made a practical point, as though I were responsible. If Dick had to transfer to another university (did Dick himself believe it would be all that easy, I was thinking? when was the right time to stop them hoping too much?), he wouldn't be able to make a contribution to the housekeeping. As it was, he had been doing so out of his student grant.

"The grants are miserable, I suppose you know that," said Dick, ready to argue another grievance.

"Take him away," said Mr. Pateman, "and he won't be able to pay a penny. There'll be nothing coming in."

I had nothing to say on this topic, but Mr. Pateman needed to finish it off. "It's diabolical," he said.

Soon afterwards a young woman came in, unobtrusively, slipping into the room. This must, I thought, be Dick's sister, whom I had just heard of, but not more than that. Although she had only recently come in from work and could not have known of the Court result, she did not make any inquiry, not even look at her brother. Instead, she was asking for jam. There wasn't any jam today, said Mr. Pateman. There must be jam, she was saying. She was sounding peevish when, with a grandiloquent air, Mr. Pateman presented me. She was a small girl, not much bigger than her mother. She had fine eyes, but she turned them away from mine in a manner that could have been either shy or supercilious. In a delicate fashion, she was pretty: but, although she was perhaps only two years older than her brother, she had that kind of femininity which throws a shadow before it: her face was young, yet carried an aura, not really a physical look, of the elderly, almost of the wizened.

They called her Kitty. There was also a mention of someone named Cora: in the conversation I gathered that she and Cora shared, and slept in, the front room. It must have been Cora who had been playing records when I entered the house, which I had only just realized was so packed with people. I had another thought, or half-memory, from something I had heard not long before. Wasn't this Cora the niece of George Passant, the daughter of one of his sisters who had died young? I asked Kitty: she looked away, gave a sidelong glance, as though she wanted to resist answering me straight.

"I think she is," she said, with what seemed a meaningless edge of doubt.

Could I have a word with her? George was a lifelong friend; by a coincidence, I should be meeting him in half an hour. It was not such a coincidence, though I didn't tell her so.

Kitty did some more shuffling, then said:

"I'll see if she can come."

In the time Kitty was out of the room, Mr. Pateman had returned to the "diabolical" results of administrative decisions. Then the two young women returned, Cora first. She was tallish, with blunt heavy features, short straight hair; under a plain straight-hanging dress, she was strong-shouldered and stoutly built. I couldn't see much look of the Passant family, except perhaps a general thick-boned Nordic air. I said that I knew her uncle. She gave an abrupt yes. I said I owed him a lot. She said:

"I like George."

There were a few more words spoken, not many. She volunteered that she didn't see George much, nowadays. She said to Kitty:

"We ought to go and clear things up. The room's in a mess."

As they went out, I did not anticipate seeing them again. More people evanescing: it had been the condition of that day. By the side of the two Pateman males, those self-bound men, the girls didn't make demands on one, not even on one's attention. True, I felt cold and shut-in: but then, the little room was cold and shut-in. It was a relief that it was not now so full of people. This "simple home," as Mr. Pateman called it, in one of his protests about Dick's contribution, pressed upon me. I was growing to dislike the sharp and inescapable smell, strong in the little room, strongest near to Mr. Pateman himself. I had now isolated it in my nostrils, though I did not know the explanation, as a brand of disinfectant.

Mrs. Pateman was clearing away the tea, Dick—whose manners could not have been regarded as over-elaborate—had gone out, shortly after the girls, and without a word. It was still early, but I could decently leave; I was anticipating the free air outside when Mr. Pateman confronted me with a satisfied smile and said:

"Now, we can talk a little business, can't we?"

Immediately I took it for granted that he was, at last, going to speak seriously about his son. That made me more friendly: I settled in my chair, ready to respond.

"I'm not very happy about things," he said.

I began to reply, the best practical step was to find Dick a place elsewhere—

He stopped me. "Oh no. I wasn't thinking about him."

"I don't understand."

"He'll be all right," said Mr. Pateman. "I've done my best for my family and I don't mind saying, no one could have done more."

He looked at me, as usual so straight in the eye that I wanted to duck. He wasn't challenging me, he was too confident for that.

"No," he went on, "I'm not very happy about *my* position."

So that was it. That was why I had been invited, or enticed, to the house that evening.

"Do you realize," he asked, "that those two young people in the next room are both bringing in more than I am?"

I asked what he was doing. Cashier, he said, in one of the hosiery firms, a small one. Curiously enough, what was a similar job to my father's, years before. The young women? Secretaries. Fifteen or sixteen pounds a week each, I guessed?

"You're not far off. It's a lot of money at twenty-two or three.

Mr. Pateman did not appear to have the same appreciation of the falling value of money as my father, that unexpected financial adviser. But I happened to know the economics of this kind of household, through a wartime personal assistant of mine and her young man. Though Mr. Pateman could not realize it, that acquaintanceship, in which I hadn't behaved with much loyalty, made me more long-suffering towards him and his family now.

"How much are they paying you for their room?" I said.

"If you don't mind," Mr. Pateman answered, throwing his head back, "we'll keep our purses to ourselves."

Anyway, I was thinking, he couldn't extract a big amount from them—even though, as I now suspected, he was something of a miser, a miser in the old-fashioned technical sense. I had been watching his negotiations with the tea-table food. Between them, the two young women must have money to spend: they could run a car: it was strangely different from my own youth in this town, or the youth of my friends.

"My position isn't right," said Mr. Pateman. "I tell you, it isn't right." It was true to this extent, that a middle-aged man in a clerical job might be earning less than a trained girl.

"All I need," he went on, "is an opportunity."

I had to hear him out.

"What have you got to offer?"

"If I get an opportunity," he said, with supreme satisfaction, "I'll show them what I've got to offer."

I said, he had better tell me about his career. How old was he?

Fifty last birthday.

"I must say," I told him, "I should have thought you were younger."

"Some people," said Mr. Pateman, "know how to look after themselves."

Born in Walsall. His parents hadn't been too "well endowed with this world's goods" (they had kept a small shop). They had managed to send him to a grammar school. He had stayed on after sixteen: the intention was that he should one day go to a teachers' training college.

"But you didn't?"

"No."

"Why not?"

A very slight pause. Then Mr. Pateman said defiantly:

"Ah, thereby hangs a tale."

For the first time that evening, he was dissatisfied with his account of himself. I wondered how often I had heard a voice change in the middle of a life story. A platitude or a piece of jargon suddenly rang out. It meant that something had gone wrong. His "tale" seemed to be that he wanted to make money quick. He had had what he called a "brainwave." At twenty he had become attached to a second-hand-car firm, which promptly failed.

"Why did it fail?"

"It isn't everyone who is fortunate enough to have capital, you know."

Then he had become a clerk in an insurance office in Preston.

"You may be thinking I've had too many posts. I was always looking for the right one."

He had got married. ("I'm a great believer in taking on one's responsibilities early.") Unfit for military service. Both children born during the war.

Another brainwave, making radio sets.

"My ship didn't come home that time either," said Mr. Pateman.

"What happened?"

"Differences of opinion." He swept his arm. "You know what it is, when the people in command don't give a man his head."

"What would you have done if they had given you your head?"

"They never intended to. They asked me there on false pretenses. My schemes never got beyond the blueprint stage."

A new venture—this time in patent medicines. It looked as though all was well.

"Then we met a very cold wind. And I don't want to accuse anyone, but my partner came better than I did out of the financial settlement."

By that time, in his early forties, he had lived in a dozen towns and never made more, I guessed, than a few hundred a year. He descended further, and for eighteen months was trying to sell vacuum cleaners house to house. He brought it out quite honestly, but as though with stupefaction that this should have happened to him. Then—what he admitted, with a superior smile, had seemed like a piece of luck. An acquaintance from his radio days had introduced him to his present firm. He had moved to the town, and this house, five years before. It was his longest continuous job since his young manhood.

"And I'm still getting less than my own daughter. It isn't right. It can't be right."

I should have liked to avoid what was coming. Playing out time, I asked if his firm knew that he was considering another move. He gave a lofty nod.

"Are they prepared to recommend you?"

"They certainly are. I have a letter over there. Would you like to read it?"

It did not matter, I said. Mr. Pateman gave me a knowing smile.

"Yes, I should expect you to read between the lines."

I was saying something distracting, meaningless, but he was fixing me with his stare:

"I want an opportunity. That's all I'm asking for."

I said, slowly: "I don't know what advice I can possibly give you—"

"I wasn't asking for advice, sir. I was asking for an opportunity."

Even after that higgledy-piggledy life, he was undefeated. It was easy to imagine him at the doors of big houses, talking of his vacuum cleaners, impassively, imperviously, not down and out because he was certain the future must come right.

Nevertheless, I was thinking of old colleagues of mine considering him for jobs. Considering people for jobs had to be a heartless business. No man in his senses could think Mr. Pateman a good risk. They mightn't mind, or even be interested in, his odder aspects. But he carried so many signs that the least suspicious would notice—he had been restless, he had quarreled with every boss, he had been unrealistically on the make.

Still, nowadays there was a job for anyone who could read and write. Mr. Pateman was, in the mechanical sense, far from stupid. He had a good deal of energy. At his age, he would not get a better job, certainly not one much better. He might get a different one.

He was sitting with his hands on his knees, his head back, a smile as it were of approbation on his lips. He did not appear in the least uneasy that I should not find an answer. The slack fire smoked: the draught blew across the room: among the fumes I picked out the antiseptic smell which hung about him as though he had just come from hospital.

"Well, Mr. Pateman," I said. "I mustn't raise false hopes." I went on to say that I was out of the official life for good and all. He gazed at me with confident disbelief: to him, that was simply part of my make-believe. There were two places he might try. He could possibly get fitted up in another radio firm: I could give him the name of a personnel officer.

"Once bitten, twice shy, thank you, sir," said Mr. Pateman.

Alternatively, he might contemplate working in a government office as a temporary clerk. The pay would be a little better: the work, I warned him, would be extremely monotonous: I could tell him how to apply at the local employment exchange.

"I don't believe in employment exchanges. I believe in going somewhere where one has contacts at the top."

He seemed—had it been true before he met me?—to have dreamed up his own fantasy. He seemed to think that I should say one simple word to my old colleagues. I tried to explain to him that the machine did not work that way. If the Ministry of Labor took him on, they would send him wherever clerks were needed. He could tell them that he had a preference, but there was no guarantee that he would get what he wanted.

Anyone who had been asked for such a favor had to get used to the sight of disappointment—and to the different ways men took it. There were a few who, like Mr. Pateman now, began to threaten.

"I must say, I was hoping for something more constructive from you," he said.

"I am sorry."

"I don't like being led up the garden path." His eyes were fixed on mine. "I was given to understand that you weren't as hide-bound as some of them."

I said nothing.

"I shall have to consider my course of action." He was speaking with dignity. Then he said: "I expect that you're doing your best. You must be a busy man."

I got up, went into the back kitchen, and shook hands with his wife. She could have overheard us throughout: she looked up at me with something like understanding.

Mr. Pateman took me down the passage (the record player was still sounding from the front room), and, at the door, threw out his hand in a stately goodbye.

FIVE

TIME AND A FRIEND

Owing to the single-mindedness of Mr. Pateman, I was a few minutes late for my appointment with George Passant. I arrived in the lounge of the public house where we had first drunk together when I was eighteen, nearly forty years before: the room was almost empty, for the pub was no longer fashionable at night and George himself no longer used it, except for these ritual meetings with me.

There, by the side of what used to be a coal-fire and was now blocked up, he sat. He gave me a burst of greeting, a monosyllabic shout.

As I grew older, and met friends whom I had known for most of my lifetime, I often thought that I didn't see them clearly—or rather, that I saw them with a kind of double vision, as though there were two photographs not accurately superposed. Underneath, there was not only a memory of themselves when young, but the physical presence: that lingered in one's sight, it was never quite ripped away, one still saw them—through the intermittence of time passing—with one's own youthful eyes. And also one saw them as they were now, in the present moment, as one was oneself.

Nowadays I met George three or four times a year, and this double vision was still working. I could still—not often, but in sharp moments—see the young man who had befriended me, set me going: whose face had been full of anger and hope, and who had walked with me through the streets outside on nights of triumph, his voice rebounding from the darkened houses.

But, more than in any other friend, the present was here, too. There he sat in the pub. His face was in front of me, greeting me with formal welcome. It was the face of an old sick man.

Not that he was unhappy. On the contrary, he had been happier than most men all his life, and had stayed so. Not that he behaved as though he were ill. On the contrary, he behaved as though he were immortal. If I had been studying him for the first time, I should have been doubtful about guessing his age. His fair hair was still thick, and had whitened only over his ears, though it was wild and disarranged, for his whole appearance was dilapidated. His face was lined, but almost at random, so that he had no look of mature age. His mouth often fell open, and his eyes became unfocused.

He was actually sixty-three. I had tried to get him to discuss his health, but he turned vague, sometimes, it seemed to me, with a deliberate cunning. He spoke casually about his blood-pressure and some pills he had to take. He admitted that his doctor, whose name he wouldn't tell me, had put him on a diet. From what I noticed, he didn't even pretend to keep to it. He still ate gargantuan meals, somehow proud of his self-indulgence, topping off—in a fashion which once had been comic but was now frightening—a meal larger than most of us ate in two days with four or five cream-cakes. He drank as much, or more, than ever. He had always been heavy, but now was fat from his upper chest down to his groin. He must have weighed fifteen stone.

None of that had interfered with his desire for women. I had an uncomfortable suspicion that, as he grew old, he wanted younger girls: but, with the same elderly cunning with which he dissimulated his health, he had long ago concealed those details from me. I knew that his firm of solicitors had pensioned him off a couple of years before. Once again, he was vague in telling me the reasons. It might have been that his concentration had gone, as his body deteriorated. It might have been that what he called his "private life," that underground group activity by which he had once started out to emancipate us all, had become notorious. And yet, in this middle-sized town, none of the members of the Court that morning would have been likely even to have heard his name.

He kept his strange diffident sweetness. When he forced himself, his mind became precise. He liked seeing me. Yet, I had to admit it (it was an admission that for years I had shut out), he had become quite remote. Whenever we met, he asked the same set of hearty mechanical questions, as he did that night. How was Margaret? Well, I said. Splendid, said George. Was I writing? Yes, I said. Splendid, said George. How was Charles? Getting on fine, I said. Here the formula took a different course. "I'm not concerned about his academic prospects. I take those for granted," said George. "I'm asking you about his health."

"He's very tough," I said.

"I hope you're certain about that," said George, as though he were a family doctor or the best-qualified censor of physical self-discipline.

"He's fine."

"Well, that's slightly reassuring," said George. "It's his health that I want to be convinced about, that's the important thing."

That conversation, in very much the same words, took place each time we met. It expressed a kind of formalized affection. But it had set in a groove something like ten years before. So far as there was meaning in the questions about Charles, they referred to the fact that he had been seriously ill in infancy. Since then, he had been as healthy as a boy could be: but George, who wanted to show his interest, couldn't find an interest in anything that had happened to him since.

"Drink up!" cried George. I had another pint of beer, which, except with him, I never drank.

I should have liked (I had enough nostalgia for that) to settle down to talk. I mentioned my singular experience with Mr. Pateman. George, happy with some internal reverie, gave a loud but inattentive laugh. I said that I had, for a moment or two, come across his niece. At that he showed some response, as though breaking through the daydream which submerged him.

"I'm afraid I haven't been able to see much of my family," he said.

I understood his language too well to ask why not. There were esoteric reasons manifest to him, though to no one else. In fact, he had had three sisters: all had married, and one, Cora's mother, was now dead. Another one was living in London, and the third had stayed in the town. All three of them had borne nothing but daughters; I had met none of George's nieces until that afternoon, and he himself seldom referred to them.

"This one"—Cora—"seems to be pretty bright," he said. "She even tagged along with some of my people not so long ago—"

"My people" were the successors to the group of which, in my time, he had been the leader and inspirer. All the years since, he had been surrounded by young men and women, his own self-perpetuating underground.

"What happened?"

"Oh, somehow she seemed to lose touch." He went on: "I've never inquired into the lives of any of my family. And I've never told them anything about my own."

He said that with the simplicity of Einstein stating that "puritanical reticence" was necessary for a searcher after truth.

I started to speak about a concern of mine. After all, he was my oldest friend, and it had been a jagged year for me, as my father didn't know but my young son did—and as George had barely noticed. When I got out of public life, soon after Roger Quaife's defeat, I had expected to get out of controversy also. But it hadn't happened like that. Some of the enmity had followed me, and had got tangled up with my literary affairs. A few months before, I had been accused, in somewhat lurid circumstances, of plagiarism. This had made the news, and kept recurring. As I told George, understating the whole business, if you live in public at all, you have to take what's coming: but, though I could imagine almost any other kind of accusation against me having some sort of basis, this one hadn't. That, however, didn't make it any more pleasant.

My brand of sarcasm washed over him.

"I remember seeing something or other in the papers," he said. "Of course, I couldn't take part. Who's going to listen to a retired solicitor's clerk? Anyway, as you say, you've nothing to complain about."

That was not what I had really said: he had forgotten my tone of voice. "If anyone's got anything to complain about," said George, warming up, "I have. Do you realize that I've spent forty-two years in this wretched town, and they've kept me out of everything? They've seen to it that I've never had a responsible position in my whole life. They've put a foot across my path ever since I was a boy. And at the end, if you please, they don't say as much as thank you and they give me a bit more pension than they need just to stop feeling ashamed of themselves."

In the first place, "they" meant his old firm of solicitors. But "they" also meant all the kinds of authority he had struggled against, detected conspiracies among, found incomprehensible and yet omnipotent, since he was a boy. All the authority in the country. Or in life, as far as that went. It sounded like persecution-mania, and he had always had a share of it. Yet like many people with persecution-mania, he had something to feel persecuted about. Perhaps the one allured the other? Which came first? He was the cleverest man whom I had seen, in functional terms, so completely wasted. But now I had seen more, I speculated on the kind of skill, or whether there was any, which would have been needed not to waste him—or not to let him waste himself.

"I never got anything, did I?" he said, with a gentle puzzled smile.

"No, you didn't."

"I suppose I didn't want it very much." Just for an instant, all the paraphernalia of his temperament was thrown aside, and that dart of candor shot out.

"Anyway," he shouted, in a great voice, not the voice of a sick man, "they won. *They won*. Let's have another drink on it."

He was happy and resigned. Did he realize—probably not, he was too happy to go in for irony—that, in a different sense, it was he who had won? All those passionate arguments for *freedom*—which meant sexual freedom. The young George in this town, poor, unknown, feeling himself outside society, raising the great voice I had just heard. "Freedom from their damned homes, and their damned parents, and their damned lives." Well, he had won: or rather, all those like him, all the forces they spoke for (since he was, as someone had said during one of his ordeals, a "child of his time") had won. How completely, one could not escape at the Court that morning. The freedom which George had once dreamed about had duly happened: and, now it had happened, he took it for granted. He didn't cherish it as a victory. He just assumed that the world was better than it used to be.

I had expected that we should have a meal together—but George was looking at his watch.

"I'm afraid," he said, "that I'm rather pressed tonight."

He had the air, which one sometimes saw in businessmen or politicians, of faint estrangement from those not regulated by a timetable.

I did not ask where he was going. I said I should attend the Court in June, and that we could meet as usual. Splendid, said George. Splendid, he repeated, with immense heartiness. He got up to leave me. As he went to the door, I noticed that he was making one, though only one, concession to his physical state: he was walking with abnormal slowness. It was deliberate, but from the back he looked like an old man.

When I myself left the pub, I didn't stroll through the streets, as I often liked doing. That meeting with George had had an effect on me which I didn't understand, or perhaps didn't want to: it hadn't precisely saddened me, but I didn't want my memory to be played on. It was better to be with people whom I hadn't known for long, to be back in the here and-now. So I returned to the Residence: this time the drawing-room lights, seen from the drive, were welcoming. The sight of Vicky was welcoming too. They had had an early dinner, she said, and her father had gone off to his manuscripts. She said: "When did you eat last?"

Not since breakfast, I replied. She clucked, and said that I was impossible. Soon I was sitting in front of the fire with a plate of sandwiches. Vicky curled up on the rug. I was tired, but not unpleasantly so, just enough to realize that I had had a long day. It was all familiar and comfortable, the past pushed away, no menace left.

Vicky wouldn't talk, or let me, until I had eaten. Then she said that her father had told her about the Court proceedings. She knew the result, and she was relieved: anyway, we had time to work in: perversely, she was enough relieved to be irritated with me.

"You two"—she meant her father and me—"had an up-and-a-downer, didn't you?"

"Not exactly."

"That's his account, anyway."

I told her that I thought I deserved a bit of praise. She said:

"I must say, I should like to knock your heads together."

It appeared that Arnold Shaw had told her of a violent argument, in which he had prevailed. Actually, she was pleased. Pleased because she was protective about her father and trusted me. She was hopeful about the next moves. I said that the academics were being sensible, and I myself would try to involve Francis Getliffe.

She was sitting on her heels, her hair shining and her face tinted in the firelight.

"Bless you," she said.

I had not mentioned Leonard Getliffe's name, but only his father's. That was enough, though, to set her thoughts going, as if I had touched a trigger and released uncontrollable forces. Her expression was softened; when she spoke her voice was strong but had lost the touch of bossiness, the doctor's edge.

Could she make a nuisance of herself again? she said. She knew that I understood: questions about Pat had formed themselves. My first impulse, before she had said a word, was of pity for Leonard Getliffe.

Though I knew, and she knew that I knew, she started off by seeming unusually theoretical. Was a marriage, all other things being good, likely to be affected if the wife was earning the livelihood? Even for her, the most direct of young women, it was a pleasure to go through a minuet, to produce a problem in the abstract, or as though she were seeking advice on behalf of a remote acquaintance. I gave a banal answer, that sometimes I had known it work, sometimes not. In my own first marraige, I added, my wife had contributed half the money: and, though it had been unhappy, it had not been any more unhappy, perhaps less, because of that. She hadn't heard of my first marriage: and, after what I had just said, she still really hadn't heard. She said:

"So you're not against it?"

I said, once more banal, that any general answer had no meaning. Then I asked:

"Are you going to get married then?"

"I hope so."

I had another impulse, this time of concern for her. She was speaking with certainty. I wished that she was more superstitious, or that she had some insurance against the future.

"You see," said Vicky, "I can earn a living, though it won't be a very grand living, while we see if he can make a go of it. Is that a good idea?"

"Isn't he very young—" I began carefully, but she interrupted me.

"There is a snag, of course. You can't do a medical job with young children around. I'm too wrapped up in him to think about children now. You know how it is, I can't believe that I shall ever want anything but him. I have to tell myself, of course I shall." She gave a self-deprecating smile. "I'm just the same as everybody else, aren't I? I expect I shall turn into a pretty-doting mother."

"I expect you will," I said. I was easier when she got down from the heights.

"If we wanted to start a family in three or four years' time, and we oughtn't to leave it much later, because I shall be getting on for thirty, then he might not be able to keep us, might he?"

Practical plans. Delectable practical plans. As delectable as being on the heights, sometimes more so.

"However good he is," I said, "it's hard to break through at his game—"

"I know," she said. "Well, what else can he do on the side?"

I said it would be difficult for his father to allow him anything. Martin had a daughter still at school, and apart from his Cambridge salary, not a penny. As for myself—

"Oh, I couldn't possibly let you give us money."

Her young man quite possibly could, I thought. I nearly said it: but she, like George in the pub an hour or two before, would not have recognized my tone of voice.

In any case, there was something that I ought to say.

"Look, Vicky," I began, as casually as I could, hesitating between leaving her quite unwarned and throwing even the faintest shade upon her joy, "I told you a minute ago, he is a very young man, isn't he?"

"Do you know, I don't feel that."

"*Your* character's formed," I went on. "You're as grown-up as you'll ever be." (I wasn't convinced of that, but it was a way to talk of Pat.) "I'm not so sure that's true of him, you know."

She was looking at me without apprehension, without a blink.

"I mean," I said, "parts of people's character grow up at different rates. Perhaps that's specially so for men. In some ways, Pat's mature. But I'm not certain that he is in all. I'm not certain that he's capable of knowing exactly what he wants for his whole life. He may be too young for that."

She smiled.

"You're wrong," she said.

She smiled at me affectionately, but like someone in the know, with a piece of information the source of which cannot be revealed.

"He's a very strong character," she said.

All my hesitation had been unnecessary. I hadn't hurt her. She was no less fond of me, and also no less joyous. She was totally unaffected. She was confident—but that was too weak a word, for this was the confidence of every cell in her body— that she knew him as I could never do, and that she was right.

We did not say much more about Pat that night. Some time

afterwards, while we were still sitting by the fire, Arnold Shaw came in, rubbing his hands.

"Couple of hours' good work," he announced. "Which is more than most of my colleagues will do this term."

With the utmost friendliness and good nature, he asked me if I had spent a tolerable afternoon, and invited me to have a nightcap. Vicky was watching us both with a blank expression. She had heard him talk of a bitter quarrel: if I knew Arnold Shaw's temper, he had denounced me as every kind of a bad man: here he was, convivial, and treating me as an old friend. She admired him for being a museum specimen of a seagreen incorruptible (in that she was her father's daughter): here he was, looking not incorruptible but matey and malicious, and certainly not seagreen. Here we both were, drinking our nightcaps, as though we wanted no one else's company. Yet she didn't for an instant doubt that he would never budge an inch, and that I too would stick it out. Here we were, exchanging sharp-tongued gossip. It struck her as part of a masculine conspiracy which she could not completely comprehend.

When Arnold Shaw was disposed to think of a second nightcap, she roused herself and, daughterlike, doctorlike, said that it was time for bed.

SIX

DESCRIBING A
TRIANGLE

Back in our flat, the sunlight slanting down over the Hyde
Park trees, my wife was listening to me. I had been telling
her about the past two days: we had our own shorthand, she
knew where I had been amused and where I was pretending
to be amused.

"It's a good job you've got some stamina, isn't it?" she
said.

It sounded detached; it couldn't have been less so. She was
happy because I was well and not resigned, any more than
she was herself. She had always looked younger than her age,
and did so still. Her skin remained as fine as Vicky Shaw's.
The only open sign of middle-age were the streaks of gray
above her temples. I had suggested that, since she looked in
all other respects so young, she might as well have them
tinted. She had been taken aback, for that was the kind of
intervention which she didn't expect from me. But she said
no: it was the one trivial thing she had refused me. She wore
those streaks like insignia.

In some ways she had changed during our marriage: or
rather, parts of her temperament had thrust themselves
through, in a fashion that to me was a surprise and not a
surprise, part of the Japanese-flower of marriage. To others,
even to friends as perceptive as Charles March or my brother,
she had seemed over-delicate, or something like austere. It
was the opposite of the truth. Once she had dressed very

simply, but now she spent money and was smart. It might have seemed that she had become vainer and more self-regarding. Actually, she had become more humble. She didn't mind revealing herself, not as what she had once thought suitable, but as she really was: and if what she revealed was self-contradictory, well then (in this aspect true to her high-minded intellectual ancestors, from whom in all else she had parted) she didn't give a damn.

Earlier, she used to think that I enjoyed "the world" too much. Now she enjoyed it more than I did. At the same time, in the midst of happiness, she wanted something else. She had thrown away the web of personal relations, the aesthetic credo, in which and by which her father, whom she loved, had lived his life. That was too thin for her: and as for the stoical dutifulness of many of my political or scientific friends, she could admire it, but it wasn't enough. She would have liked to be a religious believer: she couldn't make herself. It wasn't a deep wound, as it had been for Roy Calvert, for she was stronger-spirited, but she knew what it was—as perhaps all deep-natured people know it—to be happy, to count her blessings, and, in the midst of content, to feel morally restless, to feel that there must be another purpose to this life.

With Margaret, too clear-sighted to fabricate a purpose, this gave an extra edge to her responsibilities. As a young woman she had been responsible, with a conscience greater than mine: now she was almost superstitiously so. Her father, who had been ill for years—she wouldn't go out at night without leaving a telephone number. Her son by her first marriage. Charles and me at home. Her sister. Margaret tried to disguise it, because she knew her own obsessions: but if she had believed in prayer, she would have prayed for many people every night.

So she took it for granted that I ought to do my best for Arnold Shaw and Vicky. She took it for granted that I should

be as long-suffering as she could be—for after the years together, some of my behavior had shaded into hers, and hers
into mine. Further, she was herself involved. She seemed controlled, whereas I was easy and let my emotions flow, so that
people were deceived: her loves and hates had always been
violent, and below the surface they were not damped down.
She was exhibiting one of them now, against my nephew Pat.
She thought he was a waster. She was sorry for any woman
who married him. Yet, although she scarcely knew Vicky, she
believed me when I said that she was totally committed.

There wasn't much one could do in others' lives: that was a
lesson I had taught her. But there was no excuse for not
doing the little that one could: that was a lesson she had
taught me. At the least, I could put in a word for Arnold
Shaw. It would be better for both of them if he kept his job.
It was worth going to Cambridge, just to get Francis Getliffe's support, Margaret agreed. We didn't like being parted,
but she couldn't come while her father was so ill: for some
time past she had been tied to London, and consequently in
the last twelve months I had spent only six or seven nights
away from home.

This time I need not stay in Cambridge more than one
night—and that I could put off until Charles went back to
school. There were a few days left of his holidays, and he was
still young enough to enjoy going out with Margaret and me
to dinner and the theater, the pleasant safeguarded London
evenings.

Those days passed, and I was in a taxi, driving out along
the Backs to the Getliffes' house, within a week of my visit to
the Court. So that, by chance, I had completed the triangle of
the three towns that I knew best—in fact, the only three
towns in England that I had ever lived in for long. The sky
was lucid, there was a cold wind blowing, the blossom was
heavy white on the trees: it was late afternoon in April, the
time of day and year that I used to walk away from Fenner's.

This was the "pretty England" with which I had baited my son, the prettiest of pretty England. Nowadays when I saw Cambridge, I saw it like a visitor, and thought how beautiful it was. And yet, when I lived there, I seemed scarcely to have noticed it. It had been a bad time for me, my hopes had come to nothing, I was living (and this had been true of me until I was middle-aged) as though I were in a station waiting-room: somehow a train would come, taking me somewhere, anywhere, letting my hopes flare up again. But that wasn't what I remarked first about Cambridge: instead, it was the distractions, or even the comforts, that I had found. One of the most robust of men, who was given to melancholy, told a fellow-sufferer to light bright fires. Well, I had had enough to be melancholy about, but what I remembered were the bright fires. There had been times when I didn't know what was to become of me: yet it had been a consolation (and this was the memory, unless I dug deeper against my will) to call on old Arthur Brown, drink a glass of wine, and get going on another move in college politics. Even if I had been content, I should nevertheless, I was sure, have got some interest out of that power-play. I enjoyed watching personal struggles, big and small, and I couldn't have found a better training-ground. But, all that admitted, if I had been content, I shouldn't have become so passionately absorbed in college politics. They were my refuge from the cold outside.

The Getliffes' drawing room was, as usual, untidy and welcoming: perhaps a shade more untidy than it used to be, since now they had half a dozen grandchildren. It had been welcoming in the past, even when my relations with Francis had been strained, once when we were ranged on different sides, and again more recently when, led by Quaife, we had been on the same side and lost. It had been welcoming even when he was torn by ambition, when his research was going wrong or his public campaigns had wrecked his nerves. One could see the traces of those tensions in his face to this day, the lines, the folds of sepia flesh under his eyes. But the tensions had themselves all gone. Of my close friends, he had had the greatest and the most deserved success. Quite late in life, he had done scientific work with which he was satisfied. That was his prime reward. The honors had flowed in: he was no hypocrite, and he liked those too. There had never been anything puritanical about his radicalism. On a question of principle, he had not made a single concession: his integrity was absolute: but, if orthodoxy chose to catch up with him, well, then he was ready to enjoy sitting in the House of Lords.

The stiffness, the touch of formality which looked like pride and which had developed during the worst of his struggles, had almost vanished. Sometimes in public it could recur. I had recently heard some smart young debunker pass a verdict on him. The young man had met him precisely once, but felt morally obliged to dispose of an eminent figure. "He's the hell of a prima donna, of course, but he does know how to land the jobs." I hadn't been infuriated so much as stupefied. Each of us really is alone, I thought. And now I was greeting my old friend and his wife, in their own home, in the happiest marriage I had ever seen.

I embraced Katherine. She had, with unusual self-discipline, been dieting recently and had lost a stone or two: but she remained a matriarch. When Francis was surrounded by the three married children and assorted grandsons and granddaughters, he became a patriarch. Yet now he and Katherine were smiling at each other with—there was no need to diminish or qualify the word—love. They had been married for well over thirty years: it had been a lively active marriage, the support—more than support, the inner validity—in all his troubles. They had gone on loving each other, and now, when the troubles were over, they did so still.

It would have been easy, one would have expected, to envy

Francis. He had had so much. And yet, curiously enough, he had not attracted a great deal of envy. Nothing like as much as our old colleague, Walter Luke: not as much as I had at times myself. What makes a character envy-repellent? On the whole, the people I had known who attracted the least envy were cold, shut in, mildly paranoid. But none of that was true of Francis, who was—at least in intimacy—both kind and warm. So was she, and they were showing it that evening.

Though Katherine complained that she hated entertaining, and had given that as a reason why Francis should not become Master of the college (the hidden reason was that he shrank from the in-fighting), this house had, with the years, taken on a marked resemblance to the ground floor of an American hotel. One son and one daughter lived in Cambridge; and they, their children, their friends, their friends' children, paid visits as unpredictable as those in a nineteenth-century Russian country house. In the midst of the casual family hubbub, the Getliffes took care of others: they knew that Margaret would want news of her son Maurice, and so, along with a party of young people, some of whom I couldn't identify but who all called Francis by his Christian name, he had been brought in for a pre-dinner drink. By one of the sardonic tricks of chance, it was just that same considerate kindness which had brought ill-luck to their eldest son: for, on a similar occasion, when Leonard first brought Vicky Shaw to see them, they had invited my nephew Pat: and it was in this drawing room that she had fallen in love.

In a corner of the room, I was talking to Maurice about his work.

"I wish I were brighter," he said with his beautiful innocent smile, as he had said to me before, since for years Margaret and I had had to watch him struggle over one scholastic hurdle, then another. He bore no malice, even though the rest of us found these hurdles non-existent. He was fond of his stepbrother, who was a born competitor. Sometimes I

couldn't help thinking—it was a rare thought for me—that he
was naturally good. He had been a beautiful child, and now
was a good-looking young man. I should have guessed, when I
first saw him as an infant, that by now he would appear
indrawn: but that had proved dead wrong. He had turned
out good-looking in an unusual fashion, as though the world
hadn't touched him: fair, unshadowed, with wide-orbited
idealist's eyes. Yet the world probably had touched him, for
those were the kind of looks that at school had brought him
plenty of attention. And he would get the same from women
soon, I thought. He gave affection very easily: he might be
innocent, but he accepted all that happened round him. He
liked making people happy.

Margaret was devoted to him. Partly with the special devotion, and remorse, that one feels for the child of a broken
marriage: partly because there was something of her own
spirit in him. But none of her cleverness, nor of his father's.

I was trying to discover how things were going. He was in
his first year. He hoped to become a doctor, like his father.
Psychologically, that would be a good choice for him. He
wanted to look after others: given the faith which he, like
Margaret, didn't find, he would have made a priest.

The trouble was, the college had told us that he was unlikely to get through the Mays (the Cambridge first-year examinations). I was inquiring what he thought, and which
subjects were the worst.

"I'm afraid I'm pretty dense," he said.

"No, you're not," I said. I let some impatience show. Often
I felt that, just as he accepted everything else, he accepted his
own incompetence.

"You believe I'm doing it on purpose, don't you?" He was
teasing me. He and I had always been on friendly terms. He
wasn't in the least frightened of me: nor, so far as I had ever
seen, of anyone else. He had his own kind of insight.

At last the Getliffes and I were left alone. For once there was no one else present when we went into dinner. Francis, who had seen me spend a long time with Maurice, began talking about him.

"I'm afraid," he said, "he isn't going to make it."

"He's very nice," said Katherine.

"He's not even stupid," said Francis. "I know, it must be a worry for you both."

The two of them were not only loving parents, they took on the duties of parents at one remove. It seemed like a way of giving thanks for their own good fortune. The problems of friends' children—not only those of intimate friends like us—they spent their time upon. About Maurice, Francis had had interviews with his tutor and supervisors. Francis and Katherine hadn't known the inside of a broken marriage; but their sympathy was sharp, they could feel for both Margaret and me; in different senses, it made us more vulnerable through Maurice.

They were sympathetic, but also practical. With a creased, unsentimental smile, Francis said that, come hell, come high water, we had to get the young man through some sort of course. Damn it, he had to earn a living. His supervisors said he didn't seem to possess any approach to a memory. He couldn't memorize anything. "I should have thought," said Francis, "that's going to make medicine pretty well impossible. The anatomy they learn is sheer unscientific nonsense, but still they've got to learn it."

He gave me some consolatory examples to tell Margaret, of intelligent people who had nothing like a normal memory, and there we had to leave it, Katherine reluctantly, for she, like all her relatives I had once known so well, couldn't resist coming back to test an aching tooth.

The dinner was good. Francis, who had been so gaunt and quixotic right into his mid-fifties, was at last beginning to put on a little weight. I was comfortable with them both, and more than that. But I should have to leave in an hour or two, for I was staying with my brother. It was time to discharge what I had come for.

"Francis," I said, "I wonder if you can give a hand about old Arnold Shaw."

He had heard most of the immediate story—though neither he nor Katherine were above inquiring about the details of the students' goings-on. I told him that the present issue was effectively steeled: it looked as though two or three of the students would be placed elsewhere: and then Shaw would get a confirmatory vote and, in form, a victory. But, I said, it might be an expensive victory. He had had plenty of enemies before. Now there would be more. There might come a point, not too far off, when his position became untenable. Could Francis use his influence as Chancellor? Could he talk to the academics in private? And to some of the dignitaries? After all, he could speak with real authority. He just had to tell them that, in spite of his faults, Shaw was doing a good job.

Francis had been listening as carefully as he used to listen in Whitehall. He passed the decanter round to me, and watched me fill my glass. He said:

"I don't think I can tell them that."

"Why not?"

"Quite simply, I don't believe he is."

"Oh come," I said. Incautiously, I hadn't been prepared for this. "Look, I know he's an awkward customer, I have to stand more of it than you do, but after all he has put the place on the map."

"I don't believe," said Francis, "that a man ought to be head of a university if he gets detested by nearly all the students and most of the staff."

It was years since I had seen him in action: I had half-forgotten how decisive he could be.

"Remember," I said, "that he's brought in the staff—at least, he's brought in all of them that are any good."

"He is a good picker." Francis was irritatingly fair. "Yes, that's been his contribution. But now he's got them, he can't get on with them. It's a pity, but the place will be at sixes and sevens so long as he's there."

He added:

"It's a pity, but he's cut his own throat."

"He's got some human quality," I said.

Katherine broke in:

"You said that before. About the other one. And we said his wife was appalling. So she was, but I suppose she was attached to him in her own fashion. When he died, it was just before Penelope had her second baby, she stayed with the coffin and they had to pull her away from the grave."

For the moment, I had lost track. Who was she talking about?

"And then she died within three months, though no one troubled to know about her and so no one knew what was the matter. As for Walter Luke, it didn't do him any harm. He went to Barford and got into the Royal Society and nearly got killed—"

"No connection." Francis smiled at her, though he looked as mystified as I was.

"And finished up perfectly well and got decorated and had another child."

She ended in triumph:

"You did make a frightful ass of yourself that time, Lewis."

That was a phrase her father used to brandish. I had been quite bemused, but now I had it. She was indulging, as she did more often, in a feat of total recall, just as her father used to. What she had been saying referred to an argument about the Mastership in that house, no less than twenty-six years before. It was the candidate I had wanted, Jago, who had died, and his wife after him—but that was not twenty-six years before, only two. When Katherine got going, she existed, just as her father had, in a timeless continuum when the present moment, the three of us there at dinner, was just as real, no more, no less, than the flux of memory.

Francis was slower than I to take the reference. Then he gave her a loving grin, and said to me:

"She's right, you know. You did make an ass of yourself that time."

It was true. It had been bad judgment. But, though my candidate had lost, though it was so long ago, Katherine and Francis often liked to remind me of it.

"Two can play at that game," I began, ready to try rougher tactics, but in fact Katherine's performance had taken the sting from the quarrel, and also, realistically, I knew that Francis, once he had taken up his stance, would be as hard to move as Arnold Shaw himself. So when he said that I was now making the same mistake, that I got more interested in people than in the job they had to do, I let it go. It wasn't without justice, after all. And it wasn't without justice that he spoke of Arnold Shaw. Something would have to be done for him, if and when he resigned: the university would give him an honorary degree: he could be found a research appointment to help out his pension. That would be better than nothing, I said. Then I mentioned that I had met Leonard, and the three of us were at one again.

"I'm getting just a little tired," said Francis, "of people telling me that as a scientist he is an order of magnitude better than I am." But he said it with the special pride of a father who enjoys his son being praised at his own expense. To give an appearance of stern impartiality, as of one who isn't going to see his family receive more than their due, he said that their second son, Lionel, wasn't in the same class. "I don't think he's any better than I am," said Francis judiciously. "He ought to get into the Royal before he's finished though."

I said that they were abnormally lucky: but still, the genes on both sides were pretty good. Francis said, not all that good. His father had been a moderately competent barrister at the Parliamentary Bar. Katherine said: "There's not been a single March who's ever produced an original idea in his life. Except, perhaps, my great-uncle Benjamin, who tried to persuade the Rothschilds not to put down the money for the Suez Canal."

Anyway, said Francis, who wanted to talk more of Leonard, a talent like his must be a pure sport. High level of ability, yes, lots of families had that—but the real stars, they might come from anywhere, they were just a gift of fate. "It must be wonderful," he said, half-wistfully, "to have his sort of power."

They were proud of him, as I should have been, or any sentient parent. They were pleased that he was as high-principled as they were: he had recently defied criticism and appointed Donald Howard, who had once been a fellow of the college, to his staff, just because he had been badly treated—although Leonard didn't even like the man. But, despite their close family life, they seemed to know little or nothing of his unhappiness over Vicky. "It's high time he got married," said Katherine, as though that were his only blemish, an inexplicable piece of wilfulness. They wondered what sort of children he would have.

After Francis had driven me to the college gate, I walked through the courts to the Senior Tutor's house. I had walked that same way often enough when Jago was Senior Tutor. Now I was accustomed to it again, since my brother, after Arthur Brown's term, got the succession. Lights were shining, young men's voices resounded: the smell of wistaria was faint on the cool air: it brought back, not a sharp memory, but a sense that there was something I knew but had (like a name on the tip of the tongue) temporarily forgotten.

My brother's study was lit up, curtains undrawn, and there

he and Irene were waiting for me. She fussed round, yelping cheerfully: Martin sat by the fireside in his slippers, sharp-eyed, fraternal, suspecting that there was some meaning in this visit.

Another home, another marriage. A settled marriage, but one which had arrived there by a different route from the Getliffes'. She had been a reckless, amorous young woman: in their first years she had had lovers, had cost him humiliation and, because he had married for love, much misery. But he was the stronger of the two. It was his will which had worn her down. It was possible—I was not certain—that as she grew to depend upon him utterly, she in her turn had been through some misery. I was not certain, because, though he trusted me more than anyone else and occasionally asked me to store away some documents, he preserved a kind of whiggish decorum. If there had been love affairs, they had been kept hidden. Anyway, their marriage had been settled for a long time past, and Martin's anxiety had its roots in another place.

On my way down to Cambridge, I hadn't been confident that I should get him to talk. As soon as I entered his study we were easy together, with the ease of habit, and something stronger too. But he had been controlled and secretive all his life, and in middle age he was letting secretiveness possess him. I still didn't know whether I should get an answer, or even be able to talk at all.

By accident, or perhaps not entirely by accident, for she understood him well, it was Irene who gave me the chance.

We had begun by gossiping. Nowadays the college changed more rapidly than it used to in my time. There were twice as many fellows, they came and went. Many of my old acquaintances were dead. Of those who had voted in the 1937 election, only Arthur Brown, Francis, and Nightingale were still fellows. Some I had known since hadn't stayed for long. One who hadn't stayed—it was he that Irene was gossiping about—

was a man called Lester Ince. He had recently run off with an American woman: an American woman, so it turned out, of enormous wealth. They had each got divorces and then married. The present rumor was that they were looking round for a historic country house.

"A very suitable end for an angry young man," said Martin, with a tart smile. I was amused. I had a soft spot for Lester Ince. It was true that, since he had started his academic career by being remarkably rude, he had gained a reputation for holding advanced opinions. This had infuriated both Francis and Martin, who believed in codes of manners, and who also remained seriously radical and had each paid a certain price.

"He's quite a good chap," I said.

"He hasn't got the political intelligence of a newt," said Martin.

"He's really very amiable," I said.

"If it hadn't been for that damned fool," Martin was not placated, "we shouldn't have been in this intolerable mess."

That also was true. Before Crawford, the last Master, retired, it had been assumed that Francis Getliffe would stand and get the job. That would presumably have happened—but Francis had suddenly said no. The college had dissolved into a collective hubbub. Lester Ince had trumpeted that what they needed was an *independent man*. The independent man was G. S. Clark. Half the college saw the beauty of the idea: G. S. Clark was an obsessed reactionary in all senses, but that didn't matter. Martin, who was an accomplished college politician, did his best for Arthur Brown, but the Clark faction won by a couple of votes. It had been one of the bitter elections.

"It's got to the point," Martin was saying, "that when the Master puts his name down to dine, half a dozen people take theirs off."

"What about you?"

"As a rule," said Martin, without expression, "I dine at home."

That had its own eloquence. He was both patient and polite: and once he had been on neighborly terms with Clark. Yes, he replied to my question, they were saddled with him for another seven years.

Irene was more interested in Lester Ince's future.

"Think of all that lovely money," she said.

She told me about the heiress. It appeared that Lester Ince had at his disposal more money than any fellow (or ex-fellow, for he had just resigned) of the college in five hundred years.

"Money. We could do with a bit of that," she said.

She said it brightly, but suddenly I felt there was strain, or meaning, underneath. To test her, I replied: "Couldn't we all?"

"*You* can't say that to us, you really can't." Her eyes were darting, but not just with fun.

"Is anything the matter?" I wasn't looking at Martin, but speaking straight to her.

"Oh, no. Well, the children cost a lot, of course they do."

Their daughter Nina, who was seventeen that year, went to a local school: she was a gentle girl, with a musical flair which her brother might have envied, and had cost them nothing. It was Pat on whom they had spent the money—and, I guessed, more than they could spare, although Martin was financially a prudent man. It was Pat about whom she was showing the strain. She had to risk offending Martin, who sat there in hard silence.

I risked it too.

"I suppose it'll be some time before he's self-supporting, won't it?" I asked.

"Good God!" she cried. "We shouldn't mind so much if we were sure that he would ever be."

She went on talking to me, Martin still silent. I must have known young men like this, mustn't I? What could one do? She wasn't asking much: all she asked was that he should come to terms, and begin to behave like everyone else.

This was the strangest game that time had played with my sister-in-law. It had played a game with her physically, but that I was used to: she had been a thin, active young woman, and then in her thirties became the victim of a pyknic practical joke: so that, although her face kept an avid girlish prettiness, she had, as it were, blown up like a Michelin tire man. But that was a joke of the flesh, and this was odder. For only a few years before, as she contemplated her son, she was delighted that he seemed "as wild as a hawk." She had enjoyed the prospect of a son as "dashing" as the young men with whom she had herself racketed round. Now she had it. And she was less comfortable with it than respectable parents like the Getliffes might have been.

She seemed specially horrified about his debts, though, again oddly, she had no idea how big they were.

"Don't worry too much about that," I said. "Perhaps I can help."

"That isn't necessary." For the first time since his son was hinted at, Martin spoke.

Irene looked at him: either she did not choose, or did not dare to talk any further. In a moment, with a bright yelping cry, she announced that she was tired. "You boys can sit up if you want, don't mind me," she said, on her way to the door.

Martin was sitting with his shoulders hunched, his fingers laced together on one knee. His scalp showed where the hair was thinning: between us, in the old grate, gleamed one bar of the electric fire. Behind Martin was a bookcase full of bound scientific journals, photographs of teams he had played for in his athletic days: as I glanced round, in the constrained and creaking quiet, on his desk I noticed the big leather-covered tutors' register which Arthur Brown used to keep.

Then he began to talk, in the tone of a realistic and experienced man, as though we were talking, not having to explain ourselves, about an acquaintance. He interrupted himself, seeming more deliberate, to light a pipe. It was easy to exaggerate these things, wasn't it? (He might have been echoing my talk with Vicky.) People grew up at different rates, didn't they? Young men who were sexually mature often weren't mature in other ways. And young men who were sexually mature found plenty of opportunities to spend their time. "Most of us," said Martin, in a matter-of-fact ironic fashion, "would have welcomed a few more such opportunities, wouldn't we?"

In an aside, he mentioned my first marriage. When I met Sheila, I was nineteen: if I had known more about women— Martin said, with dry intimacy—I should have been spared a lot.

"In his case"—he did not call his son by name—"it's the other way round."

He was looking away from me, with his forehead furrowed.

"I don't know where I made the mistake. I wish I knew where to blame myself." Quite suddenly his realism had deserted him. His tone had changed. His voice, as a rule easy and deep, had sharpened. If he had sent his son to a different school—they hadn't been clever at handling him, they had certainly misunderstood him. If he had never started at the university—that was Martin's fault. It was just the kind of harking back that Martin must have listened to many times in that room: from parents certain that their young man was fine, that circumstances had done all the havoc, or his teachers, or a particular teacher, or their own blindness, lack of sympathy, or bad choice.

"There's only one rule," I said, trying to console him. "Whatever you do is wrong."

"That's no use. I've got to make sure where I've made the mistakes—so that I can get him started now."

Not only his realism had deserted him, so had his irony. That last remark of mine, which he might have thought to himself, listening to parental sorrows, was just a noise in his ears. For neither I nor anyone else could be any good to him. Irene, who was an affectionate mother, worried about her son, but practically, not obsessively; Martin's love was different in kind. People sometimes thought him a self-contained and self-centered man: but now, more than in sexual love, he was totally committed. This had been so all through his son's life. It was a devotion at the same time absolutely possessive and absolutely self-abnegating.

It was possible that Martin might not have been so vulnerable if his own life had gone better. He had started with ambitions, and he had got less than he or the rest of us expected. Here he was, as Senior Tutor, dim by his own standards, and that was, in careeristic terms, the end. Martin was a worldly man, and knew that he was grossly undercast. He had seen many men far less able go much further. To an extent, that had made him wish to compensate in the successes of his son. And yet, I thought it might have happened anyway: it was men like himself, stoical and secretive, who were most often swept by this kind of possessive passion.

It was a kind of passion that wasn't dramatic; to anyone outside the two concerned, it was often invisible, or did not appear like a passion at all: and yet it could be weighed with danger, both for the one who gave the love and for its object. I had seen it in the relation of Katherine Getliffe's father with his son. It had brought them both suffering, and to the old man worse than that. It was then that I picked up the antique Japanese phrase for obsessive parental love—darkness of the heart. Nowadays the phrase had become too florid for my taste; nevertheless, that night, as I listened to Martin, it might still have had meaning for someone who had known what he now felt.

I had seen this passion in old Mr. March. But I had felt it in myself. I had felt it for one person, and—in his detached moments the reflection might strike him as not without its oddity—that was Martin. Sitting there in his study, we were middle-aged men. Although I was nine years the older, in many ways he was the more set. But when we were young, that wasn't so; I was deprived of the children whom I wanted, and, less free than I had later become, I transferred that parental longing on to him. Once again, it had brought us suffering. It had separated us for a time. It had helped bring about crises and decisions in his career, in which he had made a sacrifice. As he spoke of his son, I didn't bring back to mind that time long past: yet, for me at least, it hung in the air: I did not need telling, I did not need even to observe, that this parental love can be, at the same moment, both the most selfless and the most selfish of any love one will ever know.

I couldn't give him any help. In fact, he didn't want any. This was integrally his own. When he had brushed off my offer of money, he had done it in a way quite unlike him. Usually he was polite and not over-proud. But this was his own, and I didn't offer money again that night. The only acceptable help was that I might arrange some more introductions for his son.

At last I was able, however, to talk about Vicky: and he replied simply and directly, more so than he had done that night, as though this were a relief or a relaxation. Did he know her?

"Oh yes, she's been here."

"What do you think of her?"

"She's in love with him, of course."

"What about him?" I asked.

"He's fond of her. He's been fond of a good many women. But still—he's certainly fond of her."

He was speaking quietly, but with great accuracy. It struck me that he knew his son abnormally well, not only in his nature but in his actions day to day. Whatever their struggles or his disappointments, they were closer, much closer, in some disentangleable sense, than most fathers and sons. It struck me—not for the first time—that it took two to make a possessive love.

"She's expecting him to marry her, you know," I said.

"I think I realize that."

"She's a very good young woman."

"I agree," said Martin.

"I've got a feeling that, if this goes wrong, it may be serious for her. I'd guess that she's one of those who doesn't love easily."

"I think I'd guess the same." Martin added, quite gently: "And that's not a lucky temperament to have, is it?"

"God knows," I said. "I don't blame the boy if he doesn't love her as she loves him."

"He's a different character. If he does love her—I can't say for sure—it's bound to be in a different way, isn't it?"

"Of course," I said, "I don't blame him if he doesn't want to be tied."

"It might be what he needs," said Martin. "Or it might be a disaster."

"I tell you, I don't blame him. But if she goes on expecting him to marry her—and then at the end he disappears—well, it will damage her. And that may be putting it mildly."

"Yes."

"She is a good young woman, and she doesn't deserve that."

"I hope it doesn't happen."

"And yet," I said, "you don't care, do you? You don't really care? So long as he isn't hurt—"

Martin replied:

"I suppose that's true." Since we were speaking naturally, face to face, a flicker of his sarcasm had revived. "But it isn't quite fair, is it? One can't care *in that way* for everyone, now can one? I'm sure you can't. You wait till your son has a girl who is besotted on him."

He gave me a friendly, fraternal smile.

"In any case," he went on, "whatever do you want me to do?"

"No. I don't think there is anything you could do."

"I'm certain there isn't."

"But if he's going to drop her in the long run, it would probably be better for her if he did so now."

"I couldn't influence him like that," said Martin. "No one could." Again he smiled. "Coming from you, it doesn't make much sense, anyway. I don't pretend to know what's going to happen to them. You seem to have made up your own mind. But you may be wrong, you know. Haven't you thought of that?"

SEVEN

A QUESTION OF LUCK

The afternoon was so dark that we had switched on the drawing-room lights. The windows were rattling, the clouds loomed past. It was the middle of June, and Charles was at home for a mid-term holiday. He lay on the sofa, without a coat or tie, long legs at full stretch. Margaret was out having her hair done: I had finished work, and Charles had just mentioned some observation, he told me it was Conrad's, about luck.

Of course, I was saying. Anyone who had lived at all believed in luck. Anyone who had avoided total failure had to believe in luck: if you didn't, you were callous or self-satisfied or both. Why, it was luck merely to survive. I didn't tell him, but if he had been born twenty years earlier, before the antibiotics were discovered, he himself would probably be dead. Dead at the age of three, from the one illness of his childhood, the one recognition-symbol which his name evoked in George Passant's mind.

Charles had set me daydreaming. When I thought of the luck in my own life, it made me giddy. Without great good luck, I might shortly be coming up for retirement in a local government office. No, that wasn't mock-modest. I had started tough and determined: but I had seen other tough determined men unable to break loose. Books? I should have tried. Unpublished books? Maybe. By and large, the practical luck had been with me. On the other hand, I might have been unlucky in meeting Sheila. And yet, I should have been certain to waste years of my young manhood in some such passion as that.

Something, perhaps a turn of phrase of Charles's or a look in his eye, flicked my thoughts onto my brother Martin. He had been perceptibly unlucky: not grotesquely so, but enough to fret him. If I had had ten per cent above the odds in my favor, he had had ten per cent below. Somehow the cards hadn't fallen right. He had never had the specific gift to be sure of success at physics: unlike Leonard Getliffe, whose teachers were predicting his future when he was fifteen. Martin ought to have made his career in some sort of politics. True, he had renounced his major chance; it seemed then, it still seemed, out of character for him to make that sacrifice, but he had done it. I believed that it was a consolation to him, when he faced ten more dim years in college: he had a feeling of free-will.

But still, he had all the gifts for modern politics. You needed more luck in that career, of course, than in science, more even than in the literary life. Nevertheless, if Martin had been a professional politician, I should have backed him to "get office," as the politicians themselves called it. He would have enjoyed it. He would have liked the taste of power. He would have liked, much more than I should, being a dignitary. And yet, I supposed, though I wasn't sure, that he didn't repine much: most men who had received less than their due didn't think about it often, certainly not continuously: life was a bit more merciful than that. There were about ten thousand jobs which really counted in the England of that time. The more I saw, the more I was convinced that you could get rid of the present incumbents, find ten thousand more, and the society would go ticking on with no one (except perhaps the displaced) noting the difference. Martin knew that unheroic truth as well as I knew it. So did Denis Geary and other half-wasted men. It made it easier for them to laugh it off and go on working, run-of-the-mill or not, it didn't matter.

Charles said:

"You remember at Easter, when we came away from your father's, what I said? I told you it wasn't quite what I expected."

He had a memory like a computer, such as I had had when I was his age. But his conversational openings were not random, he hadn't introduced the concept of luck for nothing.

"Well?" I said, certain that there was a connection, baffled as to what it was.

"I expected to think that you'd had a bad time—"

"I told you, I had a very happy childhood."

"I know that. I didn't mean that. I expected to think that you'd had a bad start."

"Well, it might have been better, don't you think?"

"I'm not sure." He was smiling, half-taunting, half-probing. "That's what I was thinking when I came away. I was thinking you might have had better luck than I've had."

I was taken by surprise. "What do you mean?"

"I mean, you were a hungry boxer. And hungry boxers fight better than well-fed boxers, don't they?"

However he had picked up that idiom, I didn't know. In fact, I was put out. I was perfectly prepared to indulge in that kind of reflection on my own account: but it seemed unfair, coming from him.

"I should have thought," I said, "that you fight hard enough."

"Perhaps. But I've got to do it on my own, haven't I?"

He spoke evenly, good-temperedly, not affected—though he had noticed it—by my own flash of temper. He had been working it out. I had had social forces behind me, pressing me on. All the people in the back streets who had never had a chance. Whereas the people he had met in my house and grown up among—they had been born with a chance, or had made one. Achievement didn't seem so alluring when you met it every day. He was as ambitious as I had been: but, despite appearances, he was more on his own.

I was talking to him very much as nowadays I talked to Martin. Sometimes I thought he bore a family resemblance to Martin, though Charles's mind was more acute. Yes, there was something in what he said. I had made the same sort of observation when I met my first rich friends. Katherine Getliffe's brother Charles—after whom my son was named—had felt much as he did. The comfortable jobs were there for the taking: but were they worth it? Books were being written all round one: could one write any good enough? I was twenty-three or more before I met anyone who had written any kind of book. "And that," I observed, "was a remarkably bad one."

Charles gave a friendly grin.

When I first went into those circles, yes, I had comforted myself that it was I who had the advantage. For reasons such as he had given. And yet—I had had to make compromises and concessions. Too many. Some of them I was ashamed of. I had sometimes been devious. I had had to stay—or at any rate I had stayed—too flexible. It was only quite late in life that I had been able to harden my nature. It was only quite late that I had spoken with my own voice.

"But all that," said Charles, "kept you down to earth, didn't it?"

"Sometimes," I said, "too far down."

"Still, it has come out all right." He insisted: "It's all come out more than all right, you can't say it hasn't?"

"I suppose I'm still more or less intact," I said.

He knew a good deal about what had happened to me, both the praise and blame. He was a cool customer, but he was my son, and he probably thought that I was a shade more monolithic than I was.

"Don't overdo it," he said.

"I thought I should have a placid old age. And I shan't."

"Of course you will in time. Anyway, do you mind?"

I answered: "Not all that much."

"The important thing is, you must live a very long time."

That was said quite straight, and with concern. His smile was affectionate, not taunting. The exchange was over. I said:

"Of course, if it will make things easier for you, I can disown you tomorrow. I'm sure you'd get a nice job in the sort of office I started in."

We were back to the tone of every day. The clouds outside the window were denser, Margaret had not yet come in. Charles fetched out a chess set, and we settled down to play.

Not that afternoon, perhaps at no moment I could isolate, I realized that there was another aspect in which I was luckier than Martin. Anyone who knew us in the past, in the not-so-remote past, would have predicted that, if either of us were going to be obsessively attached to his son, it would be me. I should have predicted it myself. I was made for it. All my life-history pointed that way. I had deliberately forewarned myself and spoken of it to Margaret. But, though I was used to surprises in others' lives, I was mystified by them in my own. It hadn't happened.

When first, a few hours after he was born, I held him in my arms, I had felt a surge of animal insistence. His eyes were unfocused and rolling; his hands aimlessly waving as though they were sea-plants in a pool: I hadn't felt tender, but something like savage, angrily determined that he should live and that nothing bad should happen to him. That wasn't a memory, but like a stamp on the senses. It had lasted. In the illness of his infancy, I had gone through a similar animal desolation. Soon, when he learned to drive a car, I should be anxious until I heard his key in the lock and saw him safely home.

But otherwise—I didn't have to control myself, it came by a grace that baffled me—I didn't want to possess him, I didn't want to live his life for him or live my own again in him. I was glad, with the specific kind of vanity that Francis Getliffe showed, that he was clever. I got pleasure out of his triumphs, and, when he let me see them, I was irritated by his setbacks. Since there was so little strain between us, he often asked my advice, judging me to be a good professional. He had his share of melancholy, rather more than an adolescent's melancholy. As a rule, he was more than usually high-spirited. The tone of our temperaments was not all that different. I found his company consoling, and often a support.

I could scarcely believe that I had been so lucky. It seemed inexplicable and, sometimes, in my superstitious nerves, too good to be true. Call no man happy until he is dead. Occasionally I speculated about an event which I should never see: whether my son, far on in his life, would also have something happen to him which was utterly out of character and which made him wonder whether he knew himself at all.

EIGHT

RED CAPSULES

Two evenings later—Charles was still at home, but returning to school next day—a telegram was brought into the drawing room as we were having our first drinks. Margaret opened it, and brought it over to me. It read: Should be grateful if you and Lewis would visit me tonight Austin Davidson.

Austin Davidson was her father. It was like him, even in illness, to sign a telegram in that fashion. It was like him to send her a telegram at all: for he, so long the champion of the 'twenties' artistic *avant garde*, had never overcome his distrust of mechanical appliances, and in the sixteen years Margaret and I had been married, he had spoken to me on the telephone precisely once.

"We'd better all go," said Margaret, responsibility tightening her face. She didn't return to her chair, and within minutes we were in a taxi, on our way to the house in Regent's Park.

Charles knew that house well. As we went through the drawing room where Margaret had once told me I could be sure of her, I glanced at him—did he look at it with fresh eyes, now he had seen how his other grandfather lived? In the light of the June evening, the Vlaminck, the Boudin, the two Sickerts, gleamed from the walls. Charles passed them by. Maybe he knew them off by heart. The Davidsons were not rich, but there had been, in Austin's own phrase, "a little

money about." He had bought and sold pictures in his
youth: when he became an art critic, he decided that no
financial interest was tolerable (Berenson was one of his lifelong hates), and turned his attention to the stock market.
People had thought him absent-minded, but since he was
forty he hadn't needed to think about money.

In his study, though it was a warm night, he was sitting by
a lighted fire. Margaret knelt by him, and kissed him. "How
are you?" she said in a strong maternal voice.

"As you see," said her father.

What we saw was not old age, although he was in his seventies. It was much more like a youngish man, ravaged and
breathless with cardiac illness. Over ten years before, he had
had a coronary thrombosis: until then he had lived and appeared like a really young man. That had drawn a line across
his life. He had ceased even to be interested in pictures.
Partly, the enlightenment that he spoke for had been swept
aside by fashion: he had been a young friend of the Blooms-
bury circle, and their day had gone. But more, for all his
stoicism, he couldn't come to terms with age. He had gradually, for a period of years, got better. He had written a book
about his own period, which had made some stir. "It's not
much consolation," said Austin Davidson, "being applauded
just for saying that everything that was intellectually respectable has been swept under the carpet." Then he had weak-
ened again. He played games invented by himself, whenever
Margaret or his other daughter could visit him. Often he
played alone. He read a little. "But what do you read in my
condition?" he once asked me. "When you're young, you
read to prepare yourself for life. What do you suggest that I
prepare myself for?"

There he sat, his mouth half-open. He was, as he had always been, an unusually good-looking man. His face had the
beautiful bone structure which had come down to Margaret,
the high cheekbones which Charles also inherited. Since he
still stumbled out to the garden to catch any ray of sun, his

skin remained a Red Indian bronze, which masked some of
the signs of illness. But when he looked at us, his eyes, which
were opaque chocolate-brown, quite different from Margaret's, had no light in them.

"Are you feeling any worse?" she said, taking his hand.

"Not as far as I know."

"Well then. You would tell us?"

"I don't see much point in it. But I probably should."

There was the faintest echo of his old stark humor: nothing wrapped up, nothing hypocritical. He wouldn't soften
the facts of life, even for his favorite daughter, least of all for
her.

"What can we do for you?"

"Nothing, just now."

"Would you like a game?" she said. No one would have
known, even I had to recall, that she was in distress.

"For once, no."

Charles, who had been standing in the shadows, went close
to the fire.

"Anything I can do, Grandpa?" he said, in a casual easy
fashion. He had got used to the sight of mortal sickness.

"No, thank you, Carlo."

Austin Davidson seemed pleased to bring out the nick-
name, which had been a private joke between them since
Charles was a baby, and which had become his pet name at
home. For the first time since we arrived, a conversation
started.

"What have you been doing, Carlo?"

"Struggling on," said Charles with a grin.

There was some talk about the school they had in common.
But Austin Davidson, though he had been successful there,
professed to hate it. How soon would Charles be going to
Cambridge? In two or three years, three years at most,
Charles supposed. Ah, now that was different, said Austin
Davidson.

He could talk to the boy as he couldn't to his daughter. He

wasn't talking with paternal feeling: he had little of that. All of a sudden, the cage of illness and mortality had let him out for a few moments. He spoke like one bright young man to another. He had been happier in Cambridge, just before the first war, than ever in his life. That had been the *douceur de la vie*. He had been one of the most brilliant of young men. He had been an Apostle, a member of the secret intellectual society (Margaret and I had learned this only from the biographies of others, for he had kept the secret until that day, and had not given either of us a hint).

"You won't want to leave it, Carlo." Davidson might have been saying that time didn't exist, that he himself was a young man who didn't want to leave it.

"I'll be able to tell you when I get there, shan't I?" said Charles.

Again, all of a sudden, timelessness broke. Davidson's head slumped onto his chest. None of us could escape the silence. At last Davidson raised his head almost imperceptibly, just enough to indicate that he was addressing me.

"I want a word with you alone," he said.

"Do you want us to come back when you've finished?" asked Margaret.

"Not unless you're enjoying my company." Once again the vestigial echo. "Which I should consider not very likely."

On their way out, Margaret glanced at me and touched my hand. This was something he would not mention in front of Charles. She and I had the same suspicion. I said, as though a matter-of-fact statement were some sort of help, that I would be back at home in time for dinner.

The door closed behind them. I pulled up a chair close to Davidson's. At once he said:

"I've had enough."

Yes, that was it.

"What do you mean?" I said automatically.

"You know what I mean."

He looked straight at me, opaque eyes unblinking.

"One can always not stand it," he said. "I'm not going to stand it any longer."

"You might strike a better patch—"

"Nonsense. Life isn't bearable on these terms. I can tell you that. After all, I'm the one who's bearing it."

"Can't you bear it a bit longer? You don't quite know how you'll feel next month—"

"Nonsense," he said again. "I ought to have finished it three or four years ago." He went on: he didn't have one moment's pleasure in the day. Not much pain, but discomfort, the drag of the body. Day after day with nothing in them. Boredom (he didn't say it, but he meant the boredom which is indistinguishable from despair). Boredom without end.

"Well," he said, "it's time there was an end."

He was speaking with more spirit than for months past. He seemed to have the exhilaration of feeling that at last his will was free. He wasn't any more at the mercy of fate. There was an exhilaration, almost an intoxication, of free-will that comes to anyone when the suffering has become too great and one is ready to dispose of oneself: it had suffused me once, when I was a young man and believed that I might be incurably ill. At the very last, one was buoyed up by the assertion of the "I," the unique "I." It was that precious illusion, which, on a lesser scale, was a consolation, no, more than a consolation, a kind of salvation, to men like my brother Martin when they make a choice injurious (as the world saw it) to themselves.

"You can't give me one good reason," he said, "why I shouldn't do it."

"You matter to some of us," I began, but he interrupted me:

"This isn't a suitable occasion to be polite. You know as well as I do that you have to visit a miserable old man. You feel better when you get outside. If I know my daughter, she'll have put down a couple of stiff whiskies before you get back, just because it's a relief not to be looking at me."

"It's not as simple as that. If you killed yourself, it would hurt her very much."

"I don't see why. She knows that my life is intolerable. That ought to be enough."

"It isn't enough."

"I shouldn't expect her," said Davidson, "to be worried by someone's suicide. Surely we all got over that a long while ago."

"I tell you, it would do more than worry her."

"I thought we all agreed," he was arguing now with something like his old enthusiasm, "that the one certain right one has in one's own life is to get rid of it."

When he said "we all," he meant, just as in the past, himself and his friends. I had no taste for argument just then. I said no more than that, as a fact of existence, his suicide would cause a major grief to both his daughters.

"Perhaps I may be excused for thinking"—he said it airily, light-heartedly—"that it really is rather more my concern than theirs."

Then he added:

"In the circumstances, if they don't like the idea of a suicide in the family, then I should regard them as at best stupid and at worst distinctly selfish."

"That's about as untrue of Margaret as of anyone you've ever known."

It was curious to be on the point of quarreling with a man so sad that he was planning to kill himself. I tried to sound steady: I asked him once again to think it over for a week or two.

"What do you imagine I've been doing for the last four years?" This time his smile looked genuinely gay. "No, you're a sensible man. You've got to accept that this is my decision

and no one else's. One's death is a moderately serious business. The least everyone else can do is to leave one alone."

We sat in silence. Though his head had not sunk down, he
did not seem oppressed by the desolating weight that came
upon him so often in that room. He said:

"You'll tell Margaret, of course. Oh, and I shall need a
little help from one of you. Just to get hold of the necessary
materials."

That came out of the quiet air. He might have been asking
for a match. I had to say, what materials?

Davidson took out of his pocket a small bottle, unscrewed
the cap, and tipped onto his palm a solitary red capsule.

"That's seconal. It's a sleeping drug, don't you know."

He explained it as though he were revealing something
altogether novel—all the time I had known him, he explained
bits of modern living with a childlike freshness, with the kind
of Adamic surprise he might have shown in his teens at the
sight of his first aeroplane.

He handed the capsule to me. I held it between my fingers,
without comment. He said:

"My doctor gives me them one at a time. Which may be
some evidence that he's not quite such a fool as he looks."

"Perhaps."

"I could save them up, of course. But it would take rather
a long time to save enough for the purpose."

Then he said, in a clear dispassionate tone:

"There's another trouble. I take it that I'm somewhere
near a state of senile melancholia. That has certain disadvan-
tages. One of them is that you can't altogether rely on your
own will."

"I don't think you are in that state."

"It's what I think that counts." He went on: "So I want
you or Margaret to get some adequate supplies. While I still
know my own mind. I suppose there's no difficulty about
that?"

"It's not altogether easy."

"It can't be impossible."

"I don't know much about drugs—"

"You can soon find out, don't you know."

I said that I would make inquiries. Actually, I was dis-simulating and playing for time. I twiddled the seconal be-tween my fingers. Half an inch of cylinder with rounded ends: the vermilion sheen: up to now it had seemed a com-fortable object. I was more familiar with these things than he was, for Margaret used them as a regular sleeping pill. Per-haps once or twice a month, I, who was the better sleeper, would be restless at night, and she would pass me one across the bed. Calm sleep. Relaxed well-being at breakfast.

Up to now, these had been innocent objects. Though there were others—mixed up in my response as for the last few minutes I had listened to Davidson—which I had not chosen to see for many years. Another drug: sodium amytal. That was the sleeping drug Sheila, my first wife, had taken. Oc-casionally she also had passed one across to me. She had killed herself with them. Davidson must once have known that. Perhaps he had not remembered, as he talked lucidly about suicide. Or else he might have thought it irrelevant. At all times, he was a concentrated man.

When I told him I would make inquiries, he gave a smile—a youthful smile, of satisfaction, almost of achievement.

"Well then," he said. "That is all the non-trivial conversa-tion for today."

But he had no interest in any other kind of conversation. He became withdrawn again, scarcely listening, alone.

When I returned to the flat, Margaret and Charles were sitting in the drawing room. Margaret caught my eye: Charles caught the glance that passed between us. He too had a suspicion. But it had better remain a suspicion. Margaret had had enough of parents like some of her father's friends, who in the name of openness insisted on telling their chil-dren secrets they did not wish to hear.

It was not until after dinner that I spoke to Margaret. She went into the bedroom, and sat, doing nothing, at her dressing table. I followed, and said:

"I think you'd guessed, hadn't you?"

"I think I had."

I took her hands and said, using my most intimate name for her:

"You've got to be prepared."

"I am," she said. Her eyes were bright, but she was crying. She burst out:

"It oughtn't to have come to this."

"I'm afraid it may."

"Tell me what to do." She was strong, but she turned to me like a child.

All her ties were deep, instinctual. Her tongue, as sharp as her father's, wasn't sharp now.

"I've failed him, haven't I?" she cried. But she meant also, in the ambiguity of passionate emotion, that he had failed her: because his ties had never been so deep.

"You mustn't take too much upon yourself," I said.

"I ought to have given him something to keep going for—"

"No one could. You mustn't feel more guilty than you need." I was speaking sternly. She found it easy to hug guilt to herself—and it was mixed with a certain kind of vanity.

She put her face against my shoulder, and cried. When she was, for an instant, rested, I said:

"I haven't told you everything."

"What?" She was shaking.

"He wants us to help him do it."

"What do you mean?"

"He's never been too good at practical things, has he?" I spoke with deliberate sarcasm. "He wants us to find him the drugs."

"Oh, no!" Now her skin had flushed with outrage or anger.

"He asked me."

"Hasn't he any idea what it would mean?"

Again I spoke in our most intimate language. Then I said: "Look, I needn't have told you. I could have taken the responsibility myself, and you would never have known. There was a time when I might have done that."

She gazed at me with total trust. Earlier in our marriage I had concealed wounds of my own from her, trying (I thought to myself) to protect her, but really my own pride. That we had, with humiliation and demands upon each other, struggled through. We had each had to become humbler, but it meant that we could meet each other face to face.

"Can you imagine," she cried, "if ever you got into his state—and I hope to God that I'm dead before that—can you imagine asking young Charles to put you out?"

All her life, since she was a girl, she had been repelled by, or found quite wanting in human depth, the attitude of her father's friends. To her, they seemed to apply reason where reason wasn't enough, or oughtn't to be applied at all. It wasn't merely that they had scoffed at all faiths (for despite her yearning, she had none herself, at least in forms she could justify): more than that, they had in her eyes lost contact with—not with desire, but with everything that makes desire part of the flow of a human life.

"Tell me what to do," she said again.

"No," I replied, "I can't do that."

"I just don't know." Usually so active in a crisis, she stayed close to me, benumbed.

"I will tell you this," I said. "If it's going to hurt you too much to give him the stuff; that is, if it's something you think you won't forget, then I'm not going to do it either. Because you'd find that would hurt you more."

"I don't know whether I ought to think about getting hurt at all. I suppose it's him I ought to be thinking about, regardless—"

"That's not so easy."

"He wants to kill himself." Now she was speaking with her father's clarity. "According to his lights, he's got a perfect right to. I haven't got any respectable right to stop him. I wish I had. But it's no use pretending. I haven't. All I can do is make it a bit more inconvenient for him. It would be easy for us to slip him the stuff. It would take him some trouble to find another source of supply. So there's no option, is there? I've got to do what he wants."

The blood rushed to her face again. Her whole body stiffened. Her eyes were brilliant. "I can't, she said, in a voice low but so strong that it sounded hard. "And I won't."

I didn't know what was right: but I did know that it was wrong to press her.

Soon she was speaking again with her father's clarity. The proper person for him to apply to for this particular service would be one of his friends. After all—almost as though she were imitating his irony—there was nothing they would think more natural.

Obviously he had to be told without delay that we were failing him. "He'll be disappointed," I said. "He's looking forward to it like a treat."

"He'll be worse than disappointed," said Margaret.

"I'd better tell him," I said, trying to take at least the load from her.

"That's rough on you." She glanced at me with gratitude.

"I don't like it," I said. "But I can talk to him, there's no emotion between us."

"There's no emotion between him and anyone else now, though, is there?" she said.

Once more she stiffened herself.

"No, I must do it," she said.

She looked more spirited, brighter, than she had done that night. Hers was the courage of action. She could not stand the slow drip of waiting or irresolution, which I was better at enduring: but when the crisis broke and the time for action had arrived, when she could do something, even if it were distasteful, searing, then she was set free.

So, with the economy of those who know each other to the bone, we left it there. We returned to the drawing room, where Charles, who was reading, looked at us, curiosity fighting against tact. "You're worried about him, I suppose," he allowed himself to say.

NINE

TRICK OF MEMORY

All through those weeks, I was being badgered by messages from the Pateman family. One had arrived during Charles's break; another the evening after Austin Davidson made his request, the same day that Margaret went to him with our answer. Dick Pateman's messages came by telephone, in the form of protracted trunk calls (who paid the bills? I wondered): he had been found a place at a Scottish university, but that made him more dissatisfied. But his dissatisfaction was not so grinding as that of his father, who wrote letters of complaint about his son's treatment and his own. There was, I knew it well, a kind of blackmail of responsibility: once you did the mildest of good turns, natures such as these—and there were more than you imagined—took it for granted that you were at their mercy. Well, after the June Court, I had decided to pay them a last visit and say that that was the end.

Meanwhile, Margaret had faced her father: and the result was not what we expected. True, he had been bitter, he had been intellectually scornful. He regarded what he called her "mental processes" as beneath contempt. And yet, she could not be sure, was he also feeling relieved, or perhaps reprieved? At any rate, he seemed both more active and less despairing: and physically, after his announcement to us and his quarrel with her, he had, for days which lengthened into weeks, something like a remission. If that had happened to anyone else, he would have thought it one of fate's jokes, though in slightly bad taste. During Margaret's visits, daily though uninvited, he produced ironies of his own, but didn't speculate on that one. As for her, she dared not say a word, in case this state were a fluke, something the mind-body could hold stable for a little while, before the collapse.

On the day of the Court meeting, which was the twenty-second of June, I arrived at the station early in the afternoon and went straight out to the university. The Court was to meet at 3:00: the proceedings would be formal: but (so I had heard from Vicky) Leonard Getliffe and two of the younger professors had decided that, since it wasn't necessary for them to attend, they wouldn't do so. Arnold Shaw had expressed indifference: he was going to get his vote of support, there would be no dissension. Had the man no sense of danger? I thought. The answer was, he hadn't. Among his negative talents as a politician, and he had many, that was the most striking. If one had watched any king of politics, big or little, one came to know that a nose for danger was something all the real performers had. They might lack almost every other gift, but not that. Trotsky, like Arnold Shaw, whom he didn't much resemble in other respects, had singularly little nose for danger. He got on without it for a few years. If he had had it, he might have held onto the power for longer.

Thus I was sitting in Leonard Getliffe's office (they used the American term by now) in the physics department. Out-side, it was a bright midsummer afternoon, just like the weather twenty-two years before, when Leonard was nine years old, the day we heard that Hitler's armies had gone into Russia. A motor-mower was zooming over the lawn, and through the open window came the smell of new-cut grass. In the room was a blackboard covered with symbols; there were three or four photographs, among whom I recognized Einstein and Bohr: on the desk, notebooks, trays, another photograph, this time of Vicky Shaw. Not a flattering one. She wasn't photogenic. In the flesh she had both bloom and vital force, but in two dimensions she looked puddingy.

There the picture stood, in front of him. I said, wouldn't he reconsider and come along to the Court? After all, we had done what we could for the students. Yes, said Leonard, even Pateman had got fitted up. "The Scots can cope with him now," I said.

"No, not the Scots." Leonard gave the name of a university close by, only twenty miles away. "They've accepted him," said Leonard.

"Are you sure?"

"I don't see why he should invent the story, do you?" Leonard's grey eyes were regarding me cat-humorously through his glasses. "Especially as it stops us exerting ourselves."

No doubt that was why I hadn't been badgered on the telephone for several days. It hadn't been thought necessary to tell me that I wasn't to trouble myself further.

"Well then," I said. "It's only a formality today. Why not come along?"

"It's only a formality," said Leonard. "Why come along?"

"You know as well as I do. Just to patch things up."

"In that case, it's not precisely a formality, is it?"

It resembled an argument with his father—over tactics, or principles, or choices—such as we had had since we were young men. But it wasn't quite like that. Leonard was just as immovable, but gentler and at the same time more certain. The matter had been mishandled. He and his colleagues (but I now felt sure that his was the authority behind them) weren't willing to appear placated, until they had made their own terms. They weren't being noisy. They were merely abstaining. It was the quietest form of protest. Maybe others would understand.

"What about the Vice-Chancellor?"

"He's only got to see reason, hasn't he?" said Leonard.

Vicky had told me that, if she had appealed to him to go easy on her father, he would have done it. She (for once confident) was sure that she could do anything with him. But that was the one appeal she couldn't make. One oughtn't to use love like that, unless one can pay it back. And also I, having heard her secrets, couldn't use it either: she had said so, direct as usual. Well, that did credit to the decency of her feelings. And yet, for once confident, she was for once over-confident. Listening to him, I didn't believe that, if she had promised to marry him tomorrow, she would have changed one of his decisions about Arnold, or even his tone of voice.

Was it possible that, miserable about her, he—who was as decent as she was, and no more malicious—was taking it out of her father? I didn't believe that either. It was hard to accept, but personal relations often counted not for more, but for far less than one expected. There were people who in all human affairs, not only politics but, say, the making of a painter's reputation, who saw a beautiful spider's web of personal connections. Such people often seemed cunning, abnormally sophisticated in a world of simple men: but when it came to practice, they were the amateurs and the simple men were the professionals.

"Can't you really go a step or two to meet him?" I asked.

"I think it is for him to meet us."

Dead blank. So, killing time before the Court, I chattered about some of the scientists I knew of his father's generation —Constantine, O——, B——, Mounteney. As usual, I found an obscure amusement in the way in which Leonard and his contemporaries discussed fellow-scientists twenty or thirty years older than themselves. Amiable dismissal: yes, they had done good work; once, they deserved their awards and their Nobels: but now they ought to retire gracefully and cease cluttering up the scene. Mounteney— "It's time," said Leonard, "that he was put out to grass." With the same coolness, Leonard remarked that he himself, at thirty-one, might

very well be past his peak. His was probably the most satisfy-
ing of all careers, I said: and yet, for the reason he had just
given, I was glad that it had not been mine.

Somehow, casually, I mentioned Donald Howard. It was
good of Leonard to have found him a niche. No, merely
sensible, said Leonard. Of course, he added vaguely, you knew
something about that affair in your college, didn't you? Yes, I
knew something, I said (I felt sarcastic, but Leonard, like
other conceptual thinkers, had a thin memory, didn't store
away the things he heard). I even knew Howard a bit. Would
I like to see him for a minute? Out of nothing but curiosity, I
said yes. Leonard spoke to the apparatus on his desk, beside
Vicky's picture. Within minutes, Howard came, head bent,
into the room. He shook hands, conventionally enough. He
wasn't quite as graceless as I remembered, though he had
some distance to go before he became Lord Chesterfield. His
shock of hair, which used to push out from his brow, had
been cut: he looked more like the soldier that most of his
family had been. He wasn't cold to me, but equally he wasn't
warm. Did he like living in the town? He'd seen worse, he
said, without excess. How did he enjoy the university? It was
better than a technical college, he said, without excess. He
seemed to think that some conversational initiative of his
own was called for. What was I doing in this place, he ven-
tured? I had come down for the Court, I replied. I shouldn't
have thought that was worth anyone's time, said Howard.
After that, he felt that he had done his duty, and escaped.

Leonard grinned at me.

"How good is he?" I asked.

"Oh, he's better than Francis"—the Getliffe family, like
Edwardian liberals, called their parents by their first names—
"used to think. By a factor of two." Leonard went on to say
that at the time of his dismissal from the college, and during
the research which led up to it, Howard had been paralyti-
cally lacking in confidence: so much that it made him look a

scientific fool. But that he wasn't. Now he had been given a "good problem" and was having some success, he showed a certain amount of insight. He'd never be really first-rate: he'd probably never make the Royal Society, said Leonard, as though that were the lowest limit of man's endeavor. But he could develop into a competent professor, conscientious with his students and with half a dozen respectable scientific papers to his name.

That sounded like a firm professional judgment. When I asked about other parts of Howard's life, Leonard had picked up or remembered little. He didn't know—as I had heard and believed to be true—that Howard had ceased to be a fellow-traveler. He hadn't gone through a dramatic conversion, he had just moved without explaining himself into the center of the labor party. About his marriage—yes, Leonard did know, man who should be married himself, that Howard had divorced his wife. She had gone off with Eric Sawbridge, who, unlike Howard, had stayed a communist, pure and un-budgeable, and wouldn't budge until he died. He had served nine years in jail, after passing on some of the early atomic information, and had come out unchanged.

"One of the bravest men I ever knew," I said to Leonard.

"Francis says the same," Leonard replied. But to him all this, all those crises of conscience which had riven his scientific predecessors, all the struggles, secret and public, in which his father and I had spent years of our lives, seemed like history. If he had been our age, he would have felt, and done, the same as we did. As it was, he signed the "liberal" letters, but otherwise behaved as though there were nothing else that a man of goodwill could do.

It was getting on for three, and I got up.

"I still can't persuade you to come?" I said.

"I'm afraid not, Lewis," he answered, with an unyielding but gentle smile.

In the Court room, one side wide open to the afternoon
sun, in fact so open that curtains had to be drawn to avoid
half the table being blistered, the first item on the agenda
took three minutes. And those three minutes were the stately
minuet. *Resolution of confidence in Disciplinary Committee.*
The secretary reported that three of the students had found
accommodation elsewhere: Miss Bolt had announced her engagement, and did not wish to undertake further study. "Any
discussion?" said Arnold Shaw, sharp eyes executing a tra-
verse. Not a word. "May I ask for a motion?" This had been
prearranged: resolution of confidence, moved by a civic dignitary, seconded by an academic. "Any further discussion?"
Not a word. "Those in favor?" Denis Geary looked across at
me while hands were going up. No, there was no point in
indulging oneself, though he, unlike me, wasn't interested in
guarding Arnold Shaw. His hand went up, so did mine.
"Unanimous," said Shaw, giving a pursed smile, with a satisfaction as great as Metternich's after one of his less commonplace maneuvers.

The whole of the rest of the proceedings was dedicated to
the October congregation. Flummery, of course; but then
people, even serious people like Denis Geary, enjoyed flummery: there were wafts of pleasure, as well as mildly dotty
practical suggestions, in the air. Lord Getliffe would preside.
Honorary degrees would be presented. The Court had already approved the names of the honorary graduands. Dinner. Speeches. Who should speak? That particular topic took
up a long time. I sat absent-minded, while the general enjoyment went on. At last (though it was actually only about
half-past four) I got out into the summer air. Would I have
tea? Shaw was pressing me. No, I had an engagement soon.
That was embroidering the truth. For the first time on any of
my visits to the town, George Passant had sent me a note—
like all the letters I had ever received from him, as short and
neat as a military dispatch—saying that he was otherwise oc-

cupied and couldn't meet me for our usual drink. All I had
to do was call on the Patemans, when the father was home
from work, and settle my account. Then I could go to the
Residence, obligations fulfilled, though (I was still thinking
of Leonard) not in a fashion anyone could congratulate himself upon.

Still, it was pleasant to walk by myself round the campus
(that word also had swept eastward in the still sunshine. The
students were dressed differently from those I used to know:
young men and girls in jeans, long hair, the girls' faces un-
painted and pale. Transistor radios hung from a good many
wrists. Pairs were lolling along, arms round each other's
waists: that too wouldn't have happened in my college before
the war. I stretched myself on the grass, not far from such a
group. The conversation, however, as much as I could catch,
was not amorous but anxious. They nearly all carried examination papers with them. This was the time of their finals:
they had just been let out of a three-hour session: they were
holding inquests. Dress changed: social manners changed:
sexual manners changed: but examinations did not change.
These boys and girls—they must have been round twenty-one,
but they were so hirsute that they looked younger—were at
least as obsessed as any of us used to be. They had another
paper next morning. One girl was saying that she must shut
herself up that night, she needed to put in hours and hours of
work. Wrong, I wanted to say: real examinees didn't behave
like that: don't look at a book, don't even talk about it. But I
kept quiet. Whoever listened to that kind of advice? Or to
any other kind of advice, except that which they were already
determined to take?

It was pleasant in the sun. I was timing myself to arrive at
the Patemans' house at six. Now that I knew the way, I managed it to the minute. But Mr. Pateman was not there. His
wife let me in, the passage dark and odorous as I entered
from the bright afternoon. From the front room the record

player was, just as last time, at work. In the parlor high tea was laid. The room was empty except for Kitty, who, cutting a slice of bread, gave a little beck of recognition.

"He's not in yet, I'm afraid," said Mrs. Pateman again.

"I told him the time I should be coming." She was the only woman of the household whom I liked: I couldn't let myself be rough with her.

"The doctor doesn't have his surgery till six, you see," Mrs. Pateman began a flustered explanation.

"I'm sorry," I had to say. "I hope there's nothing much the matter?"

"Of course there isn't." Kitty gave a fleering smile. "There's never anything the matter with him—"

"You didn't ought to say that about your father." Mrs. Pateman seemed overwhelmed in this house, this "simple home" which even to me was uncomfortably full of egos. Kitty shrugged, looked at me under her eyebrows, and informed me that Dick was camping, and wouldn't be back for a week. She said it in a manner which was little-me-ish and at the same time hostile, no, not so much hostile as remote from all of them. She might be resenting his having a higher education, while she, appreciably cleverer, had been kept out of one. I found her expression, partly because of its mobility, abnormally difficult to read. I guessed that she might, despite the fluttering, be as hard as the others. That was as far—and perhaps even this I imagined or exaggerated—as I could see that night.

Taking her slice of bread, she went back with light scampering steps to the front room, where I assumed that Cora Ross was waiting. Mrs. Pateman, naturally polite, embarrassed, continued to explain about her husband. He was always one for going to the doctor in good time. He had a stiffness in his throat which he thought might be associated with a backache (a combination, I couldn't help thinking to myself, unknown to medical science). He was always careful about what she, echoing him, called "germs." That accounted, I realized, for the disinfectant smell which hung about this room, even in his absence. He must add, to his other unwelcoming characteristics, a chronic hypochondria.

At last he came in, head thrown back, hand outstretched. He gave me a stately good-evening, and sat down to his corned beef and tomato ketchup. Meanwhile his wife was saying:

"He didn't find anything, did he, Percy?"

"Nothing serious," he said with a condescending smile. "I'm a great believer"—he turned to me—"in taking precautions. I don't mind telling you, I should recommend anyone of your age to be run over by his doctor once a month."

I said that I couldn't stay long. I wanted only to finish up this business of his son. I hadn't heard until that day that he had been accepted by ——— (the neighboring university). That completed the story, and they ought to consider themselves fortunate.

"No," said Mr. Pateman, not angrily but in a level reasonable fashion. "I can't be expected to agree with that."

"I do expect you to agree with that." I had come to break this tie. To be honest, I didn't mind a quarrel: but I wasn't getting it.

"Well then, we shall have to agree to differ, shan't we?"

"Your son," I said, "is a remarkably lucky young man. If he were here—by the by, I have not had a word from him about his news—if he were here I should tell him so. He might have been thrown out for good. As it is, this is exactly like going on at the university here as though nothing had happened."

"Ah." Mr. Pateman smiled, an all-knowing patronizing smile. "There I have to take issue with you. Do you realize that this place is twelve miles away?"

"Of course I do."

"How is he going to get there?"

I muttered, but Mr. Pateman continued in triumph:

"Someone is going to have to pay his fare."

I stared at him blank-faced. With a gesture, he said:

"But I'll grant you this. It's not so bad as Scotland. No, it's not so bad as Scotland. So we'd better let bygones be bygones, hadn't we?"

He was victorious. For the moment, he was sated. I thought—not then but later, for on the spot I was outfaced, deflated, like one working himself up to a row and finding himself greeted with applause—how people say comfortably that persecution never works. Read a little history, and you find that persecution, more often than not, is singularly effective. The same with paranoia. You might think it was a crippling affliction: live some of your life, and you find that paranoia too, more often than not, is singularly effective. Certainly the streak possessed by the Patemans, father and son, had won them, in this business, what they wanted. It also made Mr. Pateman that evening feel powerful as most of us never do. Paranoia of that kind is only placated for an interval, and then, like sexual jealousy, starts up again. But while it is placated, it—again like sexual jealousy—gives a reassurance which is utterly possessing, as though all enemies were conquered or annihilated, a reassurance of non-enmity that those of us who are not paranoid will never know.

Before I left, Mr. Pateman favored me with his views on civil servants. It was no thanks to me, but he was enjoying some new "brainwave" about a move for himself. He reiterated, he couldn't remain a cashier much longer. "I'm like a bank clerk shoveling money over the counter and not having any for himself." But he had listened to me enough to visit the Employment Exchange. As he had foreseen, he said with satisfaction, they had been useless, totally useless.

"You know what civil servants are like, do you?"

I told him I had been one, during the war and for years later.

"Present company excepted." He gave a forgiving smile. "But you've had some experience outside, you ought to know what civil servants are like. *Rats in mazes*. You switch on a light and they scramble for the right door."

I said goodbye. Mr. Pateman, standing up and squaring his shoulders, said that he was glad to have had these talks. I asked if the new job he was thinking of was an interesting one.

"For *some* people," he said, "every job is an interesting one."

He volunteered no more. His lips were complacently tight, as though he were a cabinet minister being questioned by a backbencher of dubious discretion.

Sitting in the Residence drawing room, a few minutes to go before dinner, I told Vicky that I had had a mildly punishing day. "Poor old thing," she said. I didn't say anything about Leonard Getliffe or the Pateman parlor, but I remarked that it was bleak to miss my customary drink with George. She shook her head: she didn't know him, he was just a name from the town's shadows.

"Anyway," she said, "you might meet another old friend tonight." She asked—would I let her drive me out into the country, for a party after dinner? Would that be too much for me? What was this party, I wanted to know. Parents of friends of hers, prosperous business people, not even acquaintances of mine. "But they want to collect you, you know. And it'd be a bit of a scoop for me to produce you." Vicky gave a cheerful grimace. She had a tendency, characteristic of realistic young women, to find any symptom of the public life extremely funny. I found that tendency soothing.

Before she had time to tell me who the "old friend" was, Arnold Shaw joined us, beaming with eupeptic good-humor. "Excellent meeting today, Lewis," he said. He was feeling celebratory, and had opened one of his better bottles of claret for dinner. At the table, the three of us alone, he did not once refer to the controversy. It was over, in his mind a neat, black, final line had been drawn. He talked, euphorically and non-stop, about the October congregation. Arnold loved ceremony, protocol, anything which distinguished one man from another. If the President of the Royal Society came to receive an honorary degree, should he, or should he not, on an academic occasion, take precedence over a viscount who was not receiving a degree?

As he propounded his intricate problem, Vicky was smiling. She was still amused when he went on to what for him was the fascinating topic of honorary degrees. Here he took great trouble, and, as so often, received no credit from anyone, not even her. If a university was going to give honorary degrees at all, he had harangued me before now, it ought to be done with total purity. He would make no concessions. As so often, no one believed that he was a pure soul. Yet he had done precisely what he said. No local worthies. No putative benefactors. No politicians. Men of international distinction. No one else.

"I'm glad you mentioned the man Rubin," he said to me. David Rubin was an American friend of mine, and one of the most eminent of theoretical physicists. "I've made inquiries. They say he's good. No, they say he's more than good."

"Well, Arnold, the fact that he got a Nobel prize when he was about forty," I said, "does argue a certain degree of competence."

Arnold let out his malicious chuckle.

"Leonard Getliffe thinks a lot of him. And that young man isn't very easily pleased." He was glancing meaningfully at his daughter. "I always know I shall get an honest opinion from Leonard on this sort of business. Yes, he's absolutely honest, he really is a friend of mine."

His glance was meaningful. So, in a different sense, was mine. I hadn't told Vicky about my conversation with Leonard: now I was glad that I hadn't; it would have done no good and turned her evening sour. I sipped at the admirable wine. Why was Arnold so innocent? Hadn't he noticed the abstentions from the Court? Why were he and Leonard so pure? Under the taste of the wine, a vestigial taste of black currants—a vestigial reminder of a worldly man, unlike those two, a man nothing like so pure, Arthur Brown, looking after his friends in college, giving us wine as good as this, years ago.

As soon as we had settled in her car and Vicky was driving up the London Road, out of the town, I asked who was the old friend? The old friend I was to meet?

"They didn't want to tell either of you, so that it would be a surprise."

"Come on, who is it?"

"I think her name is Juckson-Smith."

"I've never heard of her," I said.

"They said you used to know her."

"I've never heard the name."

"Have I got you on false pretenses?" Vicky glanced sideways from the wheel, to see if I was disappointed. "Juckson-Smith—I think they call her Olive."

Then I understood. I had not seen her for thirty years. Once there had been a sort of indeterminate affection, certainly not more, between us. She had been a member of George Passant's group, the only one of us from a well-to-do family. Those had been idealistic days, when George ranged about the town, haranguing us with absolute hope about our "freedom." But after I left the town, some of them worked out their freedom: Olive took a lover, and under his influence got mixed up in a scandal which—to me at least, who had to watch it—had been a signpost along our way.

She had, so far as I had heard, cut off all connections with the town. Her family was respectable, and it was not a pretty story. She had married her lover, and, some time during the war, I had been told that they had parted. Presumably she had married again. All this had happened many years before and, except to a few of us, might be submerged or forgotten.

Myself, I wasn't remembering much of it, memory didn't work like that, as Vicky drove past the outer suburbs, into the country, past the midland fields, every square foot man-made and yet pastoral in the level light. It was past nine, but the sun was still over the horizon. Swathes of warm air kept surging through the open window, as we passed, slowing down, tree after tree.

"You do know her then?"

"I knew her first husband better. He was rather an engaging man."

"Why was he engaging?"

"You might have liked him." No, I shouldn't have said that. Jack Cotery was just the kind of seducer whom this young woman had no guard against. I hurried on: "He had a knack of reducing everything to its lowest common denominator. He often turned out to be right, though I didn't enjoy it."

I began to tell her an anecdote. But this was one that I didn't mind recalling. My spirits had become higher. When I was in high spirits, and letting myself go, Vicky found it hard to decide whether I was serious or not. She drove on, her expression puzzled and even slightly mulish, as I indulged myself talking about Martineau. Martineau, when I was in my teens, had been a partner in one of the town's solidest firms of solicitors—the same firm of which George Passant was managing clerk. He was a widower, and he kept something like a salon for us all. Then, over a period of two or three years, round the age of fifty, he became invaded by religion, or by a religious search: he started wayside preaching, and before long gave up all he had, except for what he could carry, and went off as a tramp. At my college I used to receive postcards from various workhouses.

"Did you?" said Vicky, as though it were an invention.

He joined a religious community, and soon left that to become a pavement artist on the streets of Leeds. The pictures he drew were intended to convey a spiritual message. After a while, he moved to London and operated in the King's Road. The average daily take in Chelsea was three times the take in Leeds: I picked up some information about the economics of pavement artistry in the late 'thirties.

"Did you?" said Vicky once more.

The point was, I said, Jack Cotery had insisted from the start that all Martineau needed was a woman. Jack had discovered that his wife had been an invalid, he had had no sexual life right through his forties. Jack said that if he and my Sheila went off together, that would cure them, if anything could. I thought that was too reductive, too brash by half. The trouble was, about Martineau it turned out to be right.

"What happened?" Suddenly Vicky was interested.

Very simple. At the age of sixty, Martineau met, heaven knows how, a very nice and mildly eccentric woman. They got married within three weeks and had two children in the shortest conceivable time. Martineau gave up pavement artistry (though not religion) and returned to ordinary life. Very ordinary: because he became a clerk in exactly the type of soliticor's firm in which he had been a partner and given his share away. My last glimpse of him: he had been living in a semi-detached house in Reading, running round the garden bouncing his daughter on his back. He had exuded happiness, and had survived in robust health until nearly eighty.

"I can understand that," said Vicky, driving past the golden fields.

"Can you?"

"I shouldn't be so edgy if I weren't so chaste."

"You're not very edgy."

"I'm getting a bit old to sleep alone."

"You know," I said, "it isn't the answer to everything."

"It's the answer to a good many things," she said.

From the road, a mile or two further on, one could see a house standing a long way back upon a knoll, as sharp and isolated as in a nineteenth-century print. Yes, that was where we were going, said Vicky. It was a comely Georgian façade: once, I supposed, this had been a squire's manor-house. Not now. Not now, as we drove up the tree-verged drive, car after car parked right to the door: no poor old Leicestershire squire had ever lived like this. In fact, we didn't enter the house at all, but went round, past the rose-gardens, to the swimming pool. There, standing on the lawn close by, or sitting in deck chairs, must have been sixty or seventy people. Some were in the water: waiters were going about with trays of drinks. I met my hostess, middle-aged, well-dressed. I met some of the guests, middle-aged, well-dressed. I found myself trying to remember names, just as if I were in America. For an instant, looking down from the pool over the rolling countryside. I wondered how I could tell that I wasn't in America. This might have been Pennsylvania. This was a style of life that was running round the fortunate of the world. One difference, perhaps, but that was only a matter of latitude: in Pennsylvania it wouldn't have been bright daylight at half-past nine.

I had a drink, answered amiable questions, received an invitation or two: one man claimed to have played cricket with my brother Martin. My hostess rejoined me and said:

"You know Olive Juckson-Smith, don't you?"

I said, yes, I used to. She said, do come and meet her, it'll be a surprise.

We made our way, through the jostling party, the decibels rising, the alcohol sinking, to a knot of people at the other side of the pool. My hostess called: "Olive! I've got an old friend for you."

The first thing I noticed was that Olive's hair had gone

quite white. She was my own age, so that oughtn't to have disturbed me, though for a moment, after all those years, it did. She had been, in her youth, a handsome Nordic girl, bold-eyed and strong. Her eyes still shone light-blue, but her face was drawn: she had lost a lot of weight: though her arms were muscular, her body had become gaunt. The first moment was over, the shock had gone. But I was left with the expression that greeted me. It was one of hostility—no, more than that, something nearer detestation.

"How are you?" I asked, still expecting (it was the mild pleasure I had been imagining on the way out) to meet an old friend.

"I'm well enough." Her answer was curt, as though she didn't want to speak at all.

"Where are you living now?"

She brought out the name of a northern town. She was fashionably turned out. I guessed that she and her husband were as well-off as my hosts. I didn't know whether she had children, and I couldn't begin to ask. I said, trying to remain warm:

"It's a long time since we met, isn't it?"

"Yes, it is." Her voice was frigid, and she hadn't given even a simulacrum of a smile.

My hostess, who was both kindly and no fool, was becoming embarrassed. To ease things over, she said to Olive that I had done a good many things in the time between. "I've heard of some of the things you've done," Olive said to me, her face implacable.

To start with, I had thought that she was hating me because I reminded her of a past she wanted to obliterate, in which I had, quite innocently, been involved. But that seemed to be the least of it. For suddenly she began to attack me, and soon to denounce me, for parts of my public life. I had been a man of the left. My "gang," people like Francis Getliffe and the others (she knew a number of them by name, as though she had been monitoring all we said and wrote), had done their best to bring the country to ruin. We were all guilty, and I was as guilty as any man.

If she had merely become conservative, there would have been nothing astonishing in that. It had happened to half the friends, perhaps more than half, with whom I had knocked about in my youth. But she had become fanatically so. And, for the paradoxical reason that I had lived a good deal among politicians, I was all the worse prepared to cope. In Westminster and Whitehall, in political houses such as Diana Skidmore's Basset, your opponents didn't curse you in private. Sometimes, at the time of Munich or Suez, one thought twice about accepting a dinner invitation—but I had never, not once, been blackguarded like this. Except, now I came to think of it, by one of my cousins, who, discovering that I had made a radical statement, told my brother Martin that he had crossed my name out of his family Bible.

There was nothing to do. I caught the eye of Vicky, who was standing not far off, made an excuse, and joined her group. Then I moved round the pool, from one cordial person to another, cordial myself. They were drinking, so was I, it was like any party anywhere. Except that, when I next encountered Vicky, I said that I didn't want to stay too long: as soon as we decently could, I should like to slip away. She was enjoying herself, but she nodded. Before half-past eleven, she was driving back into the town. Over the dark fields, the sky was dark at last.

"That wasn't a success, was it?" she said.

"Not by the highest standards," I answered.

"I'm sorry."

"I'm sorry to have dragged you away." She didn't get enough treats, I was thinking: but she made the most of any that happened to her. She had been happy by the pool-side, as though she were a child, fascinated by her first party. Nevertheless, she had witnessed some of the scene with Olive, and

she had come away without a question. As I had told Martin,
she was a good girl.

Never mind, she was saying, she would be taking her holiday in September, she would be in London with Pat, there
would be plenty of parties. She broke off:

"Was she always like that?"

"When she was your age, people might have thought she
was a lot like you."

"Oh, that's not fair!"

"I was going on to say that they would have been dead
wrong. Sometimes she seemed to think about others, but I
fancy she was always self-absorbed."

"Of course," said Vicky in her level tone, "I suppose I am
rather conservative. Most doctors are, you know."

"But you won't get conservative like that. If you meet
Maurice"—I was choosing someone with whom she was
friendly—"in thirty years' time, you won't tell him he's the
worst man in the world."

She chuckled, then said:

"Was it nasty?"

"No one likes being hated. I've known people who pretended not to care—"

"You do have to put up with some curious things, don't
you?"

She said it in her kind, aseptic fashion, and for the rest of
the drive we talked about her father. When we came to the
suburbs, she had to stop at a traffic light, behind another car.
There was a lamp-standard on the pavement, brightening
the leaves of the lime tree close beside. Quite suddenly, without warning or cause, I had something like a hallucination.
The number-plate of the car in front, either to my eyes or in
my mind, I could not distinguish whether the transformation was vital or not, was carrying different fewer figures.
NR 8150. Those were the figures in my mind. That was the
number of Sheila's father's car, when we were twenty. She

disliked driving and seldom used it. She had driven me in it only once or twice, and nowhere near this road. The car meant nothing to either of us, and I had not thought of its number in all those years. There it was. Vicky was asking me something, but all I could attend to was that number.

It was a trick of memory that seemed utterly unprovoked. At dinner, the taste of claret had brought back an instant's thought of Cambridge, but that was the kind of sensuous trigger-pressing all of us often know. It was possible that I was hyper-aesthetized to some different form of memory after the confrontation with Olive: but it didn't strike home like that, the scene with Olive had been in the here-and-now, this was as though time itself had played a trick.

Vicky had put a hand on my arm.

"Are you all right?" she was saying.

"Perfectly."

I was speaking the truth. I had remembered a number, that was all.

II
ARRESTS OF LIFE, FIRST AND SECOND

TEN

AN EDGE
OF DARKNESS

Summer, autumn, 1963. It was a placid time for us, more so than for a long time past. My name had gone out of the news: Margaret's father stayed, by what seemed like one of fate's perversities, in better health and spirits. The world outside was more placid too. Sometimes we talked of South-East Asia, but without the smell of danger. Even suspicious and experienced men, like Francis Getliffe, were allowing themselves a ration of hope.

We turned inwards to the family—and there Margaret had a little to worry about, nothing dramatic, just a routine worry, as she watched her children's lives. Maurice had failed in his first-year examination: by a concession which in abstract justice should not have been granted, he was being allowed back for his second year. He took it with as little pique as ever. When Charles cursed a piece of work he had brought back for the holidays, Maurice said: "Now you realize that you ought to be stupid, like me."

Then he had gone off for the whole summer to work as an attendant in a mental hospital. It was not a job many young men would have taken, but he was happy. He had the singular composure which one sometimes meets in the self-abnegating. At night, when we were alone, Margaret often talked about him. Ought he to care so little for himself? Wouldn't it be better if he had more drive, and, yes, a dash of envy? She was worrying, but she felt a twisted joke at her own expense. She had come to admire the selfless virtues: and now with her first-born—whom she loved differently from Charles —she was wishing that, instead of trying to be of some good to the helpless, he would think about his future and buckle down to his books.

Yet, when they were together, he was protective towards her. Just as he was protective towards Vicky, the evening that she and Pat spent with us in the flat. It was late in September, Charles had gone back to school, the two of them came for an early drink and stayed to dinner, Maurice had not yet returned from his hospital.

Pat, who knew well enough that Margaret disapproved of him, began making up to her the moment he came in. I found the spectacle entertaining, partly because I had a soft spot for my nephew, partly because Margaret was not entirely unsusceptible. He entered, put Vicky down in one chair, made Margaret keep her place in another while he took charge of the drinks. It was all brisk, easy, and practised: and yet, in the serene evening, the mellow light, there was at once a stir and crackle in the room.

He was a shortish young man, shorter than his father, who was himself inches less tall than Charles or me. He had strong shoulders like his father's, and similar heavy wrists. His hair curled close to his forehead, he had sharp eyes, a wide melon mouth. No one could have called him handsome, or even impressive. When he made a sidelong remark to Vicky, who didn't show amusement easily, she was laughing with sheer delight.

I observed them as he bustled round with the whisky and the ice-jug. She was elated. As for him, his spirits were usually so high that it would be hard to detect a change. Frequently he called her darling, he said that "we" had been to the theater last night, that "we" were going to a friend's studio tomorrow. He was using all the emollients of a love affair. She was looking at no one else in the room: while he was sparking with energy to make Margaret like him.

He was sitting between her and Vicky, and I opposite to them, with my back to the light. Eyes acute, he was searching Margaret's face to see when he drew a response. Her father? Yes, he seemed a little better, said Margaret. "That's all you can hope for, isn't it?" said Pat, quick and surgent. Once, when he was brasher, he would have been asking her to let him call on Austin Davidson: but now Pat not only knew her father's condition, he knew also that she had been exposed all her life to young painters on the climb. With the same caution, he didn't refer, or pay attention, to the great Rothko, borrowed from her father, on the wall at their back, which from where I sat beamed swathes of color into the sunset. Pictures, painting, Pat was shutting away: as he leaned towards her, he was leaving himself out of it. He tried another lead. Maurice? Yes, he knew about the hospital. "I'm sorry he missed the Mays"—he was speaking of the examination. "But still, it doesn't matter all that much, now does it?"

"It's a nuisance," said Margaret.

"Aren't you being old-fashioned, Aunt Meg?" When I heard him call her that, which no one else ever did, I felt he was getting surer. "You all believe in examinations, like my father, don't you now?"

"Well, he's got to get through them—if he's going to do what he wants."

"But does he want to? Are you sure he does?"

"Don't you think he wants to be a doctor?" Margaret was asking a question, a genuine question.

"I don't know. I'm not sure that he does. But I'll bet you this, he'll find something, either that or something else, that he really wants to do."

He looked eagerly at Margaret, and spoke with authority. "I suppose you realize that all the people my age think he's rather wonderful? I mean, he's influenced a lot of us. Not only me. You know what I'm like. But if I'd stayed at Cambridge, and it wasn't a tragedy for anyone that I didn't, you know, he would have been one of the better things—"

"I know he's kind—"

"I mean more than that."

For the moment at least he had melted her. Next day she would have her doubts: she was too self-critical not to: and yet perhaps the effect wouldn't wear off. I was thinking, you can't set out to please unless you want to please. He had his skill in finding the vulnerable place, and yet this wasn't really skill. He couldn't help finding the way to give her pleasure. Men like Arnold Shaw would view this activity, and the young man himself, with contempt. In most of the moral senses, men like Arnold were beyond comparison more worthy. Nevertheless, they would be despising something they could never do.

I was thinking also, how old should I guess Pat to be, if I didn't know? Certainly older than he was, older than Vicky: but he had, apart from his mouth, the kind of lined, small-featured face which stayed for years in the indeterminate mid-twenties. He was taking two drinks to our one, but there again his physical temperament was odd. He showed the effect of alcohol when he had finished his first glass—and then drank hard, and didn't show much more effect, for hours to come. He seemed to live, when quite sober, two drinks over par: with alcohol, he climbed rapidly to four over par, and stayed there.

They were talking about doctoring.

"I've always thought I should have enjoyed it," Margaret was saying to Vicky. "I often envy you."

"I don't know about that," said Vicky.

"Oh, you must."

"No." Vicky persisted with her stubborn honesty. "I don't think I had a vocation. It's a job—"

"It's a job where you're doing some good, though."

"You don't feel that so much if you're dealing with out-patients nine to five," said Vicky. "I might have enjoyed being a children's doctor. Because they're going to get better, most of them."

"Maurice's father was just that. Is just that. Did you know?" I put in. It was easier for me to say it than for Margaret.

"Yes, I should have liked it too," Margaret said.

"But you don't need to be too disappointed if Maurice doesn't, isn't that right?" Pat turned to her again. "You're sure you haven't been guiding him, without meaning to?"

He told her that might be why Maurice couldn't—really couldn't, for all his sweetness and goodwill—force himself to work. Did Margaret believe it? Perhaps she would have liked to. And, though Pat was continuing to efface himself, he would have liked to believe it too. For in secret, and sometimes not so much in secret, he put the blame for his own academic disasters down to his father's fault. If Martin hadn't wanted him to be a scholarly success—

As we sat at the dinner table, Pat continued to talk comfortingly to Margaret. I didn't interrupt. As Margaret knew, or would remember when the euphoria had dropped, I couldn't accept those consoling explanations: but I didn't propose to break the peace of the evening. As for Vicky, it was the peace of the evening that she was basking in. Pat was doing well. He was being listened to. They didn't go to many dinner parties with middle-aged couples. It was all unexacting and safe. It was like a foretaste of marriage.

Happily, Vicky put in another word about child-doctoring. It had improved, out of comparison, since before the war. Children's health was better in all classes. It was lucky to have been born in the 1950's. Then she mentioned that people a mile or so from my father's house would next week be escorting their children back and forth from school. A boy of eight had disappeared a day or two before, there was a wave of anxiety going round. "I hope they find him," said Vicky.

Margaret remarked that once, when Maurice was a child, she had been beside herself when he was an hour late. Then Pat broke in and told her another story of Maurice at Cambridge.

While Pat and Margaret talked to each other, Vicky was able to pass some information on to me. Her glance sometimes left me and flicked across the table: she wanted a smile, she gave a smile back: but that didn't prevent her telling me the news. It was worrying news, and she had to tell me before the evening was over. But she didn't sound worried, her words were responsible while her face was not. Anyway, she had gathered (not, so far as I could learn, from Leonard Getliffe) that there might shortly be another resolution before the Court. The three academics, Leonard and two others, who had kept away from the vote of confidence, were growing more dissatisfied. At the least, they wanted some definition of the Vice-Chancellor's powers. No, they were being careful, they were hoping to find a technique that didn't hurt him—but they meant business.

Did Arnold know? I asked. He was quite oblivious, Vicky said. She tried to warn him, but he behaved as though he didn't want to know.

Would I make sure to come to the next Court? That was on the day of the congregation in October? Yes, I said, I intended to come.

"You might be able to make him understand," she said.

"I doubt it."

"You may have to tell him the truth."

I swore.

"But you will come? You promise me?"

"Of course I'll come."

She was content. After that, we returned to the drawing room, and were chatting like a family circle when, towards ten o'clock, Maurice came in. He kissed his mother, kissed Vicky, then sank down into an armchair with a tired easy-going sigh. When Margaret asked him, he said that he had been sitting with a schizophrenic patient all afternoon. It took a bit of effort, he said; until this holiday he hadn't known what schizophrenia could mean. He was wearing a shabby suit, his face—unlined in spite of his fatigue—pallid by the side of Pat's doggy vigor. Margaret had a plate of sandwiches ready for him, and he began to scoff them. He glanced at Pat, who was by this time at least his customary four drinks over par. "I'm a long way behind, aren't I?" said Maurice, with his objective smile. Margaret gave him a stiff whisky, which he put down at speed.

"Better," he said. It surprised some people, but he wasn't at all ascetic about alcohol. Whether he was ascetic about sex, I couldn't (it was strange to be so baffled with someone one had watched since infancy) have sworn.

Before long, he and Pat and Vicky were talking together. Any one of them was easy with Margaret or me, didn't feel, or let us feel, the gap of a generation: but together they were drawn by a gravitational pull. Curiously, their voices got softer, even Pat's, which could be strident when he was confronting his elders. Was it fancy, or did they and their friends whisper to each other more than we used to do?

Yes, Maurice said to them, he would be going back to Cambridge in a fortnight to "have another bash." A singular phrase, I thought, for that gentle young man, not one which the professionals in the family would find encouraging. Vicky was giving him some advice about medical examinations. Maurice listened acceptantly and patiently. Soon he switched off: what were they going to do? Well, Vicky said, her holiday would be over in a few days, she'd be returning to the hospital. Pat said that he'd be staying in London: he'd got some sort of job (it sounded as though he had collected a little money too), he'd be able to paint at nights and weekends.

"You'll be separated again, won't you?" said Maurice.

"It can't be helped," said Vicky.

"How do you manage?"

"Oh, we have to manage," she said.

"I suppose," said Maurice, "you get on the phone and tell each other when you're free."

He meant—so I thought—that it was Pat who told her when he was free.

"It's nice when we do see each other," said Pat, just as evenly as Maurice was speaking.

"I should have thought," said Maurice, "that it was an awful strain."

"We're getting used to it," she said.

"Are you?"

"Are you worried about me, Maurice?" Vicky asked.

"Yes, I am." He answered with absolute naturalness.

"Oh, look, I'm pretty tough."

"I don't think you ought to rely on that forever. Either of you."

He spoke to Pat. "What do you think?"

Pat replied, with no edge in his voice: "Perhaps you're right."

At dinner there hadn't been a word about their plans, partly because Pat was repressing all his own concerns, partly because neither Margaret nor I felt we could intrude. But Maurice hadn't been so delicate, and no one was upset. It might be a happy love affair, but he had picked up (as, in fact, we had also, in the midst of happiness and peace) that there was something inconclusive in the air. As for their plans, they seemed that night to have none at all. So Maurice, less involved in this world than any of us, told them that it was time they got married.

To me, as I listened to the quiet voices, the odd thing was how they took it. Pat: with no sign of resentment, as though it were a perfectly reasonable conversation about how they were going to get back to Islington when they left the flat. Well, Pat wasn't touchy. But Vicky? She too wasn't resentful, or even apprehensive. She seemed to take it as a token of kindness, but not really relevant to her and Pat. She might have been nervous about this intervention, if she hadn't been so certain that, just because she and Pat were themselves, in due course he would marry her. She had, I thought, a kind of obstinacy which no one outside could budge—obstinacy or else a faith (it was here, and nowhere else, that she showed something like conceit) in her own judgment.

Anyway, the three of them remained on the best of terms, and Maurice and Pat had another drink or two before the end of the evening.

When Maurice had gone back to Cambridge and Margaret and I were alone, she reminded me more than once of that initiative of his. She was proud of how uninhibited he was, particularly when she was worrying about him again. And also she thought he had been right. She was a little ashamed of herself, of course, for having been softened by Pat's blarney. She was, like Maurice, altogether on Vicky's side. It would be bad for her if the affair dragged on like this.

So we talked, on pleasant October evenings. There wasn't much on our minds. I was working hard, but not obsessively. On a Friday night Charles rang up, according to habit, from school. All well. I told him that, the following Wednesday, I had to go to the University Court and Congregation. "Multiplying mummery," came the deep mocking voice over the wire. Politics too, I said. That's more like it, said Charles.

The next morning I woke up, drowsy with well-being, looking forward as I came to consciousness to a leisurely weekend alone with Margaret. I was lying on my right, and through a gap in the curtains the misty morning light came in over the Tyburn gardens. As I looked at the gap, I noticed —no, I didn't notice, it hit me like a jolt in a jet plane thirty thousand feet up, the passage up to that instant purring with calm—a veil over the corner of my left eye. A black veil, sharp-edged. I blinked. The veil disappeared: I felt a flood of reassurance. I looked again. The veil was there, covering perhaps a quarter of the eye, not more.

Margaret was sleeping like a child. I got out of bed and went to the window, pulling a little of one curtain back. Outside was a tranquil autumn haze. It was the kind of morning in which, years before, it had been good to be back in England after a holiday abroad. On my left side, the black edge cut out the haze. I blinked. I went on testing one eye, then the other. It was like pressing on a tooth to make sure it is still aching. The veil remained. Now that I was looking out into the full light, there was a penumbra, orange-brown, along its edge, through which I had some sort of swirling half-vision, as through blurred smoked glass. The veil itself was impenetrable. No pain.

I tiptoed out to the bathroom, and looked at myself in the glass. A familiar eye looked back. There wasn't a mark on it, the iris was bright, the white wasn't bloodshot. The lines in my face had deepened, that was all.

I went back to bed, trying to steady myself. I was more frightened, or not so much frightened as nervously exposed, than I liked being. Later on, people made excuses for me, told me it wasn't so unnatural: the eye is close to the central nervous system, and so, they said cheeringly, eye afflictions often have their psychological effects. But I wasn't thinking of explanations or excuses then. All I wanted was to talk sensibly to Margaret.

She was still sleeping. As a rule, she slept heavily in the early morning, and woke confused. Again I left the bed, found our housekeeper already stirring, and asked for breakfast as soon as she could bring it. Then I sat looking down at my wife. I said, "I'm sorry, but I should like you to wake up now."

ELEVEN

OBJECTIVITY?

As I put my hand on her shoulder, she struggled through a dream, through layers of sleep. She managed to say, is anything the matter? I replied that a cup of tea would be arriving soon. She asked the time and, when I told her, said that it was too early. I said that I was just a little worried. What about, she said, still not awake, then suddenly she caught my tone of voice. What about? she said, only to act, slipping out of bed into her dressing gown, watching me, her face wide open.

While she had a cup of tea, smoked her first cigarette, I described my symptoms. Or rather my symptom, for there was only the one. "What can it be?" said Margaret. I was asking her the same thing. For a moment we looked at each other, each suspecting that the other had some guess or secret knowledge. Then we knew that we were equally lost.

She didn't think of saying that it might pass. We were too much at one for that. Over breakfast she was wondering what advice we could get. Clearly we needed an eye specialist. What about the man whose son was at Charles's school? No sooner had she thought of the name than she was riffling through the telephone directory. Mansel. Harley Street. No answer there. Home address. She got through, and, listening, I gathered that Mr. Mansel was away. At an eye surgeons' conference in Stockholm. He would be back very late tomorrow, Sunday, night.

"That's probably time enough," I said.

She said: "I want to know what you've got."

I argued, with the perverse obstinacy of shock, that he was said to be first-rate and that at casual meetings we had both liked him. We could ring him up on Monday morning: that would, I said again, be time enough.

"I want to know," she said. Couldn't we find a doctor who might have an idea? The curious thing was, we couldn't really be said to have a doctor. Since my breakdown as a young man, I had been, apart from bouts of lumbago, abnormally healthy: so had she been, and she hadn't yet entered the change of life. So far as we had a doctor, it was my old friend Charles March, but he hadn't visited us professionally for something like ten years.

Still, she would talk to him, she said. Once more I listened to her on the telephone. Dr. March was on holiday, was he? Back in a fortnight? He had a locum, of course? Could she have his telephone number?

"No, leave it now," I said.

She did not mention the name of her first husband. He was an excellent doctor, she had complete faith in him—but no, she couldn't, she couldn't disturb, not the peace of the moment, but the insulation of the moment in which we sat together.

But there were other doctors. Later it seemed to us inexplicable—or out of character for either of us, especially her, so active and protective—that we spoke to none of them through that long weekend. She was used to a kind of pointless stoicism which sometimes, in bad trouble, came over me. As a rule, if we expected harsh news, she wanted to find out the worst and get it over: my instinct was to wait, it would come soon enough, other miseries had passed and so might this. That weekend, though, she behaved as I did myself. I was worried enough but, perhaps because I had a physical malaise to preoccupy me, she was worse. For once, she did not want to brave it out and discover our fate.

During the morning, I went into the study and found her there. In a hurry, she put her hand over what she was reading. It was a medical dictionary. I had come for exactly the same purpose. I gave her a smile. It was the sort of grim joke old Gay's saga-men would have enjoyed. She smiled back, but she was having to control her face.

Before lunch we went for a walk in the park. It was a day of absolute calm, the sun warm enough to tinge the skin, the mist still lying in the hallows. The grass smelt as welcoming as on a morning in childhood. Margaret, clutching my arm, was watching me shut and open my left eye.

"How is it?"

"No better," I said. In fact, it was worse. The veil had spread and now covered between a third and a half of the eye. The orange penumbra flickered dizzily as I tried to gaze into the benign autumn sky. When I closed the eye, I could walk as comfortably as on the afternoon before, the time that Margaret and I had taken a stroll in the same beautiful weather.

It was a long weekend. I couldn't write or even read: as for looking at television, that became an exercise in calculating whether the veil was creeping further. We talked a good deal, but only about what had happened to us, us together, us alone. Those we were interested in, or responsible for, we didn't talk about at all. The exchanges of habit, as soothing as a domestic animal one loved, those we had thrown away: not a word about Charles's next Sunday at home. Sometime before the Sunday morning Margaret had made her own diagnosis. I didn't ask to know it. And yet at moments, as in all strain, time played tricks. We were back on Friday evening, having our drinks after Charles's telephone call. This hadn't happened. And then Margaret was watching me as I opened my eye.

On Monday morning, after a drugged and broken night, I woke early. I found Margaret looking at me. With a start, I stared at the window. The veil was black: no larger, but like a presence on the nerve. I turned towards her, and said: "Well, we shall soon know."

"Yes, we shall," she said, steady by now.

When could I decently ring this man up? She was even prepared to smile at the "decently": now the time had come, we had something to do.

Over breakfast we decided on nine o'clock. But when I tried his office, I heard that he had been in hospital since six. "Mr. Mansel gets on without much sleep," said his secretary, with proprietorial pride. I could get him there: which, fretted by the delays, in time I did.

"I'm sorry, I didn't arrive home till late last night. They gave me your message." The voice was brisk, light, professional. "What's gone wrong with your eye?"

I told him. "That's a very clear description," the voice said with approval, rather as though I were a medical student walking the wards and making a report. I had better see him that morning. He was doing an operation at 9:30. He would be at Harley Street by 11:30. Too early for me?

No, not too early, we thought as the minutes dragged. I couldn't block out the bad eye enough to read the newspapers. Margaret went through them for me: nothing much: a Kennedy speech: oh yes, the body of that child who was missing, the one in your home town, that's just been found, poor boy: an old acquaintance called Lord Bridgwater (once Horace Timberlake) had died on Saturday. We were not interested. Margaret sat beside me in silence and held my hand.

Just as, still silent, she held my hand in the taxi on the way to Harley Street. It was only a quarter-of-an-hour's trip from the north side of the park. We hadn't been able to discipline ourselves; we arrived at 11:10. No, Mr. Mansel wasn't in yet: empty waiting-room, the smell of magazines, old furniture, the smell of waiting. All Margaret said was that, when he examined me, she wanted to be there.

At last the secretary entered, comely, hygienic, and led us in. Mansel was standing up, greeting me like a young man to an older; the room was sparkling with optical instruments, and Mansel himself was as sharp as an electronic engineer. Although our sons were in the same year at school, he was not more than forty, tall, thin, handsome in an avian fashion. Did he mind my wife staying? Not in the least. He showed her to a chair, me to another beside his desk. He had in front of him a card about me, name, age, address, clearly filled up: he asked a question.

"Should you say your general health was good?"

I hesitated. "I suppose so," I said with reluctance, as though I were tempting fate.

No illnesses? Latest medical examination? Long ago. "Then we won't waste any time on that," he said with impersonal cheerfulness, and chose, out of a set of gadgets, what looked no more complicated than a single lens. Left eye? Firm fingers on my cheek, lens inches away, face close to mine. His eyes, preternaturally large, like a close-up on the screen, peered down: one angle, another, a third.

He took perhaps a minute, maybe less.

"It's quite straightforward," he said. "You've got a detached retina."

"Thank God for that," I heard Margaret say.

"As a matter of fact," he said coolly, "I could have diagnosed it over the telephone."

"If you had," I said, sarcastic with relief, "it would have saved us a bad couple of hours."

"Why, what did you think it was?"

Margaret and I glanced at each other with something like shame. Ridiculous fears we hadn't spoken. Fears uninformed. Fears out of the medical dictionary. Brain tumor, and the rest.

Mansel was speaking as though cross with us.

"I understand. It's easy to imagine things." Actually, he

was cross with himself. He hadn't been sensitive enough. He wouldn't make that mistake again. He wasn't only a technician, I thought, he was a good doctor. From her corner by the surgical couch, Margaret broke out: "Mr. Rochester."

"What?" I said.

"He must have had exactly your condition. Don't you remember?"

The point seemed to me well taken. Mansel found this conversation incomprehensible, and got down to business. He would have to operate, of course. What were the chances? I asked. Quite good. Statistically, I pressed him. Not worse than seventy-five per cent, not better than eighty-five per cent, he said with singular confidence. I wasn't to expect too much: they ought to be able to give me back peripheral vision.

"What does that mean?"

"You won't be able to read with it. But you'll have some useful sight."

If he could have operated on Saturday, he said, in an objective tone, just after the eye went, he might possibly have done better: it was too late now. Still, he had better get me into hospital that afternoon, and perform next morning.

"That's a little difficult," I said. To myself, my voice sounded as objective as his. I felt collected, exaggeratedly collected, as though, after the anticlimax, I had to compete on equal terms.

"Why is it difficult?"

I said that I had an engagement on Wednesday which I was anxious to keep. He interrogated me. I explained that I wouldn't have thought twice about the formal ceremony at the university, but there was a Court meeting which I had given a serious promise to attend. Margaret, her face intent but hard to read, knew that I was referring to Vicky and her father.

"Some promises have to be broken," said Mansel.

"I've got some responsibility this time. Some personal responsibility, you understand."

"Well, I can't judge that. But I've got to give you medical advice. You ought to have this operation tomorrow. The longer we put it off, the worse the chances are. I've got to tell you that."

He was a strong-willed man. Somehow I had half-memories of the times I had clashed with men like this, both struggling for what I used to think of as the moral initiative.

"I'm not going to be unreasonable," I said. "But you must be definite about the chances. Is that fair?"

"I'll be as definite as I can."

"If we delay three days, what difference will it really make?"

"Some."

"Would it, say, halve the chances? In that case, of course, it's off."

His will was crossed by his professional honesty. He gave a frosty smile.

"No. Nothing like that."

"Well then. Can you put it into figures again? Tomorrow you said it would be an eighty per cent chance. What would it be on Thursday?"

"A little worse."

"How much worse?" I said.

"Perhaps ten per cent."

"Not more than ten per cent?" I went on. "Less rather than more?"

"Yes," said Mansel without palaver." "I should say that was true. Less rather than more."

Then I asked, would he mind if I had a word with my wife alone? With his courtesy which was both professional and youthful, he said that he would be delighted: he was sure she would be the wisest of us all.

We looked into the waiting-room, but there were by now

several people in it. So, her fingers interwoven with mine, we walked up and down the pavement outside the house. The mist had lifted, the air was pearly bright.

"Well," I said, "what do I do?"

"I must say," said Margaret, "I'd be happier to see you tucked up in hospital."

"And yet, if you were me, you wouldn't even hesitate, would you?"

"That's a bit unkind."

"No. The idea that you wouldn't take a tiny bit of risk—"

She understood, without question, that I wasn't being quixotic, as she might have been. If she had been asked, she might have said that I was showing defiance, taking my revenge for feeling helpless. In both of us as we grew older, there emerged a streak of recklessness which she had always had and which I loved in her. But this wasn't a time, we took it for granted, to discuss motives. We had both got tired of the paralysis of subjectivism, when every action became about as good or about as bad as any other, provided that you could lucubrate it away.

She knew that if she asked me to go into hospital that night, I should do so. She understood me, and didn't ask.

We returned to Mansel's consulting room. He stood up, polite and active, looking expectantly at Margaret.

"No," I said. "I'm at your service at any time from Thursday morning."

"Right," said Mansel, without a blink or sign of disapproval. "You'll go in sometime that afternoon, will you? I'll deal with you early on Friday."

TWELVE

MONOCULAR VISION

With Margaret there to look after me, I arrived at the university robing-room half an hour before the morning ceremony. She had fitted me with a patch which shut out my left eye, and when Francis Getliffe saw it—he was already dressed in his chancellarial regalia—he walked across to us, frowning with concern. When Margaret explained what had happened, he said angrily:

"You ought never to have come."

"Francis," I said, "you know perfectly well why I've come." On the agenda for the Court that afternoon, over which he was to preside, there was an innocent-looking item standing in his son's name. Shaw still hadn't picked up the significance, so far as I had heard: but Francis knew, so did the group of young professors, and so did I.

We couldn't speak any more, the room was bumbling with a kind of Brownian movement of human beings in fancy dress. Scarlet hoods, azure hoods, cheflike hats of French universities: hoods of this university, all invented by Shaw himself, one of which, the D.Sc., was a peculiarly startling yellow-gold. Soon I was in fancy dress myself, regarding the scene with monocular detachment: I could see perfectly well, as well as with two eyes, but somehow the sheer fact of physical accident kept me in a bubble of my own. People I knew, Shaw, Leonard Getliffe, Geary, did not look quite real. Nor did my old acquaintance, Lord Lufkin, who, since he was to be invested with a hood later in the morning, stood subfusc, among the blur of colors, in a black gown. He was well into his seventies by this time, and had at last been persuaded, or perhaps financially coerced, into retiring. But that hadn't taken the edge off his public persona. He had taken to going about with someone I saw at his side in this milling, be-hooded mob; a man of fifty who acted as something like Lufkin's herald, producing pearls of wisdom from Lufkin's past, while the master himself stood by in non-participating silence.

That morning we came together in the crush. Untypically, Lufkin kissed Margaret's cheek. "I'm glad to see your charming bride," said Lufkin, who disapproved of American business idioms and often used them.

He was not above taking an interest in my misfortunes. Once more we had to explain.

"If they're going to use the knife on you," said Lufkin creakingly, "you'd better get the best man in London. I always believe in getting the best man in London."

"He's always said that," said the herald, pink-faced, well-tubbed, plump beside his hero's bones.

"Who is your man, then?" Lufkin said.

I produced the name of Mansel.

"Never heard of him," said Lufkin, as though that removed Mansel from the plane of all created things.

After a patch of conversational doldrums, he had another thought.

"I have it," he said. He turned to the herald. "Go and ring up ———." Lufkin gave the name of the President of the Royal College of Surgeons — "and find out how this fellow's thought of."

The herald trotted off. The curious thing was, as Margaret and I had discovered, that he was a successful solicitor, and not Lufkin's solicitor at that. He had appointed himself Lufkin's handyman, not for money or any other sort of benefit (Lufkin's patronage had gone by now), but just because he loved it.

Lufkin considered that he had done his duty by me, and passed on. His parting shot, as he gazed at some honorary graduands, was:

"I never have believed in giving people degrees they haven't worked for."

In which case, one would have thought, he ought not to have been present to receive one himself that morning. Most men would have thought so: but not Lufkin.

The academic procession got into line, a mace-bearer led us, caps dipping, hoods glaring, into the university hall. It might have been any one of two thousand academic processions that year in the English-speaking world, all copied, or not so much copied as refabricated, from processions of corporations of clergymen four hundred years before. It wasn't really a tradition, it was man-made. Man-made, not woman-made, Margaret used to say: women couldn't have kept their faces straight long enough to devise colleges and clubs, the enclaves and rituals which men took shelter in.

Anyway, with solemnity this particular ritual pattered on. We climbed up the steps onto the platform, we took off our caps to Francis Getliffe, Francis Getliffe took off his cap to us. We sat down. For a moment or two, the order of proceedings was interrupted, for some students had become amused by the patch over my eye and started to cheer. Then Francis Getliffe delivered the invocation: more standing up, sitting down, taking off of caps.

At last the public orator was beginning to make his speech in praise of Lufkin. The orator stood towards the edge of the dais, and Lufkin, standing opposite, did not turn his face towards him. Lufkin just remained there, immutable, with an assessing expression—just as he used to sit at his own table, in the days of his industrial power, surrounded by his court of cherubim and seraphim. He listened now, as he used to listen then, to the story of his virtues and achievements, as though he could, if he felt inclined, point out where certain important features were being omitted. About his virtues, Lufkin's view of his own character was different from any other person's: about his achievements, the maddening thing was, he was right. He made his claims for himself, and he sounded like, and perhaps sometimes was, a megalomaniac: yet objectively the claims were a little less than the truth.

Lufkin was duly hooded, the citations fluted on, an orientalist was being celebrated: I was only half-listening, with my eye regarding David Rubin, whose turn was still to come. At each academic pun, a smile crossed his clever, sad, Disraelian face. One might have thought that he enjoyed this kind of jocularity or that he was intoxicated by the occasion, never having been honored before. If one did think either of those things, one couldn't have been more wrong. I had known him for a good many years, and I sometimes thought that I now knew him less well than at our first meeting: but I did know one thing about him. He felt, underneath his beautiful courtesy, that his time was being wasted unless it was spent in his own family or with one or two colleagues whom he accepted as his equals. He had been adviser to governments, he had had all the honors in his own profession, he was courted by the smart, and he was so unassuming that they believed they were doing him a favor: it must have seemed, people said, a long way from his Yiddish momma in Brooklyn. Not a bit of it. His skin was like parchment, there were pandalike colorations under his eyes, he had never looked satisfied either with existence or himself. But, satisfied or not, Rubin was one of the aristocrats of this world. He walked among us, he was superlatively polite, and (like Margaret's forebears) he didn't give a damn.

Another citation; looking out over the hall, I felt, or imagined, that my sound eye was getting tired. I didn't observe that a note was being passed up to Lufkin: in fact, during that ceremony no one but Lufkin would have had a note passed up to him. I was surprised to be tapped on the arm by my neighbor and be given a piece of paper. On it was written, in a great sprawling hand, the simple inscription: *Mansel is all right. L.*

Rubin, last on the list, had returned to his seat with his scroll; Francis Getliffe gave the valedictory address, and Margaret led me away. I had begged myself off the mass luncheon, and she and I ate sandwiches in an office. I told her, not that she needed telling, that I should be glad when the Court was over. She knew that I couldn't rely on my energy that afternoon, that I, who had been to so many committees, was nervous before this one.

Because I was nervous, I arrived in the Court room too early, and sat there alone. I read over the agenda: it was a long time since any agenda had looked so meaningless. Item Number 7 read: Constitution of Disciplinary Committee. It would take a couple of hours to get down to it. Previously I had thought that Leonard Getliffe and his friends had been well-advised, the tactics were good: now the words became hazy and I couldn't concentrate.

The others clattered in noisily from the luncheon, some of them rosy after their wine. Francis Getliffe took the ornamental chair, looking modestly civilian now that his golden robes were taken off. Arnold Shaw, flushed and bobbish, sat on his right hand. Francis was just going to rap on the table when his son came and whispered to me: "I'm very sorry that you had to come." Civil of him, I thought without gratitude. Did he know that, if you are in any kind of conflict, the first law is—be present in the flesh?

Francis Getliffe cleared his throat and said that, before we began, he would like to say how sorry the entire Court was to hear of my misfortune, and how they all wished me total success in my operation. Several voices broke in with "my lord chairman," saying how they wished to support that. I duly thanked them. Down below the words, I was cursing them. Just as energy had seeped away, so had good nature. The last thing I could take was either commiseration or kind wishes.

As though at a distance from me, the meeting lumbered into its groove. Lumbered, perhaps, a little more quickly than usual, for Francis, though a stately chairman, was surreptitiously an impatient one. Someone by my side crossed, one by one, five items off. The sixth was *Extension to Biology Building*, and even Francis could not prevent the minutes ticking the afternoon away. The voices round me didn't sound as though they could have enough of it. The U. G. C.! Architects! Appeals! Claims of other subjects! Master building plan! Emotions were heated, the voices might have been talking about love or the preservation of the peace. Of all the academic meetings I had attended, at least half the talking time, and much more than half the expense of spirit, had been consumed in discussions of building. Whatever would they do when all the buildings were put up? The answer, I thought, though not that afternoon, was simple: they would pull some down and start again.

At length I heard the problem being referred (by an exercise of firmness on Francis's part) to the Buildings Sub-Committee. Sharply, Francis called out "Item Number 7." I gripped myself: I had to be with them now. It was hard to make the effort.

Focusing on Francis, I was puzzled that he didn't ask the Vice-Chancellor to leave us. Whether Shaw knew it or not, he was going to be argued over.

Instead, Francis gazed down the table.

"Professor Getliffe," he said to his son, "I think you have something to say on this matter."

"Yes, my lord chairman," Leonard said to his father. "My colleagues and I want to suggest that we postpone it. We should like to postpone it until next term."

"That would give me a chance," said Shaw briskly, automatically (Good God, I was thinking again, still not reacting, how many months would he have survived in Whitehall?), "to send round a paper on the present arrangements for discipline. And how I propose to make one or two changes."

"Thank you, Vice-Chancellor," said Francis, who might have been thinking as I did. "Anyway," he addressed the room, "I must say, I think there is some merit in Professor Getliffe's suggestion, if it appeals to the Court. I know this seems an important piece of business to some of us, and it would be a mistake to rush it. I'm anxious that everyone should have the opportunity to give us his views. I believe Sir Lewis is interested, isn't that so?"

"Yes, I am rather interested."

"Well then. We hope you'll be able to attend the Court next term. Completely recovered. Then I shall propose we might set aside the first part of the meeting for this business. We shall very much want to hear your opinion."

I said, yes, I should try to attend the Court. In temper, in ultimate let-down, I could keep to the official language. Would anyone to whom the official language might as well have been Avar or Estonian realize that they were considering me, that this was a put-up job between father and son?

Leaving the meeting in time to escape conversation, I got a university car to myself to take me to the Residence. There, among the smell of leather (to me an anxious smell), I sat in a state both harsh-tempered and depressed. The let-down, yes. The wasted effort, yes. The physical discomfort, yes. But this was a state, concealed from others, that I used to know, and didn't often now. The bizarre thing was, I had got my way. Through the Getliffes' indulgence, I had won Shaw four months' grace. If I had been at my most competent, I shouldn't have done better than that. I might easily have done much worse (there would be time, there was still the residue of a planner working within me, to lobby Denis

Geary and some of the others). I should never know whether
—if the Getliffes hadn't treated me with pity—I could have
made my effort that afternoon at all.

When Margaret saw me enter our bedroom at the Residence, she said, "You've been doing too much." I said, "I've
been doing nothing at all." Before I told her the story, she
made me lie on the bed: then, reassured, she let me talk. This
time I wasn't using the official language: Margaret was used
to me when I wasn't giving events the benefit of the doubt.
She sat beside me, looking down with a curious expression,
clear-eyed.

She told me it was six o'clock, nearly time to dress for the
dinner that night. Was I going to be able to manage it? I
nodded. She didn't protest: she just remarked that a drink
would help, and she would find one. Soon she returned, with
Arnold Shaw following her, in his shirt-sleeves and carrying a
tray, eupeptic, enjoying himself as butler. He poured a large
whisky for her, and an even larger one for me. He splashed in
soda, spooned the ice. Then, as he picked up the tray, ready
to depart, he said to me, with a wise reproving frown: "It was
irresponsible of you. To come here today. It was irresponsible, you know."

The door shut behind him, brisk executive feet pattered
down the passage. I took a gulp at my glass, and then I
laughed. It was a sour laugh, but it was at least a laugh.

Margaret joined in. "I've been wanting to do that for quite
some time," she said. "I've been wondering just when you
wouldn't mind."

Since I couldn't knot a tie easily one-eyed, she did it for
me, and I went down before her into the drawing room.
David Rubin and Francis Getliffe had already arrived, and as
I joined them Rubin was saying that sometimes, this autumn,
he had felt that his intellectual analysis might be wrong. He
meant his analysis of the chances of peace. It had always been
blacker than either of ours, more pessimistic than that of

anyone we met. Yet he knew as much as we did, and more. He said he was inclined to trust his analysis, not his feelings: said it with a shrug and began to cachinnate. He was not the lightest of company when the cachinnation broke out and he was predicting the worst. Still, he said, sometimes he felt that he might be wrong. If so, he went on sarcastically, it wouldn't be any thanks to people like us. We had, all three of us, done our best, we had spent months and years of our lives, we had tried to find ways of action. It hadn't affected the situation, said Rubin, by one-hundredth of one per cent. If things did go right, it would be no thanks to us: it would be due to something as random and as incalculable as a change in the weather.

Others came up to us. Francis was being less fatalistic, when David Rubin took me aside. In a corner of the room he indicated my patched eye and said:

"This is a nuisance, Lewis."

It sounded brusque. But it wasn't so. He looked at me with monkey-sad eyes, incongruous above his immaculate dinner jacket (his colleagues gossiped, why should a man of his morbid pessimism appear to be competing as the Best Dressed Man of the Year?) His eyes were sad, his nerve-ends were as fine as Margaret's. He wasn't going to harass me with sympathy, or with alternative plans for surgical treatment.

"Yes," I said, without any bluff.

"These retinas are getting rather common."

I asked him why.

"Quite simple. We're all living longer, that's all. You've got to expect bits of the machine to break down."

He had judged it right, he was being a support.

"You've played your luck, you know," he said.

He went on: he had a check-up every six months. When did I last have a check-up?

I said something about American hypochondria.

"Maybe," said Rubin, with astringent comradeship.

"They'll find something sooner or later. Let's see, you're ten years older than I am. But remember, I did my best work before I was thirty. I bet you I've felt older than you have—I bet you I have done for years."

But, when we had gone into dinner, the courses clattering in the most lucullan of all Arnold Shaw's feasts, I sat with Rubin's brand of consolation wearing off. The amnesia of the first drinks wore off too: going into hospital next day, I had to stop drinking early in the meal, though I didn't want to. The mechanics of politeness jangled on: I turned from the honorary graduate's wife on my right to the one on my left and back again: they found me dull: I just wanted the day to end.

There was one diversion, though. Vicky had led the women out, and the rest of us had reseated ourselves at Shaw's end of the table. Shaw was in excelsis. He had made four distinguished scholars honorary graduates. There was also Lufkin, who had been forced upon him by the engineers, but still he was good enough. Shaw saw them all round him. He was a man of uncomplicated pleasures, and he was content. He was also content because he had given them splendid wine, and drunk a good deal of it himself. Again, Lufkin was an exception. True to his bleak rule, he had drunk one whisky before dinner, another with the meal, and now, while the others were enjoying Shaw's port, he allowed himself a third. But it was he who dominated the table. He was explaining certain circumstances, to him still astonishing though they had happened a couple of years before, surrounding his retirement.

"I decided it was right to go. Before there was any risk of being a liability to my people. Not that I wasn't still at my best, or I should have got out long before." He sat there skull-faced, still youthful-looking for a man in his late seventies. He delivered himself as though indifferent to his audience, completely absorbed in his own drama, projecting it like something of transcendental importance and objective truth.

"What do you imagine happened?" It was the kind of rhetorical question no one could answer, yet by which men as experienced as Rubin and Francis Getliffe were hypnotized.

"Nothing happened," Lufkin answered himself with stony satisfaction.

He went on:

"I made that industry." It sounded gigantesque: it was quite true. He had possessed supreme technological insight and abnormal will. He had made an industry, not a fortune. He had more than enough money for his needs, but he had nothing to spend it on. By the standards of his industrial colleagues, he was not a rich man. "I made that industry, and everything inside it. I used to tell my people, *I am your best friend*. And they knew, *I was their best friend.*"

Heads, hypnotized, were nodding.

"What did they do?" Silence again. Again Lufkin answered himself. "Nothing." He spoke with greater confidence than ever. "When any of my managers retired, the whole works turned out. When my deputy retired, the whole organization sent a testimonial. What did they do for me?"

This time he didn't give an answer. He said:

"I wasn't hurt. I was surprised."

He repeated:

"I wasn't *hurt*. I was *surprised.*"

When we joined the women, it was only minutes before Margaret spoke to Vicky and Arnold Shaw and took me off to bed. Alone in our room, I said to her: "Paul Lufkin is lonely." I was wondering, how used were the others to this singular display of emotion? Horizontal fission, we used to call it. Lufkin sincerely believed that he wasn't hurt. And yet, even he must realize at least that he felt lost. After great power for forty years, power all gone. After a lifetime of action, nothing to do. Once he had talked of retiring to

Monaco. Now, so far as I knew, he lived in Surrey and came to London once a week for the committee of a charity. "Paul Lufkin is lonely," I said.

"He's not the only one," said Margaret.

I asked what she meant.

"Didn't you realize that Vicky was waiting for a telephone call all night, poor girl?"

In the solipsist bubble in which I had gone through that day, I had scarcely noticed her.

"Did she hear?"

Margaret shook her head.

"That nephew of yours. I'm afraid he's throwing her over, don't you think so?"

"It doesn't look good." I was sitting on the bed, just having taken off the eye-patch. I was trying to speak about Vicky, but the black edge cut out the light, the orange fringe was giddily swimming, and I let out that complaint only for myself.

THIRTEEN

HOMAGE TO SUPERSTITION

The next morning, tea-trays on our bed, Margaret sketched out the day's timetable. There was a train just after one, we could be in London in a couple of hours: that would bring us to the hospital before tea. The less time I had in the dark, the better, I said. I knew that I should have to lie on my back, both eyes blindfolded, to give the retina hours to settle down.

When I had agreed to Margaret's program, I said:

"In that case. I think I'd like to see my old father this morning."

For an instant, she was caught open-mouthed, her looks dissolved in blank astonishment. Her own relation with her father had been so responsible, she had sometimes been shocked by mine. She had never seen me in search of a father, either a real one or a surrogate, in all our time together. She gazed at me. She gave a sharp-eyed intimate smile and said:

"You know, it isn't much more than having a few teeth out, you do know that?"

It sounded like free association gone mad, but her eyes were lit up. To others I seemed more rational than most men; not to her. She had lived with a streak of superstitiousness in me as deep as my mother's, though more suppressed. She had watched me book in, year after year, at the same New York hotel, because there I had heard of a major piece of luck. She had learned how I dreaded any kind of pleasure on a Tuesday night because one such evening I had enjoyed myself and faced stark horror on the Wednesday morning. Sometimes, in fact, I infected her. She wasn't sorry, she was relieved, to hear this atavistic desire of mine. It might be a longish operation, Margaret had said: there was a shrinking from unconsciousness which was atavistic too. She, as well as I, wasn't disinclined to make an act of piety, to make the sort of insurance for which one prays as a child. The fact that it was an incongruous act of piety might have deterred her, she had more sense of the fitness of things, but she took me in my freedom, and didn't wish it to deter me.

So, by the middle of the morning, she had said our good-byes, and we were driving out through the back streets along which, the preceding spring. I had walked with Charles. The cluster of shops, the chapel, the gentle rise. When I was a boy, cars didn't pass those terraced windows once a day; and even that morning, when the university Daimler stopped outside Aunt Milly's old house, there were curious eyes from the "entry" opposite.

I led Margaret in by the back way. Passing the window of my father's room, I stood on tiptoe but could see only darkness. When I went up the steps to the French window, I found the room was empty. We returned along the passage. I rang at the familiar front door (pulling the hand bell, perhaps it was still the same bell, as when I came back one night, late from a school debate, found our own house empty and rang Aunt Milly's bell: there was my mother pretending to laugh off a setback, lofty in her disappointed pride). The bell jangled. After a time, footsteps sounded, and a middle-aged man in his shirt-sleeves opened the door. I had seen him before, but not spoken to him: he was always referred to by my father as Mr. Sperry. He was called my father's "lodger," though he occupied the entire house except for the single room.

I told him my name and said that I was looking for my

father. Mr. Sperry chuckled. He was long and thin, with a knobbly Adam's apple and a bush of hair. He had a kind, perplexed, and slightly eccentric face. I thought I remembered hearing that he was a jobbing plumber.

"I expect the old gentleman's doing his bit of shopping," he said.

"When do you think he'll be back?"

Mr. Sperry shook his head. "It's wonderful how he does for himself," he said. He had the most gentle manners: but it was clear that, though he had occupied the house for ten years, he didn't know much about my father, and was puzzled by what little he did know. "I can't tell you when he'll be home, I'm sure. Would you care to come in?"

I exchanged a glance with Margaret. I said we hadn't many minutes, there was a train to catch, we'd just hang about outside for a little while. That was true: and yet, kind as Mr. Sperry was, he was a stranger, and I didn't want to sit in childhood's rooms with him.

Standing outside the car, Margaret and I smoked cigarettes. It would be bad to miss my father now. I kept looking along the road to the library, down the rise to the chapel. Then Margaret said:

"I think that's him, isn't it?"

I was watching the other direction. She was pointing to a tiny figure who had just turned into sight, by the chapel railings.

She wasn't certain. Her eyes were perfect: she could make out that small figure as I could not: but she couldn't be certain because, owing to my father's singularity, she had met him only twice.

Slowly, with small steps, the figure toddled on. Yes, it was my father. At last I saw him clearly. He was wearing a bowler hat, beneath which silky white hair flowed over his ears: his overcoat was much too long for him, and his trousers, as wide as an old-fashioned Russian's, billowed over his boots. At each short step, a foot turned outwards at forty-five degrees. He was singing, quite loudly, to himself. He seemed to be looking at nothing in particular. He was only four or five houses away when he noticed us.

"Well, I declare," he said.

Away from him, how long was it since I had heard that phrase? It was like listening at a college meeting when I was a young man: one heard usages, long since dead, such as this one of my father's, stretching back three generations. "I declare," he repeated, gazing not at me but at Margaret, for he kept his appreciative eye for a good-looking woman.

I explained that we had had to attend a university function the day before, and thought we would look him up. It would be easier if he had a telephone, I grumbled.

"Confound it," said my father, speaking like a national figure who would not dare to have an entry in the directory, "I should never have a minute's peace. Anyway"—he fumbled over Margaret's name, which he had forgotten, but went on in triumph—"you tracked me down, didn't you? Here you are as large as life and twice as natural."

We followed him in, down the passage again, up the steps to the French window, saying that we would stay just a quarter-of-an-hour. In the dark odorous little room, my father switched on a light. To my mother, who had never seen it in that house or her own, electric light had been one of the symbols of a higher existence: and anyone who thought that proved her unspiritual didn't know what the spirit was.

He offered to put the kettle on, and make us some tea. No, we didn't want to drink tea at twelve o'clock in the morning. But he had to give us something. At last, with enormous gratification, he produced from a cupboard a bottle about one-third full of tawny port. "I've always liked a drip of port," he told Margaret, and proceeded to tell her a story about going out with the waifs at Christmas "when Lena was alive," being invited into drawing rooms and figuring as the hardened drinker of the party. That was one of the daydreams in which I didn't believe. I looked out into the stone-flagged yard. There was a stump of a plum-tree still surviving near his window. As far back as I could remember, that tree had never borne any fruit.

My father was talking with animation to Margaret. So far he hadn't commented on the patch over my eye. Either he hadn't noticed, or he thought that it was the kind of idiosyncrasy in which I was likely to indulge. I interrupted him:

"As a matter of fact, I've got to have a minor operation tomorrow."

"You've ruptured yourself, have you?" he said brightly, as though that was the only physical mishap he could imagine happening to anyone. It had happened, apparently, to Mr. Sperry.

"No," I said with a faint irritation, tapping my patch. "I've got a detached retina."

My father had never heard of the condition. In fact, he had only the haziest notion of where the retina was. Margaret, very patient with him, drew a diagram, which he studied with an innocent expression.

"I expect he'll be all right, won't he?" he asked simply, as though I wasn't there.

"Of course he will. You're not to worry."

Not, I couldn't help thinking, that he seemed over-whelmed by anxiety.

"I've never had any trouble with my eyes, you know," he was ruminating. "I've got a lot to be thankful for, by gosh I have." In fact he had kept all his senses into his late eighties. He surveyed me with an air of preternatural wisdom, or perhaps of cunning.

"You ought to take care of your eyes, that you ought. I tell people, I must have told you once upon a time, be careful, you've only got one pair of eyes. That's it. You've only got one pair of eyes."

"At this moment," I said, "I've got exactly half of that."

This was a kind of grim comment in which Martin and I, and young Charles after us, occasionally indulged ourselves. My father was much too amiable a man to make such comments: but whenever he heard them—it had been true in my boyhood, it was just as true now—he appeared to regard them as the height of humor. So he gave out great peals of his surprisingly loud, harmonious laughter.

"Would you believe it?" he asked Margaret. "Would you believe it?" He kept making remarks about me, directed entirely at her, as though I were a vacuum inhabited only by myself. "He's a big strong fellow, isn't he?" "He'll be all right, won't he?" "He's a young man, isn't he?" (I was within a week of my fifty-eighth birthday.) "I wish I were as young as he is."

At that reflection, his face, usually so cheerful, became clouded.

"I'm not so young as I used to be," he turned his attention from Margaret to me. "I don't mind for myself, I poddle along just as well as ever. But people are beginning to say things, you know."

"What people?"

"I'm afraid they're beginning to say things at the choir."

I felt a stab of something like animal concern, much more as though he were my son than the other way about.

"What are they saying?"

"They keep telling me that they're sure I can manage until Christmas. I don't like the sound of that, Lewis, I don't like the sound of that."

"Do they know how old you are?"

"Oh no. I haven't told them that." He regarded me with the most extreme shrewdness. "If anyone asks, I just say I'm a year older than I was this time last year."

He burst out:

"They're beginning to ask if the walk home isn't too much for me!"

It wasn't an unreasonable question, addressed to a very old man for whom the walk meant a couple of hours on winter nights. It wasn't an unreasonable question: but I hoped that that was all. I said I was ready to arrange for a car each time he had to attend the choir. Anything to prevent them getting rid of him. Anything.

"That's very good of you, Lewis," he said. "You know, I don't want to give it up just now."

His tone, however, was flat: and his expression hadn't regained its innocent liveliness. My father might be a simple old man, but he had—unlike that fine scholar and man of affairs, Arnold Shaw—a nose for danger.

FOURTEEN

THE DARK AND
THE LIGHT

A voice was saying:

"You're waking up now."

It was a voice I had not heard before, from close beside me. I had awakened into the dark.

"What time is it?" It was myself speaking, but it sounded thick-tongued in the dark.

"Nearly three o'clock."

"Three o'clock when?"

"Three o'clock in the afternoon, of course. Mr. Mansel operated this morning."

Time had no meaning. A day and a bit since that visit to my father, that had no meaning either.

"I'm very thirsty."

"You can't have much. You can have a sip."

As I became conscious, I was aware of nothing but thirst. I was struggling up to drink, a hand pressed my shoulder. "You mustn't move." I felt glass against my lips, a trickle of liquid: no taste, perhaps a dry taste, a tingle in the throat: soda-water?

"More."

"Not yet."

In the claustrophobic dark, I was just a thirsty organism. I tried to think: they must have dehydrated me pretty thoroughly. Processes, tests, injections, the evening before, that morning, as I lay immobilized, blinded: reduced to hebetude. This was worse, an order of magnitude worse, than any thirst after a drunken night. I didn't want to imagine the taste of alcohol. I didn't want to touch alcohol again. Lemon squashes: lime juice: all the soft drinks I had ever known: I wanted them round me as soon as I got out of here, dreaming up a liquid but teetotal elysium.

Through the afternoon I begged sip after sip. In time, though what time I had no idea, the nurse said that my wife had come to see me. I felt Margaret's hand in mine. Her voice was asking after me.

"I don't like this much," I said.

She took it for granted that it wasn't discomfort I was complaining of. Yesterday's superstition, today's animal dependence—those I was grinding against.

"It won't be long," she said.

"Too long."

Her voice sounded richer than when I could see her: she told me Mansel had reported that the operation had gone according to plan. It would have been easier if he could have done it earlier in the week. ("Obstinate devil," I said, glad to be angry against someone.) It had taken nearly three hours—"One's playing with millimeters," he had said, with a technician's pride. He wouldn't know whether it had worked or not for about four days.

"Four days."

"Never mind," she said.

"That's easy to say."

"There isn't much I can say, is there?" she replied. "Oh, they're all convinced you're remarkably well. That's rather a comfort, isn't it?"

I didn't respond.

"At least," she said, "it is to me."

Patiently, she read to me out of the day's papers. At last she had to leave me, in the dark.

Yet, though my eyes were shut and blindfold, it wasn't the

familiar dark. It wasn't like being in a hotel room on a black night, thick curtains drawn. It was more oppressive than that. I seemed to be having a sustained hallucination, as though deep-scarlet tapestries, color glowing, texture embossed and patterned, were pressing on both my eyes. I had to get used to it, until the nightly drug put me to sleep, just as I had to get used to my thoughts.

Early next morning, time was still deranged; when I switched on the bedside radio it was silent. I heard Mansel's greeting and felt skilled fingers taking off the bandages, unshielding the eye. Five minutes of light. The lens, the large eye peering, the aseptic: "It looks all right so far," the skilled fingers taking the light away again. A few minutes of his shop: it was a relief to get back into someone's working life. What hours did he keep? Bed about 10:00, up at 5:30, first calls, like this one, between 6:00 and 7:00. Training like a billards player, he couldn't afford to take more than one drink a night: three operations that morning, two more after lunch. He enjoyed his job as much as Francis Getliffe enjoyed his: he was as clever with his hands. Nearly all his techniques were new. Thirty years ago, he told me, they couldn't have done anything for me at all.

That was an interlude in the day. So was Margaret's visit each afternoon, when she read to me. So was the radio news. Otherwise I lay there immobile, thinking: or not really thinking so much as given over to a plasma of mental swirls, desires, apprehensions, resentments, sensual reveries, sometimes resolves. It wasn't often that this plasma broke out into words: occasionally it did, but the mental swirl was nearer to a dream, or a set of dreams. Dreams in which what people called the "unconscious" lived side by side with the drafting of a letter. Once when I was making myself verbalize, I thought—as I had often done—that the idea of the unconscious as "deep" in our minds had done us harm. It was a bad model. It was just as bad a model as that of a "God out there," out in space, beyond the clouds. We laughed at simple people and their high heavens, existing in our aboriginal three-dimensions: yet, when he turned our minds upon our own minds, we fell into precisely the same trap.

Thoughts swirled on. To anyone else, even to Margaret, I should have tried to make some sort of show of sarcasm. To myself, I hadn't got the spirit. I didn't like self-pity in myself or others. There were times, in those days, when I was doing nothing but pity myself. I had known that state before, ill and wretched, as a young man. I had more excuse then. This wasn't enough excuse for one's pride to break. Yet I couldn't pretend.

Margaret asked if I wanted other visitors. None, I said, except her. That was an attempt at a gesture. Yes, I should have to see Charles March: as he was my doctor, I couldn't keep him out. When he came in on the second morning, I told him, putting on an act, that it was absurd anything so trivial should be such a bore.

In his kind harsh voice (voices came at me out of the dark, some from nurses whom I had never seen), he replied:

"I should find it intolerable, don't you think I should?"

He was closer in sympathy than any of my friends, he could guess how I was handling my depression. As though casually, he set to work to support me by reminding me of the past. He had been thinking only the other day, he said—it gave him a certain malicious pleasure—of the way we had, in terms of money, exchanged places. When we first met, he had been a rich young man and I was penniless. Now he was living on a doctor's income and I had become distinctly well-to-do.

"It would have seemed very curious, the first time you came to Bryanston Square, wouldn't it?"

The irony was designed to provoke me. The voice went on:

"You've had an interesting life, Lewis, haven't you?"

"I suppose so," I said.

"All those years ago, if you had been told what was going to happen to you, would you have compounded for it?"

"Would you have done, about yourself?"

"I wasn't as insatiable as you, you know. In most ways, yes."

I didn't have to explicate that answer. He hadn't chosen to compete. His marriage, like mine to Margaret, had been a good one. He had two daughters, but no son. He envied me mine. But he was trying to be therapeutic, he didn't want to talk about himself.

"You had a formidable power in you when you were young, we all knew that. We were all certain you'd make your name. You can't say you haven't, can you? But it must have been surprising when it happened. I know some of it's been painful, I couldn't have taken what you've had to take. Still, that was what you were made for, wasn't it?"

I heard the friendly smile, half-sardonic, half-approving.

"You didn't find your own nature," he was saying, "altogether easy to cope with, did you?"

"You know I didn't."

"You started out subtle and tricky as well as rapacious. You had to make yourself a better man. And the trouble with that sort of effort is that one loses as well as gains. We're both more decent than we were at twenty, Lewis, but I'm sure we're nothing like so much fun."

At that I laughed. That was the primordial Charles March. He might have become more decent, but his tongue hadn't lost its sadistic edge.

"Still, I've told you before," he went on, "it's impossible to regret one's own experience, don't you agree?"

"I used to agree with you. Which you thought entirely proper, of course." Just for an instant I had caught the debating tone of our young manhood. Then I said: "But in this I'm beginning to wonder whether you are right."

He was glad to have revived me a bit, to have led me into an argument: but he was taken aback that I had spoken with feeling, and that my spirits had sunk down again. Quickly he switched from that subject, although he stayed a long while, casting round for other ways of interesting me, before he left.

Claustrophobia was getting hold of me. It had been a nuisance always. The scarlet tapestries pressed upon my eyes, the pillows were built up so that I couldn't move my head more than a few degrees.

Blindness would be like this. Did one still have such hallucinations? Was it the absolute dark? Of all the private miseries, that was one I was not sure I could endure. None of us knew his limits. Once, when young Charles was conceived, I thought it might be beyond my limit if the genes had gone wrong, if he were born to a suffering one could do nothing about.

I shouldn't be able to read with my left eye. That was practical. If this could happen to one eye, it could happen to the other. Peripheral vision (Mansel's voice). Useful vision. A great deal of my life was lived through the eye. How could I get on without reading? Records, people reading to me. It would be gritty. How could I write? I should have to learn to dictate. It would be like learning a new language. Still.

The machine wearing out (Rubin's voice). People talked about getting old. Did anyone believe it? Aging men went in for rhetorical flourishes: but were they real? One didn't live in terms of history, but in existential moments. One woke up as one had done thirty years before. Certainly that was true of me. Men were luckier than women. There was nothing brutal to remind one of time's arrow. Perhaps men like Rubin, physicists, mathematicians, remembered they had had great concepts in their youth: never again, the power had gone. I had seen athletes in their thirties, finished, talking like old men and meaning it. But for me, day by day, existence hadn't altered. Memory faltered a little: sometimes I forgot a name. The machine wearing out.

As I pushed one fact away, another swam in. Living in

public. Attacks. That year's attack, people saying that I had stolen other men's writing. They could have accused me of many things, but, as I had told George Passant, not of that. That couldn't have done. You had to make yourself a better man (Charles March's voice). Yes, but even when I was as he first knew me, when I was "tricky and rapacious," that I could never have done. Not out of virtue, but out of temperament. It was one of my deficiencies—and sometimes a strength—that I had to stay indifferent to what I didn't know at first-hand. Yet the accusation hurt. It seemed to hurt more than if it had been true.

In the red-dark: motionless: there came—for instants among the depression or the anger—a sense of freedom. This was as low as I had gone. There was a kind of exhilaration, which I had known just once before in my life, of being at the extreme.

Then the vacuum in my mind began to fill itself again.

Early in the fifth morning, Mansel's greeting. The clever fingers: the reprieve of light. The lens, the large eye. He was taking longer than the usual, examining from above, below, and the right.

Crisply he said:

"I'm sorry, sir. We've failed. The retina hasn't stuck."

It was utterly unanticipated. I had prepared myself for a good deal, not for this. At the same time it sounded—as other announcements of ill-luck had sounded—like news I had known for a long time.

"Well," I said, "this is remarkably tiresome."

"That's putting it mildly," said Mansel. He spoke in bad temper, blaming himself and me, just as I heard scientists taking it out of their lab-assistant after an experiment had gone wrong. He was recalculating. There was an element of chance in these operations. There was an element of human error. He couldn't trace the fault.

"Anyway, inquests are useless," he said snappily. He became a doctor, a good doctor, again.

"There's no reason why you should be uncomfortable any longer," he said, taking the cover off my good eye. We shall have to look after that one, he remarked, in reassurance. It would have to be inspected regularly, of course. He would ring up my wife, so that she could take me home. I should feel better there. It would do me good to have a drink as soon as I arrived.

"What will happen to this?" I pointed a finger towards the left eye.

"For the present, it will probably be rather like it was before we operated. Then, if we did nothing further—I shall have to talk to you about that, you understand, but not just now—if we did nothing further, it would gradually die on you. That might take some time."

After he had gone, I sat up in bed and drank a cup of tea. Lying flat, I had been scarcely about to eat a sandwich, and I was hungry. Obviously, Mansel wanted to try another operation. It was dark to face the thought of going through all that again. Just to get some minor vision. A little sight was better than no sight. The bad eye would die on me. That might be the right choice. He was a strong-willed man, he wouldn't have me let it go without a conflict. In my way I was stubborn too. I had to make my own forecasts.

Yet, in the middle of indecision, I got an animal pleasure out of being in the light. My left eye Mansel had bound up again, but the other was free. It was good to see the roofs outside, and a nurse's face. She had spoken to me each morning, and now I saw her. If I had met her in the street, I should have thought she looked sensible enough, with the map of Ireland written on her. But now her face stood out, embossed, as though I had not seen a face before.

It was she who told me that I had a visitor. I looked at my watch. Still not ten o'clock. I thought that Margaret had been in a hurry. But the nurse held the door open, not for her, but for young Charles.

"How are you?" I asked mechanically.

"No, how are *you?*" he said.

I asked if he had seen Margaret. I was hoping that she had broken the news to him. No, he had come straight from school: he had begged the morning off to visit me.

He sat by the bedside, watching me. I saw his skin, fresh from an adolescent shave. I had to come out with it. I said, more curtly than I intended:

"It hasn't worked."

His face went stern with trouble.

"What does that mean?"

I answered direct:

"I think it means that I shall go blind in that eye. But you're not to worry—"

"Good God, why aren't I to worry? What's your sight going to be—"

I interrupted, and began to talk as reassuringly as Mansel. The good eye was perfectly sound. One could do anything, including play games, with one eye. Nature was sensible to give us two of everything. "We've got to take reasonable precautions, obviously," I went on. "Mansel will have to check that eye, we shall lay on routine—"

"How often?"

"Once a month, perhaps—"

"Once a week," said Charles fiercely. I had never seen him so moved on my behalf.

I tried to distract him. Going back to one of the reflections that rankled when I lay in the dark (going back and deliberately domesticating it), I produced the kind of question that normally made him grin. Being accused of something which is untrue—one feels a sense of moral outrage. But being accused of something which is dead true—one also feels a sense of moral outrage. Which is the stronger? I told him a story of Roy Calvert and me, traveling with false passports in the war, masquerading as members of the International Red Cross, and being accused by French officials at the Lyon airport of being frauds. Just as in fact we were. I had never felt more affronted in my life, more morally wronged.

Charles gave a faint absent smile, and then his face became stern again. I had a suspicion that he was hiding some trouble of his own. Love, perhaps—or, equally possible, some essay that in his professional fashion he thought had been under-marked. In any case, he would have kept his own secrets: but that morning he wanted to conceal even the expression on his face. Could he take me home? It was foolish to bring Margaret all this way. He would ring her up while I dressed.

Soon he was leading me through the corridors—the hospital smell threatening, the walls echoing and gaunt. He was supporting me, unnecessarily, on his arm, as he led me through the corridors down to the waiting taxi.

FIFTEEN

SUAVE MARI MAGNO

Back in the flat, with Charles returned to school, I lay on the sofa, not talking much. Now at last I was beginning to feel it. Margaret, unselfregarding, gave me books that might snag my attention and brought in trays when I didn't want to sit down to meals.

It went on like that for three days. On the morning after I left hospital, Mansel came in and took off the bandages, saying that the operation cut had healed. He also said that I should probably be more visually comfortable if I went on wearing a patch over the eye.

So I lay about in the drawing room during those days, not able to rouse myself. Occasionally I inched up the patch for an instant, shutting the good eye, puzzled by the impact of light and what I did or did not see.

Exactly four days after Mansel had stood over my hospital bed and clipped out the verdict, I woke. It was half-past seven. Out of habit I looked towards the chink of light between the curtains. I had taken off the patch when I went to bed. I closed the good eye and with the left eye open stared towards the chink. I dropped the eyelid, looked again. I did that several times, as if performing an exercise or doing an optical experiment. Then I got up, as I had nearly a fortnight before, pulled one of the curtains aside, shut my good eye again, and looked. Just as I had done nearly a fortnight before, I went back to bed. This time, I didn't disturb Margaret, but waited for her to wake. At last she did so. Even then I did not speak at once, but waited until she was alert.

I said:

"Something odd has happened."

"What is it now?" Her voice was quick and anxious.

"No, nothing bad." I went on carefully, as though my words might be quoted or as though I were touching wood: "The eye seems to have cleared itself up. At least, there doesn't seem to be any black veil this morning."

She cried out:

"What can you see?"

"I can see a bit. Not very well. But anyway I do seem to have a full field of vision."

It might be temporary, I warned her, trying to warn myself. In fact, for a couple of days past, I had been wondering each time when I squinted past the patch, where the black edge had gone to. Just for the moment, the eye appeared to be behaving something as Mansel had promised me it would, if the operation worked. I could see the shape of the room, Margaret's face, I could make out the letters in the masthead of *The Times,* nothing else. Above all, there was no blackness pressing in. That made me hopeful, unrealistically, in relation to what the eye could do.

"It would be better than nothing." Again I was choosing the words.

Margaret also was trying to be cautious. Action was neutral, action didn't mean false hope: the best thing she could do was telephone Mansel. He could come at half-past one, she reported. Margaret and I talked the morning away, waiting until he arrived, spotless as David Rubin, always busy, never in a hurry, sacrificing the solitary sandwich and the half-hour off in his obsessive way.

Lying flat, I assisted (in the French sense) in the familiar routine. The lens, the scrutinizing eye. It went on longer than usual, longer than the morning of decision four days before.

"Well, I'm damned," said Mansel. He broke out: "Look, I am glad! You're quite right. The retina has got itself back somehow."

He had spoken simply, like one who was enjoying someone else's good luck. Then he became professional once more, professional with a problem on his mind.

"You haven't got much to thank me for. I think you ought to understand that. I've never seen anything quite like this. By all the rules, that retina ought to be floating about. But there's a great deal we don't understand in this business. We're really only in at the beginning. It's a great deal more hit-and-miss than it ought to be. I hope it will be a bit more scientific before I've finished."

He was preoccupied with the problem, absent-minded as he gave me instructions. Inspections. This might be a fluke, he had better see me within the week. Premonitory symptoms, flashes of light before going to sleep: I must see him at once. His mind still absent upon the physics of the retina, he told me to avoid any risk of knocks on the head—such as in boxing or association football. I said mildly that those risks weren't in my case so very serious. Mansel had the grace to give a sheepish youthful grin.

"You must think I've made a mess of things," he said. He said it with the detachment of a man who knew that he was a master of his job: and who assumed that I knew it too.

After he had departed, Margaret burst out crying. Her nerves were strong when we were in trouble. Trouble over, she was left with the aftermath. Comforting her, I didn't feel any aftermath at all. This had been an arrest of life. It was already over. I went for a walk in the park that afternoon, looking with mescalin-sharp pleasure (sometimes shutting my good eye) at the autumn grass. I felt full of energy, eager to escape from the solipsistic bubble in which I had been immersed for those last days. Life goes on, young Charles had told me consolingly after we paid that visit to my father. Had he ever heard of an arrest of life? When would he know one? Anyway, it was time to get back into the flow.

Though I didn't often write in the evening, I put in a couple of hours' work before dinner. Later, I was busy with the letters that had stayed unread. Often I became irked by claims upon my time, other people's dilemmas: not that night. I was back with them again.

As I read, I called out the news to Margaret. Nothing to vex either of us, as it happened. Just the balm of getting back into good nick, as Martin and the other games players used to say. A note from Maurice's tutor—no, nothing worrying, in fact he seemed to be doing a little better. W———— (the tutor) would like a chat about future plans for him, just that. Margaret wasn't listening to any arrangements of W————'s: she was suffused with a tender, unprotected, abjectly loving smile. At the most vestigial suggestion of good news—practical good news—about Maurice, she blushed as she did when she was first in love. How did one become a favorite child? Why had I, not Martin, been my own mother's? Margaret loved young Charles because he was himself and because he was mine. But she took his academic skill for granted, just as she did her own. She could judge his ability with detachment. After all, she came from a family of professionals, where, when one got a first, someone like her father or one of his brothers came up and said, Well, it's nice for you know that you're not altogether a fool. Maurice she loved, though, with all her tenacious passion. She loved him in a light of his own. She responded like the simplest mother who had scarcely heard of universities and who was bedazzled to find her child was there. If Maurice could struggle through to any kind of degree, she would be so proud.

Yes, of course I would see W————, I was saying. But I wasn't prepared to go out of London yet awhile. After the past fortnight, I needed to get back into my own particular nick. Four hours' work from 10:00 A.M. each morning, no lunch anywhere. Then I was at anyone's disposal for the rest of the day. W——— could call the next time he was in London.

Margaret blushed again. When I took the most prosaic administrative step on Maurice's behalf, she was over-grateful. She asked if I had got through my pile of letters, and then produced another from her bag. "This is from Vicky," she said. "I wasn't to trouble you with it unless you were quite well."

She went on:

"She rang up this afternoon. When you were out on your walk. She's been ringing up every day."

As she handed me the letter, she said:

"If you'd been free, you know, that girl would have fallen for you."

"No," I said, "for once you're wrong."

"I'm not jealous."

"No, you're not jealous, but you're wrong."

Margaret was happy, affectionate, and obstinate. In snatches, as I went through the letter, I persisted: I should have been the first to know. What Vicky needed was not someone to love (we had seen her taste), but a father to talk to. If a young woman had Arnold Shaw as a father, it wasn't entirely unnatural that she should need to talk to someone else.

The letter was actually concerned with Arnold. I wasn't to make any effort until I had had a holiday (Vicky could not resist giving me some medical advice). But afterwards, if I could talk to people at the university before the Lent-term Court, it might be a precaution. As far as she could gather, feeling hadn't changed. The last Court meeting had gained time, but hadn't altered the situation.

"I must say," I cried, "everything seems preposterously normal!"

At the end of her letter, Vicky wrote that she might be coming to London before Christmas, but she wasn't sure.

"That means that she's hoping he will ask her," said Margaret. "That's normal too."

We looked at the big round handwriting, the oddly stilted, official-sounding phrases. "I wonder what her love-letters are like," said Margaret. Sitting together on the sofa, we discussed whether there was anything we could do for her. Of course there wasn't. But it was a luxury to show concern. To be just to us both, we each felt some concern. We were fond of her, and respected her. Yet, warming us both that night, there was an element of *suave mari magno*. We were on the shore, watching the rough sea and someone else being tossed about in the storm. We had been through it ourselves, alone and together. That night we were by ourselves, in our own home, trouble past. It was a luxury to show concern.

Back in the flow, it wasn't long before I was talking to Francis Getliffe about the university quarrels. It happened in a private room at Brown's Hotel. We were attending a dinner party, but not a social one. We had been attending that same kind of dinner party for a good many years past. This was a group of eminent scientists, in which I was included because I had worked with them for so long. They had been meeting several times a year to produce ideas on scientific policy. They were entertained, with some lavishness, by a wealthy businessman who was both sweet-natured and a passionate follower of the opposition politicians. The scientists didn't pay much attention to the lavishness, being most of them abstemious: but they were interested in the politicians, for by that autumn it was certain that there would be an election next year and probable that the opposition would win it. This group of scientists had been men of the left all their lives; and they still hoped that, if that happened, some good things could be done.

There they sat round the table, our host's good wine going, very slowly, down uncomprehending crops. Constantine, his head splendid and at the same time Pied Piper-ish: Mounteney, granitic, determined not to be appeased: Francis Getliffe: Walter Luke: my brother Martin: several more: our host and a couple of the opposition front bench. Most of the scientists had international reputations, two were Nobel prizewinners, and all except Martin were Fellows of the Royal. At one instant, while Constantine was talking—which didn't differentiate it from a good many other instants—I had a sense that I had been here before. I was seeing the haze of faces as in a bad group picture—striking faces most of them—of my old acquaintances. Very old acquaintances: for they had all (and I along with them) been at common purposes for getting on for thirty years. We had, as young men, sat round tables like this, though not such expensive ones, trying to alarm people about Hitler: then preparing ourselves for war: then, when the war came, immersing ourselves in it. That had been, in the domain of action, their apotheosis. They had never been so effective before or since. But they hadn't given up. Nearly all of them had risked unpopularity. Some, most of all Constantine, had paid a price. Some, like Francis Getliffe, had become respectable, though politically unchanged. The truth was that the youngest at the table was Martin, a year off fifty. Why was the evening such a feat of survival? There was scientific ability about, comparable with theirs, but either the younger professionals didn't take their public risks, or there was something in the climate which didn't let such roughhewn characters emerge.

That night, they didn't sound in the least like sheer survivals. There were candles lit on the dinner table, but they insisted on the full lights above. One or two, like Francis Getliffe, were talking good political sense. As usual, Mounteney didn't infer, but impersonally pronounced, that if the politicians and I were eliminated, then some progress might be made. Two of the less cantankerous had brought memoranda with them. The chief politician was listening to everyone: he was as clever as they were, yet when they were at their most positive he didn't argue, but stowed the ideas away. They thought they were using him: he thought he could use some of them. That made for general harmony. All in all, I decided, it wasn't a wasted evening.

After the rest had gone, Francis and Martin, not so frugal as their colleagues, stayed with me for a final drink. But Martin, when I mentioned Arnold Shaw, did not take any part in the conversation. He and Francis, though they were sometimes allies, were not friends. There had always been a constraint between them, and now, for a simple reason, it was added to. Francis had come to know of the misery that Vicky was causing his son. Francis also knew that she was infatuated with Pat, whom he thought a layabout. In all that imbroglio, Francis could not help remembering that Pat was Martin's son: and—with total unfairness from a fair-minded man—he had come to put the blame on Martin and regard him with an extra degree of chill.

As I tentatively brought in the name of Arnold Shaw, I got a response from Francis which surprised me. In his own house in the spring, he had had no patience with me. This night, sitting by the littered table in Brown's, he answered with care and sympathy. "Of course," he said, "I still think you over-rate the old buffer. You're putting yourself out too much, I'm certain you are. But that's your lookout—"

I said that I hadn't any special illusions about Arnold: but I didn't want him to be pushed out in a hurry, hustled out by miscellaneous dislike.

"Leonard doesn't dislike him," Francis was saying. "He thinks he's a damned bad Vice-Chancellor, but otherwise he's rather fond of him."

He looked at me with a considerate smile, and went on:

"I don't believe you're going to alter the situation there. It's gone too deep. But what do you really want?"

I replied, I too accepted that there wouldn't be peace until Arnold left. The decent course was to make it tolerable for him, to ease him out, with a touch of gratitude, over the next three years.

Francis shrugged. "Nice picture," he said. But, in a

friendly fashion, he continued: "Look, I think the only hope
is for him to come to terms with the young Turks. I don't
imagine it will work, mind you, but I'm sure it's the only
hope." That is, according to Francis, Shaw would have to
take the initiative (as anyone fit to be in charge of an institution, he added tartly, would have done long ago). He would
have to face Leonard and his colleagues, no holds barred.
They were used to harsh argument, they would respect him
for it. Couldn't I pass on the word, that this was worth trying? "You know, if he doesn't try it," said Francis, "there'll
be the most God-almighty row."

Francis was speaking as though he were on my side: yet in
principle he wasn't. And when he disagreed in principle, he
wasn't often as sympathetic as this. It occurred to me that he
might be affected by my physical misadventure. Most people
when you were incapacitated or ill tended insensibly to write
you off. They took care of you in illness, but did less for you
in action. Your mana had got less. With a few men, particularly with strong characters like Francis—perhaps by a deliberate effort—the reverse was true. They seemed to behave, or
tried to behave, as though your mana had increased.

After we had said goodnight to Francis, who was staying at
the Athenaeum, Martin and I sat in the dark taxi, swerving
in the windy dark through empty Mayfair streets. Nothing
eventful had happened to him, but we went on talking in my
drawing room, talking the small change of brothers, anxiety-
free, while the windows rattled. He had nothing to report
about Pat, but for once he spoke of his daughter Nina. Yes,
she seemed to have a real talent for music, she might be able
to make a living at it. She was a great favorite of mine, pretty,
diffident, self-effacing. If the luck had fallen the other way,
and Pat had had that gift, Martin would have been triumphant. But he was composed and happy that night, and,
though he was an expert in sarcasm, that specific sarcasm
didn't get exchanged.

SIXTEEN

DECISION ABOUT
A PARTY

Now I had started moving about again in London, I had to pay a duty visit to Austin Davidson. It was not such an ordeal as it had been, Margaret told me. She, except when I was in hospital, went to him each day. In fact, when we called at tea-time, passing by the picture-hung walls, he was able to meet us at his study door and return to his armchair without help or distress, though he waited to get his breath before he spoke.

In the study, strangely dark, as it always seemed, for a connoisseur of visual art, the only picture I could make out hung above his chair. I thought I had not seen it before: a Moore drawing? The December night was already setting in, the reading lamp beside Davidson lit up nothing but our faces.

He looked at me from under his eyebrows: from the cheekbones, the flesh fell translucently away. His eyes, opaque, sepia, bird-bright, had, however, a glint in them.

"I'm sorry about your catastrophe," he said.

"It's all over," I replied.

"You notice that I used the word 'catastrophe?' "

"Yes," I said.

"Old men get a remarkable amount of satisfaction out of the physical afflictions of their juniors." He gave his old caustic grin. "There's nothing to make an old man feel half his age—as much as hearing that someone twenty years younger has just died."

It might have been an effort. If so, it was a good one. It had the note of the unsubdued, unregenerated Davidson. Margaret and I were laughing. If most men had said that—certainly if I had—it would have sounded guilty. Not so with him. It sounded (just as his talk about his own suicide had sounded) innocent and pure.

He leant back, brown eyes sparkling. He was delighted that he could entertain us. For the next couple of hours except when he heard himself gasping, he forgot to be morose. Another friend of his came in, whom Margaret and I had often met, a man about my age called Hardisty. He had been a disciple of the set to which Davidson belonged: he was clever, miscellaneously cultivated, good-looking apart from being as nearly bald as a man can be: he believed that Davidson and his friends had been the new Enlightenment, and that it would be a long time before there was another. He did most of the talking, while Davidson nodded, for they formed a united front. Neither Margaret nor I wanted to be abrasive, so we left them to it, Davidson occasionally making some reflection which gave Hardisty a chance to eat a tea young Charles wouldn't have thought contemptible. Savory toast: Chelsea buns: éclairs. Davidson's housekeeper had provided tea for us all. The rest of us ate nothing, but the tea disappeared, and Hardisty chatted away between mouthfuls, the sort of man who did not put on weight.

Davidson recalled when, just before the 1914 war, he had seen his first Kandinsky. It had been uncivilized of the Russians not to understand that that was a step forward. Yes, said Hardisty, perfectly in tune, art, any art, had its own dynamic, nothing could stop it. You mightn't like it, you mightn't understand it, but since the first abstracts were painted nothing could have stopped the art of our time. A little later, he said, just as easily, morals had their own dynamic too. In a few years, for example, we should all regard drugs, or at least most drugs, as we now regarded alcohol. It was much too late for any of us to start on them, he said, brimful of health, but still—. Again Davidson nodded. Yes, he said, it was interesting how the tabus had been vanishing in his own lifetime.

"In my young days at Cambridge, don't you know," he went on, "homosexuality was a very tender plant."

Hardisty gave an acquiescent smile. For as long as Margaret and I could remember, he had been living with another man. This partner I had seen only once: I had an idea that he didn't fit into our sort of company: but the arrangement had been as stable as most marriages. Certainly Hardisty was a happy man.

"By and large, this has been a dreadful century," Davidson was saying. "But in some ways we have become a bit more civilized."

He seemed satisfied, either by the reflection or because he had not been too tired by the effort to talk. Do you know, he said to his daughter, "I think I'm going to allow myself a drink?"

On the way home, Margaret, just because his spirits had lifted (she had begun to feel justified in not giving way to him that summer), looked youthful and gay: youthful, gay, maternal, as though she had just heard that Maurice had passed an examination.

We kept another social engagement that week, this time at one of Azik Schiff's theater parties. As the party joggled for position in front of the Aldwych, the lights were washing onto the streaming pavement, but an attendant, hired by Schiff, was waiting with an umbrella, another attendant, hired by Schiff, was waiting in the foyer to lead us to our place. Our place, to begin with, was a private room which led out of the near-stage box. Waiters were carrying trays loaded with glasses of champagne. On the table were laid out mounds of pâté de foie gras. In the middle of it all stood Schiff, looking like an enormous, good-natured, and extremely clever frog. By his side stood his wife Rosalind, looking like a lady of Napoleon's Empire. Her hair was knotted above her head, her mouth was sly, her eyes full. She was wearing an Empire dress, for which, in her fifties, she didn't have the bosom. On each of her wrists, thin and freckled, glittered two bracelets, emerald and diamond, ruby and diamond, sapphire and diamond, and (as a modest concession) aquamarine. Jewelry apart, skin-roughening apart, she had not changed much since I first met her. For she was an old acquaintance: she had been Roy Calvert's wife. But, although immediately after Roy's death I had written to her for a time, it was not on her initiative that, a few years before this theater party, we had met again. It was on her second husband's.

No doubt Azik thought that, in some remote fashion, I might be useful. I didn't mind that. He had the knack, or the force of nature, to think one might be useful and still have plenty of affection to spare for one on the side. I had a lot of respect for him. He had had a remarkable, and to me in some ways an inexplicable, life. In the 'thirties, when Roy Calvert had been working in the Berlin oriental libraries, Azik also had been in Berlin, a young student, ejected from the university under the Hitler laws. He had escaped to England with a few pounds. Somehow he had completed an English degree, very well. Somehow, when the war came, he escaped internment and fought in the British army, also very well. He finished the war in possession of several decorations, a first-class honors degree, and what he had saved out of his pay. He was thirty-three. He then turned his attention to trade, or what seemed to be a complex kind of international barter. Eighteen years later, by the time of this party, he had made a fortune. How large, I wasn't sure, but certainly larger than the fortunes of Charles March's family or the other rich Jewish families who had befriended me when I was young.

It seemed like a conjuring trick, out of the power of the rest of us, or like an adventure of Vautrin's. I once told him that if our positions had been reversed, and I had had to become a refugee in Berlin, I should—if I had been lucky— have kept myself alive by giving English lessons, and I should have gone on giving English lessons till I died. Azik gave an avuncular smile. Obviously he thought rather the same himself.

He was not in the least like my old March friends. They had become undistinguishable, by my generation, from rich upper-middle-class gentile families, rather grander Forsytes. Azik was not indistinguishable. To begin with, he went to synagogue, whether he believed or not. He was a devoted Zionist. He would not have considered anglicizing his first name. Unlike the Marches, who, in common with their gentile equivalents, had taken to concealing their money, Azik enjoyed displaying his. Why not? He was an abundant man. No one could be less puritanical. So long as he could leave young David—Rosalind, late in life, had given him a son, by this time ten years old—well off, he liked splashing money about as much as making it. Anyway, he created his own rules: he wasn't made to be genteel: sometimes I thought, when people called him vulgar, that in following his nature he showed better taste than they. As another oddity, he was politically both sophisticated and detached. He made large contributions not only to Israel but to the labor party: and in private treated us to disquisitions as to what social democratic governments were like and exactly what, if we got one next year, we could expect from ours.

His entertainments were no more understated than the rest of him. He had a passion for the theater, and he had a passion for trade. So he mixed the two up. Theater boxes, plus this gigantic running supper: snacks before the play, snacks in the intervals, snacks after the play. Other people went to ambassadors' parties: ambassadors got used to going to his. There were several present in the private room that night. It was no use being finicky. There was more Strasbourg pâté on view than I remembered seeing. One waded in, and ate and drank. It bore a family resemblance to a party at a Russian dacha, when the constraints had gone, the bear-hug was embracing you, the great bass voices were getting louder and the lights appeared to be abnormally bright.

While listening with one ear to a conversation on my left (a Hungarian was asking Azik what effect on world politics Kennedy's assassination would have—it had happened a fortnight before), I talked to Rosalind. Once she had made up to me because I was Roy Calvert's closest friend: all that was forgotten. I was one of many guests, but she liked to please. How were my family? Like a businessman, or a businessman's wife, she had docketed their Christian names. She always read everything about us, she said, with a dying fall. That was more like old times. At close quarters she looked her age: the skin under her eyes was delicately lined. (I heard Azik saying robustly that he didn't believe single individuals affected world politics. Whatever had been going to occur before Kennedy's death, would occur, for good or bad.) She was using a scent, faint but languorous, that I didn't recognize. Even before she married her first rich man, she had always been an expert on scents.

"Unless I get another glass of champagne, I shall just collapse," she said, with another dying fall. That was still more like old times. Soon she was talking about Azik, with adoration, but her own kind of adoration. Except that the name happened to have changed, she might have been talking about Roy Calvert thirty years before. To an outsider's eyes, they seemed distinctly different men. A good many women had thought Roy romantic. He had been gifted, but he had had to struggle with a manic-depressive nature, often so melancholy that he detested his own life. He had been, at least potentially, a great scholar. Rosalind had adored him. She had learned something about his profession, and could talk as the wife of a scholar should. When she spoke of him, there was no one else in this world: and there was also, in the midst of the worship, a kind of debunking twinkle, as though she alone could point out that, though he was everything a woman could wish for, he could do with a bit of sense.

On the other hand, Azik was not a romantic figure, except in the eyes of someone like Balzac. It would be stretching a point to suggest that he had an over-delicate or tormented nature. But once again, when Rosalind spoke of him, there was no one else in this world. Once again she had learned something about his profession, and could talk as the wife of an international entrepreneur should. And once again, in the midst of the worship, there was a kind of debunking twinkle, as though she alone could point out that, though he was everything a woman could wish for, he could do with a bit of sense.

It was a great gift of hers, I thought, to fall in love so totally just where it was convenient to fall in love. Though she wasn't an adventuress, she had done better for herself than any adventuress I had met. Roy had been well-off, at least by our modest academic standards of the time (I had seen his father's name over a hosiery factory when I walked to school as a boy): Azik was perhaps ten times richer. She had loved each of them in turn. She herself said that night, in the sublime flat phrase of our native town: "No, I can't say that I've got much to complain about."

In the throng of the party Muriel joined us, Roy Calvert's daughter, born a few months before he was killed, so that she was over twenty now. I had seen her, intermittently, in the last few years. As a child she promised to get the best out of both her parents' looks, but by now, though she had a kind of demure attractiveness, that hadn't happened. Her nose was too long, her eyes too heavy-lidded. Usually those eyes were averted, her whole manner was demure: but when she asked a question, one received a green-eyed sharp stare, perhaps the single physical trait that came from her father. No, there was another: her face one wouldn't notice much, now she was grown up, but when she walked she had his light-footed upright grace.

Rosalind chatted on about Azik's exploits. Muriel, eyes sidelong, put in a gentle command. On the face of it, she thought Rosalind was under-rating him. Whether this was Muriel's way of amusing herself, I didn't know.

The bells were ringing, we went into our box. Azik's passion for the theater was an eclectic one, and we were seeing a play of the Absurd. Within a few minutes I tried, in the darkness of the box, to make out the hands of my wristwatch: how long before the first interval? In time it came. Back into the private room. Back to more champagne, the table restocked, dishes of caviar brought in. But back also to a sight I had had no warning of. One of the diplomats had taken charge of Margaret, I was in another group with Azik—when I saw, in the corner of the room, dinner-jacketed like the rest of us, my nephew Pat. He was talking, head close to head, with Muriel. I put my hand on Azik's massive arm, and drew him aside. I indicated the couple in the corner, and in an undertone said:

"How do you know that young man?"

"It was impossible to fit him into the boxes," said Azik, misunderstanding me, as though apologizing for not doing his best for Pat. "So I asked if he would not mind to join us for our little drink—"

"No," I said. "I meant, how did you come to know him?"

"I must say," replied Azik, "I think he presented himself to my wife. Because his father was such a great friend of Calvert."

He moved his great moon face nearer to mine, with a glance of friendly cunning. Did he have any suspicions about that story? In fact, it was quite untrue. Martin had known Roy Calvert only slightly: they might have walked through the college together, that was about all. Of course, it was conceivable that Pat had picked up a different impression. Family legends grow, he must have heard a good deal about

Roy both from me and his father. As for Rosalind, I doubted whether she had known, let alone remembered, many of Roy's Cambridge friends.

"I did not raise objection," Azik said. He added, putting a finger to the side of his squashed and spreading nose: "Remember, I am a Jewish papa."

I told him, I sometimes felt I should have made a pretty good Jewish papa myself. But some of our thoughts were in parallel, and one at right angles.

"Your brother's is a good family, I should say," said Azik.

I would have disillusioned him, if it had been necessary. But it wasn't. He knew as well as I did that the Eliots were not a "good family" in the old continental sense. He knew precisely where we came from. But he meant something different. Azik saw, much more clearly than most Englishmen, what the English society had become. It was tangled, it was shifting its articulations, but in it men like Martin had their place.

I asked Azik whether he had seen much of Pat.

"Ach, he is very young," said Azik, with monumental good nature and a singular lack of interest. Our thoughts still did not meet. Azik began to speak, quietly but without reticence, about money. Muriel's money. "I have to be careful, my friend. Mu will have something of her own when she is twenty-one." Calvert (as Azik always called Roy) had not had much except a big allowance: but what he left had been "tied up" for Mu. "He was a very careful man," said Azik with a kind of respect. "However, that is chicken feed." Azik, totally unprudish about money, unlike most of my rich English acquaintances, told me the exact sums. "But Calvert's father, no, that isn't such chicken feed." Rosalind had been bequeathed a life-interest in half of it; the rest was in trust for Muriel, and would come to her next year. "Fortunately, she has her head screwed on."

Before we parted, Azik could not resist explaining to me

how different his own dispositions were. "I have made over a capital sum to Rosalind with no strings attached. So she can walk out on me tomorrow if she can't stand me any longer." He gave an uxorious chuckle. As for David, well, need anyone ask? Though I did not need to ask, Azik insisted on telling me of a magniloquent settlement.

After another instalment of the Absurd, we returned for the second interval in the private room. This time, seeing that Pat had reappeared and was once more close to Muriel, I went straight to them.

"Hello, Uncle Lewis," said Pat, treacle-brown eyes wide open and cheeky. "Who'd ever have thought of seeing you here?"

"Daddy would have hated it if you weren't here, you know that, Sir Lewis," said Muriel, precisely. She was utterly composed.

I asked them how they liked the play. Muriel smiled, lashes falling close to her cheeks. Pat began: "I suppose we can't communicate, at least that's the idea, isn't it?"

Yes, that was the idea.

He looked at Muriel. "But I can communicate with you sometimes, can't I?"

"I think," she said, "I can communicate with Daddy."

For a moment, I had cursed myself for mentioning the play. It was true that for two acts it had been expressing noncommunication: but at the end of the second, as though for once human beings could make themselves clear to one another, there had been a lucid and in fact a lyrically eloquent description of fellatio. I had been with Pat in company where he would have found this an occasion too hilarious to resist. But no, now he was holding his tongue: was he being protective toward her, or was it too early to frighten her?

I watched her, her eyes meekly cast down. She did not appear to be in need of protection. She was so composed, more than he was. I knew that Rosalind, like other mothers whose own early lives had not been unduly pure, had taken extreme care of her. She hadn't gone unsupervised, she had had to account for any date with a young man. And yet I should have guessed—though I wouldn't have trusted any of my guesses about her very far—that she was one of those girls who somehow understand all about the sexual life before they have a chance to live it.

"Uncle Lewis," said Pat, "are you open on New Year's Eve this year?"

This time he was really being brash. I had to answer that I had been pretty much occupied that autumn, we hadn't made up our minds. That was, in literal terms, true. But Margaret and I had got into the habit of asking our families and close friends for New Year's Eve: neither of us had suggested breaking it. The point was, he was begging for the two of them—as though Vicky, who had been invited the year before, could be dropped, or as though they might all have an amicable time together.

"I think," put in Muriel, quick, sure-footed, "Daddy said that we're having dinner with you soon, aren't we?" (She meant Azik, Rosalind, and herself.)

Yes, I said.

"That will be nice."

Pat looked at me, as though he would have liked to wink. He wasn't used to anyone as cool as this—who could, so equably, declare his proposition closed.

As Margaret and I were given a lift home in one of the diplomatic cars, acquaintances beside us, we couldn't have our after-the-play talk. In the lift, going up to our flat, she was silent, and stayed so until she had switched on the drawing-room lights and poured herself a drink. She asked if I wanted one, but her tone was hard. Sitting in the chair the other side of the fireplace, she said:

"So that's the way it is!"

Her face was flushed: the adrenalin was pouring through her: she was in a flaming temper.

"What do you mean?"

"You know what I mean."

"I haven't any idea."

"You have," she said. "Your nephew. What does he think he's up to?"

"How should I know?"

"It's intolerable!" she cried. I was thinking, yes, she was kind, she took to heart what Vicky might go through: but also Margaret was no saint, she was angry because she herself had, at intervals, been taken in by Pat. I was getting provoked, because of the disparity we both knew between Margaret's kind of temper and my own. I had to make an effort to sound peaceful.

"Look here, I don't know much about this girl"—Muriel—"but if it's any consolation to you, I fancy that she can look after herself—"

"I shouldn't be surprised," she said. But she said it with edge and meaning.

We were on the verge of a quarrel. I said:

"I don't understand."

"I was thinking of her father." She went on, with exaggerated reasonableness: "Of course he was in a higher class than your nephew Pat. But shouldn't you have said that there might be some sort of resemblance—?"

"Nonsense." This was an old argument. With the gap in age between us, she had felt shut out from parts of my youth. At times she was jealous of the friends who had known me when I was a young man. Francis Getliffe and Charles March —with those she was on close terms. George Passant, she had worked to understand. But Roy Calvert, who was dead, whom she could never know, she could not help believe that I had inflated, had given a significance or an aura that he could not conceivably, in her eyes, have possessed.

"Well, Pat does set out to be a miniature Byronic hero, doesn't he?"

"Roy Calvert," I said, "had about as much use for Byronic heroes as I have."

"But still," she said, "you do admit that he succeeded in bringing misery to everyone, literally everyone, so far as I've ever heard, who had any relations with him?"

I sat without speaking.

"I know you claim that he had a sort of insight. But I can't convince myself that the spiritual life, or the tragic sense, or whatever they like to call it, is a bit like that."

Like her, I spoke with deliberate carefulness, as though determined either to take the bite out of my voice or not to overstate my case.

"I'm not sure that nowadays I should see him quite in the same way. But of one thing I am perfectly certain. Of all the men and women I've ever known, he was the most selfless. He's the only one, and he suffered for it, who could really throw his own self away."

Now we were quarrelling. We had learned, early in our marriage, that it was dangerous to quarrel. If I had been like her, there would have been no danger in it. Her temper was hot: the blood rushed: it was soon over. But with me, usually more controlled, temper, once I had lost it, smoldered on.

Margaret, watching me, knew this bitter streak in me and knew it more acceptantly than I did myself.

"If you say that," she said, "then I've got to take it."

I accused her of making a concession. I said that neither of us wanted the other to make concessions which were not genuine. Between us there couldn't be that kind of compromise—

"Perhaps it was not quite genuine," she said with a difficult smile. "But—what am I to do?"

Somewhere, filtering towards my tongue, were words that would make us both angrier. Suddenly, as though by some inexplicable feedback, I said in a mechanical tone:

"Pat was sucking up for an invitation to our party. For both of them."

Margaret gave a shout of laughter, full-throated, happy laughter.

"Oh God," she cried. "What on earth did you say?"

"Oh, just that we hadn't decided whether we were going to give one."

"It must be wonderful to be tactful, mustn't it?"

Margaret went on laughing. We were certainly going to give a party, she said. After all (her mood had changed, she was still flushed, but now with gaiety), we had a lot to be thankful for, this past year. My eye. Young Charles's successes. Maurice's survival. Her father better. Various storms come through. It would be faint-hearted not to give a party. But one thing was sure, she said. He was not going to bring that girl. Was that all right? Yes, I said, caught up by her spirits, that was completely all right. Without a pause between thought and action, she went to the study, brought back a sheet of paper, and, although it was late, began writing down a list, a long list, of names.

SEVENTEEN

EVENING BEFORE
THE PARTY

For the next four days, Margaret enjoyed planning the party. It had become a token of thanksgiving. Every evening we sat in the drawing room and added some more names. The list grew longer; we knew a good many people, most of them in professional London, but wider-spread than that. We had changed the date to Christmas Eve. This was partly because there was another New Year's party, to which we felt inclined to go: but also because we calculated that Pat would be back with his family in Cambridge, and so we could invite the Schiffs. That calculation, however, went wrong. Martin and Irene decided to come for the night, and, together with their children, to have Christmas dinner with us next day. Margaret swore: would anything get rid of that young man? But she was in high spirits, the party occupying her just as it might have done when she was a girl. There weren't enough refusals, I complained. The senior Getliffes couldn't come, but Leonard could. Others accepted from out of London. There's nothing like an operation to make people anxious to see one, I said.

Still, it was agreeable, when Maurice had come down from Cambridge and Charles had returned from school, to have the four of us sitting before dinner, talking about this domestic ritual. Maurice had young men and girls he wanted to invite, some of them lame ducks. Charles had school friends who lived in the London area. Throw them all in, we agreed.

The age-range of the party would be about sixty years. As we sat there in the evening, the week before Christmas, I thought that in contrast to Maurice's untouched good looks, Charles already appeared the older. He had just won a scholarship, very young: but sometimes, as on the morning he visited me in hospital, he seemed preoccupied. I noticed that, instead of staying in bed late, as he used to do in the holidays, he got up as early as I did, riffling through the letters. I had been older than that, I thought, when I was first menaced by the post. But he was controlled enough to live a kind of triple life: his emotions were his own, but, as the Christmas nights came nearer, curtains not yet drawn at tea-time, black sky over the park, he sat with us, teasing Margaret, dark-eyed, ironic, enjoying the preparations as much as she did.

It was the afternoon of 23rd December, about five o'clock. Margaret had not got back from visiting her father, the boys were out. I was, except for our housekeeper, alone in the flat. I had been reading in the study, the light from the angle-lamp bright across my book. There were piles of papers by the chair, a tray of letters on the room-wide desk, all untidy but findable, at least by the eye of memory; all the grooves of habit there. The telephone rang. I crossed over to the far side of the desk. "This is George." The strong voice, which had never lost its Suffolk undertone, came out at me. I exclaimed with pleasure: I had not seen him for months. "I'd rather like to have a word," the voice went on robustly. "I suppose you're not free, are you?"

I replied that I was quite free: when would he like—? "I can come straight round. I shan't be many minutes."

Waiting for him, I fetched the ice and brought in a tray of drinks. I was feeling comfortably pleased. This was a surprise, a good end to the year. I hadn't seen him for months, I thought again, no, not since the April Court. That hadn't been my fault, but it was good that he should invite himself. He might come to the party the following night, that would be better still; there was something, not precisely nostalgic, but reassuring in going back right through the years. My brother hadn't really known me when I was in my teens: but George had, and he was the only one, when I was in the state young Charles was approaching now.

I let him in, and took him to the study. Would he have a drink? I hadn't seen him in full light, I had my back towards him as I heard a sturdy yes. I splashed in the soda, saying that it was too long since we had had an evening together.

Then I sat down opposite him.

"I ought to explain. This isn't exactly a social visit," he said.

I began to smile at the formality, so like occasions long ago when he wished to discuss my career and behaved as if there were some mysterious etiquette that he, alone among human-kind, had never been properly taught. I looked into his face as he lifted the glass, ice tinkling. He was staring past me; his eyes were unfocused, which was nothing new. His hair bushed out over his ears, in blond and whitening quiffs, uncut, unbrushed. The lines on his forehead, the lines under his eyes, made him appear not so much old as dilapidated: but no more old or dilapidated than when I had last seen him in our traditional pub.

Over the desk, on his right, the window was uncovered, and I caught a glimpse of his great head reflected against the darkness.

It was all familiar, and I went on smiling.

"Well, what's the agenda?" I asked.

"Something rather unpleasant has happened," said George.

"What is it?"

"Of course," said George, "it must be some absurd mis-take."

"What is it?"

"You know who I mean by my niece and the Pateman girl?"

"Yes."

"They've been asking them questions about the boy who disappeared. The one who was done away with."

For an instant I was immobilized. I was as incapable of action as when I stood at the bedroom window, blinked my eye, and found the black edge still there. That edge: the noise I had just heard, the words: they were all confused.

Without being able to control my thoughts, I stared at George, wishing him out of my sight. I heard my voice, hard and pitiless. Who were "they?" What had really happened?

George, face open but without emotion, said that detectives had been interviewing them: one was a detective-superintendent. "He seems to have been very civil," said George. Statements had been taken in the Patemans' house. The young women had been told that they might be questioned again.

"Of course," said George, "it's bound to be a mistake. There's a ridiculous exaggeration somewhere."

I looked at him.

"There must be," I said.

"I'm glad you think that," said George, almost cheerfully.

From the instant I had heard the news, and been frozen, I had taken the worst for granted. With a certainty I didn't try even to rationalize. Yet here I was, giving George false hope. When, thirty years before, he had faced me with his own trouble—trouble bad enough, though not as unimaginable as this—I had been maddened by his optimism and had tried to destroy it. Here I was doing the opposite. But it was not out of kindness or comradeship. Even less out of gratitude. I couldn't find a thought for what he had once done for me. Forebodings from the past, linked with this new fact, at the same time incredible and existential, drove out everything else. I wanted not to see him, I wanted to agree with him and have him go away.

I tried to do my duty.

"I suppose," I said, "I've got to ask, but I know it isn't necessary, you can't be touched in any way yourself?"

"Well"—George's tone was matter-of-fact—"they've been in on the fringe of our crowd. If anyone wanted to rake up stories of some of the crowd, or me as far as that goes, it might be awkward—"

"No, no, no. Not in this sort of case." This time my reassurance was honest, impatient.

"That's what I thought myself." He spoke amiably but vaguely; he had once been a good lawyer, but now he seemed to have forgotten all his law. He went on:

"I ought to have kept more of an eye on them, I grant you that. But the last two or three years, since my health went wrong, I've rather gone to pieces."

He said it with acquiescence, without remorse: as though "going to pieces" had been a vocation in itself.

"What steps have you taken? About those two. What practical steps?"

I heard my own voice hard again.

"Oh, I've put them in touch with solicitors, naturally."

"What solicitors?"

"Eden & Sharples. I didn't need to look any further."

Just for a moment, I was touched. Eden & Sharples was the present name of the firm of solicitors where George had been employed, as managing clerk, all his working life. When he was a young man of brilliant promise, they hadn't been generous to him. Sometimes I used to think that, had they treated him better, his life might have been different. Yet even now, made to retire early, pensioned off, he still thought of the firm with something like reverence. In this crisis, he turned to them as though they were the only solicitors extant. It was misfits like George—it was as true now as when I first met him—who had most faith in institutions.

"Well then," I said. "There's nothing else you can do just now, is there?"

That was a question which was meant to sound like leave-taking. I hadn't offered him another drink: I wanted him to go.

He leaned forward. His eyes, sadder than his voice, managed to converge on mine. "I should like to do something," he said. "I should like to ask you something."

"What is it?"

"I told you, I've rather gone to pieces. I can't look after this business. I'm relying on you."

"I don't see what I can do."

"You can make sure—if things get more serious, which is ridiculous, of course—you can make sure that they get the best advice. From the senior branch of the legal profession." George brought out that bit of solicitor's venom, just as he used to do as a rebellious young man. But he was more lucid than he seemed. As so often, he both believed and disbelieved in his own optimism. He was anticipating that they would go to trial.

"I can't interfere. You've got to trust the solicitors—"

Once more, George had become lucid. He could admit to himself how the legal processes worked. He said:

"I just want to be certain that we're doing everything possible. I just want to be certain"—he looked at me with resignation—"that I'm leaving it in good hands."

I had no choice, and in fact I didn't want any. I said:

"All right, I'll do what I can."

"That's very nice of you," said George.

I had to give him his second drink. He did not say another word about the investigation. For a few minutes he chatted amicably, made his formal inquiry about Charles, and then announced, with his old hopeful secretive restlessness, that he must be off.

When I had seen him to the lift, I went straight into the bedroom, so as to avoid meeting either of the boys. There I sat, neither reading nor thinking, until Margaret returned. She was taking off her hat as she opened the door. At the sight of me she said:

"What's happened?"

I told her, dry and hard.

"This is dreadful." Still wearing her coat, she had come and put her arms round me.

"I'm sorry for George," she said.

"I don't know who I'm sorry for."

She was listening to each inflection. Even she could not totally divine why I was so much upset. George was my oldest friend, but she knew that we met seldom and couldn't really talk. Even so, even if the relation had been closer, George himself was not in danger nor involved. It was all at one remove, startling that it should come so near, perhaps—

"You won't tell the boys tonight, will you?"

"They'll read it in the papers—"

"Don't tell them tonight, though."

She meant, she didn't want their spirits quenched before tomorrow's party.

"You'll find," I said, "that they can take it. People can take anything. That's the worst thing about us. Those two will take it. Maurice will take it because he's naturally good—and Charles because, like us, he isn't."

I had spoken roughly, and she frowned. She frowned out of bafflement and concern. Still she could not divine why I was so much upset. Nor could I. I couldn't have given a reason, either to her or to myself, why this had struck me like another arrest of life. Not so near the physical roots as the blinded eye—but somehow taking hold of more of my whole self, stopping me dead.

Maybe (I tried to explain it as I lay awake, later that night) a physical shock one could domesticate, it was part of the run of this existence, it wasn't removed from Margaret and my son, it was in the nature of things. But George's announcement didn't happen to one, it didn't happen even when one heard it and, at the same instant, foresaw what was to come. Nevertheless, I couldn't reach, any more than Margaret, what I really felt.

Back in our bedroom—hours before the time I lay awake —Margaret was still asking me to keep the news from the boys, at least for a couple of days. Of course I would, I promised. She searched my face, wondering what that would give away. Then I snapped back to this home of ours, and told her she ought to know me better: didn't she remember times, nearer the bone than this, when I had been able to pretend?

EIGHTEEN

THE CHRISTMAS
GREETING

Just before nine on Christmas Eve, as we sat round waiting, Charles wanted to arrange a sweepstake on the first guest
to arrive. Martin, Irene, and Pat had been dining with us:
Pat, to whom parties were like native air, was making sure
that the hired waiters knew their job. Standing in the drawing room, decorous, empty, expectant, paintings throwing
back the light, Margaret, Irene, and Martin were taking their
first drinks. As for me, I should have to be on my feet for the
next few hours: anyway, it was better not to drink that night.

If Charles's sweep had been arranged, no one would have
won it. The bell rang on the stroke of nine: the first guest
entered: it was Herbert Getliffe, whom only I knew and
whom most of the others had scarcely heard of. He entered, a
little dishevelled, his glance at the same time bold and
furtive. He was in his mid-seventies by now, years older than
his half-brother Francis. When I first entered his chambers
(and found myself exploited until I learned the tricks of one
of the trickiest of men), most people prophesied that he
would be a judge before he finished. Herbert would have
prophesied that himself: it was his ambition. But it hadn't
happened. He had, fairly late in life, got onto the snakes
instead of the ladders. He might pour out his emotions, but
he was pathologically tight with money. That put him on the
final snake. For, although it was hushed up, he had been over-
ingenious with his income-tax returns. After that no judge-

ship. He had carried on with his practice until a few years before. He made more money, and, when his wife died, saved it by living in a tiny Kensington flat and inviting himself out to meals with his friends. They did not mind having him, for, though his ambition had failed him, his ebullience hadn't. As he grew old, most of us—even while we remembered being done down—became fond of him.

With great confidence, he called my wife Marjorie. He seemed under the impression that she was an American. Breathlessly, with extreme gusto, he told her a story of his daughter, who was living "in a place called Philadelphia." His style of conversation had become more mysteriously allusive: Margaret, who had met him just once before, looked puzzled. Helpfully he explained: "Pa. U.S.A."

In the morphology of such a party, four people had come in by ten past nine, and then something like fifty in the next few minutes. Expectancy left the rooms, the noise-level climbed. I had to walk round, looking after the strangers. An African friend of Maurice's, lost among the crowd. As I talked about his work, I saw Douglas Osbaldiston, fresh-faced, still young-looking, standing among a group of young women. There were long tables, laid with food and glasses, in each of the bigger rooms: but within half an hour a hundred bodies stood round them, more were coming, one had to push one's way. I couldn't spend time with my own friends. Lester Ince, who had been drinking before he arrived, introduced me to his new wife, ornamental, a couturier's triumph. She was full of enthusiasm for any of Lester's acquaintances, but he was chiefly occupied with hilarity because I was going about with a glass of tomato juice.

In a crowd, the noise, trying to spot the lonely, I put last night's news out of mind. Yet once—as though it were unconnected—I was thinking as I introduced Vicky to Charles March, that Christmas Eve was an unlucky night. Why had we fixed on it? There had been one Christmas Eve, at another party, which even now I couldn't forgive.

I shook hands with Douglas Osbaldiston in the press. Friendly, kind, competent, he asked about an acquaintance: could he help? Was any night a lucky night for Douglas? He was at the top of the Treasury by now, as had been predictable long before. Some of the young people in these rooms thought about him as the high priest—unassuming, yes, but stuffy and complacent—of what they still called "the Establishment." Early next morning, as on every morning, he would go to his wife's bedside. The paralysis had, after six years, crept so far that she could not light a cigarette or turn the pages of a book. He had loved her as much as anyone there would ever love.

In the innermost room, one of the opposition front bench, who had attended the scientists' dinner, was holding court. No, not holding court, for he was as matey and unassuming as Douglas himself. Standing there, listening to the young, chatting, tucking away names in a computer memory.

In another room, Monty Cave, who had in July become a Secretary of State, held his own court. It had needed staff-work by Martin, assisted by Pat—who had been amiable to Vicky but became over-conscientious in his party duties—to keep the front benches apart. Not because the two of them were political opponents, but because they were personal enemies. We didn't want a battle of practiced distaste, even though Monty, who was not a favorite with many, would come off worst.

Gilbert Cooke, plethoric, hot-eyed, like a great ship in sail, burst through to me. He was in search of my son Charles, intent on talking about the old school. But when I saw them together, Charles was politely slipping away. Their school was for Gilbert the most delectable of topics of conversation, but Charles did not share that view, especially if there were comely girls close by. For Charles, whatever letter he was waiting for in the mornings, was on the lookout that night. There was a daughter of Charles March's, shy and pretty, whom he knew I should have liked him to take out. Instead, I kept noticing his head close to that of Naomi Rubin, David Rubin's youngest, who was working in London and who was years older than Charles. She looked bright, nothing like so pretty as the March girl: but she was listening, and I didn't doubt that he was dissimulating his age.

There were swirls through the rooms as a few people left or others came in late. Caro, who used to be Roger Quaife's wife, made an entrance with her new husband. It was surprising that she came, for normally she moved entirely in a smart circle with which Margaret and I had only a flickering acquaintance. Her second husband, unlike Roger, came from an ambience as rich and rarefied as her own—though to some that was concealed under the name of Smith. He was cultivated, much more so than Caro, and, of all those I had talked to that night, he was the only one who could identify our paintings.

We were standing in the dining room, which had at that stage of the party become the central lobby, so congested that I found it hard to direct Smith's Hanoverian head to a newly acquired Chinnery, when I heard scraps of a conversation, loud and alcoholic, nearer the middle of the room.

"That's all we need to say," Edgar Hankins was declaiming, in the elegiac tone he used for his literary radio talks. His rubbery blunt-featured face was running with sweat. "That's all we need to say. Birth, copulation, and death. That's all there is."

He was declaiming to, or at least in the company of, Irene. Once, and it had overlapped the first years of her marriage to Martin, she had been in love with him. All that was long since over. She gave a cheerful malicious yelp (was there, out of past history, just the extra edge?), and replied:

" 'He talks to me that never had a son.' "

It was true (aside, someone was complaining about quotations from the best authors) that Hankins, who had married after their love affair, had no children. Hankins, with elevated reiteration, answered:

"Birth, copulation, and death."

"If you must have it," cried Irene triumphantly, "birth, copulation, children, and death! That's a bit nearer."

Hankins went on with his slogan—as though he had reached one of the drinking stages where the truth is ultimately clear and only needs to be pronounced. As I pushed away, seeing someone alone, I heard Irene's antiphon.

"Birth, copulation, children, and death! If anyone leaves out the children, he doesn't begin to know what it's all about."

Quite late, about a quarter to twelve, when the rooms were beginning to thin, Sammikins, in a dinner jacket with a carnation in his buttonhole, walked in. He asked loudly after his sister Caro, who had already left. Their father had died a couple of years before, and Sammikins had come into the title. So he had had to give up his seat in the Commons, which to him, though to no one else, appeared his proper occupation. He told me—or rather he told the room—that he had lost "a packet" at poker an hour or two before. I hadn't seen him for months: I thought he looked drawn and that the flesh had fallen in below his cheekbones. When I got him to myself, I asked how he was.

"Just a touch of alcoholic fatigue, dear boy," he said in his brazen voice. But he was quite sober. Apart from me and some of the very young, he seemed the only person present who had not had a drink that night.

Many people in the swirl were well and happy. Some, I knew, were heartsick. With Douglas, from a cause that couldn't be cured. Others, like Vicky, who couldn't restrain herself from begging ten minutes alone with Pat, might someday look on at this kind of party, just as the content now looked at her. Leonard Getliffe had been and gone. There must have been others there, not only among the young, who—without the rest of us knowing—were putting a face on things. It was part of the flux. Just as it was part of the flux that, in the public eye, some were having the luck and some the opposite. Douglas, in spite of his organic grief, had reached the peak in his job. The master-politician was confident that, before this time next year, he would have reached the peak in his. An American playwright, who had been modestly drinking in a corner, had just had a spectacular success. And there was another success, the most bizarre of all. Gilbert Cooke, who had been fortunate to be kept in the civil service after the war, had managed to become deputy head of one of the security branches. It couldn't have been a more esoteric triumph: except to Douglas, one dared not mention the name of the post, much less of its occupant. I had not the slightest conception of how Gilbert had made it. For him, who was not able even to suggest that he had been promoted, it was his crowning glory.

Whereas Herbert Getliffe was not the only one for whom the snakes had been stronger than the ladders. Edgar Hankins's brand of literary criticism, which had been rooted in the 'twenties, had gone out of fashion. He could still earn a living, one saw his name each week, he still wrote with elegiac eloquence: but the younger academics sneered at him, and in the weeklies he was being referred to as though he were a dead Georgian poet. There was another turn-up for the book (Sammikins, in another context, had just been blaring out those words), the most unjust of all—as though anything could happen either way. Walter Luke had stepped in for half an hour, grizzled, crisp. Yes, he had got honors, but what did they mean? Apart from Leonard Getliffe, he had a greater talent than anyone there. But for years past, he had thrown up everything to lead the project on plasma physics. Now, so all the scientists said, it was certain that the problem would not be solved for a generation. Walter Luke knew it, and knew—making jaunty cracks at his own expense—that he had wasted his creative life.

At midnight, as I was saying some goodbyes at the hall door, another guest, the last of all, emerged from the lift. It was Ronald Porson. He hadn't been invited by me—but he was one of those, living alone in bedsitters in the neighborhood, whom Maurice and the local parson went to visit. The parson had been at the party, but had left some time before to celebrate Christmas mass. I guessed, from the first sight, that I should need some help with Porson, but Maurice was nowhere near.

, He came lurching up. In the passage light there was the gleam of an MCC tie.

"Good evening, Lewis," he said in a domineering tone. I asked him to come in. As we walked into the dining room, he said:

"I was told you had a champagne party on."

Not quite, I said. But there was the bar over there—

"I insist," said Porson. "I was told it was a champagne party."

As a matter of fact, I said, there were lots of other liquids, but not champagne.

"I insist," began Porson, and I told him that, if he wanted champagne, I would find a bottle. He had come to pick a quarrel: I didn't mind his doing so with me, but there were others he might upset. Immediately he refused champagne, and demanded gin.

"I don't like large parties," said Porson, looking around the room.

"Can't be helped," I replied.

He took a gulp. "You've got too many Jews here," he announced.

"Be careful."

"Why should I be?"

Martin, who had been watching, whispered, "You may need a strong man or two." He beckoned Sammikins, and they both stood near. Porson was in his seventies, but he could be violent. None of us, not even the clergyman, knew how he survived. He came from a professional family; he had eked out his bit of capital, but it had gone long since. He had once been convicted of importuning. But all that happened to him made him fight off pity and become either aggressive or patronizing or both.

"Who is he?" He pointed to Sammikins.

I said, Mr. Porson, Lord Edgeworth.

"Why don't you do something about it?" Porson asked him.

"What are you talking about?"

"Why don't you do something about this country? That's why you're supposed to sit there for, isn't it?" Porson put out his underlip. "I've got no use for the lot of you."

"You'd better calm down," said Sammikins, getting hot-eyed himself.

"Why the hell should I? I had an invitation, didn't I? I *suppose* you had an invitation—"

Then Maurice came up, and greeted him amicably. "Hallo, young man," said Porson.

"I expected you'd be in church," said Maurice.

"Well, I thought about it—"

"You promised Godfrey"—the parson—"you would, didn't you?"

"To tell you the bloody truth," said Porson, "it's a bit too spike for me." He began, self-propelled, onto another griev-ance, on what "they" were doing to the Church of England, but Maurice (the other's rage dripped off him) said he would drive him round, they would still arrive in time for the Christmas greetings. Gentle, unworried, Maurice led him out: although the last I saw, looking through the hall towards the lift, were Porson's arms raised above his head, as though he were inspired into a final denunciation of the whole house.

About an hour later, the crowd had gone, Pat and the waiters had cleared the glasses from the drawing room, the windows were open to the cold air. Again in the morphology of parties, there was still the last residue remaining, not only remaining but settling down. Edgar Hankins reposed on cushions on the drawing-room floor: so did the playwright: Margaret and I sat back in our habitual chairs. Martin and Irene, since they were staying with us, remained too. Their daughter had gone to bed, Pat had disappeared, but Charles wanted to look as though the night were just beginning. Also fixtures, unpredictable fixtures, were Gilbert and Betty Cooke.

Martin, cheerful, said to me:

"Look, you're about eighteen drinks behind the rest of us. Won't you have one now?"

I hadn't been able to tell him about George Passant's news. It would have been a relief to do so. But now I was tired, sedated by the to-and-fro of people, not caring: yes, I said, I might as well have a drink. When he brought it to me, it was very strong. That was deliberate, for Martin was a vigilant man.

Someone cried, "Happy Christmas!"

From the floor, Edgar Hankins, who was far gone, raised a dormouselike head.

"Not the English greeting," he muttered, fluffing the words.

"What's the matter?" said Irene.

"Not 'Happy Christmas.' Insipid modernism. Vulgar. Genteel taste. Merry Christmas—that's the proper way. Merry Christmas."

Hankins subsided. Gilbert Cooke, with Charles sitting beside him, could at last indulge his insatiable passion for talking about their school. Charles wanted to hold inquiries about people at the party, but was trapped.

For a few minutes Betty and I were in conversation, quietly, with talk all round us. We were fond of each other, we had been for years. In bad times for us both, we had tried to help each other. Her love affairs had gone wrong: she was diffident but passionate, she hadn't the nerve to grab. We had thought, certainly I had, that she deserved a better man than Gilbert, or at least a different one. Yet somehow the marriage had worked.

That night, as we whispered, she was watching me with her acute splendid eyes, the feature which, more in middle-age than youth, gave her a touch of beauty.

"You've had enough," she said.

I protested.

"Now, now, now," she said. "I used to notice one or two things, didn't I?"

I had to give a smile.

"I'll get rid of them," she said, glancing round the room. It was the sort of practical good turn which, even in her bleakest times, she had often done for me.

Next morning I woke up early. Through the window came the sound, very faint, of church bells. I stretched myself, feeling well, with the vague sense, perhaps some shadow of a memory from childhood, of a pleasing day ahead. Then, edging into consciousness, suddenly shutting out all else—as sharp, as absolute as when, a few weeks before I had awakened in well-being and then seen the veil over my eye—was the brute fact. There was nothing to keep away nor soften what George had told me; and what I felt as I listened, I felt waking up that morning, as though the passage of hours hadn't happened or couldn't do its work.

III
QUESTIONS WITHOUT ANSWERS

NINETEEN

A FAIR QUESTION

A milky blue sky, a bland and sunny afternoon, very mild for the second week in January. There was a blazing fire in the Residence drawing room, and I was sitting on the window-seat. Neither Vicky nor Arnold Shaw had been in the house when I arrived an hour before, but all the matter-of-fact comforts had been arranged, and, looking out at the bright daylight, I did not want to leave them. In fact, I had an appointment with Eden & Sharples, George's old firm, at half-past three.

My old colleagues who had to live the disciplined official life had taught me, not that I was good at it, to cut off my thoughts. Douglas Osbaldiston went each morning to see the wife he loved able to move only her lips and eyes: he arrived at the Treasury as immersed in the day's timetable as when he was happy. At times it was better to think of the timetable. I was to call on my father that night. That would be no tax: I had received a letter from him just after Christmas (he had written to me not more than half a dozen times in my whole life), saying that he would like to see me.

I had one more thing to do before I went to the solicitors. As soon as the young women were charged, which happened on the last day of December, I had telephoned George, telling him that I would keep my promise, but that in return I needed to know about his health. It sounded harsh, or even irrelevant: George was angry and then evasive: I insisted. I couldn't explain, but I had to know what I was taking on, and where I could draw the limits: how much responsibility was he fit for himself?

So, in the hall at the Residence, I did some more telephoning. George had at last given me his doctor's name. He had also undertaken to tell the doctor that I was authorized to inquire.

Over the telephone I heard a jolly, lubricated, courteous voice. Yes, Passant was a patient of his. Yes, he knew about me, of course, but he didn't remember Passant mentioning my name. I said (George, whom I shouldn't see till next day, had either forgotten or been deceitful) that I was a very old friend.

"Well, anyway, I'm glad to talk to you." The voice was forthcoming, relaxed. "He hasn't any close relations, has he?"

I said that he had two sisters alive, but, so far as I knew, saw nothing of them.

"He's not as well as he ought to be, you know."

I asked what was the matter.

"Physically, he's a good deal older than his age."

Was he really ill?

"No, I can't say that. But I can't say either that he's a specially good life."

Was he in a condition to take serious strain?

That the doctor couldn't guess. Passant was a happy man. His arteries, though, were hardening: his blood-pressure, despite medication, stayed high.

"He's his own worst enemy, you know." The voice was kind, that of someone fond of George. "He's a very self-indulgent chap, isn't he? We all like a drop to drink, but I fancy that he takes more than most of us. And I'm certain that he eats too much. If you could persuade him to lose a couple of stone, he might live ten years longer. He ought to have a wife to look after him, of course." It was all compassionate, brotherly, down to earth: but this was one patient out of many, he had no idea of George's secret life. Nevertheless, he went on talking. It was a relief to know that George had someone who thought about him. "He's a good soul, isn't he? Do what you can to make him sensible, won't you?"

It was a relief to the doctor, maybe, that there was someone who thought about George. Yet, an hour later, standing in the outer office at Eden & Sharples, where I had often waited for him, I was asking questions as though this were a routine visit to a solicitor's. Mr. Eden was expecting me? Mr. Eden was sorry, the secretary said, he had been called away at short notice. Could I see someone else? Yes, Mr. Sharples would be free in a minute. I looked round the office: still frowsty, shelves of books, metal boxes with clients' names painted in white. Although the practice was going on, I should have guessed that it had diminished, that there must be twenty bigger firms in the town by now.

The present Eden was the nephew of the senior partner whom I had known. Neither of them had been over-energetic; this one (though I wasn't quite a stranger) was avoiding a distasteful interview that afternoon. Probably George had always inflated the standing of the firm. It must have made, I thought mechanically, a fair living for the two partners, not much more.

The inner door opened, and a big man, taller than I was and much more massive in the shoulders, stood on the threshold. He uttered my name as though it were a question.

"Come you in," he said.

It was meant to sound cordial. In effect, it sounded like the standard greeting of someone indrawn.

I sat down in an armchair in his office, which had once been Martineau's. More shelves of law books. Double windows, so that there was no noise from the street beneath.

Sharples took the chair behind his desk. He was in his

forties, handsome in a somber deep-orbited fashion. He had the forearms of a first-class batsman, and the hair grew thick and dark down to the back of his hands.

"Well—" he addressed me by name again, gazing at me under his eyebrows"—what can we do for you?"

He seemed both formal and awkward.

I said: "I think I mentioned in my letter, anyway I'm fairly sure that Aubrey Eden knows, that I'm a friend of George Passant's."

Sharples said:

"Mr. Passant left our employment some time ago."

That told me enough of his attitude to George.

"If it weren't for that connection," I said, choosing the words, "I shouldn't have any right to be here at all."

"We're very glad to see you. Any time you care to come."

"You are acting for these two women, Passant's niece and the other one, aren't you?"

He looked at me with deep sad eyes. He detested George, but he was determined to be courteous to me. In his own manner, he was a courteous and not unfriendly man. On the other hand, he was equally determined not to say a word out of place.

After a pause, he replied:

"That is not quite accurate."

"What isn't quite accurate?"

"We are acting for Miss Ross, that's true." That was the minimum he could tell me: it wasn't a professional secret, it would be on the record by now. "But we're not acting for Miss Pateman."

"You mean, you've passed that on to another solicitor?"

"You will find that another firm is handling her case."

"Why is that?"

"You're familiar with our trade, Sir Lewis."

In fact, the answer was obvious. There might be a conflict of interest between the two. It was standard procedure to give them different lawyers from the start.

"Can you tell me this," I said (it was like talking to a wall), "have you briefed counsel yet?"

He paused again. then said:

"Yes."

"Who?"

Once more he was working out that I could get the information elsewhere. At length he produced a name, Ted Benskin. It was a name that I recognized, for during the few years I practiced at the Bar, I had been a member of the Midland Circuit, and still, rather as men read about their old school, I watched for news of it. Not that Benskin had been a contemporary of mine. He was one of the crop of young men who had become barristers after the war and who were now making reputations for themselves.

"He took silk not long ago, didn't he?" I said.

For once Sharples could answer without brooding. In 1960, he said. He then added that Benskin was well-thought-of.

I asked: "Have they got a counsel for Miss Pateman (I was falling into Sharples's formality) yet?"

"I'm afraid I oughtn't to answer that."

That seemed like the end of the road. I tried one more slant: had he any idea, assuming that the case went for trial, who would be leading for the Crown? The question was not innocent. If the case was grave enough, or had roused enough horror, then the Attorney-General might elect to appear himself. Sharples was on guard.

"It isn't very profitable to speculate, I should have thought," he said. "We'd better cross that bridge when we come to it."

Against the far wall, visible to both of us, stood an old grandfather clock. It said a quarter to four. I had been shown into the room at 3:35. The interview was over. He seemed more embarrassed than at the start, now that we were both silent: I found it hard to jerk myself away. I turned to the window on my right, watching the traffic pass soundlessly below, where the tramlines used to run, and pointed to the building opposite. I told Sharples that I had worked there as a youth. "Did you, by Jove?" he said, with excessive interest and enthusiasm.

When I went out into the street, my timetable had gone all wrong: my next date, the only one that evening before I went to my father's, was not until six o'clock. There was a stretch of empty time to kill, and I didn't want a stretch of empty time. Absently (I didn't expect much from the next meeting, I didn't know where to find hard news, it was a foggy meaningless suspense, without the edge of personal anxiety), I walked a few hundred yards into Granby Street, in search of a café that I remembered. There was still a café nearby, but neon strips blared across the ceiling, people were queuing up to serve themselves. Close by, a block of offices was going up, the landmarks were disappearing, this street was reaching above the human scale. I went on another few hundred yards and crossed into the market place. There, all seemed familiar. The shops grew brighter as the afternoon darkened: doors pushed open, smells poured out, smells of bacon, cheese, fruit, which didn't recall anything special to me—perhaps there was too much to recall. For an instant all this gave me a sense of having cares sponged away. Best of all, the old grinding machine was working on, the smell of roast coffee beans flooded out, bringing reassurance and something like joy.

But even there, where we had once entered past the machine and into the café, there was no café left. I walked along the pavement, opposite the market stalls. Alongside me, facing me, women in fur coats, redolent of bourgeois well-being, just as the whole scene was, were bustling along. The cafés of my youth might have vanished, but such women had to go somewhere, after their shopping, for a cup of tea: so I finished up in a multiple store, scented and heated as Harrods, where I found a restaurant full of well-dressed women, most of them middle-aged, myself the only man. There was not a face in the room that I recognized, though once I might have passed some of those faces in the streets.

Over my tea, reading the local evening paper, I was preparing myself for Maxwell. It was one way of pushing away the suspense, any practical thought was better than none. Otherwise, I hadn't any reason to think he would help me. In the days after Christmas, beating round for any kind of action, I had remembered that he had become the head of the local C.I.D. I had known him, very slightly, when I was pleading one or two criminal cases and he was a young detective-sergeant. Then I had met him again, during the war, after he had been transferred to the special branch. Why he had moved again, back to ordinary police work, I hadn't any idea. I hadn't seen him since just after the war; this present job must be the last of his career.

There were bound to be half a dozen of his subordinates busy on a case like this. The police weren't stingy about manpower. It would be detective-inspectors who had done the investigations, not their boss. He might not know much, but he would certainly know something. That was no reason, though, why he should talk to me. I was not a special friend of his. Further, I should have to declare that I had some sort of interest. He was far too shrewd, and also too inquisitive, a man not to discover it. If I had been there out of random or even out of sadistic curiosity, I should have stood a better chance.

I had asked him to meet me at a pub in the market place. There, in the saloon bar, immediately after opening time, I waited. But I didn't have to wait long. The door swung open, and Maxwell entered with a swirl and a rush of air. He was a man both fat and muscular, very quick on small, strong, high-arched feet. He turned so fast, eyes flashing right and left until he saw me, that the air seemed to spin round him. "Good evening, sir," he said. "How are you getting on?"

I said, come and have a drink.

We sat in an alcove, tankards on the table in front of us. When he lifted his tankard, wishing me good health, Maxwell's eyes were sighting me. He had a strange resemblance to my old colleague Gilbert Cooke. Maxwell, too, was smooth-faced and plethoric, so much so that a doctor might have worried, though he was particularly active for a man in his mid-fifties. His great beak nose protruded violently from the smooth large face. His eyes were of the color that people called cornflower-blue, and so wide open that they might have been propped. The resemblance to Gilbert was so strong that it had previously, and had again that night, a curious effect on me: it made me feel that I knew him better than I did. Because I had an affection for Gilbert, I felt a kind of warmth, for which in reality I had no genuine cause, for this man. In upbringing, though, they weren't at all the same. Gilbert was the son of a general, while Maxwell's mother had been a charwoman in Battersea. He had himself started as a policeman on the beat, and one could still hear relics, by now subdued, of a south-of-the-river accent.

"Are you getting on all right?" he began—and then didn't know what to call me. When we had some dealings together in the war, he had come to use my Christian name. Now my style had changed; he was uneasy, and cross with me because he was uneasy. That was the last thing I wanted, to begin the evening. Not for the first time, I cursed these English complications. I told him, as roughly as I could, to drop all that. Underneath his inquisitive good manners, he could be rough himself, as well as proud. He gave a high-pitched laugh, drained his tankard, called me plain Lewis, and whisked off to fetch two more pints, although I was only half-through mine.

He went on with his inquiries about my fortunes. I retaliated by asking about his; all was well, he had just had a grandson. But with Maxwell the questions tended to flow one way.

"What are you here for, anyhow?" His eyes were unblinking and wide.

"That's almost what I've come to ask you."

"What's that, then?"

"Your people have been dealing with this murder, haven't they? I mean, the boy who disappeared."

He stared at me.

"What's the point?" he asked.

I thought it better not to hedge. "I happen to know a relative of one of those young women—"

"Do you, by God?"

Across the table his big face was looking at me, open, not expressionless, but with an expression I couldn't read. His reactions, like his movements, were very quick. He was wondering whether to tell me that he couldn't speak. Yes or no. I had no idea of the motives either way.

As though there hadn't been a hesitation, he said:

"You'd better come to the office. Too many people here."

He looked round the bar with his acquisitive glance, the same glance, I guessed, that he had used as a detective in London pubs, picking up gossip, talking to his informers, just as much immersed in the profession of crime as if he were a criminal himself. Nowadays he was too conspicuous a figure to do that magpie collecting job. Yet the habit was ingrained. Leave him here, and he would find someone who would gossip, and information, irrespective of value (perhaps about the domestic habits of commercial travelers), would be docketed away.

"When you've finished your beer—" Now that he had made up his mind, he was eager to be off.

Through the familiar market place he walked with short quick steps, faster than I should have chosen. Then up the street where the recognition-symbols were disappearing: the pavements were crowded, every third or fourth face seemed to be colored; I mentioned to Maxwell that when I was a boy it was an oddity to see a dark skin in the town.

"Mostly Pakistanis," said Maxwell. "Don't give much trouble."

Keeping up his skimming steps, he was telling me, as it were simultaneously, that the police headquarters weren't far off and that the town had less than the nation's average of crime. On one side of the street were a few shops whose names hadn't changed: on the other, a building vast by the side of its neighbors, bare and functional. Maxwell jerked his thumb.

"Here we are," he said, taking my arm and steering me across, as though the traffic didn't exist.

In the great entrance hall, policemen said, good evening, Superintendent. The lift was painted white, so was the fourth-floor corridor. Maxwell opened a door, whisked through a stark office where sat men in plain clothes, opened another door into his own room. After all the austerity, it was like going into a boudoir. The furniture, I imagined, was official issue, though, at that, he had a couple of armchairs. There were flowers on his desk and on a long committee-table. Flanking the vase on his desk stood two photographs, one of a middle-aged woman and one of a baby.

"That's the grandson," said Maxwell. "Have you got any yet?"

"No," I said.

"They'll give you more pleasure than your children," said Maxwell. "I promise you they will."

We had sat down in the armchairs. He pointed to a cigarette box on the desk, then said, without changing his tone of voice:

"I want you to keep out of this."

I replied (despite his quiet words, the air was charged): "What could I do anyway, Clarence?"

He looked at me with an intent expression, the meaning of which again I couldn't read.

Suddenly he said:

"Who is this relative?"

He was speaking as though we were back in the pub, the past twenty minutes wiped away.

"Cora Ross's uncle. A man called Passant."

"We know all about him."

I was taken aback. "What do you know?"

"It's been going on a long time. Corrupting the young, I should call it."

I misunderstood. "Is *that* why you want me out of the way?"

"Nothing to do with it. We can't touch Passant and his lot. Nothing for us to get hold of."

"Then what are you warning me about?"

For once his response wasn't quick. He seemed to be deliberating, as in the pub. At last he said,

"Those two women are as bad as anything I've seen."

"What have they done?"

"You'll find out what they've done. I tell you they are bad. I've seen plenty, but I've never seen anything worse."

I had heard him speak pungently before, but not like this. His feeling came out so heavy that I wanted to divert it, to return to the matter-of-fact.

"You can prove it, can you?" I said.

"We've brought them in, haven't we?" At once he was a professional, cautious, repressed, telling me that I ought to know the police didn't arrest for murder unless they were sure.

"And can you prove it?"

"We can prove enough," he said in a businesslike fashion, a good policeman at the end of his career, one who had brought so many cases to the courts. "You can trust us on that."

"Yes," I said, "I can trust you on that."

"They'll go down for life, of course. There's just one dodge they might pull. And you know that as well as I do." He stared at me, with meaning and, at last I realized, with suspicion.

He said, in a level, controlled tone:

"I'm going to tell you something. I mean every word of it. Those two are as sane as you or me. When we had them in here and found out what they'd done, if I could have got away with it, I'd have put a bullet in the back of both their necks. It would have been the best way out."

Once more I wanted to get back to something matter-of-fact, or innocent.

"They'll get life, you said. This isn't a capital murder, then?"

At this time we were still governed by the 1957 Act, a bizarre compromise under which the death penalty was kept, but only for a narrow range of murders, depending on the choice of weapon and the victim: that is, poisoning was not capital, unless you poisoned a police officer; but murder by shooting was.

"No," said Maxwell.

"How did they do it?"

"They beat him to death. In the end."

"You may as well tell me—"

"We don't know everything. I doubt if we ever shall know."

I said, once again, tell me.

"We're pretty sure of this. They played cat-and-mouse with him. He wasn't a very bright lad. They picked him up at random, they don't seem to have had a word with him before. They've got a hideout in the country, they took him there. They played cat-and-mouse with him for a weekend. Then they beat him to death."

He wasn't being lubricious about the horrors, as I had heard other policemen or lawyers round the criminal courts, telling stories of killings which I remembered clinically, as though they had happened to another species: I had to re-

member them clinically just to remember them at all, and
yet I believed that, despite appearances, I was less physically
squeamish than Maxwell.

"The worst they can get for that," he said, "is life. Which
doesn't mean much, they'll be let out all right, you know
that. But it's the worst they can get, and by God they're going
to get it."

"The alternative is—"

"The alternative is, a nice comfortable few years in a
blasted mental hospital. Diminished responsibility. They'll
try that. What do you think I've been talking to you about
tonight?"

Yes, he had been suspecting me. He had seen me in action
as an official, he could imagine me going round to doctors,
talking to them about "diminished responsibility," which
was another feature of the 1957 Act.

"Yes, they'll try that, Clarence," I said. "On the strength of
what you tell me, any competent lawyer would have to."

"They don't want any help," he said.

"But don't you think they'll get it—"

"I told you something else a minute ago. Those two are as
sane as you and me."

"How are you so certain?"

"I've seen them."

"That's not enough—"

"If you'd seen them and talked to them as I have, you'd be
certain too. You'd be as certain as that you're sitting there."

He went on:

"If anyone pretends they didn't know what they were
doing, then we've all gone mad. We might as well give up the
whole silly business. Will you listen to me?"

He was more intense. And yet, I had been misjudging him.
Yes, he was inclined to see conspiracies, he thought I might
be one of those standing in his way. He was a policeman: he
had "brought them in," he wanted his conviction. But, star-

ing open-eyed at me in the flowery office, he didn't want only, or even mainly, that. Strangely, he was making an appeal. It was deeper than his professional pride, or even moral outrage. He wanted to feel that I was on his side. He wanted to drag me, with all the force of his great strong body onto what to him was the side of the flesh, or (to use a rhetorical phrase which he would have cursed away) of life itself.

In a sharp but less passionate tone, he asked:

"You don't believe in hanging, do you?"

"No."

He gazed at me, unblinking.

"Don't you think you might be wrong?" he asked.

"I've made up my mind."

He still gazed at me.

"I'll give you one thing," he said. "I don't believe in all the crap about deterrence. It deters some of them from carrying guns, that's about all. Nothing in the world would have deterred those two."

"And you go on saying they're quite sane."

"By God I do. They just thought they were cleverer than anyone else. They just thought, I expect they still think, they're superior to anyone else and no one would ever find them out or touch them."

There was a silence.

"I can't get away from it," he said. "There are some people who aren't fit to live."

I replied: "We're not God, to say that."

"I didn't know you believed in God."

"It might be easier if one did," I said.

Maxwell shook his head. "Either those two aren't fit to live," he said, "or else the rest of us aren't."

"Why did they do it?" I broke out. "Have you any idea why they did it?"

"I think it was a sort of experiment. They wanted to see what it felt like."

His lip was thrust out, his face, interrogating, confronted mine. After a moment, he said: "I told you, when we had them in and discovered what they'd done, I'd have put a bullet in them both. What would you do with them? That's a fair question, isn't it? What would you do with them?"

I had a phantom memory of another conversation, a loftier one, in which a character more tormented than Maxwell asked a similar question of someone better than me. But I was living in the moment, and I had no answer ready, and gave no answer at all.

TWENTY

TWO CLOCKS

As I looked up from the road outside my father's house, the winter stars were sharp. I had gone there straight from the police headquarters: looking up at the stars, I had a moment of relief. I was getting ready for the mutual facetiousness which, as a lifetime habit, I expected with my father.

When I got inside his room, though, it wasn't like that. First, there was something unfamiliar about the room itself which, to begin with, I couldn't identify. Then his voice was toneless as he said, hello, Lewis. He was watching a kettle beginning to boil on the hob. He was ready to make himself a cup of cocoa, he said. Would I have one?

No, I said (the flicker of how I usually addressed him still showing through), I wasn't much given to cocoa.

"I don't suppose you are," said my father.

His spectacles were at their usual angle from forehead to cheek, the white hair flowed over the wings. Through the lenses, his eyes were lugubrious.

"How are you getting on?" he said, not half-heartedly, nothing like so much as half.

"How are *you* getting on?"

"They've given me the sack, Lewis." Suddenly his eyes looked magnified: tears began to glisten down his face. They were the tears, as abject and shameless as a child's, of extreme old age. And yet, watching them, I wasn't shameless myself, but the reverse. I had never seen him cry before. Not in all his misfortunes or his humiliations: not when he went bankrupt, or when my mother died.

I said: Hadn't he told the people at his choir that I would provide transport? That it was all arranged? In fact, immediately after my last visit and before the operation, I had, through Vicky, made contact with a car-hire firm in the town. They were to produce a car and driver any time he asked. I had written to my father, spelling out precisely what he had to do. I had had no answer: but then, that was nothing new.

"I did tell them," said my father, sniffling, defensive, as though I were angry with him for incompetence, as his wife and sister used to be. "I did tell them, Lewis."

"Well then?"

"It was no good.

"They had me on a piece of string," he added, lachrymose but acceptant.

It turned out, he went on to explain, that they persuaded him not to find his own car. They drove him forth and back every Sunday night until Christmas. Then they told him— one of the older men had to break the news—that it was "getting too much" for him.

"It wouldn't have done any good, Lewis. Even if you'd driven me yourself. They thought it was time to get rid of me. They thought it was time I went."

I couldn't comfort him. Wouldn't they let him go on somehow, wouldn't it be something if he just attended the choir, when he felt like it?

"It's no use. There's nothing I can do any more."

He went on:

"I told you what they were up to. You can't say I didn't tell you, can you?"

For an instant, that pleased him. He said:

"I suppose you can't blame them. They've got to think about the future, haven't they?"

"You've got to think about yourself."

He answered:

"I haven't got anything to think about."

As I heard that, I was left silent.

"Mind you," he said, "they made a bit of a fuss of me. They had a party, and they drank my health. Sherry I think it was. You'd have enjoyed that, Lewis, that you would. And what do you think they gave me?"

I shook my head.

"Over there," he pointed.

The little room had struck strange: but in the dim light, taken up by my father's wretchedness, I hadn't noticed the clock in the corner, although it had been ticking, I now realized, heavily away, racket-and-whirr. It was a large old-fashioned grandfather clock, glass-fronted, works open to sight. When I drew my chair nearer, I could see that it was a good specimen of its kind, with gold work on the face and gilt inlays in the woodwork. They had made a handsome, perhaps a lavish, present to the old man.

"Two clocks," said my father, indicating the familiar one, on the mantelpiece. "That's what I got."

"They can't have known you'd had another one—"

"I've only had two presentations in my live-long days," he said. "Both clocks."

I couldn't be sure whether he was ready to clown, or making an effort to. I said, anyway, they had spent a lot of money this time, the gift was well-meant.

"They don't even tell the same time," said my father. "You ought to hear them strike, they go off one after the other. When they wake me up in the morning, I think, confound the clocks."

Not for the first time, I was beating round for something to interest him. Wouldn't he at least let me send him a television set? No, he said with meek obstinacy, he would never look at it. How did he know till he tried? He did know.

Everything else I could think of, record-player, books, he met with the same gentle no. Wasn't there anything at all I could get for him?

"Nothing I can think of, thank you, Lewis," he said.

Absently, quite remote from me, he seemed to be thinking again about his clocks.

"I don't know why people should fancy that I always want to know the time. Time doesn't matter all that much now, does it?"

He went on:

"After all, I shouldn't be surprised, I might go this year."

He was speaking without inflection, and in fact as though I were not present. He didn't say much more, apart from offering to put the kettle on again and make some more cocoa, or tea if I preferred it. Whether he was glad to have told me of his demission, I couldn't guess, but he was calm and affable as we said goodbye.

Outside the house, I remembered the visit with my son Charles the previous spring. When I thought of the old man, I should have been grateful for my son's company, all of us part of the flow. But then Maxwell's question drilled back into my mind: that was what I was here for: no, it was better to be alone.

TWENTY-ONE

"IS IT AS EASY
AS THAT?"

The following afternoon, there was a light in George Passant's sitting room at three o'clock. When I lived in the town,
that light had often welcomed me late at night: he had taken
lodgings in this dark street of terraced houses—similar to the
Patemans' and less than half a mile away—as soon as he got
his job in the firm of solicitors, and had kept them ever since.
Though I had not visited him there for a good many years, it
was my own choice, and a deliberate one, to go that afternoon. I did not want to meet in a pub, and give him an
excuse to have a drink and break—restlessly? secretively?—
away. At least that would have been my rationalization. Perhaps I did not want to be reminded of hearty evenings and
the grooves of time.

At the front door he greeted me with his robust, cordial,
impersonal shout. Although he had kept the same lodgings
for so long, I couldn't help but notice that those lodgings had
changed for the worse. There was a violent, attacking smell of
curry percolating the whole house, reaching inside his own
sitting room. Once he had been looked after by a landlady.
When she died, her heirs had split up the house into tiny
apartments: George had no one to cook a meal for him, and
in his sixties was more uncomfortable than as a young man. I
glanced round his sitting room, littered with papers, pipes,
ashtrays, undusted, newsprint on the floor. Like my father, he
was having to "make do" for himself. Unlike my father, he

didn't produce a vestige of order, but seemed to imbue the derelict room with an air of abandon or even of intent.

Over the mantelpiece stood a steel engraving of the Relief of Ladysmith, which had been there getting on for forty years before. Since his parents died, a few of his personal documents had accrued to him and been hung round the walls: his Senior Oxford certificate, the records of his solicitor's examinations (showing him always in the highest class), a photograph of himself when he first qualified, and a diploma stating that he had been incorporated as a member of the Independent Order of Rechabites. I knew the Rechabites from my own childhood; they were one of the teetotal movements that sprang up in the nineteenth century, just as the upper fringe of the working class tried to become respectable; my own Aunt Milly had held high office in the organization, just as she had in any teetotal organization within her reach. Once, long ago, after a night when George and I had been racketing round the town, we had discovered that each of us had "signed the pledge" before the age of ten. I was as hilarious as he was, and as determined to celebrate with another drink. But, in cold history, the pubs were already shut.

As I sat down, on the other side of the fireplace in which glowed one bar of an electric fire, I looked into his face. The skin under his eyes was dark and corrugated: that had been so for long enough. I couldn't be sure that there was any change in him at all, any visible change, that is, from the night before Christmas Eve. He said, in a loud but formal tone:

"Well, how do you think things are going?"

I answered:

"Worse than anyone could have imagined."

His reply was automatic:

"Oh, I'm not entirely prepared to accept that."

"You must."

"You can't expect me to assume that whatever your set of informants have been telling you—"

"George," I said, "there have been times when I've let you comfort yourself. I may have been wrong, I don't know. Anyway, this time I can't."

I told him that I had had an interview with the superintendent. George interrupted, protesting about "these policemen." But, as so often, his optimism, and the lack of it, seemed to co-exist in the same instant. When I said, "You must listen to me," he fell silent, his eyes blank.

I told him, just as clinically as I had remembered killings in Maxwell's office, what the police believed the two young women had done. His face was frowning and deliquescent with pain. Physically, he had always been easily moved: he could be upset by the thought of suffering trivial by the side of this.

When I finished (I was as curt as I could be), he said:

"Do you believe this too?"

"Yes."

George gazed at me with a helpless expression, the sound of his breathing heavy, and said, as though it was all he could find to say:

"It's very bad."

There were no words for me either. But I could not let him slip, as I had once seen him in a disaster of his own in that same room, into the extreme lethargy which was more like a catatonic state.

After a time, I said:

"There's almost nothing that anyone can do."

"I'm leaving it to you," he said.

"I can't do anything."

"You're not backing out, are you?"

I did not reply at once. I said:

"No. For what it's worth, I'm not."

For an instant his face shone with one of his old, expansive smiles. Then he asked:

"Will you go and see her? My niece, I mean?"

I said, as gently as I could manage:

"I think that's your job, you know."

He replied:

"I'm afraid I'm not up to it any more."

Looking at him, I knew that I had no option. This might be a surrender of his, he might, if forced, still be capable of an effort. But I was obliged to do what I had come for. She must be in the local jail, I assumed. George nodded. I wasn't certain whether any but relatives would be allowed to visit her. If it could be arranged, I would go.

George thanked me, but as though he took it for granted. Ever since he collected his first group of young people round him, ever since he was to them—which included me—the son of the morning in this town, he had been used to a kind of leadership. Even now he felt it natural that anyone who had been close to him should do as he asked.

There was something I wanted to find out. As if casually, I said:

"How well do you know her?"

George's voice was more animated than it had been that afternoon. "Oh, about as well as some of the others on the fringe of our crowd. She was rather interesting at one time, but then she began to slip out of things. And of course there were always a lot of lively people coming on—"

"What is she like?"

George responded with an air of distraction, even irritation, speaking of someone far away:

"She didn't join in much. I suppose she used to listen. I thought she took things in."

"Is that all?"

"I didn't notice anything special, if that's what you mean. Of course, some time or other she took up with the Pateman girl. Some of the young men seemed to like the Pateman girl, I never could see why."

"George"—I was speaking with full urgency by now—"you

must have talked to your niece, you must know more about
them than this?"

He said, suddenly violent:

"I refuse to take any responsibility for either of them. You
know what I've told them. I told them what I've told everyone else, that they ought to make the best of their lives and
not worry about all the neutered rubbish round them who've
denied whatever feeble bit of instinct they might conceivably
have been endowed with. Do you think I cared if they lived
together? Not that I knew for certain, but if they did they
were just acting according to their nature. And that's more
than you can say for the people you've chosen to spend your
time among. I suppose you're trying to put the responsibility
onto me. If they'd never been told to make the best of their
lives, they'd have been just as safe as everyone else, would
they? None of this would ever have happened to them? I
won't accept it for a single instant. It's sheer brutal hypocritical nonsense. If that's all you've got so say, I'm not prepared
to be attacked any more."

As his voice died down, I replied:

"I didn't say it."

After his outburst, he sank back, exhausted, drained.

I went on:

"But there is something I ought to say. It's quite practical."

"What's that?" he said without interest.

"The police know a good deal about your group. For God's
sake, be careful."

"How have you heard this?" His attention had leapt up;
his eyes were cautious and veiled.

"Maxwell told me."

"What did he say?"

"He only talked vaguely about corrupting the young. But
they've been watching you."

"What do they call corrupting the young?"

I said:

"Never mind that. For God's sake, don't give them the slightest chance—"

When I was a young man, I had failed him by not being harsh enough. Now, too late, I meant to be explicit. After this case, the police would have no pity. They were well-informed. Either he ought to break up the group once for all: or else it had to be kept legally safe. No drugs (not that I had heard any rumor of that). No young girls. No homosexuality.

George gave a dismissive nod. "I'll see about it."

"Do you mean that?"

Once more he nodded.

"You've got to mean it," I said.

"I'm sorry if I've got people into a mess," he replied.

It was a response that seemed extraordinary: inadequate, detached, as though he were not at all involved or had no need to look into himself. All along, perhaps, even when I first knew him, he had been alienated (though at that time we didn't use the word) from the mainstream of living: now he had become totally so. I had to believe, against my will, that nothing could have changed him. It wasn't just chance, or the accidents of class and time. There were plenty who had lived alongside him, who thought they shared his hopes—like my brother Martin or me, when we were in our teens—who, whatever had happened to us, were not alienated at all. But George had gone straight on, driven by passions that he didn't understand or alternatively were so pre-eminent that he shrugged off any necessity to understand them. I was not sure, though I guessed, how he had been spending his later years. He was a man of sensual passion. Of that there was no doubt, he was more at its mercy than most men. But equally it was sensual passion more locked within himself, or his imagination, than most men's. He was in search, not really of partners, but of objects which would set his imagination alight. But that solipsistic imagination (as self-bound as mine when I was lying in the hospital dark) was linked—and that may have been the most singular thing about him—to a peculiarly ardent sexual nature. And so he had finally come to desire young girls, one after another, each of them lasting just as long as they didn't get in his imagination's way. It had meant risks. Yet he seemed to be stimulated by the risks themselves. There had been his disaster, where I had been a spectator, of years before. That hadn't stopped him. There had been, though I didn't learn the details until after his death, warnings and near-catastrophes since. In secret, after each one, he seemed driven, compelled, or delighted to double his bets.

It was a sexual temperament which only a man in other respects abnormally controlled could have coped with. That he wasn't, and—so it seemed—in his later life didn't want to be. In the past I had thought that, despite his gusto and capacity for joy, he too had known remorse and hadn't cared to look back at the sight of what he had once been. I had thought so during the time, long before (it was strange to recall, after my last meeting with her), when Olive and I were friendly, and she, who gave none of us the benefit of the doubt, jeered at me for giving it to George. I had believed that she didn't understand faith or aspiration, that she looked at men as strange as George through the wrong end of the telescope. That was true: and yet her view of George wasn't all that wrong, and mine had turned out a sentimentality. Curiously enough, it would have seemed a sentimentality to George himself. To borrow the phrase he had just employed, he had lived "according to his nature." For him, that was justification enough. He wasn't one who felt the obligation to reshape his life. *Of course* he could look back at the sight of what he had once been. If I—because of comradeship or my own moral needs—wished to invest him with the signs of remorse, then that was my misfortune: even if, as I sat with him

that afternoon, it meant the ripping away of—what? part of
my youth, or experience, or hope?

I still had an answer to get out of him, though part of it
had come through what he hadn't said.

"The legal line, I take it, will be pretty obvious," I said.
"The defense for those two, I mean."

"I thought you were suggesting that there wasn't any," said
George, withdrawn again.

"Oh, it'll all depend on their state of mind, won't it?"

Intentionally, I said it in a matter-of-fact tone, like one
lawyer to another. But George ceased to be lacklustre, he
straightened himself, his voice was brisk with action.

"Of course it does!" he cried. "I suppose everyone realizes
that, you'd better make sure they do."

I said, it looked as though counsel would have no other
choice.

"Of course, they must be mad," said George.

"You didn't say so, when I asked you about them, did
you?"

I had said that as an aside, and George took no notice.

"Of course, they must be mad," he repeated, with an in-
crease of vigor.

"What makes you think so?"

"That's the answer!" George shouted.

"Did you ever see any signs in either of them which make
you think so?"

"Damn it, man," he said, "I'm not a bloody mental doctor."

"What sort of signs did you see?"

"I tell you, I'm not a mental doctor."

I asked: "Why do you think they are mad?"

George stared at me, as he used to when he was young, face
protesting, defiant, full of hope.

"I'm assuming they've done what you say," he said. "No
sane person could have done it. That's all."

"Is it as easy as that?"

"Yes!" he cried. "It's as easy as that. They're criminal lunatics, that's what they are. Only lunatics could behave as they
did. They're nothing to do with the rest of us—"

I had to tell him: "The police don't think so. They think
they're as sane as any of us."

George cursed the police, and said: "They're not bloody
mental doctors either, are they?"

"I expect," I said, "that those two are being watched by
doctors all the time."

"Well," he said, fierce and buoyant, "we've got to bring in
our own. I can rely on you, can I, that the lawyers get hold of
the right people—"

He went on, as though he had realized the truth from the
moment I broke the news; the comforting and liberating
truth. He was active as I had not seen him for a long time.
Happy again, he went on examining me about the defense.

"It stands to reason," he cried, "they must be as mad as
anyone can possibly be!"

Soberly, firmly, he began to talk about the trial. The
committal proceedings wouldn't take long. He wasn't going
to ask me to come. But when it came to the assizes, George
said, he would have to attend himself.

"It won't be very pleasant, I accept that," he said.

He asked, with a half-smile:

"Can you be there?"

I said, "What use would that be?"

"I should feel better if you were somewhere round, you
know," he said.

TWENTY-TWO

OUT OF PRISON

It occurred to me that Maxwell, for reasons of his own, would be in favor of my paying a visit to the jail. So, back at the Residence, I rang him up. Passant wanted me to talk to his niece, I said: he wasn't in a fit state to do it himself: it wasn't a job I welcomed, but what was the drill? Maxwell said that he would speak to the governor. If she wouldn't see me, they couldn't force her, that was the end of it.

Later in the evening, the telephone rang, and Vicky, who was sitting with me, went into the hall to answer it. In a moment she returned and told me: "It's for you. Police head-quarters."

I heard Maxwell's voice, brisk, sounding higher-pitched than when one met him in the flesh. All fixed. I could go to the jail at four o'clock the following afternoon. She hadn't shown any interest. They had asked if she objected, and she said she didn't mind whether I went or not.

When I got back to the drawing room, Vicky inquired: "All right?"

"I suppose so," I said.

She knew why I was staying in the town, but she hadn't asked about any of the details. She assumed that I was trying to help old friends. She might have noticed that I was unusually silent. Perhaps not: she had her own concerns, she didn't think there could be anything wrong with me. In any case, she was not inquisitive.

Instead, she was talking in high spirits about her father's dinner party next day. Her spirits were high because she had heard from Pat (who, I thought, either got fond of her in absence or was keeping her in reserve) that week. She was also pleased because her father, instead of resisting the advice which I relayed from Francis Getliffe, had, contrary to all expectation, taken it. He had actually invited Leonard and his other young academic critics to dinner. It was to be an intimate dinner so that he could put "his cards on the table," as he had told both of us euphorically, implying that we should have to keep out of the house. Vicky was herself euphoric. She couldn't help but think of Leonard and her father as clever, silly, squabbling men, and now perhaps they would take the opportunity to stop making idiots of themselves.

Next afternoon, just before four, I was outside the main gate of the jail. Above me the walls stretched up, red brick, castellated, a monument of early-nineteenth-century prison architecture—and a familiar landmark to me all through my childhood, for I passed it on the route between home and school. Passed it without emotion, of course: it just stood there, the gates were never open. And yet, even before the inset door did open that afternoon, let me in, closed behind me, I felt the nerves at my elbows tight with angst—the sort of tightness one felt visiting a hospital, perhaps, as though one were never going to escape? No, more shameful than that.

A policeman met me, gave me the governor's compliments, told me the governor was called away to a meeting but hoped that next time I would have a glass of sherry with him. The policeman led me up flights of stone stairs, right up to the top of the building, along a corridor, white-painted, to a door marked CONFERENCE ROOM.

"Will you wait here, sir?" said the policeman. "We'll get her along."

The room was spacious, with a long table: it was dark here, but through the window I could see the russet wall of the prison, and over the wall the bright evening sky.

After a time there were footsteps outside, and two women entered. One was in police uniform: in the twilight she seemed buxom and prettyish. Should she switch on the light? she asked. Yes, it might be better, I replied. Her voice sounded as uneasy as mine.

The exchange of domesticities went on. Should she send for a cup of tea? I hesitated. I heard her ask her companion— though with the room now lit up, I had glanced away— whether she would like a cup of tea. Some sort of affirmation. You can sit down, said the policewoman to her companion. I took the chair on the other side of the table: and then, for the first time, I had to look at her.

"May I give her a cigarette?" I called to the policewoman, who had gone right to the end of the room.

"Yes, sir, that's allowed."

I leant over the table, as wide as in a board-room, and offered a packet. The fingers which took the cigarette were square-tipped, nails short, not painted but neatly varnished. I had not really looked at her before, not in the few minutes in the Patemans' living room; her eyes met mine just before I held out a match, and then were half-averted.

Her face was good-looking, in a strong-boned, slightly acromegalic fashion, more like her uncle's than I had thought, though unlike him she did not have a weight of flesh to hide her jaw. Her hair, side-parted, cut in a thick short bob, was the same full blonde. But it was her eyes, quite different from his, from which I could not keep my own away. George's were a light, almost unpigmented blue, the kind of color one sees only in Nordic countries: hers were a deep-umber brown, so heavily charged that, though they stayed steady while averted from me, they seemed to be swimming in oil.

"What have you come here for?" she asked.

"George asked me to."

"What for?"

I didn't answer until two cups of tea had been placed on the table. I sipped mine, weak, metallic-tasting, like White-hall tea.

I had to submerge or discipline what I felt. Going into the jail, preparing for this visit, I had been nervous. In her pres-ence, I still was. It might have been anxiety. It might have been distaste, or hatred. But it was none of those things. It was something more like fear.

"He wanted me to see if there was anything I could do for you."

"I shouldn't think so."

She had been wearing a half-smile ever since I looked at her. It bore a family resemblance to the expression with which George, at our last meeting and often before that, asked me for a favor, but on her the half-smile gave an air, not of diffidence, but of condescension.

"He asked me to come," I repeated.

"Did he?"

"He wanted me to see if you needed anything."

My remarks sounded, in my own ears, as flat as though I were utterly uninterested: and yet I was longing to break out and make her respond. (*What have you done? What did you say to each other? When did that child know?*)

"I like George," she said.

"Did you see much of him?"

"I used to. How is he?"

"He's not too well."

"He doesn't look after himself."

The flat words faded away. Silence. The other questions were making my pulses throb (*Who suggested it? Didn't you ever want to stop? Are you thinking of it now?*) as, after a time, I asked in the stiff mechanical tone I couldn't alter:

"How are they treating you?"

"All right, I suppose."

"Have you any complaints?"

A pause. Her glance moved, not towards me, but down to her lap.

"This dress they've given me is filthy."

It was a neat blue cotton dress, with a pattern of white flowers and a pocket. I could see nothing wrong with it.

"I'll mention that," I said.

Another pause.

"Anything else?" I asked.

"I shouldn't mind seeing a doctor."

"What's the matter?"

She wouldn't reply. Was she being modest? I looked at her body, which, contradicting her face, was heavy, deep-breasted, feminine. (*Did you ever feel any pity? Will you admit anything you felt?*)

"I'll tell them."

Flat silence. Forcing myself, I said:

"I used to be a lawyer. I'm not sure if you know that."

She gave the slightest shake of her head.

"If I can be any help—" (*Did you do everything they say? What have you done?*)

"We've got our lawyers," she answered, with what sounded like contempt.

"Have you talked to them?"

"They've asked me a lot of questions."

"Are you satisfied?"

"It didn't get them very far," she said.

Silence again. I was trying to make another effort, when she said:

"Why have we got different lawyers?"

For an instant I thought she was confused between solicitors and barristers, and started to explain; but she shrugged me aside and went on:

"Why have Kitty and me got different lawyers?"

"Well, the defense for one of you mightn't be the same as for the other."

"They're trying to split us up, are they?"

"It's common practice—"

"I thought they were. You can tell them they're wasting their time."

She went on, bitter and scornful:

"You can go and tell the Patemans so."

I began, this must have been the solicitors' decision, but she interrupted:

"Yes, those Patemans have always wanted to come between me and Kitty. That's all they're good for, the whole crowd of them."

Her anger was grating. She went on:

"You wanted to know if there was anything you could do for me, didn't you? Well, you can do this. You can tell that crowd they're wasting their time."

She went on, nothing was going to split her and Kitty. With bitter suspicion, she said:

"I suppose you'll get out of it, won't you? You won't go and tell them so."

I said, if it was any comfort to her, I would.

"I should like to see their faces when you did."

Once more, angrily, she said that I should slip out of it. I said without expression that I would tell them.

"I hate the whole crowd of them," she said.

After that, she seemed either exhausted or more indifferent. My attempts to question her (the internal questions were dulled by now) became stiffer still. I gave her a cigarette and then another. To eke out the minutes, I kept raising the cup to my lips, saving the last drops of near-cold tea.

At last I heard the policewoman moving at the far end of the room (for some time we had been left alone). "Afraid

your time is up, sir." I heard it with intense relief. I said to
Cora that I would come again, if she wanted me.

She didn't say a word: her half-smile remained. Outside
the jail, in the fresh night air, I still felt the same intense
relief, mixed with shame and lack of understanding. The
great walls, which dominated the road in daytime, were now
themselves dominated by the neon lights. I didn't clearly remember, five minutes afterwards, what it was like inside.

Some time later, when I met Vicky in the town—I was
taking her out for dinner in order to leave the Residence free
for Arnold Shaw's private party—she did not so much as ask
me what I had been doing. Some young women would have
noticed that I was behaving with a kind of bravado, but
Vicky took me for granted. Which was soothing, just as it was
to see her happy. The small talk of happiness, merely the
glow, still undamped, of a letter from Pat. The pleasure of
sitting at a restaurant-table opposite a man. The pleasure,
incidentally, of a very good meal. She had nominated an Italian restaurant which had not existed in my time, and she
tucked into hearty Bolognese food with a young and robust
appetite. When I lived in the town, we couldn't have eaten
like this, even if we had had the money, but since the war
people had learned to eat. Restaurants had sprung up: there
was even good English cooking, which I had never tasted as a
boy. Other things might go wrong, but food got better.

The pink-shaded lamp made her face look more delicate,
as faces look when the light is softening after a sunny day. She
was talking more than usual, and more excitedly. Once I
wondered if she was wishing—as a good many have wished in
the lucky lulls in a love affair—that time could stand still. No,
I thought. She was too brave, too positive, not apprehensive
enough for that.

We had to spin the evening out. Arnold Shaw's dinner
party had started early, but we were not to arrive back until
eleven. "Anyway," said Vicky, "it'll be nice to have them stop

nattering at each other, won't it? He ought to have patched it up months ago." Although I was dawdling over our bottle of wine, I couldn't do so for another hour and more.

"What shall we do?" I said.

"I know," said Vicky with decision.

"What?"

"Don't you worry. Leave it to me."

After we left the restaurant, she led me down a couple of side streets past a window which was darkened but, as in the wartime blackout, had a strip of light visible along the top edge. On the door, also in dimmed light, was the simple inscription HENRY'S.

"We go in here," said Vicky.

Inside it was as dark as in a smart New York restaurant. If it hadn't been so dark, Vicky and I might have looked more incongruous, for her skirt was much too long and my hair much too short. But the young people, lolling about at crowded tables drinking coffee, were too polite or good-natured to notice. They pushed along, made room for us, settled us down. It was not only dark, the noise was deafening: a record player was on full blast, couples were twisting on a few square yards of floor. It was so noisy that some young man, hair down to his shoulders, had to point to a coffee-cup to inquire what we wanted.

Soon afterwards the same young man patted Vicky's knee and jerked his thumb towards the floor. To my surprise, she gave an enthusiastic nod. When she started to dance, she appeared much older than anyone there: she wasn't dressed for the occasion, she was as out of place as someone arriving in a lounge suit at a function with all the others in white tie and tails. But, again to my surprise, she danced as one who loved it: she had rhythm from the balls of her feet up to her pulled-back hair: she had more animal energy than the boys and girls round her. It was a strange fashion to end that day, watching Vicky enjoy herself.

"Nice," she said in the taxi going home. It occurred to me that all this was a legacy of Pat's, and that she might be thinking of him.

It was not, however, quite the end of that day. When we arrived at the Residence, the windows were shining but there were no cars standing in the drive. We seemed to have timed it right, said Vicky efficiently. As we went into the hall, Arnold Shaw came out of the drawing room to greet us. His color was high, his melon-lips were pursed and smiling. They've gone? she asked. He nodded with vigor, and said, expansively, come in and get warm.

In the bright drawing room, used glasses on the coffee-tables, Shaw stood on the hearth-rug, braced and grinning.

"You've been in prison this afternoon, Lewis, haven't you?" he said to me. He said it with taunting good-nature, eyes bright, as though this was the sort of eccentric hobby I should indulge in, having no connection with serious living.

I said that I had.

"Well, I'm out of prison myself, you'll be glad to know," he announced. "And that means that I'm going to give us all a drink."

At a quick and jaunty trot, he left the room. As we waited for him, Vicky was happily flushed but didn't speak. For me, his one casual question had triggered other thoughts.

He returned balancing a tray on which shone two bottles of champagne and three tulip glasses. While he was twisting off the wire from one bottle, Vicky burst out:

"So everything is all right, is it?"

"Everything is all right," he said.

The cork popped, carefully he filled a glass, watching the head of bubbles simmer down.

"Yes," he said, "I shall be going at the end of the term."

"What?" cried Vicky.

"I'm resigning," he said, filling another glass. "I've told

them so. Of course, they'll treat it as confidential until I get the letter off tomorrow. I had to explain the protocol—"

"Oh, blast the protocol," said Vicky. Tears had started to her eyes.

I had been jolted back into the comfortable room, into their company.

"You can't do it like this, Arnold—" I began.

"You'll see if I can't. It's the right thing to do."

"You must give yourself a bit of time to think." I was finding my way back to an old groove, professional concerns, the talk of professional men. "This is an important decision. You've got to listen to your friends. You haven't even slept on it—"

"Quite useless." He spoke with mystifying triumph. "This is final. Full stop."

Vicky, cheek turned into her chair, was crying. For once, she was past trying to boss him: she wasn't often like a child in his presence, but now she was. She couldn't make an effort to dissuade him. She didn't seem even to listen as I said:

"Hadn't you better tell us what has happened?"

"It's simple," said Arnold Shaw. "They were all very friendly—"

"In that case, this is a curious result."

"They were all very friendly. No one minded speaking out. So I asked them whether, if I went on as Vice-Chancellor, I had lost their confidence."

"And they said—"

"They said I had."

"In so many words?"

"Yes. In so many words." Arnold refilled his glass, looking at me as though he were master of the situation.

"I must say, it all sounds very improbable," I told him.

"They were absolutely direct. I respected them for it."

"You must find respect very easy."

"I don't like double-dealing," said Arnold Shaw.

"But still—why have you got to listen? These are only three or four young men—"

"No good, Lewis." Shaw's expression was happy but set. "They're my best young professors. Leonard is alpha double plus, but the others are pretty good. They're the people I've brought here. They're going to make this place if anyone can. A Vice-Chancellor who has lost the confidence of the men who are going to make the place hasn't any business to stay."

"Look here, there are some other arguments—"

"Absolutely none. It's as clear as the nose on your face. I go now. And I'm right to go."

Arnold, like one determined to have a celebration, poured champagne into my glass. He was so exalted that he scarcely seemed to notice that his daughter was still silent, huddled in her chair. At a loss, I drank with him, for an instant thinking that of all well-meant interventions, Francis Getliffe's had been the most disastrous. It was the only advice I could remember Arnold Shaw taking. Without it, he would have battered on, unconscious of others' attitudes, for months or years. Yet, though unlike my old father he had no nose for danger, he took it far more robustly, in fact with elation, when he was rubbed against it. Of course, he was many years the younger man. My father, when his own dismissal came, had nothing else to live for. But still—it was an irony that I didn't welcome—it was often the unrealistic who absorbed disasters best.

"I remember, Lewis, I told you one night in this house," Arnold pointed a finger, "I told you I should decide when it was right to go. No one else. It didn't matter whether any of the others, or any damned representations under heaven, were aiming to get rid of me. If I thought I was doing more good than harm to this place, then I should stay and they would have to drag me out feet first. But I told you, do you remember, that the moment I decided, myself and no one else, that I was doing more harm than good, then I should go, and that would be the end of it. Well, that's the position. I can't be any more good in this job. So I go at the earliest possible time. That's the proper thing to do."

He was just as intransigent as when he was resisting any compromise or moderate suggestion in the Court. He was more than intransigent, he felt victorious. He was asserting his will, and that buoyed him up: but more than that, he was behaving according to his own sense of virtue or honor, and it made him both happy and quite immovable. He had scarcely listened to anything I said: and, as for Vicky, perhaps she realized at once, when first she heard his news and began to cry, how immovable he was.

At last she had roused herself and, eyes swollen, began to talk about their plans. Yes, they would be moving from the Residence, they would have to find another house. She didn't say it, but she was becoming protective again. How much would he miss his luxuries, and, much more, all the minor bits of pomp and ceremony? Would he be impregnable when once he knew that he had really lost his place? Vicky said nothing about that, but instead, in a factual and prosaic manner, was calculating how much income they would have.

Arnold insisted on opening the second bottle of champagne. I didn't want it, but he was so triumphant, in some way so unshielded, that I hadn't the heart to say no.

TWENTY-THREE

THE FRONT ROOM

The Patemans' house was not on the telephone, and I sent a note that I should call on them at half-past six, at Cora Ross's request, before I caught my train back to London. That was the day after my visit to the jail. The clear weather had broken, it was raw and drizzling in the street outside, the street lamps shone on the dark front window, curtains left undrawn.

Mrs. Pateman let me in. The light in the passage was behind her, and I could not see her face. She said nothing except that my overcoat was wet. I put down my suitcase and went into the parlor, into claustrophobia and the disinfectant smell. There, sitting at the table, plates not cleared away, were both Mr. Pateman and his son. Dick nodded, Mr. Pateman, head thrown back, gave me a formal good-evening. I sat down by the slack fire, no one speaking. Then Mr. Pateman said, in a challenging, more than that, attacking tone:

"I hope you're bringing us good news, sir."

"I'm afraid not," I said.

He stared at me.

"I don't want you to make any mistake from the beginning. I don't credit a single word that anyone brings up against my daughter." He was hostile and at the same time his confidence seemed invulnerable. But now I could, though the room was dim, watch Mrs. Pateman's face: it was washed youthful by fear. I said:

"I've got nothing to say about her."

"I didn't expect it," said Mr. Pateman. "Some of us don't need telling about our children."

"I've only come," I said, "to give you a message from her friend."

"Mind you," said Mr. Pateman, ignoring me, "I know that certain people want to drag her through the courts." With confidence, with the brilliance of suspicion, he went on: "I've got my own ideas about that."

I tried to speak gently, in the direction of his wife: "You've got to prepare yourselves for the trial, you know."

"Thank you," said Mr. Pateman, "we are prepared for more than that. My daughter's room"—he pointed towards the front of the house—"is waiting for her as soon as this trial is over. It's waiting for her empty, with not a penny coming in."

How soon would the trial be? Mrs. Pateman asked in a timid voice. I explained that they would be sent from the police court to the assizes—that would be two or three months ahead. To my surprise, Mr. Pateman accepted this information without protest: perhaps he had discovered it already. Would he accept a different kind of information, if I warned him that his hopes were nothing but fantasy and that he was going to hear the worst? I might have warned him, if we had been alone: in the presence of his wife, certainly frightened, maybe clinging to his hopes, I hadn't the courage to speak.

"I've only come," I repeated, "to give you a message from Cora Ross."

"I don't want anything to do with that woman," said Mr. Pateman.

"It was just this—when it comes to the trial, she wants you to know, they're going to be loyal to each other."

"I shouldn't expect anything else. From my daughter," said Mr. Pateman, with complete opacity, dismissing the news as of no interest, getting back to his own suspicion: "I never liked the look of that woman, she was a bad influence all along. I always had my own ideas about her."

He stared at me accusingly:

"I don't want to say this, but I've got to. I never liked the look of that woman's uncle. He's a friend of yours, sir, I've been told?"

"That's true," I said.

"I don't want to say this, but he's been the worst influence of all. Even if he is a friend of yours, he's a loose liver. There's bad blood in that family, and it's a pity my daughter ever came anywhere near them. That's why certain people want to drag her through this business. They think anyone who goes round with that woman must be as bad as she is. And that woman wouldn't have turned out as bad if it hadn't been for her uncle."

"I don't agree with that," said Dick Pateman, who had been sitting with an expression as aggressive as his father's.

"Some of us," said Mr. Pateman, "have spent a lifetime summing people up."

"Passant would have been all right," Dick went on, "if only they'd given him a chance."

"I can't agree."

Dick continued. "They" were to blame, "the whole wretched set-up," the racket, the establishment, society itself. We should have to break it up, said Dick. Look what they had done to his father. Look at what they were doing to him. His discontent was getting violent (I gathered he was having more trouble with examinations at his new university). Kitty would be happy in a decent society. There was nothing wrong with her. As for Cora Ross, if she'd "done anything," that was their fault: no one had looked after her, she'd never been properly educated, she'd never been found a place.

I didn't answer. What did he believe about the crime? Certainly not the naked truth. He was more lucid than his father, and more angry. He seemed to accept that Cora Ross was involved. But his indignation comforted him and at the

same time deluded him. It removed some of the apprehension he might have had about his sister. So much so that I had
to ask one question: had he talked to her solicitors? No, he
said, his father had done that.

All the news in that home, then, had come from Mr. Pateman. He and Dick must have sat in the parlor arguing with
no more sense of the fatality than they showed tonight. It was
intolerable that they should be so untouched. The dark little
room, with its single bulb, pressed upon one. We were shut
in, they didn't mind being shut in. Their faces were as bold
as when I had first seen them. The disinfectant smell seemed
to become stronger, mixed with the sulphuretted smell of the
slack fire.

"Yes," said Mr. Pateman, "I've done my best with those
people"—the solicitors to whom Eden & Sharples had sent
Kitty's case.

He confronted me with glass-bright eyes.

"And thereby hangs a tale," he announced.

For an instant, I thought he was going to give some of their
opinions.

He said:

"They're running up their bills, those people are. I want
to know, where is the money coming from?"

It was a question for which I was totally unready. I hadn't
even asked George about the legal costs for his niece. In the
midst of shock, I hadn't given it the vestige of a thought. Yet
it was certain that George couldn't afford to pay himself. His
friends in the town were better-off than they used to be:
perhaps they had already supported him, but I didn't
know.

"It will cost some money," I said.

"That doesn't get me very far."

I said that the whole expenses wouldn't be less than several
hundred pounds.

"You're not being very helpful, sir."

I said: "I'm just telling you the facts."

"Do you think it's helpful to mention a sum like that to me, after the way I've been treated?"

I said (I was recalling that the structure of legal financing had changed since the time I practiced) that they were not to worry. Legal aid would be forthcoming. In a case like this, no one had to think about solicitors' and barristers' fees.

"Oh no," said Mr. Pateman, "we've already been granted legal aid. So has the other one, they tell me."

"Then what are you worrying about?"

"Charity," said Mr. Pateman with a superior smile. "I don't like my family receiving charity."

My patience was snapping. "You can't have it both ways—"

"I always believe in exploring avenues," he went on, still invulnerable.

"I don't know what you're thinking of."

"Newspapers. That's what I'm thinking of."

Yes, he had heard of newspapers paying for the defense in a murder case, and getting an article out of it afterwards. Wasn't that true?

"Do you really want that to happen?" I asked.

"It would recoup us all for some of our losses. It would mean my daughter was paying her way."

He appeared to want, though he didn't specifically say so, advice about the popular press, or perhaps an introduction. I had no intention of giving either, and got up to leave; once more Dick nodded and Mr. Pateman and I exchanged formal goodnights. In the passage Mrs. Pateman, who had followed me out, plucked at my sleeve.

"Please," she whispered. "Come in here a minute."

With quick scurrying steps (such as I had noticed in my glimpses of her daughter) she opened the door of the front room. It looked, as soon as the standard-lamp was switched on, bright, frilly, feminine: the lamps gleamed behind painted Italian shades: from the passage one could see straight across the room to a long low dressing-table, looking-glass shining under the lights. The floor was swept and polished, just as on an afternoon when the young women were returning from their work. And yet I had an instant of holding-back before I could cross the threshold, an instant which was nothing but superstitious, as though I were entering a lair.

Furtively, she closed the door behind us. I sat on one divan, Mrs. Pateman on the other, which lay underneath the window: in the black uncovered glass, one of the lamps was reflected full and clear. Close to me stood the latest model of a record player. There were other gadgets, well cared-for, stacked neatly on the shelves, a tape-recorder, a couple of transistor radios.

Mrs. Pateman gave me a wistful ingratiating smile.

"Are you sure?" she said.

Taken aback, I stammered a reply:

"Am I sure of what?"

"Are you sure what's happened?"

The eyes in the small wrinkled face were fixed on mine.

I said, "No." She was still gazing at me.

"It's a good job he doesn't believe she's done anything, isn't it?"

"Perhaps it is," I answered.

"He won't believe it, whatever happens. It's just as well. He couldn't face it if he did."

She said it simply. She was speaking of the husband who dominated her as though he were sensitive, easily broken, the soul whom she had to protect.

"Are you sure yourself?" she asked again, just as simply.

I hesitated.

"I should have to be absolutely sure to tell you that." It was as near a straight answer as I could give. It seemed to satisfy her. She said:

"I can't bear to think of her in there."

The words sounded unhysterical, unemotional, almost as though she were referring to a physical distress.

"I can understand that."

"She's got such nice ways with her when she tries, Kitty has."

I mentioned—we were both being matter-of-fact—that I had met her once or twice.

"And she often did good things for people, you know. She was always free with her money, Kitty was."

She added:

"Her father used to tell her off about that. But it went in one ear and out of the other."

Her face was so mobile, for an instant there was the recollection of a smile.

"I've been worrying about her a long time, as far as that goes."

"Have you?"

"I thought there was something going wrong with her. But I couldn't find out what it was. It wasn't just having a good time—"

"Did she talk to you?" I put in.

She shook her head.

"That's the trouble with children. They're your own and you want to help them and they won't let you."

She went on, without any façade at all:

"I don't know where I went wrong with her. She always kept herself to herself, even when she was a little girl. She had her secrets and she never let on what they were. I didn't handle her right, of course I didn't. She was the clever one, you know. She's got more in her head than the rest of us put together."

"You mustn't blame yourself too much," I said.

"Wouldn't you?"

I replied in the same tone in which she asked:

"Yes, if anything bad happened to my son, I know I should."

"I can't bear to think of her in there," she repeated.

"I'm afraid you've got to live with it."

"How long for?"

"You don't need me to tell you, do you?"

Her face was twisted, but no tears came. All she asked me was that, if I saw her during the trial, I should tell her any news without her husband knowing. She wouldn't understand the lawyers, she said, it would be over her head. That was all. Very quietly she opened the door of the room, and then the front door. She whispered a thank you, and then saw me into the street without another word.

TWENTY-FOUR

QUARREL WITH
A SON

The sky over Hyde Park, as Margaret and I sat together in the afternoons, was free and open, after the Patemans' parlor. The lights of the London streets were comfortable as we drove out at night. It might have been the only existence that either of us knew. But Margaret was watching me with concern. She saw me go into the study to work each morning: she didn't need telling that I had never found it harder. She didn't need telling either that I was making excuses not to dine out or go into company.

One night, she had persuaded me to accept an invitation. At the dinner-party, her glance came across to me more than once, seeing me behave in the way she used to envy when she herself was shy. Back in our own flat, she said:

"You seemed to enjoy that."

I said that for a time I did.

"You've still got more than your share of high spirits, haven't you?"

"Other people might think so," I said. "But they don't know me as well as you do."

"I think so too," she replied. "It's been lucky for both of us. But—"

She meant, she knew other things. A little later, after we had fallen silent, she said, without any warning:

"What's the worst part for you?"

"The worst part of what?"

"You know all right. The worst part of this horror."

I met her eyes, brilliant and unevadable. Then I looked away. It was a long time before I could find any words. It was as hard to talk as in the dark period before we married, when we each bore a weight of uncertainty and guilt.

"I think," I said haltingly at last, "that I'm outraged because I am so close to it. I feel it's intolerable that this should have happened to me. I believe it's as selfish as that."

"That's natural—"

"I believe it's as petty as that." Yet to me that outrage was as sharp as a moral feeling.

"But you're not being quite honest. And you're not being quite honest at your own expense."

"It's surprising how selfish one is."

"Particularly," she said, "when it's not even true. I don't believe for a moment that that is the worst of it for you."

She added: "Is it?"

I was mute, not able to answer her, not able to trust either her insight or my own.

On another topic, however, which came up more than once, it was not that I wasn't able to answer her, but that I wouldn't. Just as, during my conversation with Cora Ross, so flat and banal, there had been questions pounding behind my tongue, so there were with Margaret. *What did she do? What did they say to each other? What was it like to do it?* For me in the jail, for Margaret in our drawing room, those questions boiled up: out of a curiosity which was passionate, insistent, human, and at the same time corrupt. She was no purer than I was, and more ready to ask. I felt—with what seemed like a bizarre but unshakable hypocrisy—that she oughtn't even to want to know. I didn't give her, or alternatively muffled, some of the information that I actually possessed. I showed her the reports of the committal proceedings which, although they made a stir in the press, were tame and inexplicit.

Throughout those weeks I took no action which had any bearing on the case. It would have been easy to talk to counsel, but I didn't choose. I had one of George's neat impersonal notes, telling me the name of a psychiatrist who was to be called in his niece's defense. It would have been easier still to talk to this man. He was a distant connection of Margaret's, her mother having been a cousin of his. They both came from the same set of inter-bred academic families, and I had met him quite often. He was called Adam Cornford, and he was clever, tolerant, easy-natured, someone we looked forward to seeing. He was also, I told myself, a man of rigid integrity: nothing that I or anyone else said to him would alter his evidence by a word. That was true: but it wasn't the reason why I shied away from speaking to him and even—as though he were an enemy whose presence I couldn't bear—avoided going to a wedding at which he might be present.

My mood, I knew, was wearing Margaret down. I told her so, and told her I was sorry. She didn't deny it. If I could have been more articulate, it would have been easier for her. She accepted—there was no argument, she took it for granted—that I should have to attend the trial. But she thought I oughtn't to be left alone there, with no one to turn to. Would it be useful if she came herself? She would come for part of the time anyway, if her father didn't need her. Who else? There weren't many people, as I grew older, to whom I gave my intimacy. Charles March, perhaps Francis—but they were too far away from the roots of my youth. Without my knowing it at the time, Margaret rang up my brother Martin. He would understand it as the others couldn't. Her relation with Martin had always been close: they couldn't have been each other's choice, and yet there was a tie between them as though it might have been pleasant if they had. She talked to him with that kind of trust. Yes, he was ready to hang about the trial in case I wanted him. But—and again I didn't know it at the time—she found, as they talked, that he too, underneath his control and irony, seemed unusually affected.

One Sunday, when we had fetched Charles from school to have lunch at home, Margaret mentioned the date of the trial. The assizes would be beginning in April: how long would the trial take? Anyone's guess, I was saying: probably three or four days, perhaps a week or two, depending on how the defense played it. Margaret told Charles that meant he might not be seeing much of me during the Easter holidays. I said, he could possibly endure that extreme deprivation. Charles gave a preoccupied grin.

After lunch, he and I were alone in the drawing room. He was looking out of the window: it was a serene milky day in late February, smoky sunshine and mist, the branches on the trees just showing the first vestigial thickening.

Charles turned away and said:

"So you're going to this trial, are you?"

"Yes, I've got to."

"Why have you got to?"

"One of those women is a niece of old George's, you know."

"I knew that." He was sitting on the arm of the chair: his face was clouded. "But you can't do any good."

"I can't desert him now," I said.

"You won't do any good. You won't make any difference to him."

"Perhaps a little," I said.

"I doubt it," said Charles. In a hard minatory tone he went on: "I don't think you ought to go."

"I don't understand you."

"This trial will have all the press in the world. They'll be after you."

"I shall just be there in the court, that's all—"

"Don't fool yourself. You're a conspicuous figure."

"They might notice I was there," I said. "Still—"

"This is going to be the horror of horrors. Don't fool yourself. You ought to have learned by now that you'll land yourself in trouble. Don't you realize that someone is going to link you up with the Passants? There'll be a lot of mud flying round. Some of the mud will stick. On you."

His expression was so dark that my temper was rising. I tried to seem casual.

"I think you're exaggerating," I said. "But even if you weren't, does it matter all that much?"

"I should have thought you'd had enough of it," he replied, not with kindness so much as reproach.

"Look here, I've known George since I wasn't much older than you are now. Do you really expect me to leave him absolutely alone *now?*"

"If you could do any good, no."

"Whether I can do any good or not—" I was speaking harshly.

"That's sentimental. You're taking a stupid risk which won't do any good to him and will do you some harm. There's no justification at all."

"Good God, Carlo!" I cried. "You're talking like a Chief Whip—"

"I don't care what I'm talking like. I'm telling you, you're being sentimental, that's all."

"You really think I ought to abandon an old friend just to avoid a bit of slander—"

"That's not a good piece of translation."

"Put it any way you like."

"I'll accept it your way. And I say—if you can't be any good to him, the answer is yes."

I was bitterly angry with him. Was it because he reminded me—too nakedly—of an aspect of myself when young, when I was rapacious and at the same time calculating the odds? Was it also because, with a cowardice of the nerves, I should have liked to agree with him and follow his advice?

"Do you believe," I said, my temper grinding into my voice, "that you'll be able to live your own life without taking this kind of risk? My God, if you can be that cold, what sort of life are you going to have?"

Charles had become angry in his turn. His skin, which, different from mine or Margaret's, didn't color in the sun, took on a kind of pastel flush. He said:

"I shall take more risks than you ever did."

"Say that when you've done it."

"I shall take more risks than you did. But I shall know what I'm taking them for."

"As for being cold," he went on, eyes black with resentment, "I think you're wrong. I'm not sentimental, if that's what you mean. I never shall be. I'm not going to waste so much of myself."

For some time we sat in mutinous silence, each of us hurt, each of us throwing the blame upon the other. Then Margaret entered, the low sunlight streaming onto her face, which unlike ours was tranquil and bright. In an instant, though, she felt the fury in the room. It astonished her, for she had scarcely heard Charles and me exchange a bad-tempered word.

"Whatever's the matter with you two?" she burst out.

"Carlo's been telling me that I oughtn't to go to the trial," I said, shrugging it off.

"No," she spoke to Charles, "he's right to go." She said it soothingly, but Charles, smothering his pride, began to tease her: why was she always so certain of her moral position? The teasing went on, light and easy. He could talk so easily because of the difference between them. That afternoon he couldn't have talked to me like that. He didn't give a glance in my direction. He was responding to her with fondness and detachment. He couldn't have told, or wanted to know, how he was responding to me: and nor in reverse could I.

TWENTY-FIVE

A QUIET OPENING

As Margaret and I approached the old Assize Hall, there was a smell of moist grass, sweet and taunting. It was the kind of April morning which, when one is happy, is lit up with hope: on the patch of lawn beside the steps, dew sparkled in the wave of sunlight. In front of the Georgian façade, policemen were standing, faces fresh in the clear light. The smell of grass returned, sweet and seminal. Looming behind the building was a gothic wall, a relic of the historic town: we were half a mile away from the shopping streets, and close to the quarter where I had taken Charles for a walk the year before.

The entrance hall was high, bright from the lofty windows, crowded, people hurrying past. There were spectators making their way into the courtroom, policemen in plain clothes, rooted on thick legs, policemen in uniform stationed by the doors. At the far end of the hall, barristers, in gowns but not yet wearing their wigs, pushed to and from the robing-room. The hall fell into shade, as the spring wind outside drove clouds across the sun. Then bright again. On the wall-panels stood out the arms of the county regiments. Across the far end, near where the barristers appeared and disappeared, a long trestle table carried a couple of tea-urns and plates of sandwiches, cakes, and sausage rolls, as though at an old-fashioned church fête.

Margaret was seeing all that for the first time. She had

279

never been inside this place before—in fact, she had never been inside a criminal court. The curious thing was, I seemed to be seeing it for the first time too. And yet, when I was studying law in the town, I had gone into this entrance hall a good many times. Later, when I was practicing, I had appeared in several cases at these assizes, using that same robing-room at the far end, walking through to the courtroom in the way of business. Once, in the minor financial case which had involved George Passant: often we had forgotten that, or at least acted, despite the premonitions, as though it had signified nothing.

In all those visits, I seemed to have noticed very little. Was it that I had been blinkered by my own will? When I had been a "hungry boxer," to use Charles's phrase, there were scenes I had wanted to rush through, like one passing in a train.

That morning, just as Margaret was looking round, so was I. One or two acquaintances said good-morning, knowing me by sight. I was more familiar to them than they to me. It reminded me that my presence wasn't unobserved. So it did when a young man came up, telling me that he worked in the Deputy Sheriff's office. The Deputy Sheriff would be pleased to find places for us in his own box, near to the bench. I glanced at Margaret. We were waiting for George Passant: we should have to sit in the public court beside him. I thanked the young man and explained that we should have other people with us. Margaret said, surprising me, that if her husband was on his own later in the trial, he would certainly take advantage of the offer.

It was about twenty past ten. Through the door of the entrance hall George Passant trod slowly in. He was wearing an old bowler hat, as he used to do on formal occasions, though there had not been many in his life: underneath the bowler, his hair bushed wildly out. Before he saw us, his face looked seedy and drawn. But, at the sight of Margaret, he took off his hat and broke into a smile—almost of pleasure, of astonished pleasure. He gave a loud greeting, asked how we were, asked after Charles's health. It might have been a meeting on one of his visits to London, running into us by a lucky chance, somewhere between our flat and the Marble Arch.

I went to one of the doors leading into the courtroom. A policeman told me it was quite full down below but that perhaps there was still room in the gallery. We climbed up the stairs, and there, at the extreme wing, found seats which looked down into the packed and susurrating court. Packed, that is, except for a gaping space in the dock and for the empty bench.

From the gallery, we looked down at the line, not far away, of the backs of barristers' wigs. Behind them the solicitors, Sharples massive among them, were sitting, one of them leaning over to talk to his counsel. The courtroom was small and handsome, dome-roofed, the eighteen-twenties at their neatest. It struck lighter than in my time: that I did, all of a sudden, notice. Turning round, I saw that a vertical strip of window, floor to ceiling, had been unblocked. The whole court might have been a miniature Georgian theater in a county town, except that light was streaming in from the back of the auditorium.

Without noise (only those used to the courts heard the order, *put them up*), a policewoman had appeared in the dock, coming up from the underground passage. It happened so unobtrusively that Cora Ross's head also came up before people were looking. A catch of breath. Then Kitty Pateman was sitting beside her, another policewoman following behind.

The courtroom was quiet. Heads were pushed forward, trying to get a glimpse of them. It wasn't a natural silence. Something—not dread, more like hypnosis—was keeping us all still.

Cora Ross sat straight-backed in the dock. She was wearing a chocolate dress with white sleeves. That, together with her thick bobbed hair, made her look severe, like some pictures of Joan of Arc. Her face was turned towards Kitty, with a steady undeviating glance. Kitty's glance, on the other hand, was all over the place. To say she didn't look at Cora wasn't true. She looked at everyone, her eyes darting round lizard-quick. She must have seen her parents, whom I had identified just below. She showed no recognition, but her expression was so mobile that it was impossible to read. She seemed prettier than I remembered, in her small-featured peaky fashion: the skin of her neck and forehead, though, appeared stretched, ready to show the etchings of strain. She was wearing a pale-blue blouse of some silky material. She rested her elbows on the front of the dock but shifted about as though she could not find a comfortable position; from above, I could see that one of her legs was entwined with the other.

The silence didn't last long. From the side door, a couple of barristers hurried in, took their seats, muttered something matey, desultory, to their colleagues, one of them wearing an apologetic smile.

The courtroom clock, high up at the back of the gallery, had turned half-past ten. Margaret touched my hand. She didn't know how casual the timekeeping of a court could be: but she did know that I was irked by unpunctuality, more so when I was anxious, more so still that morning. We had to wait another five minutes before we heard the ritual cry. As we were all rustling to our feet, the assize procession entered, close by the box where Margaret and I had been invited to sit. The old judge limped to his place of state: he was old, but as he faced us, in his red robe and black waistband, he had the presence of a strong and active man. With an amiable Punchlike smile, he made a becking bow to the court in front, to the jury on his left.

He had been a high-court judge for many years. The last of

the gentlemen judges, so legal acquaintances of mine used to call him. He lived like a country squire, but he was still doing his duty on the assize round—a *red* judge, my mother would have said with awe—at the age of getting on for eighty. Just as through a chance resemblance I felt I knew Detective-Superintendent Maxwell better than I did, so I felt with this man, Mr. Justice Fane, whom I had actually met only once, at an Inn guest night. For he reminded me of a man of letters who had done me a good turn: the nutcracker face with the survivals of handsomeness, the vigorous flesh, the half-hooded eyes, tolerant, worldly, self-indulgent, a little sad. He didn't pretend to be a great lawyer, so my informants said. But he had tried more criminal cases than anyone on the bench, and no one had been more compassionate.

In a full effortless voice, the Clerk of Assize, just below the judge's place, was speaking to the prisoners:

"Are you Cora Helen Passant Ross?"

"Yes."

"Are you Katharine Mavis Pateman?"

"Yes."

"Both of you are charged together in an indictment for murder. It is alleged that you, Ross, and you, Pateman, on a day unknown between September 20 1963, and October 9, 1963, murdered Eric Antony Mawby. Ross, are you guilty or not guilty?"

"Not guilty," said Cora Ross in a hard unmodulated tone.

I had heard that indictment a fair number of times (Kitty Pateman was pleading not guilty, her voice twittering and birdlike): when I was a pupil in chambers in London, with nothing to do, I had attended several murder cases. But there was a difference that morning. In the courtroom—although all of us knew the shadow of horror behind those charges—the air was less oppressive. There was none of the pall upon the nerves, at the same time shameful and thrilling, which in those earlier murder trials I had sensed all round me and not

been able to deny within myself. For there was no chance of
these two being sent to their own deaths. That was the
chance which had, at least in part, in earlier days enticed us
to the courts. Yes, young lawyers like myself had gone there
to pick up something about the trade: yes, there was the
drama: but we had also gone there as men might go, lurking,
ashamed of themselves, into a pornographic bookshop. In the
mephitic air, the sentence of death would be coming nearer.

That morning, the air was not so dense. There was one
specific sensation less. In fact, as the jury were being sworn, I
thought that there had been an attempt, despite the excite-
ment in the press, to damp down other sensations. As I
learned some time before, the Attorney-General was not taking charge of the prosecution himself. It had fallen to the
leader of the Midland Circuit, and when, just after eleven, he
began his opening speech, he was as quiet and factual as if he
were proposing an amendment to the Rent Act. The judge
had spoken just as quietly a moment before, in telling the
jury what the timetable would be: 10:30–1:00, then 2:30–
4:30. "We shall not sit longer, because of medical advice in
relation to Miss Pateman, you understand."

We had heard no mention of that, and later discovered
that she had nothing worse than an attack of rheumatism.
The judge was being elaborately considerate: just as when he
called her Miss he seemed to be rebuking the old custom of
the courts, which the clerk had had to follow, of charging
prisoners by their bare surnames.

Bosanquet began: "My Lord and Members of the Jury, on
September 20, last year, 1963, a child disappeared. His name
was Eric Mawby. He was eight years of age. He was an only
child, and he lived with his parents at 37 Willowbrook Road,
which is part of the housing estate in ———" (he mentioned
one of the outer suburbs). "You will hear that he told his
mother that he was going to play in the recreation-ground
about half a mile away from their house. You will also hear

that, on most summer and autumn evenings, at about half-past five o'clock, he went to the same recreation-ground for an hour or so's play. He was always expected back before seven o'clock, and had never failed to do so until the evening of September 20, which was a Friday."

To a foreigner, this lead-in could have sounded like English under-statement. But a foreigner might not have known the transformation in English rhetoric, both in Parliament and in the law courts, since about the middle of the 'thirties, when Bosanquet was starting to practice. He was using the tone of speech which was becoming common form. He had actually joined this circuit not long after I gave it up and went to an academic job. He had already been referred to in court as "Mr. Recorder," which had made Margaret give me a puzzled glance: he worked, besides having his solid practice, as Recorder, which meant in effect judge of a lower court, in a city close by. As he stood a couple of yards away from the dock on his right hand, he was looking at the jury with an expression unmoved and unassuming. Distorted by the wig, as some faces are, his appeared preternaturally foreshortened, round, and Pickwickian.

The quiet unaccented voice went on:

"He did not return by seven o'clock that evening. His parents became anxious, as any of us with children would be. They made inquiries of their neighbors and their neighbors' children. At nine o'clock they got in touch with the police. At once there was set in motion the most thorough of searches, of which you will hear more. I think you will agree that the police forces at all levels deserve many congratulations for their devotion and efficiency in this case. There was no news of Eric for over a fortnight, although many thousands of reports had been investigated and already certain lines of investigation were in train. But Eric had not been found, and there was no direct news of him. Where the news did come, it was the worst possible. His body had been discovered, through a very remarkable piece of fortune, if I may use the word in happenings such as these. It was the only piece of fortune that the police had throughout their massive investigations. There is, I think, no reason to doubt that, without this accident, they would shortly have discovered the burying place. However, something else happened. Very early in the morning of October 9, a pack of hounds belonging to the"—he gave the name of a local hunt—"were out cubbing in a wood or covert to which the nearest village is Snaseby, though that is some distance away. The wood is known locally as Markers Copse."

Like most people, perhaps everyone, in the court, I had heard of the bizarre incident which he was—without a trace of acceleration—coming to. During the police court proceedings, it had been carried, more than any single feature of the case, all over the press. He was telling us nothing new. But up till now I hadn't read or heard the name of the exact spot. Now I did hear it, and it meant something to me. The place was a few miles out of Market Harborough, where, as a boy, I used to stay with my uncle Will. On these holiday visits I went walking over the countryside and sometimes followed the hunt on foot (which my uncle approved of, considering it in some obscure fashion good for his estate agency). I knew Markers Copse well enough. There had been, and presumably still was, an abandoned church down in the next fold of the gentle rolling country: a church with an overgrown graveyard, relic of a village long deserted. Below the church ran a stream, in which a friend and I often went to fish. It had been pretty country, lonely, oddly rural: sometimes I, who was used to townscapes, had liked to imagine that I was back in the eighteenth century.

"In Markers Copse, then, in the very early morning of October 9, Mr. Coe, the huntsman, took his hounds. In a short time he found that two of them had got loose from the pack. They were well-trained hounds and he was naturally irritated. He had to go some distance through the copse to find them. They were smelling, apparently without any reason, at a patch of earth between two of the trees. Mr. Coe couldn't understand their behavior. It took him considerable effort, and a good deal of discipline, to draw them away. Later that same day, when his work was done, Mr. Coe was still puzzled by their behavior. He is an extremely experienced huntsman and knows his hounds. He will tell you that he felt silly, but he had to make sure whether there was any explanation or not. So he went back that evening to Markers Copse with a neighbor and a couple of spades. He could remember the precise location where the hounds had been smelling. He and his neighbor started to dig. It didn't take them long to find the body of Eric Mawby—although the grave was fairly deep and had been carefully prepared."

Bosanquet's expression hadn't changed, nor had his stress. Conversationally he informed the jury:

"You will hear medical evidence that the child had been dead since approximately the time that he disappeared. You will also hear, however, that he did not die on that first night and probably not for forty-eight hours afterwards. The pathological experts will tell you that he had received several mortal injuries, through his skull having been battered in, though with what precise implement or implements it is impossible to say. The pathological experts will also tell you that there were signs of lacerations and other wounds on his body, not connected with the mortal blows, which may have been inflicted many hours before death.

"That is something of what happened to Eric, though I am afraid that I shall have to tell you more later. I now come to the connection between him and the defendants in the dock."

He made the slightest of gestures to his right, but continued to gaze steadily at the jury.

"So far as is known, Eric had not spoken to either of them before the evening of September 20. He may never have seen them before. There is evidence, however, that they had seen him. These two young women share a room in the house of Miss Pateman's parents. They have also, for two years past, rented a cottage in the country, where they have been accustomed to go at weekends. You will hear more, I am afraid, of Rose Cottage. It is near Melton Mowbray, and some considerable distance from Markers Copse. It has, however, become not uncommon, as you will hear, for their acquaintances, or members of a circle to which they belong, to rent cottages similar to theirs at convenient distances from the town, and they are known to have visited one in the Market Harborough direction, in fact in Snaseby."

That was a reference, which some besides me must have picked up, to George Passant's group. Bosanquet left it there, and went on:

"It may sound as though Miss Ross and Miss Pateman were living a luxurious life. I might remind you that they were each drawing good salaries, Miss Pateman as a secretary, Miss Ross as a trained clerical worker. They had left school with their O-levels, Miss Pateman with seven and Miss Ross with four, and in the normal run of things they were regarded as valuable employees whose security wasn't in doubt. For two years past they had been able to run a car, a Morris saloon. As it happens, that car had its own part, a negative but finally a significant part, in the story of Eric's disappearance."

Patiently, meticulously, he described the police investigations. They had interviewed some thousands of people who might have seen Eric on the evening of September 20. There had been several hundred reports from others who thought they had (or, though he didn't say it, couldn't resist either exhibiting themselves or taking the sadistic bait). Witnesses, sound and level-headed, were almost certain that they had seen Eric walking off with a pair of men or a single boy. Others believed they had noticed him catching a bus. Several had caught sight of him in various makes of car. These stories took weeks to sift, and all turned out to be false.

The careful words tapped gently into the court. The minute hand was getting round to twelve. The judge leaned forward and asked:

"Is all this quite necessary, Mr. Recorder?"

"There is a great deal of complexity, my lord."

"But do we need all of it?"

"I'm inclined to think it may be as well."

The voices were courteous, silky, and just perceptibly tense. There might be some past history between the two men: or was the judge simply impatient! He knew, of course, everything the lawyers knew. No one on either side believed there could be any challenge to the facts. He had presumably expected that there would be a short opening speech, after which the defense, instead of trying to disprove the facts, pleaded diminished responsibility at once. Bosanquet stood there, amiable, obstinate. This was his case: he wasn't going to be hurried or budged. It might be that he had a double motive. I thought, and later had it confirmed, that he must have heard that the defense were still uncertain about their plea: though at that time I didn't guess the reason. And also he could be insuring against the medical evidence, once diminished responsibility was brought in: by being so rational himself, he was underlining how calculated the crime had been, just as he had, as though by accident, reminded everyone that the two women were of more than average intelligence.

Without altering his pace, he persevered. Many reports of persons who thought themselves eye-witnesses had been analyzed and discarded. But two, which had been received in the third week of the investigation, had something in common. In both, the witnesses thought they had seen a child sitting between two people in the front seat of a car, with a woman driving. One of these sightings had taken place not far from the recreation-ground. The child, as Mrs. Ramsden would testify, appeared to be smiling and waving, the other adult's arm round his neck and shoulders. Was the other adult a man or a woman? That Mrs. Ramsden hadn't been sure, since the face was obscured by dark glasses. The second sighting had been a mile away from Rose Cottage. Mr. Berry, who was working in his garden, had seen a car traveling very fast: he had noticed a child on the front seat but could not be positive about the other occupants. He had several times before observed Miss Rose and Miss Patemen driving to Rose Cottage: but he did not bring these occasions to mind, and this was not the car he had seen previously. It was in fact a brown Austin, and the number-plate was not noticed at either sighting, or else was obscured.

"Those were the first indications which brought the defendants within the scope of the inquiry. I have to remind you that the police had many leads which seemed far more positive and more worth pursuing. But the police routine could not overlook even the most unpromising of suggestions. And so, as a matter of routine, Miss Ross and Miss Pateman were interviewed for the first time on October 6; that is, three days before Eric's body was found. They were, as you will hear, both calm and cooperative. They expressed themselves as horrified by the disappearance and anxious to help. They denied any knowledge of the boy, but were very willing to account for their movements in the weekend of September 20–22.

"Their car had, as it happened, needed repairing, and they had left it in their usual garage. So they had gone out to Rose Cottage by bus and spent their usual quiet weekend. On the Saturday morning Miss Ross had done a little shopping in the village. They had returned to the Patemans' house by the last bus on the Sunday night.

"All this sounded quite natural. As a matter of routine, the police checked one or two details of their account. Miss Ross was remembered as shopping in the village as usual on the Saturday morning. No one had noticed anything unusual, outside their ordinary weekend habits. In the same way, an inquiry was made at their garage, the Wyvern Garage in Whitehorse Street, and their car had duly been left there for repair during the weekend, as they had stated. But here Detective-Constable Hallam, whom you will hear in evidence, asked some further questions. He wanted to know what had been wrong with the car. The answers did not satisfy him. The garage proprietor, Mr. Norman, had been slightly puzzled himself. There had been a small jamming in the gear-change, but only of the kind which experienced car-owners like the defendants could put right in a few minutes themselves. This was simply a straw in the wind, but Detective-Constable Hallam was not satisfied."

The inquiries went on, Bosanquet leaving nothing out. The car was conspicuous, it was well-known in the neighborhood. It occurred to the detective-constable to discover whether it had ever been noticed on the other side of the town, in the vicinity of Eric Mawby's house. He had found witnesses who had seen such a car patrolling, not one evening but three or four evenings consecutively, the route between Eric's house and the recreation-ground.

"This was still a straw in the wind," said Bosanquet, with no emphasis at all. "But Detective-Constable Hallam's superiors thought it justified a visit to the Patemans' house, at a time when Miss Ross and Miss Pateman were present. We have now come to December last, when, of course, Eric's body had already been discovered. At this second interview Miss Ross and Miss Pateman were not as cooperative as at the first. They refused to discuss the repairs to the car, and after a while refused to answer further questions."

Silence. The hallucinations of fact. Cora had her gaze still turned on Kitty, who had begun, in a frenetic fashion, to scribble notes and push them forward to her solicitor. She was writing as assiduously as the judge himself.

"There followed a third interview, this time at Rose Cottage," Bosanquet said. "During the questioning of Miss Ross and Miss Pateman, which was being conducted by Detective-Inspector Morley, other officers were searching the cottage and the garden. For some time this search revealed nothing. The cottage was swept and garnished. But in due course one of the officers, Detective-Sergeant Cross, discovered a small metal object pushed into the corner of a shelf. He recognized it as an angle joint which might have come from a Meccano set. He asked them to explain why it was there. At that point, Miss Pateman said or screamed something across to her companion—something like, though no one can be definite about the exact words, 'You blasted fool!'

"Neither of the defendants produced any explanation about the presence of this Meccano unit. They said it had nothing to do with them. After a further interval, officers searching the garden found, buried in the bushes, the box of what appeared to be a new Number One Meccano Set, containing most of its components, and carrying on the lid a tab from the Midland Educational Company. At this stage the defendants were separated, cautioned, and brought back to police headquarters for further inquiries."

Bosanquet glanced at his wristwatch. As though under suggestion, others of us did the same. It was ten minutes to one.

"By this time, since the officers had spent some hours at Rose Cottage, it was Saturday afternoon. Nevertheless, the manager of the Midland Educational Company was immediately contacted, and search, of course, continued at the cottage. The bill for the purchase of a Number One Meccano Set was traced, bearing the date of September 18 last year; that is, two days before Eric's disappearance. The shop assistant who had made this transaction was visited at her home. She was able to remember the purchaser as someone answering to the description of Miss Ross.

"Meanwhile Miss Ross was being examined alone by Detective-Superintendent Maxwell. He will tell you that she was still denying knowledge of the Meccano set, although in a parallel examination Miss Pateman was providing explanations, such as that it was a long-forgotten present which had never been delivered. The detective-superintendent was given the information from the Midland Educational Company. He told Miss Ross and asked her to account for it. Then she said: 'Yes, we took him out to the cottage that Friday night. We borrowed a car to do it.' "

In a tone indistinguishable from that in which he quoted her, he spoke to the judge:

"I'm inclined to think, my lord, this might be a convenient time to break off."

"As you like, Mr. Bosanquet."

The politeness, the bowing judge, the ritual, Cora's blonde head disappearing underground. When I had followed George and Margaret downstairs, the entrance hall was full, people were pushing towards the refreshment table. Outside, in the spring air, cameras clicked. Some were press cameras, but the journalists had not emerged yet, and I led the other two away, trying to hurry George's invalid pace. I heard some whispers and thought I could pick one out as "that's her uncle."

We walked, Margaret in the middle, George's heavy slow step with feet out-turned delaying us. Neither Margaret nor I could find anything to say. Instead, George spoke:

"It's nasty," he said.

His words, like all the words spoken that morning, could not have been more matter-of-fact.

"It's nasty, of course," he repeated.

"I'm sorry, George," said Margaret.

He smiled at her, a diffident gentle smile.

"Still," he went on, "wait till you hear the answer."

Margaret couldn't reply, nor could I. Was he whistling up his old unextinguishable optimism, or was he just pretending? Wait till you hear the answer. I had heard politicians growl that identical phrase across the floor of the Commons, after the bitterest attack from the other side.

"I must say," said George, "I thought that ——"—he brought out his curse as though the word had just been invented or as though the carnal reality were in front of his eyes—"was unnecessarily offensive."

Now he wasn't pretending. He was speaking out of the hates of a lifetime. I didn't answer. This was no time to argue, though in fact I thought the exact opposite. I thought also that Bosanquet, in his own fashion, was a master of his job.

"Well," said George, "where are we going to eat?"

Margaret and I looked at each other, hesitating. We didn't want much, she said. George, with a kind of boisterous kindness, said that we must eat something. He knew of a good place.

It turned out to be a pub which sometimes we used to visit (he showed no sign of remembering that) at the end of a night's crawl. Nowadays it served hot lunches: and there, in a small and steaming room upstairs, George, giving out an air of old-fashioned gallantry, placed Margaret in a chair and insisted that she eat some steak-and-kidney pie. His pleasure was extreme, pathetic, when she was ready to join him in drinking a double whisky.

He was fond of her, because she never blamed him. He had told her a good deal about his life, and found that she casually accepted it. "I hope that's really all right for you," he said, looking at her plate of meat and pastry, like a proud, considerate, but slightly anxious host.

It was not we who were trying to support him, but the reverse. He might be behaving so out of a residue of robustness greater than most men's—or out of indifference or a lack of affect. All we knew was that he was behaving like a brave man. He even told a long complicated funny story, so quirky that it didn't seem unfitting that day.

He did ask me—in an aside—whether Bosanquet (whom he never referred to by name, but always by the Anglo-Saxon curse, as though it were a kind of title) was going to "drag in" any of the crowd. George hadn't missed the single oblique reference. I said that it seemed unlikely. Perhaps the people who lent the car might be mentioned—were they connections of George's?

George shook his head, his expression for an instant lost and suffering, and said that he didn't know. "I don't want anyone else to get into a mess," he muttered, repeating the words that had chilled me the day before Christmas Eve.

He turned his attention to Margaret again, trying to think of another treat for her, before we returned to the Assize Hall. Again the crowded entrance, the barristers in the courtroom seen from above, the ascent of those two into the dock. A little delay, only three minutes this time. The ritual bowing. Bosanquet on his feet beginning:

"My lord, and members of the jury, we now turn for a moment to certain statements of Miss Pateman—"

TWENTY-SIX

TEACHING A CHILD
TO BEHAVE

"Miss Pateman made a number of statements to police officers during the period when Miss Ross was being examined by Detective-Superintendent Maxwell," said Bosanquet in a level tone, without a flick of sarcasm. "On the following day, Detective-Superintendent Maxwell decided to take her out once more to Rose Cottage and question her himself. By this time, of course, the search in and round the cottage had been intensified. Traces of blood, small traces, had been found in the bedroom. This blood, as you will hear from experts of the forensic laboratory, did not belong to the blood groups of either Miss Ross or Miss Pateman. It did, however, belong to the blood group of Eric Mawby. In the garden were found the remains of a nylon blouse not completely burnt, a blouse which witnesses recognized as having been worn by Miss Ross. On this were detectable some stains of the same blood group.

"In due course, as Detective-Superintendent Maxwell interrogated her"—How long had they been alone together? When was she told that Cora had broken down?—"Miss Pateman withdrew her denials that the child had never been inside the cottage. She now told what appeared to be a coherent and self-consistent account of those events. She and Miss Ross had for some time past wanted to have a child alone, by themselves, to be in control of. She gave a reason for this desire. They wanted to teach it to behave."

For the first time in the long and even speech, Bosanquet laid a stress, it sounded like an involuntary stress, upon the words. In an instant he had controlled himself. "They had accordingly, so it appears, picked out a boy at random. For some time they had driven round the city, in places where they were not familiar, looking for a suitable subject. It was the misfortune of Eric Mawby and his parents that they settled on him. They decided on the weekend of September 20. They bought the Meccano set two days before in order to give him something to do. They picked him up on the Friday evening without difficulty. According to Miss Pateman's account, Eric was pleased to go with them." Bosanquet paused. "That we cannot, of course, deny or establish. We also cannot establish at what stage exactly they began to ill-treat him. Possibly early on the Saturday. You will hear expert evidence about the many wounds on his body. He suffered them, according to expert judgment, many hours before death. These body wounds were healing when he was finally beaten to death by at least seven blows on the head, probably with something like a poker or a metal bar and also with a wooden implement.

"About the wounds on the body, Miss Pateman said that they had—what she called 'punished' him. They wanted to teach him to behave.

"I should say that neither she nor Miss Ross have ever admitted that they actually killed him. They have each given accounts of what happened to Eric on the Sunday night. The accounts are different. One is, that he was put on a bus to take him back to the town. The other, which is Miss Ross's, is that they drove him back themselves in the borrowed car, and dropped him at the corner of the road leading to his parents' house. Needless to say, neither of these stories deserves a moment's thought. That same night, and early the following morning, that same car was seen, as will be sworn by two witnesses, very close to Markers Copse. Further, when the car was ultimately examined—I must tell you that its real owners had no conceivable connection with this crime—there was evidence of blood, blood of Eric's group, on the floor of the back seat."

He turned to the judge, and remarked:

"I think I need to go no further at present, my lord. It would be my duty, if there were any conceivable doubts about the facts of this case, to make the position clear to members of the jury. But there is no doubt. We know most of what happened to Eric Mawby from the Friday evening until the time that he was buried. I haven't any wish to add to the intolerable facts you are obliged to listen to. You can imagine for yourself the suffering of this child. There is no doubt about the way he was killed, nor about who killed him. All I need say is that this has been proved to be a deliberate, calculated, premeditated crime. That is enough."

During the last few minutes of Bosanquet's speech, I had flinched—and this was true of Margaret and everyone round me—from looking at the two women in the dock, although, keeping my gaze on Bosanquet, I could not help noticing with peripheral vision the fingers of Kitty obsessively scribbling her notes.

A witness was being sworn, a man in his twenties, soft-faced, soft-voiced. It turned out that, with the indifferent businesslike bathos of the legal process, he was being examined about the loan of his car.

The box was on the judge's right hand, a couple of yards away from where Bosanquet had been standing: so that prosecutor, dock, witness, were all exposed to the same light. The young man's fair hair shone against the paneling.

"Your name is Laurence Tompkin? You are a schoolteacher employed by the local education authority? You know both the defendants?"

Yes, said the young man in a gentle, ingratiating manner, as of one who was trying to win affection, but he knew Miss

Ross better than Miss Pateman. Do you remember either of them saying they might want to borrow your car? Yes, he remembered that it was Miss Ross. When was that? In the early summer, last year. In the summer, not September? No, much earlier, more like July. What did she say? She just said they might want to borrow it sometime, she wanted to be sure that it was available. Then, some time later, she did borrow it? Yes. For a weekend in September? Yes. Can you tell us the date? The weekend beginning September 20. Was the car returned? Yes. When? The following Monday. Did you notice anything odd about it? There seemed to be a lot of mud on the number plate, although it had been a sunny weekend. You didn't examine the floor of the car, down below the back seat? No, he didn't think of doing so.

Benskin, Cora's counsel, got up to speak for the first time that day. He was a small man, with a long nose and a labile merry mouth: his voice was unexpectedly sonorous. He was asking a few questions for appearance's sake. He had, of course, understood Bosanquet's tactics; that is, to demonstrate the long-laid planning before the boy's death. As for the defense's own tactics, a good many of us were puzzled. They seemed to be in a state of indecision or suspense.

It would be perfectly reasonable to ask a friend, said Benskin, whether he could lend a car? Perfectly reasonable to ask, as a kind of insurance, if one was having any trouble with one's own? Even if the trouble didn't become serious for weeks? As for the return of the car, if Miss Ross and Miss Pateman drove it back to the town late on the Sunday night, they couldn't conveniently have returned it, could they? It was perfectly reasonable to park it outside their own house, and return it next day?

Having registered his appearance, Benskin sat down, with a grim half-smile to his junior. Kitty Pateman's counsel did not get up at all.

The young man left the box. He was one of George's

group: he had not been asked how he could afford a car, or
whether he shared it with anyone, or whether he also shared a
cottage, or at what kind of parties he and Cora Ross had met.
No one had a reason, so it appeared, to disturb that underground. This had been the guess that I made to George. I
glanced at him, heavy-faced, mouth a little open: perhaps,
even after the prosecutor's ending, not so many minutes before, he felt—as we all do in extreme calamities, when a
minor selfish worry is taken away—some sort of relief.

Another witness, this time the manager of the garage
where the women's own car had been left for repairs. When
had it been deposited? September 19. What was supposed to
be wrong?

At this the judge, shifting himself from one haunch to the
other as he spoke, became restive.

"Surely we are going into very great detail, aren't we, Mr.
Recorder?"

"With your permission, my lord, I wish to establish the
whole build-up before the child was abducted."

"I suggest we are all ready to take a certain amount for
granted."

"This is a complicated structure, my lord." Bosanquet
spoke mildly, but he didn't budge. "I require my pieces of
bricks-and-mortar."

"Spare us anything you don't require," said the judge,
with a nod which was resigned but courteous.

The garage manager's mystification: she (Cora Ross)
could have put it right in ten minutes. She was a first-class
mechanic herself.

Next witness, Detective-Constable Hallam. He was raw-
boned, quite young, and as he stood in the box his head was
bent down towards his hands. His pertinacity about the car.
"I was not satisfied," he said, for once raising his head. His
manner was stern but guilty-seeming, he hesitated over answering matter-of-fact questions. Gradually Bosanquet's ju-

nior, young Archibald Rose, dug the story out of him. How he hadn't been satisfied. How at the garage he thought something was strange. How he made inquiries all along the half-mile between Eric's home and the recreation-ground, asking if a green Morris had ever been seen. When had the car first patrolled that route? (That couldn't be answered, but it might have been as much as a month before September 20.)

The young constable, who had been a halting, unhappy witness, was given a special word of approval. Without him, it might have taken much longer to look in the direction of Rose Cottage.

Statements from persons who had noticed a green Morris, read in a strong voice by the Clerk of Assize. " 'I saw this car when I was getting home from work, but did not take its number. . . .' "

A detective-sergeant in the box, the first search of the cottage. The piece of Meccano. Exhibit. A plainclothes policeman, standing by the clerk, with a stiff robotlike movement held up his hand. From where I sat, just a glint of metal. Then he exposed it on his palm. The gesture was as mechanical as the plaything. An ordinary object, prosaic and innocent: yet it did not seem quite real, or else had its own aura. An object like Davidson's capsule.

"Was this the piece of Meccano you discovered in Rose Cottage . . . ?"

"It was."

Another detective-sergeant (the cottage and garden had been crowded with them). The Meccano box. Exhibited. The plainclothes policeman went through his drill.

"Was this the box you discovered in the garden of Rose Cottage . . . ?"

"It was."

The shop-assistant at the Midland Educational Company. The bill for a Number One Meccano Set.

"Is this bill dated September 18?"

"Yes, sir."

"Do you remember selling this set?"

"Yes, I do."

"To whom did you sell it?"

"To the one sitting there—" She glanced at Cora and away again.

"That was on Wednesday, September 18?"

"Yes, sir."

Bosanquet asked her to make sure of the date. "I'm sorry to press this, my lord, but you will see what I am establishing—" The judge turned to the jury. "Bricks-and-mortar," he said. He sounded affable and half-sardonic: but he was being fair to Bosanquet, underlining that this was evidence of intent. Following him, Benskin tried to shake the identification, but the girl was both gentle and strong-willed, and he got nowhere.

Witnesses, names, occupations, addresses came, went, were forgotten, a random slice of the town. One stood out, a Mrs. Ramsden, who testified about seeing a boy being driven in the car. She was plump, with a sharp nose poking out of the flesh: as a girl she must have had a cheerful, impertinent prettiness. As soon as she gave evidence, she gave the impression (much more so than any of the policemen) of being a natural witness. She was one of those people, and there were very few, who seemed to be abnormally observant and at the same time scrupulous. Yes, she had seen a brown Austin driving out of the city on the evening of September 20. What time? She could be fairly exact: she was hurrying home for a television program: about 5:45. Where was this? Not far from the recreation-ground? A few hundred yards away. What did she notice? A small boy sitting between two people in the front seat. She didn't know Eric: from the photographs, it could have been him, it looked very like him, she couldn't be more positive than that. A woman was driving

the car. The other person in the front seat? Might have been
a man or woman. Fair-haired, wearing dark glasses. What was
the boy doing? He seemed to be waving. He might have been
struggling? He might have been, but she didn't think of it at
the time. She thought he was laughing. The person with dark
glasses had an arm round him? Yes, round his neck. Like this?
Bosanquet beckoned one of the plainclothes policemen, who,
sheepish and red-faced, had his neck encircled by counsel's
arm. There was a titter, tight and guilty, the first that afternoon. Both defense counsel cross-examined. Kitty's, a young
silk called Wilson, his actor's face hard, masculine, frowning,
was trying to demonstrate that the boy had gone willingly.
Benskin, that the kidnapping might have taken place much
later. To most people in the court, none of this could matter,
it only dragged out the strain. All those who were used to
courts-of-law would have known by now, though, that they
were struggling with their instructions, though I for one
couldn't be certain what any of them were hoping for.

When Mrs. Ramsden had left, the judge coughed, and said
in an amiably testy fashion: "I see the clock has stopped."
Heads turned to the back of the court. "I make it," said the
judge, "very nearly half-past four. I don't want to go much
beyond the half-hour, Mr. Bosanquet. I hope you can be
brief with the next witness. After all, no one challenges the
fact that the boy was taken by car to Rose Cottage. That is so,
Mr. Benskin, Mr. Wilson?"

For the first time, Bosanquet conceded the point. He left
the witness—who swore to sighting the car near Rose Cottage
on the Friday evening—to his junior, and within minutes the
judge was bowing himself out of court.

It had been difficult to feel, since the end of Bosanquet's
speech, how much people in the courtroom had been anes-
thetized by the sheer mechanics of the trial. We soon knew.
As we walked with George through the entrance hall, there
was an air of hostility which, like a blast of freezing wind,

tightened the skin. Then came, not loud, but menacing and sustained, the sound of hissing. George threw his head erect, jamming his hat further back so that his forehead was exposed. The hisses went on. They were not directed at him as a person (at the time I didn't think of it: all I wanted was to lead him through the angry crowd). He wasn't well enough known in the town for that. But he was connected with those two, and this was enough.

We got him into the street. There were no taxis anywhere near, and we had to walk half a mile, people following us, women shouting at him, before we found one. On the way to the station, where Margaret had to catch a train back to London, none of us spoke. When we came in sight of the station building, the red brick glared like a discord in the spring sunshine.

While I paid off the taxi, George stood mute by Margaret's side. Then he said:

"Well, I'd better leave you now."

No, we each told him, he must wait and see her off.

"I'd better leave you now," George repeated.

We looked into his face. It was wild, his eyes gazing past us: and yet, how was it different from lunchtime, what did his expression mean?

"I don't want you to, you know," said Margaret.

"I think I'd better. I've got some things to do."

Without even glancing at each other, we thought we couldn't press him any further. "I'll see you tomorrow, then?" he said to me. "Of course," I replied. He said to Margaret: "It was very nice of you to come," and kissed her.

When we were alone in the booking hall—the smell of damp wood and train smoke so familiar to me, but that evening bringing back neither homesickness nor meaning—Margaret said:

"That must be the worst of it over, mustn't it?"

Her eyes were sharp with pain. All I could say was that I didn't know.

Down in the refreshment-room, gazing at me across the
marble table, she was saying that she was glad I was staying
with the Gearys. This had happened because Vicky and her
father had by this time left the Residence. Margaret had
spent the previous night with me at the Gearys' house; she
had liked them and trusted them more than she did usually
at first sight. She wasn't being entirely protective; she would
have welcomed their good nature for herself as well as for
me; she had been appalled by that day in the court. Before
she went through it, she had imagined what it would be like.
She had believed that she would be stronger than I was. Now
she didn't want (and this was true of the reporters and police
officers, more used to the horrors of fact than the rest of us)
to be alone.

We were sitting there fidgeting with the glasses on the
table, as we might have been in a love affair that was going
wrong, articulateness deserting us, pauses between the words.

She said:

"Could we have taken it?"

After a gap, I said:

"I've told you, sometimes I am afraid that one can take
anything."

"I wasn't thinking only of the little boy."

I nodded.

"I was thinking of the parents. If it had been ours—"

I didn't need to reply.

In time, she went on:

"And I was thinking of the parents of the others. The ones
who did it. If they had been ours—"

Slowly I said:

"Perhaps there, life's a bit more merciful. Somehow one
might cover it up or make excuses—"

"Do you really believe that?"

When the London train drew in, she clung to me on the
platform until the whistle shrilled.

The Gearys' house was right on the outskirts of the town,

in a district which had been open fields when I was a boy. Small gardens lay in front of the neat semi-detached pairs on both sides of the road: junior managers lived there, as well as modest professional men like Denis Geary. He and his wife were waiting for me in their sitting room, bright well-kept reproductions of Vermeer and Van Gogh on the walls, on the mantelpiece photographs of their children, groups of the family on holidays abroad.

A copy of the local evening paper under the bookshelf. Headlines about the trial. As he stood up, handsome, grizzled, Denis pointed to it.

"Now," he said, "you've got to forget all about it."

He was years younger than I was. But he was talking benevolently, as though I were a junior teacher on his staff, coming to him with some domestic trouble.

I said that it wasn't so easy.

"Lewis, you've got to forget about it." He went on, it might have happened anywhere, it had absolutely nothing to do with the normal run of things, we just had to wipe it out of our minds.

I wasn't used to being spoken to paternally. Not many men had ever tried to father me. But Denis was one of this world's fathers, and I didn't resent it.

"He's right, you know," said Alison Geary.

"I promise you," said Denis, "that we'll look after anything practical when it's all over. We'll look after old George as far as we can."

Yes, they would visit the Patemans and the two young women, wherever they were sent. It was all in the line of duty. They had visited criminals before now, they took it as naturally as talking to me.

Denis said: "Now you forget it and have a drink."

They had observed, at those dinners at the Shaws', that I enjoyed drinking. They had laid in more liquor that would be expected in a headmaster's house, and more, I couldn't help thinking, than they could comfortably afford. But I wasn't saving their pockets when I told them that, in times of trouble, I drank very little. It was true. They were so kind that I was confiding in them.

"I think I can understand that," said Denis. He said it with fellow-feeling, as though he had gone through dark nights. Just for an instant, I wondered if he were more complex than he seemed. Heartily he came back: "Still, you must have a little."

They set to work to distract me both then and through dinner, which, as on the night before, was a delectable English meal. The Vice-Chancellorship—Denis guessed that I might still be made interested in jobs. They hadn't yet found a successor to Arnold Shaw. They had offered the post to Walter Luke, but he had turned it down. Why? Denis replied, straight-faced: "He said that he didn't want to become a stuffed shirt." I couldn't resist a grin: that sounded like the authentic Walter. Someone asked him if there were other reasons. Denis said, still straight-faced: "He said he couldn't improve on the one he had already given."

Comprehensive education—they were both campaigning for it, it meant that our old school, Denis's and mine, would cease to be a grammar school. "But it's the only answer," said Alison eagerly. "It really is." She was as devoted a radical as her husband; she brought out all the arguments of the day. The lives we were wasting: we three had been lucky in our education, though we hadn't thought so, we had been lucky, compared with the neighbors round us. This was the only answer. It was also good politics; the public wanted it, whatever the tories said, and that was nothing against it; but the point was, it was right.

Although she had been talking to distract me, she was committed. Her bright sepia eyes were shining: it was easy to imagine her, quick-stepping, full-bodied, tapping at the voters' doors.

She couldn't raise an argument. She spoke about their children. The daughter had been married that winter. Did they like the man? He's a very good chap, said Denis, we think they're very happy. Where were they living? He was a schoolteacher in the town, said Alison.

"Well, you did the same," said Denis, with an uxorious grin.

"He's an extremely nice man," said Alison. "He'll make her a good husband." Then, as though she couldn't help it, her face changed. It began to wear an expression I had not seen in her before—was it wistful or shamefaced?

"But I always used to think she'd do something different, after all."

"She's going to be happy," Denis told her, like one repeating himself.

"Yes. She's a pretty girl," Alison turned to me, "though I am her mother."

From the photographs, that I could believe.

"She's got a lot of imagination too. She always used to be reaching after something wonderful. I used to think that she'd finish up by marrying—well, someone like André Malraux."

It seemed a curious dream: even though Alison, determined to be practical, explained that she meant, naturally, a younger version of M. Malraux. The Gearys' marriage was one of the happier ones: but what Alison dreamed for her daughter, she must, of course, once have dreamed for herself.

They didn't stop working to snag my interest until, very early, I went up to my room. Through the open window came faint scents of the spring. Clouds rushed across the sky, unveiling stars. At the bottom of the garden there were no houses in sight, only a range of trees. The moon, rising above one level branch, was just turning from silver to gold. In some moods, that sight would be a comfort or a cheat, telling one that there was an existence more desirable than ours.

I might have remembered, though I didn't, someone who

refused to take false comfort. We did not exist outside of time. Those were only words which drugged us, which made us blind to our condition. He said to me, on just such a night as this, that he hated the stars.

I stayed at the window, looking out at the night sky.

TWENTY-SEVEN

AN IMPERMISSIBLE
TERM

The next morning, I arrived early in the entrance hall. Through a side door I could see the courtroom, already nearly full. There was not such a queue outside as on the first day. Lawyers hustled by, swinging their briefcases, on the way to robe. Then, as I stood about, George Passant, also early, joined me. After his loud greeting, which hadn't varied in all the years, his first remark was:

"I've been thinking, I don't think I shall fag to come in today."

I was so surprised that I hardly noticed the old-fashioned slang.

"You won't?"

"I don't see any point in it today."

His manner was bold, defiant, diffident, like a young man's. As I looked at him, I didn't understand. Other people in the hall were looking at him, but there was no demonstration. One might have thought he was frightened of another crowd like that of the night before, but I knew that wasn't true. His courage was absolute, as it had always been. He was saying that tomorrow or next day, they might be getting somewhere. Then I believed I had it. He had been working out the progress of the trial. This morning or afternoon, which he wanted to escape, the medical evidence would come into court. That, though he couldn't tell me and was brazening it out, he wasn't able to endure.

"I think that I shall stay," I said.

"Well then," said George with relief, "I'll see you later on."

After I had watched him leave, I asked a policeman to take a message to the Deputy Sheriff, inquiring whether he could still find me a place. Before the answer came back, I saw, and this was another surprise, for at that time I hadn't been told of the telephoning between him and Margaret, my brother Martin. He wasn't smiling, but he said: "I thought you mightn't mind a bit of company."

I recognized the clerk from the morning before, polite and welcoming. Yes, of course there were two seats. Yes, of course the Deputy Sheriff would be delighted to invite Dr. Eliot. The clerk led us down a corridor behind the court, narrow and white-painted, past the judge's room, out to the official box.

From there our line of sight was only just above the level of the lawyers' wigs. We had to look up to see the crowd in the rake of the court, heads lit up by the long windows behind them. The row of barristers, the next row of solicitors—suddenly they reminded me of ministers on the front bench in the Commons, their PPS's whispering to them: I might have been watching them, as I had done often enough from the civil servants' box, but the angle was different, for it was like being on the wrong side of the Speaker's chair.

Somehow we were in an enclosure with the professionals, part of the machine. An official sitting beside us gave us piles of typescript, records of the police-court hearing, depositions.

The two women came up into the dock, their faces, beyond the lawyers, on a level with ours. Cora stared straight at me, without a sign of recognition. As she turned quarter-face to her left, listening to Kitty, she seemed like a painting I had once seen in the Uffizi, with a visage stormy, troubled, handsome (later I was puzzled to discover that the painting was, of all things, Lorenzo di Credi's *Venus*). Martin, who had not seen either of them before, sat forward, tense. Kitty was saying something, eyes sharp and flickering. At the end she gave a quick, surreptitious, involuntary smile. Her skin appeared to have darkened, not become paler through imprisonment, and now she looked older than her partner.

Through the door just beside our box, the procession entered. As he finished his bow to the jury, beaming, affable, the judge gave me an appraising glance.

The first part of the morning was routine: so much routine that there was a sense of let-down in the court, but Bosanquet was as undeterred as a batsman playing himself in for his second hundred. Questions from the judge: placid answers from Bosanquet, this was a matter of "filling in some pieces." So there was evidence leading to the weekend of September 20-22. Identification of Cora in the village. A good deal of car and transport evidence. Proof that the story of a bus back to the town, last on the Sunday night, was a fabrication. Sighting of the car near Markers Copse on the same Sunday night. Sighting of the car, close to the cottage, early the following morning. Examination of the car (this was the first appearance of the forensic scientists). Blood on the floor, close to the back seat. Category of blood.

Martin, like Margaret, had not attended a criminal trial before. He wasn't prepared for the patches of doldrums, the pauses for the judge to catch up with his longhand, the flatness of facts, or even the sheer numbers of the witnesses who came and went, names, addresses, occupations, units in the lonely crowd, just as we to them were units too. (How many people did one know? Intimately? A hundred, if one was lucky. Slightly? Perhaps ten thousand, if one had lived a busy life.) The witnesses came and went: so had the students before the university court the year before, most of us expecting never to see them again. There, but only by chance, I had been wrong: it hadn't been my last sight of the Patemans. So that, as I looked back, that ridiculous set-piece appeal not only loomed stiffer and more formal than this present trial, but also took on a significance, a kind of predictive ominousness that it hadn't in the slightest degree possessed when I was sitting through it.

Already half-past twelve. The court stirred. The prosecution was coming to the discovery of the body. Archibald Rose began to examine Mr. Coe, the huntsman. The evidence was, of course, a matter of form, since no one could contest it: but it took some effort to drag it out. Mr. Coe didn't appear at all like the romantic picture of an open-air worker: his face was pallid, his hair jet-black, his cheeks sunken. In addition, he was one of those witnesses who, when told to speak up, find it—just as my least favorite student had done—as impossible as a tone-deaf person asked to sing a tune. Archibald Rose had a fine resonant performer's voice: in a cheerful reproving tone, he kept saying—"You're not to speak to me, you must speak to my lord and the jury." Mr. Coe looked lugubriously across to the jury box, raised his volume for a sentence, and then let his chin descend into chest. My place was within touching distance of the jury, and though I had sharp ears I was missing one word in two. The judge broke in: he was a hunting man, and, though Coe didn't become more audible, he nodded his head once or twice less somberly, as though sensible men were talking about sensible things. It was a famous pack, the judge was saying, one of the best packs in the shires, wasn't it? The judge had never seen or heard of hounds behaving as those two had done that morning, had Mr. Coe? If they hadn't been so cussed, would Mr. Coe have thought of returning to the spot?

Coe gave a happy smile when told that he could leave the box, so happy that others smiled in response.

Exhibit. Policeman holding up a small plastic bag, testifying that within were the clothes found on the body. There was also a polyethylene wrapper, which, for some reason not explained, had been used to cover the boy's head. The bag was opened: not many had attention to spare for the sight of bits of clothing; all around, as though there never had been any other and as though it would last forever, was the charnel smell.

"Please remove that," said the judge. "And we will wait a moment before the next witness."

The next witness had to be taken care of, for it was Eric Mawby's mother. She should have given evidence the previous afternoon, but—so the Deputy Sheriff's assistant, sitting at his desk in our box, told us as we waited, the smell still in our throats—she had not been well enough to attend. However, when she did step into the box, she was erect, and her voice was firm. She was a tall woman, with a high-nosed, proud, imperious face. As the judge asked after her health and told her she would not be questioned for long, she replied like one who enjoyed having attention paid to her.

Yes, Eric always went to play in the summer and autumn before his father came home for his tea (tea in that home must have meant a substantial meal). He always went to the recreation-ground, which was a good safe place. Yes, he was always expected back by a quarter to seven. Yes, he was a good obedient boy, he'd never been more than a few minutes late. But that Friday night when he didn't return— Inquiries. The police.

Bosanquet was asking her as few questions as he could manage: but he had to say: "On October 9, did the police tell you that a boy's body had been found?"

"Yes, they did."

"Did they ask you to identify the body?"

"They did."

"It was your son's body, Mrs. Mawby?"

"It was Eric." Her head was thrown back, her tone was not so much piteous, or even angry, as commanding.

"And the clothes—they were his clothes?"

"Yes, they were his things."

Bosanquet thanked her, and finished. Defense counsel shook their heads. The judge thanked her, congratulated her on her courage, and gave her his sympathy. "Thank you, my lord," she said, taking pity from no one, proud to act as though she were used to courts.

On the way out down the corridor—the court rose after her evidence—Martin was saying that our mother would have behaved something like that. As soon as we reached the entrance hall, Archibald Rose, the junior prosecution counsel, approached us, looking boyish now that he had taken off his wig. "Hallo, I was watching out for you." He introduced himself; he was the nephew of my old chief Hector Rose. He said that Clive Bosanquet and he wondered if we would like to lunch with them.

In Rose's car, we drove into the center of the town, talking about acquaintances. All four of us had been drilled in the compact English professional world, where, if you didn't know someone, you at least knew someone else who did.

Sitting in the restaurant, the lawyers studied the menu. They had been working hard, they were hungry. Bosanquet allowed himself one drink. Close to, his expression was sadder and more authoritative than it seemed in court.

"What do you think of all this?" he said across the table, meaning the case.

I shook my head.

"If you'd stayed at the bar, you'd have done this sort of job, you know."

"Do you all get used to it?" asked Martin with hard sympathy.

"Do you imagine anyone ever gets quite used to something like this?" Bosanquet was as direct as we were. Despite his comfortable senatorial frame, there was not much padding about him. Young Rose, whose spirits were less heavy, tried to talk of another case. Bosanquet spooned away at a plate of soup.

He looked up.

"I've had about enough of it," he said.

He went on:

"I'm afraid I've got to bring it all out. I warn you, this afternoon isn't going to be pleasant."

A week before, he told us, he had thought that they could "smother some of the horrors." They weren't good for anyone to hear. But—he had to go on.

"Look here," I interrupted, "I've been puzzled all along. What are the other side expecting?"

At that, Bosanquet and Rose glanced at each other, and Bosanquet suddenly got away from his revulsion and began to talk like a man at his ease. This was professional, this was clean. Neither of them could understand it. Something had gone wrong. The case was proved to the last inch. The defense counsel knew it, of course. Their only line was to make the best deal they could about the women's mental states. ("We shall go for them there, anyway," said Archibald Rose.) Ted Benskin was a first-rate lawyer. Bosanquet was certain that was how he wanted to plead. But something had gone wrong.

"I shan't be surprised if they don't cut their losses any moment now." (That is, accept the prosecution's case and make their plea.) "I tell you, no one will be better pleased than me. As it is, I've got to plod on through all this filth."

He gave a sweet irritated smile.

"And old Jumbo doesn't make it any easier. I wish he wouldn't try to run my case for me."

"Old Jumbo" was Mr. Justice Fane. This too was professional, this was clean—in a different compartment from blood, cruelty, the smell of death. Just as Mansel was intent upon his professional problems while I, in a different compartment, was speculating about going blind. Bosanquet was happier now. Everyone loved old Jumbo, he was saying. He had been kind to Bosanquet himself all through his career. But there was no doubt about it, he hadn't much of a lawyer's sympathy with a well-built case.

Bosanquet was assessing the old judge like a man who, in the nearish future, might become a judge himself. It would be a good end to his career: and, unlike Mr. Justice Fane, he had no private means. As with a writer or an actor, he wasn't secure from illness or old age. The barrister's life had altered since my time, they told me. How much had I made in my first year? Under a hundred pounds. Nowadays one would make a decent income, getting on for two thousand. Rose said that he had done so himself. But he appeared to have some money—which surprised me, for his uncle had none, and his father was a suffragan bishop. Anyway, Rose had acquired a house in the country when he joined the circuit. He was inviting us all there, including the defense lawyers, in a couple of nights' time.

Martin, lacking my nostalgic interest in legal careers, put in a question. He said, getting back to a preoccupation of his own:

"Have you any idea which of those two was the prime mover?"

Bosanquet said, once more clouded:

"No, we don't know."

"I suppose it might have been the butch," said Rose.

"We don't know," said Bosanquet. He said it in a subdued tone, but with authority. "There are plenty of things about this case that we don't know." He addressed Martin, who might not have realized how much information police and lawyers possessed, but couldn't prove or use: "But we do know two things. They had planned this, or something like this, literally for months beforehand. And they were going to kill, right from the beginning. That was the real point all along."

Martin nodded.

"It's ten-past two," said Bosanquet, without changing his tone. "We ought to be going." He added, as old Herbert Getliffe used to say before going into court, like a captain calling to his team in the dressing room: "All aboard."

The afternoon began quietly. In the dock Kitty was sitting, pen in hand, but for the moment not writing. The first witness, examined by Rose, was an experimental officer from one of the midland forensic laboratories, an unassertive friendly man, his manner similar to those of the meteorologists who predicted the weather before the television news. Yes, he had examined samples of blood after Eric Mawby's body was discovered. These came from another laboratory. ("We shall have a deposition to establish," said Archibald Rose, more emphatic than his senior, "that these samples were taken from relics of dried blood still remaining on his head wounds and also on his clothes.") It had been possible to determine the blood group. The blood group was the same as that already given in evidence for specimens of blood found on the floor and walls of Rose Cottage.

Another experimental officer. Blood found on a piece of clothing, a woman's nylon blouse not completely burnt, in the garden of Rose Cottage. Identical blood group

Deposition about taking samples of blood from K.M. Pateman, C.H.P. Ross. Another witness, from another laboratory, tested these samples (at this stage, the scientific tests seemed mysteriously ramified). Neither belonged to the same group as that of the other specimens.

All muted, abstract as a chart of last year's trade returns, except for Rose's ringing voice.

A new witness mounted into the box, and Bosanquet stood up himself. Laurence McQuillin. Home Office pathologist. His arms were folded, he was short, sturdy, unvivacious as a Buddha. He was practiced at giving evidence, and he also enjoyed exposition: so that, though he was extremely positive, people did not react against him, but wanted to listen. Bosanquet must have examined him before, and carefully let him give an answer about the problems presented by a body buried for three weeks. "In some matters," said McQuillin, "there is an area of doubt. I shall indicate to my lord and the jury where the conclusions have to be tentative."

"But you have reached some definite conclusions?"

"I have."

One definite conclusion was that the boy's body showed two types of injury. The first type was wounds which could not have caused death and which had, with reasonable certainty, been inflicted some considerable time before death. These wounds included lacerations on the back, buttocks, and thighs. The exact number could not be decided. Well over twenty. There were also cuts on the breast and groin. A number of burns on the upper arms and shoulders. Not less than ten. Marks on the ankles and wrists.

"What were these wounds inflicted with?"

"There must have been different instruments. The lacerations on the back and buttocks could have been caused by a stick. If so, it must have been used with severe force."

"And the others?"

"The cuts would have needed a sharp instrument. A knife could have been used. Or scissors."

"The burns?"

"I cannot be certain. They are quite small in area. Perhaps a lighted cigarette-end, but that is only a speculation."

The marks on the ankles and wrists were minor. They were consistent with the child's arms and legs having been tied, but that also was a speculation.

"None of these injuries had any connection with the victim's death?"

"None at all."

McQuillin added to his answer: they would have caused extreme pain, but a healthy child, or a healthy adult for that matter, would have recovered physically in a comparatively short time.

"How do you reach your conclusion that they were incurred a considerable period before death?"

There were two reasons, McQuillin said. One was simple and didn't require technical explanation. Blood, in considerable quantity, had been found on the outside of the boy's clothes. This had come from the head wounds. Almost none had seeped through to the inside of his shirt and shorts. On the other hand, some of the body wounds, not all, but many of the lacerations as well as the cuts, had resulted in the effusion of blood. There was no trace of this blood on the inside of his clothes. He had been killed when he was fully dressed. Thus he must have received the body wounds some time before: possibly, and in fact probably, over a period of hours: presumably while he was naked.

The second reason was technical—McQuillin described the physiology of flesh wounds, and their rate of healing. If the body had been discovered sooner, he could have been precise about the relative time of the head and body wounds. As it was, all indications pointed in the same direction, that there were hours between them.

"There is no other explanation for those body wounds than the one you have given?"

"I see no other explanation except systematic torture."

McQuillin had not raised his voice. The judge, leaning forward, spoke even more softly.

"I think it is better for us, Doctor McQuillin, if you restrict yourself to your scientific findings."

"I am sorry, my lord," said McQuillin.

"I understand," said the judge.

The head injuries—these had been the cause of death? He was killed, said McQuillin, by multiple head injuries, multiple fractures of the skull. There had been seven blows, and possibly more. Any one of several blows would have been sufficient to cause death. One group of five had been delivered by something like a heavy poker or an iron bar. The others, by a solid, obtuse, weighted surface, such as the anterior wooden portion of an axe-handle. Yes, the bleeding would have been copious. "Nothing bleeds so copiously as the scalp," McQuillin added. "There must also, with such wounds, have been a discharge of brain tissue. And fragments of bone thrown out, though these have not been found. The vault of the skull showed a number of gaps."

The blows had been delivered from in front (here Mc-Quillin beckoned a policeman, like a lecturer carried away by his subject and needing to illustrate it), or at least the first one had been. The head had been held back by the hair—like this—possibly not by the person delivering the blow. The remainder of the blows could have followed when the body had sunk to a kneeling or recumbent position—

Benskin interrupted. "This doctor in my submission is going beyond the evidence of a medical expert."

The judge said: "Mr. Benskin, I think I agree with you. Doctor, you have told us your conclusions about the cause of death? You are quite certain about them?"

"I am quite certain, my lord."

"Then I hope we might leave it there, Mr. Bosanquet."

Bosanquet stood, thinking, and said: "I am content."

Both defense counsel cross-examined. They were sharp and edgy about the doctor's reconstructions. Neither of them was free from the miasma which had during his evidence settled on the court. It was a miasma which both rotted the nerves and at the same time held them stretched. Glances at the dock were furtive. The doctor had been imagining how the blows had been struck. Creeping glances at the two women. They knew whether he was right.

Head wounds, body wounds—the lawyers were doing their job, they had to bring the descriptions back before us. To some there, those would be nothing but names by now. But not to Wilson, the younger of the silks. He sounded angry: he could not, less so than Benskin, insulate himself, he took it out of the doctor, partly because it was tactically right, but also because he genuinely, and for his own sake, wanted to disbelieve. The head wounds—no one doubted they had been inflicted, no one doubted they were the cause of death. But surely the doctor's reconstruction was entirely fanciful? In any case, it was not relevant: if it had been relevant, anyone's reconstruction would have been worth about as much, which was next to nothing at all?

"I have had some experience of these matters," said Mc-Quillin impassively.

"I repeat, your reconstruction is fanciful. But that is not the point. The death happened, we all know that. I suggest to you, your conclusions about the body wounds are also fanciful?"

"I have recorded my findings. I could give further conclusions about those wounds."

"They might have been incurred very near the time of death—?"

"I regard it as most unlikely."

"It is not impossible?"

"In giving scientific evidence, it is often wrong to say something is impossible."

"That is, your picture of long-sustained wounding—I might remind you that you used an impermissible term for which my lord reproved you—your picture goes right beyond the medical evidence?"

"In my judgment, it is the only one that fits the facts."

Wilson could not leave it alone. Questions about lacerations, cuts, bloodstains, the whole pathological examination over again.

At last the judge said: "Mr. Wilson, I shouldn't put obstacles in your way if I thought we were getting any further. But I do suggest that the jury has as much information as we can give it. And perhaps this is getting burdensome for us all."

He said it aseptically. Wilson, face flushed, wiped his forehead, continued with more questions about flesh-wounds, and then sat down.

Bosanquet's re-examination was brief. He remarked that the doctor had been a long time in the box, and asked if, as a result, he wished to modify any of his statements of fact or his conclusions. McQuillin was as impassive as when he first answered to his name. He had given considered opinions, he answered. He did not wish to change in the slightest anything he had said.

It was well after half-past four, the court had over-run for the first time in the trial: the judge had watched the clock, but not interrupted.

TWENTY-EIGHT

ANOTHER QUESTION

When at last Martin and I got out into the air, we heard a voice behind us calling. It was Edgar Hankins who, nowadays turning his hand to non-literary journalism, was writing special articles on the trial for a Sunday paper. He came running after us, his face cheerful, rubbery, sweating.

"Let's all go and have tea and then a drink," he said.

Before I could reply, Martin said:

"No, not now. Lewis and I have something to talk about."

Hankins dropped back, his face still not having forgotten the smile of invitation. I hadn't often heard Martin impolite before: his tone had been colder than when I offered to help out financially over his son. As a rule with Hankins, because of their past history, he was specially considerate. He didn't speak until we were sitting in his car. Then, before he started it, he said:

"I couldn't bear his brand of nonsense tonight."

He went on:

"You know, we could write it for him. Great throbbing pieces about how we're all guilty. So really no one is guilty. So really everything is as well as could be expected in an admittedly imperfect world."

Neither of us said much more—Martin's face was hard and angry, he made another aside about "saccharine rhetoric" —until, a little later, he rejoined me in the bar of his hotel.

It was a bar which we both knew: though, since I had left

the town for good when he was a schoolboy, we had never before sat there together. It was still a meeting-place for men coming out of their offices on the way home to the prosperous suburbs: the income level had always been higher than in the pubs which George and I most often used. Though the bar had stayed geographically in the same place, it had been transmogrified, like the hotel and most of the town itself. It had become plushier and, in the American style, much darker, lights gleaming surreptitiously behind the sandwich-bar. But the people looked much the same, hearty middle-aged men, bald or greying, a good many of them carrying their weight on athletes' muscles: from some of these Martin, as we sat in a corner alcove, kept getting shouts of greeting. For while I might be recognized from photographs, he had more acquaintances here, they had played games together before the war. Amiable impersonal back-chat: how are you getting on, I'm an old man now, I can't get my arm over any more, you never did get it very high, I shall soon be taking to bowls. Some of them had made money, Martin mentioned, when we weren't observed. There was a lot of quiet money in this town. There were also one or two casualties in this bar, boyhood friends who were scrabbling for a living, or who had taken to drink. Most of them, though, had come through into this jostling, vigorous, bourgeois life. All round us he could see the well-being, the survival, and sometimes the kindness of the flesh.

Was that any sort of reassurance to him? I was wondering. We had said little to each other: to an extent, we did not need to. I had let slip a remark about the time-switch at Auschwitz, and he had picked it up, just as Margaret would have done, or often young Charles. I didn't have to explain. I meant—someone had said it before me—that at Auschwitz one could not help being invaded by the relativity of time. The relativity which was at once degrading and ironic. That is, on the same day, *at the same moment,* people had been sitting down to meals or begetting children while, a few hundred yards way, others had been dying in torture. It had been the same with this boy's death. While he was beginning to suffer fright and worse than fright, the rest of us had, at the same moment, through the switch of time, been living as healthily as those men round us in the bar, talking or making love or maybe being preoccupied with what seemed a serious worry of our own. Martin understood without my saying so. He did not understand (I did not want to explain, perhaps because it reminded me of another death) that I had been, in court, working out the hours of the boy's suffering. That might have been going on—in all probability it had been going on—during a happy dinner party at our London flat, when Margaret and I were looking forward to the children's future, making a fuss of Vicky, and being entertained by Martin's own son.

Martin did not know that. But he knew something else, when I mentioned Auschwitz. For he and I and others of our age had seen the films of the concentration camps just after the troops had entered and when the horror came before our eyes like a primal, an original, an Adamic fact. Yes, with what we possessed of decency and political sense we had made our plans, so that, if people like us had any part in action at all, this couldn't happen again: and we had gone on spending, though men like Rubin told us that we were wasting our time, a good deal of our lives in action. And yet, while we watched those films, we had, as well as being appalled, felt a shameful and disgusting pleasure. It was almost without emotion, it was titillating, trivial and (just as when Margaret asked me questions in our drawing room) seepingly corrupt. We were fascinated (the sensation was as affectless as that) because men could do these things to other men.

The wretched truth was, it had been the same in the courtroom that afternoon. Not only in us, but in everyone round us. But it was enough to know it for ourselves.

So, when I spoke, as though casually, of Auschwitz, Martin did not ask any questions. He nodded (raising one hand to a greeting from the other side of the bar), and looked at me with a glance which was grim but comradely.

In time he said:

"What people feel doesn't matter very much. It's what they do we've got to think about."

It sounded bleak, like so much that he said as he grew older. Yet, as we sat there, old acquaintances pushing by him, he was as much at the mercy of his thoughts as I was, maybe more so. We were different men, though we had our links of sympathy. What we had learned from our lives, we had learned in different fashions: we had often been allies, but then events had driven us together: perhaps now, in our fifties, we were closer than we had ever been. But Martin, whom most people thought the harder and more self-sufficient of the two, had once had the more brilliant and the more innocent hopes. I had started off in this town in the first blaze of George's enlightenment. Let the winds of life blow through you. Live by the flow of your instincts. Salvation through freedom. Like any young man, I had got drunk on those great cries. It wasn't through any virtue of mine, but simply because of my temperament and my first obsessive love affair, that I couldn't quite live up to them. But there was another side to it. George, like many radicals of his time, believed, passionately believed, in the perfectibility of man. That I could never do, from the time that I first met him, in my teens. Without possessing a religious faith, I nevertheless —perhaps because I wasn't good myself—couldn't help believing in something like original sin.

With Martin, it had gone the other way. He had in his youth, though he had never been such an intimate of George's and nothing like so fond of him, accepted the whole doctrine. He really did have the splendid dreams. Rip off the chains, and he and everyone else would break through to a better life. He enjoyed himself more as a young man than I had done. He had gone through the existence where ideals and sex and energy are all mixed up—perhaps, even now, when people thought him sardonic and restrictive, there were times when he thought of that existence with some sort of regret. It hadn't lasted. He was clear-sighted, he couldn't deny his own experience. His vision of life turned jet-black. Yet not completely, not so completely as he spoke or thought. It was what people did that mattered, he had just said, as he had often said before; if that was true, then what he did sometimes betrayed him. After all, it had been he—alone of all of us—who had broken his career, just when he had the power and prizes in his clutch. Conscience? Moral impulse? People wondered. They might have accepted that of Francis Getliffe, not of Martin. But it was he who had done it. Just as it was he who, under the carapace of his pessimism, pretending to himself that he expected nothing, invested so much hope in his son, was wide open to danger through another's life.

The bar was noisy, but neither of us wanted to leave. The place had been familiar, part of commonplace evenings, to each of us—though it had taken something not commonplace but unimaginable to seat us there together. Martin's acquaintances downed their liquor. Most of them were middled-aged, not thinking about their age, carried along, like us, by the desire to persist. They looked carefree. For all we could tell, some of them were also at the mercy of their thoughts. One, whom I knew slightly, had reminded me of a photograph in a newspaper that morning: of Margaret and me walking with George Passant, a straggle of women demonstrating behind. Did I know "that crowd," did I know those two women? The questions had been edged. Martin had answered for me, guarded and official, Passant had been a friend of ours when we were young men. Otherwise the rest of them said their good-evenings, wanted to know whether we were

staying long, offered us drinks. Someone inquired, why don't
you come back and live here, not a bad place, you know, we
could do with you.

Martin said:

"If you hadn't had your connections here, just by chance—
would this have meant much to you?"

He was talking of what we had listened to that afternoon.

"Should you have thought about it much?" he went on.

"Should we?" I replied. For Martin, in his unexpressive
manner, was using the second person when he meant the
first.

"I can't be sure."

"Could we have shrugged it off? Some people can, you
know."

I told him about the Gearys, who weren't opaque, who
longed, more than most of us, to create a desirable life.
Yes, they could dismiss it: they could still look after both the
innocent and guilty: but it seemed to them only an accident,
a freak, utterly irrelevant to the desirable life they longed for
or to the way they tried to build it.

"That's too easy," said Martin.

I said, most of our wisest friends would see it as the Gearys
did.

"I should have thought," said Martin, "we'd had enough of
the liberal illusions."

"Those I'm thinking of aren't specially illusioned men."

"Anyone is illusioned who doesn't get ready for the worst.
If there's ever to be any kind of radical world which it's
possible to live in, it's got to be built on minimum illusions. If we start by getting ready for the worst, then perhaps
we stand a finite chance."

Though to many it seemed a contradiction in his nature,
Martin had remained a committed radical. In terms of action, we had usually been at one.

Someone sent over tankards of beer, smiling at us. With public faces, Martin and I smiled back.

"Tell me," said Martin, "those two aren't mad, are they?"

"I'm not certain we know what madness means."

"Are you evading it?"

"Do you think I should choose to, now?"

I went on:

"Do you think I should? All I can tell you is, no one round them thinks they're mad."

He said: "They look—like everyone else."

I replied;

"I'm certain of one thing. In most ways, they feel like everyone else. The girl Kitty is in pain. She can't get comfortable, she's just as harassed as any other woman with sciatica having to sit there under people's eyes. I'm certain they wake up in the morning often feeling good. Then they remember what they've got to go through all day." It had been like that, I said, when I had the trouble with my eye. The moments of waking: all was fine: and I saw the black veil. I said that in the existential moments tonight, as they ate their supper and sat in their cells, they must be feeling like the rest of us.

"I suppose you're right," said Martin.

"The horror is," I said, "that they are human."

The dialogue was going by stops and jerks: soon it fell into doldrums, like an imitation of the doldrums of the trial. We dropped into chit-chat, not even the ordinary family exchange. Neither of us mentioned—and this was very rare— our children. Martin spoke (although I knew nothing of botany and cared less) about a plant he had identified on Wicken Fen. Sometimes we were interrupted, the bar was only beginning to empty. Still we didn't want to leave. Somehow we seemed protected there. We fetched sandwiches, so as not to have to depart for dinner.

In the middle of the chit-chat, Martin made another start.

"Human beings are dangerous wild animals," he said. "More dangerous than any other animals on earth."

I didn't disagree. But I added that perhaps there were some vestigial possibilities of grace. "You have to give us the benefit of the doubt. We need that, the lot of us, to get along."

"I think you've given us all far too much benefit of the doubt," said my brother.

Maybe. And yet I believed that in the end I was more suspicious than he was.

Later, as we still sat, talking about someone who had just left the bar, Martin suddenly interrupted:

"What do you hope will happen to those two?"

"What do you mean?"

"I mean, what verdict are you hoping for?"

I had explained the legal situation, and how I couldn't understand why diminished responsibility hadn't been brought in before now. Otherwise they might as well have pleaded guilty of murder and have done with it. He had already asked about diminished responsibility: what were the chances that that defense could win?

"Do you hope they win?" Martin pressed me.

I hesitated for a long time.

"I just don't know," I said.

It would be easier, of course, for their families, I went on, it would be easier for George, it would save some pain.

"It would be easier for everyone," said Martin. He asked, in a hard and searching tone:

"And you still don't know?"

"Do you?" I replied.

It was his turn to hesitate. At last he shook his head.

By this time there were, besides ourselves, only a couple of men left in the room. It had become cavernous and quiet: now the aquarium light obtruded from behind the counter. Soon, said the barman, there would be another crowd, the after-dinner crowd, coming in. In that case, Martin said, he felt inclined to stay, he didn't specially want to move yet awhile. Neither of us suggested going out, so that we could be alone, the two of us together.

IV
RESPONSIBILITY

TWENTY-NINE

A MOTHER'S REMARK

On the third morning, which was a Wednesday, Martin and I returned to our seats in the official box, having lingered about uselessly for George. In the courtroom the chandelier lights were switched on, the clouds pressing towards the windows were dense and purplish, there was a hubbub of wind and rain. Outside it was a dramatic, a faintly apocalyptic, day: but inside the court the proceedings were subdued, voices were quiet, nothing dramatic there.

In fact, police officers were giving routine evidence about the statements made by the two women. Statements which contradicted each other, but that was no news, we had heard it already. We had heard also the elaborations, the different versions, the excuses for past lies, that Kitty had made as the police played on her. None of this was new. It was all delivered flatly, with nothing like the confidence and projection of the medical witness the afternoon before. But it had the curious intimacy that sometimes descended on law courts—an intimacy in which the police, the criminals, the lawyers, the judge, seemed to inhabit a private world of their own, with their own understandings, secrets and even language, shutting out, like an exclusive club, everyone who hadn't the right of entry.

In the middle of the morning—the gale was blowing itself out, the windows were lighter—Detective-Superintendent Maxwell went into the witness box. He was, I knew well

335

enough, a formidable man: but he didn't look and sound formidable as he stood there, opposite to us, across the court. He looked less bulky, his eyes less probing and hot: he gave his evidence as flatly as the others, unassertively, almost gently.

"Yes, sir, when she was making her fourth statement, the defendant Miss Pateman told me that they had picked him up at 5:45 on the Friday night."

Bosanquet asked, in a similar tone, what she had said. "She said that he was glad to go with them."

That had been included, in identical words, in Bosanquet's opening. So had her explanation of the child's wounds. Leaning confidentially on the box-rail, Maxwell said: "She told me, we wanted to teach him to behave. She told me again, we had to teach him to behave."

He sounded like an uncle talking of a game of parents-and-children. I hadn't seen any man conceal his passions more.

The judge put in, also in an unassertive tone:

"You went just a little fast for me, Superintendent. Was it, She-told-me-we-had-to-teach-him-to-behave?"

The judge's pen moved anachronistically over his paper. Then Bosanquet again. When did they begin to ill-treat him? "She never gave me the exact time. All she said was, We started as we meant to go on."

I was watching Kitty's face, just then washed clean of lines. Was she out of pain? Her expressions changed like the surface of a pond. She was writing another of her notes.

Maxwell had led her through the Saturday and Sunday hour by hour. "We put him to bed at half-past nine on the Saturday, Miss Pateman told me. I asked her, what sort of condition was he in then? She said, we gave him three aspirins and a glass of milk before he went to bed." You couldn't elicit how badly he had been hurt by that time, said Bosanquet neutrally. Just as neutrally, Maxwell said, no, she hadn't made a positive statement. On the Sunday, she did tell him, they had been obliged to be strict. But they had let him look at television at Sunday tea-time. "What sort of condition was he in then, I asked her, but she never replied."

The defense was raising no objection. There must be an understanding, or they must have a purpose, I thought.

It hadn't been established, it still wasn't clear, at what time on the Sunday night he had been killed. It might even have been early on the Monday morning. "I asked her," Maxwell said, "did you tell him what was going to happen to him? She said he had asked them once, but they didn't say anything."

Again, the judge remarked that his pen wasn't keeping up. Maxwell, containing himself so tightly, was speaking unnaturally fast. When the judge was satisfied, Maxwell went on:

"I think—I should like to have permission to refer to my notes"—studiously, horn-rimmed glasses on his prowlike nose, he read in a small pocket book—"that on that occasion Miss Pateman stated that they hadn't any knowledge themselves of what did happen to him."

There was a sudden flurry of confusion. Comparison of statements, Kitty's fourth and fifth: the judge had mislaid Cora's second. Bosanquet steered his way through: had Miss Pateman given any account of the actual killing? No, said Maxwell. In one statement she had told him that early on the Sunday evening they had put him on a bus. That contradicted statements, not only by Miss Ross, but by Miss Pateman herself. On another occasion she said that she didn't know, or seemed to have forgotten, what had happened on the Sunday night.

"Will you clarify that?" said Bosanquet. "She actually said that she *seemed to have forgotten*—?"

"You will find that in her Statement Number 5." For an instant Maxwell's eyes flashed.

"What did you say, when you heard that?"

"I said," Maxwell replied, once more in his most domestic

tone, "Now listen, Kitty. I can't make any promises, but it will save us all a lot of worry, you included, if we get this story straight."

"How did Miss Pateman respond?"

"She said, I will only tell you. I've given you the story as far as I remember it. I don't remember much about anything that Sunday night."

Bosanquet was passing to Maxwell's interviews with Cora. The first breakdown: the first admission (it was she who had made it, not Kitty) that they had taken the child out to the cottage that Friday. All quiet and matter-of-fact. Then Benskin was on his feet, jester's face smiling at Bosanquet. "If my learned friend will permit me. My lord, Mr. Wilson and I have agreed that we shall not challenge this evidence for the Crown. Perhaps it would be advisable for us to indicate—"

The judge gave a sapient nod. "Will you please come up, Mr. Benskin, Mr. Wilson? Mr. Recorder?" The barristers moved to the space immediately below the judge's seat, and there they and the judge and the Clerk of Assize were all whispering in what, to most people in court, seemed a colloguing mystery. In our box, the Deputy Sheriff's assistant gave us a knowledgeable glance. "About time, too," he murmured. It was, we assumed, what those on the inside had expected all along: they were changing their plea: it would have been tidier, so he was saying, if they had started clean on the first morning. Meanwhile, wigs were nodding below the judge, the old man was half-smiling.

At that moment we heard a loud unmodulated shout. It was Cora, standing in the dock, palms beating on the rail. "What the hell do you think you're doing with us? What right have you got?" She was jeering at them with fury and contempt; she began to swear, sweeping round at all of us, the oaths coming out unworn, naked, as in one of George's outbursts. The air was ripped open. Most people in the court hadn't heard until that moment what anger could sound like.

"We'll answer for ourselves. We don't want you, you ————"
—again the curse crackled. "Do you think we need to explain
ourselves to a set of ————?"

Kitty was pulling at her arm, urgently, eyes snapping. The
judge spoke to Benskin, and then raised his voice, which
showed, for the first time, the unevenness of age. "Miss Ross,
you are doing yourself no good, you must be quiet."

"Do you mean to say anything will do us good among you
crowd—"

Very quietly, Benskin had moved to the dock. For an instant she stood there, towering over him: then we heard a
rasp of command, and there was a nervous relief as she sat
down. Whispers from Benskin, low and intense, which none
of us could pick up. ("He's a very tough man," the official
was commenting to Martin.) Shortly he was back in his
place, facing the judge. "My lord, I wish to express regret, on
behalf of my client," he said, with professional smoothness,
like a man apologizing for knocking over a glass of sherry.

"Very well," said the judge. Then he spoke to the jury: "I
have to tell you that you must dismiss this incident from your
minds. And I have to tell everyone in court that it must not
be mentioned outside, under penalties of which I am sure
you are well aware." He spoke to the jury again, telling them
that he now proposed to adjourn the court until the following morning. This was because the defense would then open
their case, admitting the facts about the killing, but claiming
that the defendants acted with diminished responsibility.
"That means, you understand, that they still plead not guilty
to murder, but, because of their mental condition, under our
present law, are seeking to prove to you that their crime
should be regarded as manslaughter."

The judge lingered over this piece of exposition, courteous, paternal, with the savor of an old professor, famous for
his lectures, who may soon be delivering the last one. The
jury were to realize that the trial would from now on take a

different course. The defense would not attempt to disprove the Crown evidence as to the nature of the killing. So that the jury need not worry themselves about certain questions of detail which had already taken up some time, such as precisely when the child was killed. The legal position would, of course, be explained to them carefully by counsel and by himself in his summing-up. He realized that this trial was an ordeal for them, and perhaps they would benefit by an afternoon free. "And perhaps"—he turned to the two in the dock, without altering his tone or his kindness—"you also will be able to get a little rest."

During the morning I had noticed Mrs. Pateman in the courtroom, without her husband. I followed her out, and said that, if she cared, I could visit her that afternoon. As I spoke to her (she was looking frightened, her eyes darting round like her daughter's) I noticed that two journalists were watching us. As we knew already, young Charles's forecasts hadn't been entirely wrong.

Going back to Martin, I found him among a knot of lawyers in the hall, all simmering with gossip and rumors. Yes, naturally the defense had wanted to make this plea from the beginning. The only resistance had come from the two women. Or really, said someone, with the satisfaction of a born insider, from one of them. It had been the woman Ross who hadn't cooperated with the psychiatrists. Cooperated about as much as she did in court this morning. The gossip sparked round.

She said that she despised them.

The other one had been willing to play.

But they'd stuck together up to now. If Ross wasn't agreeable, then Pateman wouldn't insist.

Tagging on behind the master, as usual.

The previous two nights, their solicitors had been working on them. So had Ted Benskin. Last night they thought that Ross had given way. If they wanted to switch the case, she'd go along.

Did she go along this morning? You saw her hit the ceiling.

Among the buzz, a quiet voice said that he was wondering whether that wasn't a put-up job. The quiet voice came from a young man, possibly a law student, about the age I had been when I first attended this assize.

He meant, if they were going to prove she wasn't responsible, she had given them something to go on, hadn't she?

An older man said, he didn't believe anyone could act as well as that. She just cracked.

She was horrifying, said another.

If you'd been to many criminal trials, said one of the clerks, you'd be ready to believe anything. She might have been acting, she might not. Everything seemed about as likely or unlikely as anything else.

Ted Benskin will have to put her in the box, won't he?

A couple of hours later, I was walking along the street, now familiar, now repelling, to the Patemans' house. The smell of curry. The wind, still high, whistled down an entry. Penciled cards, names of tenants, beside one front door: pop music from a bedroom.

When I rang the bell, Mrs. Pateman was there, as though she had been waiting in the passage.

"It's very good of you, I'm sure," she said.

In the little sitting room, the fire was bright, as I hadn't seen it when Mr. Pateman was there to supervise. Her attempt to welcome me, perhaps? The disinfectant was not so pungent, but the room was still pressingly dark, although through the single window which gave onto the back yard one could see that the sun was coming out. We were alone in the house.

"He's gone off to work today," she said. She was answering a question I hadn't asked: in his absence, she seemed less diminutive. "I told him to. It keeps his mind off it, if he's got something to do."

As for her son, I knew already that, from the day Arnold

Shaw's resignation was announced, he had been absenting himself from his new university in order to campaign at his old one. Full restitution for the four dismissed students! Dick Pateman had organized placard-carrying processions (the dismissals were a year old now, and the two bright students were doing well elsewhere). The university gave out the news that, at the summer convocation, the ex-Vice-Chancellor was to receive an honorary degree. More processions by Dick Pateman and his followers. No degree for Shaw! Insult to student body! All this was happening during the police-court proceedings against Dick's sister, and in the weeks before the trial. Could anyone be so fanatical? asked charitable persons such as the Gearys. And they found something like menace in it.

I was trying to explain to Mrs. Pateman about the trial. It was all changed now, she understood that, didn't she? The lawyers were going to admit that the boy had been killed.

"They did it, did they?" She seemed less shrewd than on the evening she took me into the empty front room.

"Never mind what happened. You won't hear much more about it."

"They took him there, didn't they?"

I said, now the whole point was, whatever had happened, they mightn't have been responsible for what they did.

"They're going to say," said Mrs. Pateman, flickering-eyed, "that she's not all there?" With a gesture curiously like a schoolgirl's, she tapped a forefinger against her temple.

"Something like that." I told her that they would put it in their own language, it would sound strange.

"She did something, of course she did. And they're going to say she's not all there."

She looked at me with an expression open, confiding, and somehow free from apprehension.

"I can't take it in," she said.

Margaret and I had been wrong, or at least half-wrong,

when we sat in the station buffet imagining her feelings. So far as I could reach her, she wasn't covering up or making excuses. But she spoke as though she were shut off from the facts, or as though they hadn't entered or touched her.

She asked:

"What will they do to her?"

I said it depended on which way the trial now went. If this new plea didn't succeed, she would go to prison ("they'll say for life, but you understand, it doesn't mean anything like that") : if the plea did succeed, then it would probably be a mental hospital.

"When will they let her out?"

"They'll have to be satisfied, you know, that she's not going to be a danger to anyone else."

"She won't be, they needn't vex themselves about that."

For an instant I misunderstood her. I thought that she was shielding her daughter.

She went on:

"I'm not saying anything for her, she's done whatever she has done. But she's got her head screwed on, has Kitty. She'll be careful, she won't let the police get hold of her again."

Now that I had understood her, I was astonished. On the instant, that struck me as the strangest thing I had yet heard during the trial.

She glanced at me, her eyes for once meeting mine. She said:

"I can't take it in. I suppose it's a blessing that I can't."

Yes, she was grateful, but she hadn't been able to pray, she said. She hadn't been able to pray much for a long time.

"He's been praying every day," she told me. He had taken to going to early morning service, and then at home, in their bedroom, he prayed out loud each night. He was praying for help against all their dangers and against all the enemies who were working to do harm to him and his.

From her account (was there, even that afternoon, while

she was lost and numbed, a trace of slyness?) it seemed he could still believe that Kitty and himself had been conspired against.

"Sometimes I get frightened about him," she said.

Not of him, though that must sometimes, perhaps often, have been true. But she was frightened for him. He might hear something in this trial that he couldn't reject or alter. He might not be able to protect himself. She had been worrying for years, worrying since the children had been young, about how much (it was her own phrase) his mind could stand.

THIRTY

FANTASY AND ACTION

That evening Martin and I did not talk in private, for we were having supper with the Gearys. I mentioned that George, for the second day running, had not turned up in court. Within minutes, Denis was on the telephone to one of his staff asking him to find out whether Passant was "all right." It didn't take half an hour before the reply came back. There was nothing the matter with him, Denis called to us from the receiver: he would return to the trial when it wasn't "a waste of time." That sounded like a direct quotation. I was glancing at Martin as Denis sat down again, giving out a satisfaction similiar in kind to Lord Lufkin's in his days of glory, demonstrating how smoothly his organization worked. We picked up the conversation, quite remote from George, all friendly in the bright clean room. Martin was so disciplined that I couldn't tell where his real thoughts were. It might have been that he had the same difficulty about me.

Next morning, once more in the official box, we were listening to Benskin's opening. It was short and subdued. Subdued out of his normal style, for he had more taste for drama than the other barristers in the case. But he was deliberately adapting himself to the tone of the trial. He had a reputation for wit, and that he had also to suppress. His expression was stiff, the humor strained out of it, as he faced the jury. "My lord told you yesterday that my learned friend Mr. Wilson and I are, on behalf of our clients, asking you to take a new consideration of this crime. I am speaking here in agreement with Mr. Wilson, because there is no shade of difference between us, nor, and I want you to remember this, between Miss Ross and Miss Pateman. We do not dispute that this young boy was killed—and everyone in court must want to express the most profound sympathy to his mother and father. We do not dispute that Miss Ross and Miss Pateman were the agents of that killing. That having been admitted by us without reserve, you can dismiss from your minds any minor matters of controversy. I have just stated the central, plain, and simple fact. But we now wish to prove to you that, while they were agents for this killing, Miss Ross and Miss Pateman were not responsible for their actions in the sense that you and I would be, if we performed such actions. My lord will instruct you about the nature of the law in relation to diminished responsibility. But perhaps it will be some assistance to you if I read to you from Clause 2 of the Homicide Act 1957. *'Persons suffering from diminished responsibility. He shall not be guilty of murder if he was suffering from such abnormality of mind (whether arising from a condition of arrested or retarded development of mind or any inherent causes or induced by disease or injury) as substantially impaired his mental responsibility. . . .'* You will notice that the definition is wide. Abnormality of mind—leading to impairment of mental responsibility. If I may, I would like to say a few words about how that clause applies to these two young women and this case. My lord will I know correct me if he finds I am at fault. When we claim, and we have no doubt that we shall prove it to you, that they perpetrated this killing with diminished responsibility, or impairment of responsibility, we do not intend to state that, either at the time or now, they were or are clinically insane. You have all probably heard of the old McNaghten rules under which a defendant was only free from guilt if at the time of his offense he couldn't tell right from wrong. We do not state that either,

for these two young women. What we do state is something
different, about which we all have to think as clearly and
with as little emotion as we can. Let me put it this way. If
you and I perform a criminal action, or any other action as
far as that goes, we can be assumed to do it in a state of
complete responsibility. Or, if you like, free choice. If, for
instance, I suddenly assault Mr. Bosanquet with this heavy
inkwell in front of me"—just for an instant that old Adam-
buffoon was leaking out—"you will consider me, and I hope
rightly consider me, fully and completely responsible for that
action. And that is true of you and me in every action, decision, and choice right through our lives." (Benskin had taken
a First in Greats, but he wasn't proposing to puzzle the jury
with any of the textbook questions.) "That," Benskin went
on, "is the normal condition of normal people. It is true of
you and me. It is true of nine hundred and ninety-nine
people out of one thousand in the world round us. There are
some, however, of whom it is not true. You will know this
from your own experience. There are some whom we cannot
consider responsible for all their actions. Through some defect of personality, or what the Act calls abnormality of mind,
they cannot stop performing actions which may be foolish or
may be anti-social or may be hellish. We suggest to you—I am
only saying we suggest because we are certain—that that is the
case with the two young women in the dock. Their actions
have been hellish. I should be the last person to minimize
how appalling and unspeakable they are. But we suggest that
Miss Ross and Miss Pateman were not responsible for these
actions. Clearly we want the help of eminent experts who
will give us their professional judgment about these young
women's personalities and mental conditions. I shall begin
straight away by calling Dr. Adam Cornford."

Adam Cornford. Qualifications. First classes, research fellowship at Trinity, membership of the Royal College of
Physicians, psychiatric training. Few groups had ever had

more academic skills than his family and Margaret's and their Cambridge relatives. Like a number of them, like Margaret herself, he looked abnormally young for his age. He was actually forty-six, within months of Margaret's age. His hair was fair, he was good-looking in a fashion at the same time boyish, affable, and dominating. His voice, as with Austin Davidson, was light and clear.

From the beginning, he spoke unassumingly, without any affectation, but also like a man who hadn't considered the possibility of being outfaced. Yes, he had been asked to examine Miss Ross. He ought to explain that he hadn't been able to make as complete a psychiatric examination as he would have wished. At their first meeting, she wouldn't communicate. We'll come to that later, said Benskin. She did talk to you at later meetings?

To some extent, said Adam Cornford. Then he went on, stitch-and-thread through the questions, Cornford easy but conscientious, Benskin as clever, trying to smudge the qualifications down. Miss Ross was in intelligence well above the average of the population. She was not in any recognized sense psychotic. She had some marked schizoid tendencies, but not to a psychotic extent. A great many people had schizoid tendencies, including a high proportion of the most able and dutiful citizens. Those tendencies were often correlated with obsessive cleanliness and hand-washing, as with Miss Ross. It was important not to be confused (Cornford threw in the aside) by professional jargon: it was useful to psychiatrists, but could mislead others. Schizophrenia was an extreme condition, which Miss Ross was nowhere near, and she was no more likely to be afflicted by it than many young women of her age.

"Nevertheless, Doctor Cornford, you would say her personality is disturbed?"

"Yes, I should say that."

"You would say that she has a personality defect?"

"I've never been entirely happy about the term."

"But, in the sense we often use it in cases such as this, it applies to her?"

"I think I can say yes."

"She has in fact an abnormality of mind?"

"Again, in the sense the law uses that expression, I should say yes."

All of a sudden there was a quiet-toned legal argument. Cornford had been called as a witness to the mental state of Cora Ross: he said that he could do it "in any sort of depth" only if he could discuss her relation with Miss Pateman. By permission of her lawyers, he had been able to conduct professional interviews with Kitty Pateman: who, so Cornford said, had been much more forthcoming than her partner and had given him most of the knowledge he had acquired. Wilson (this had, it was clear, been prearranged) told the judge that he welcomed Dr. Cornford giving any results of his examination of Miss Pateman. The judge asked Bosanquet if he wished to raise an objection. For some moments, Bosanquet hesitated: he wasn't spontaneous, he was hedging on protocol, it was, I thought, his first tactical mistake during the trial.

"I should like to give the defense every opportunity to establish the prisoners' states of mind, Mr. Recorder," said the judge.

"The position is very tangled, my lord."

"Do you really have a serious objection?"

"Perhaps I needn't sustain it against your lordship." Politely, not quite graciously, Bosanquet gave an acceptant smile.

Cornford had listened, he said, to both of them about their relationship. It was intense. Probably the most important relationship in either of their lives. That was certainly so with Miss Ross. She had said, in a later interview, when she was putting up less resistance, that it was all she lived for.

Benskin: I have to put this question, Doctor Cornford.
             This was an abnormal relationship?
Cornford: (harmoniously) I shouldn't choose to call it so
             myself.
Benskin: Why not?
Cornford: I don't like the word "abnormal."
Benskin: Most people know what it means.
Cornford: Most people think they do. But persons in my
             profession learn to doubt it. If you ask me whether
             there was a sexual element in the relation of Miss
             Ross and Miss Pateman, then the answer is, of
             course, yes. If you ask whether there was any
             direct sexual expression, then the answer is also
             yes.

But it was easy to misunderstand some homosexual relations, Cornford said. Persons outside thought the roles were
easily defined. Often they were not. In this case Miss Ross
appeared to be playing the predominantly masculine role.
When that happened, it could throw a weight of guilt upon
the other partner: for Miss Pateman was behaving like a
woman, without the full satisfactions, without the children,
that in her feminine role she was ready to demand. That
might be particularly true of her, because in her family the
women seemed to be expected to be submissively feminine,
more than ordinarily so (was that the total truth? had Cornford had any insight into Mrs. Pateman?). Perhaps that was
why she had sought a relation with a woman—so as to be
feminine, and rebel against males, at one and the same time.
But in doing so, she took upon herself more guilt, more a
sense of loss and strangeness, than Miss Ross.

For Miss Ross had lived an isolated life, without those
intense family pressures. Her father had deserted her mother,
her mother had died young. She had been supported by an
uncle. In adolescence she had been somewhere near, without
being part of, a circle without many constraints. They were

committed to a creed of personal freedom. She had made acquaintances there, but not close contacts. Perhaps she was too indrawn a character, or perhaps she was already finding it necessary to make a masculine compensation.

She had, said Cornford, an unusual degree of immaturity. For example, she preserved every scrap of printed matter— programs of cinema-shows they had attended together, even bus tickets—relating to Miss Pateman. That sometimes happened in an intense relation, but he had never seen it carried to this extent. She had drawers full of objects which Miss Pateman had touched, including handkerchiefs and sheets.

In a different fashion, Miss Pateman showed her own, not quite so unusual, signs of immaturity. She kept up a large collection of dolls, and apparently took one or two with her whenever she left home.

Through the questions and answers—Benskin was skilfully feeding him—Cornford, unflustered, equable, drew his psychological profiles. It sounded, to listeners in court not used to this kind of analysis, strangely abstract, a dimension away from the two women's bodies in the dock. Several times, in the midst of the articulate, lucid replies, I glanced at them. Cora had her head thrown back, almost for the first time in the trial. So far as she was showing emotion, it looked something like pride: but beside her, Kitty was frowning, her face crumpled with anger, her eyes sunk and glittering, as in a patient with a wasting disease, when the skin is bronzing and the eyes sinking in.

Benskin Q, Cornford A. The two young women found each other, they responded to complementary neeeds, they were driven to escape from unsatisfactory environments. Very soon they began to live in a private world. A private world with their own games, rules, fancies. That was very common in many intense relationships. It was part of a good many marriages. It could be a valuable part. The married couple got great exaltation from living in a world made for two. This happened frequently in intense homosexual relationships. Sometimes it gave them unusual depth and strength. But it had dangers, if the relationship was overloaded with guilt. As in the case of Miss Ross and Miss Pateman. When there was a component of bad sex rather than good sex. When the sexual expression was not full or free or sufficient in itself. That needn't happen in a homosexual relation: far more often than not it didn't: very occasionally it did. It was rarer, but not unknown, in heterosexual relations also.

Benskin: Can you explain the dangers you are referring to, Doctor?

Cornford: One of them is sometimes called *folie à deux*. That is, the partners may incite each other to fantasies which neither would have imagined if left to himself or herself.

Benskin: And these fantasies may be transferred into action?

Cornford: In extreme cases, there is a danger that that may happen.

We didn't know, said Cornford, why the gap between fantasy and action—which in most of us is wide and never crossed —should in those extreme cases cease to exist. If we did know that, we should understand more of the impulses behind some criminal actions. If he were going to admit the term "personality defect," he might apply it to those impelled to carry such fantasies into action.

Benskin: That would apply to Miss Ross?

Cornford: That would apply equally to Miss Ross and Miss Pateman.

They had certainly made fantasies about having children in their charge. That was not uncommon in relations like theirs, overshadowed by guilt: especially so when one of the partners was a woman deprived, or a mother *manquée*, like Miss Pateman. There was a strong maternal aspect in her feeling for Miss Ross. In many such relationships, similar fantasies existed. They had played imaginary games of parents and children (that reminded me of the superintendent's homely tone). But it was an extreme case of *folie à deux* that led them to translate that game into a plan—

They had made fantasies about ultimate freedom. They had heard of people who talked about being free from all conventions: they had met people who prided themselves on not obeying any rules. They felt superior because they were breaking the rules themselves: that was not inconsistent with unconscious guilt, in fact it often went hand-in-hand with it. But they excited each other into being freer than anyone round them. They made fantasies about being lords of life and death. They thought of having lives at their mercy. That again was not unknown—particularly in relations with a coloration of what he (Cornford) had previously called "bad sex." But it was very rare for the impulse to be so uncontrollable as to carry over into action.

Guilty relationships, the more so if the guilt was not conscious, had a built-in tendency to lead to further guilt. One had done something which one couldn't thrust away or live with peacefully or reconcile with one's nature: with many people in that position, there grew a violent impulse to do something which one could face even less. Guilty relationships pushed both partners further to the extreme. All guilt had a tendency towards escalation.

That might be true, I was thinking: it was certainly true of some that I had known. A few people, dissatisfied with their lives, tried to reshape them. But there were many more like George, who couldn't take his pleasures innocently, who felt, at least when he was young, attacks of remorse—and yet couldn't help getting more obsessed with the chase of pleasure, never mind the risks, never mind who got hurt. He knew that those who accused him or mourned over him were right: well, to hell with them, he'd give them twice as much to be right about.

The gap between fantasy and action. Those who jumped it—Benskin got back to business—had some serious—in the terms of the Act—abnormality of mind? There was some fencing about definitions. Cornford, so confident in his own line, was intellectually a conscientious and modest man. He wasn't prepared to trust himself in semantics or metaphysics, he said.

Benskin: But if we accept from you that personality defect or abnormality of mind is not an exact term, you would tell us that Miss Ross had features of her personality which drove her into living out her fantasies?

Cornford: I should say that.

Benskin: And that really does mean an abnormality of mind, doesn't it?

Cornford: In the legal sense, I should say yes, without question.

Benskin: Also she couldn't control that part of her personality?

Cornford: I should say that too.

Benskin: That is, while planning and performing those criminal actions, she had far less responsibility for them than a normal person would have?

Cornford: I'm a little worried about the words "normal person."

Benskin: Like most of the people you meet, not as patients, Doctor, but in everyday life. Compared with them, her responsibility was impaired? Very much impaired?

Cornford: Yes, I can say that.

Wilson asked permission if he could put the same questions about Miss Pateman. After Cornford had given an identical reply, Benskin finished by saying:

"I should like you to give a clinical opinion. How well, in your judgment, would Miss Ross's mental state respond to treatment?"

For once Cornford hesitated: but he wasn't hesitating because—although it was true—this was a long-prepared question by the defense.

He said: "I can't be as certain as I should like."

"You told us, you found her difficult to examine?"

"Quite unusually."

"And the first time, she wouldn't cooperate at all?"

"No."

"What happened?"

"She told me she had nothing to say."

"In what terms?"

"Pretty violent ones."

If one had heard her outburst in court, one could imagine the scene. Cornford's handsome face was wearing a faint uncomfortable smile. He was upset as a doctor: he had his share of professional vanity: and perhaps of physical vanity too.

Later meetings had been easier, but it had been hard throughout to get her to participate.

"What sort of indication is that? About her mental state being treatable?"

"Usually it is a bad sign. When a patient hasn't enough insight to cooperate, then the prognosis is bad."

Benskin thanked him and sat down. Wilson did not ask similar questions about Kitty Pateman. Cornford might have said that Kitty Pateman had more insight, and, though the whole tone of his evidence had been in her favor, at least as much as Cora's, that final word could have done her harm.

Bosanquet must have seen the chance to divide the two. But he didn't take it. His duty was to get them both. It was

more than his duty: it was, as I knew by now, what he believed to be right. Further, as he began to cross-examine
Cornford, I gained the impression that beneath the stubborn
phlegm Bosanquet was irritated. Cornford had the knack,
just as Davidson and the older generation of their families
had, of provoking a specific kind of irritation. They were
clever, they were privileged, to outsiders it seemed that they
had found life too easy: they were too sure of their own
enlightenment. Bosanquet hadn't found life at all easy: despite his name, his family was poor, he had been to a north-
country grammar school. He wasn't sure of his own enlightenment or anyone else's, after living in the criminal courts
for thirty years. His first questions were, as usual, paced out
and calm but—I thought my ear was not deceiving me—his
voice was just perceptibly less bland.

Bosanquet: Doctor Cornford, you have been telling us
            about the gap between fantasy and action,
            haven't you?
Cornford: Yes, a little.
Bosanquet: We all have fantasies, you were saying, weren't
            you, of violent actions. That is, we all have
            fantasies of putting someone we dislike out of
            the way?
Cornford: I can't be certain that we all do. But I should
            have thought that it was a common experience.
Bosanquet: Granted. But not many actually do put some-
            one they dislike out of the way?
Cornford: Of course not.
Bosanquet: As you were saying, the gap between fantasy
            and action is not often crossed?
Cornford: Precisely.
Bosanquet: And you suggest, when it is crossed, people are
            driven by forces out of their control; that is,
            they are not responsible?

Cornford: That is rather further than I intended to go.

Bosanquet: Or, at any rate, their responsibility is diminished?

Cornford: In many cases, not necessarily all, yes, their responsibility is diminished.

Bosanquet: I don't think we have heard you make exceptions before. What exceptions would you make?

Cornford: I don't want to go into the nature of responsibility in general. That's too wide to be profitable.

Bosanquet: But you are prepared to talk about responsibility in particular cases? Such as the present one?

Cornford: Yes, I am.

Bosanquet: This case is, even to those of us who have had more experience of such crimes than we care to remember, a singularly horrible one of sadistic killing. You will agree with that?

Cornford: I am afraid so.

Bosanquet: And you have stated your opinion that the two women who performed it were acting with diminished responsibility?

Cornford: Yes. I have said that.

Bosanquet: And you would say exactly the same of any similar case of sadistic killing?

Cornford: I can only talk as a psychiatrist of this particular case about which I have been asked to express a professional opinion.

Bosanquet: But you would be likely to give the same opinion in any comparable case? Of killing just for the sake of killing?

Cornford: I can't answer that question without knowing the psychiatric background of such a case.

Bosanquet: (sternly) I have to ask you as an honest and responsible man. In any such case, where a person or persons had been living in a morbid fantasy world, and then carried out those fantasies in action, you would be likely to say that that was an example of diminished responsibility?

Cornford: (after a pause) I should be likely to say that.

Bosanquet: That is really your professional position?

Cornford: That is going too far. It might, in a good many cases, be my professional position.

Bosanquet: Thank you, Doctor Cornford. I should like to suggest to you that this is a curiously circular position. You are saying that, when people commit certain terrible crimes, they wouldn't do this unless there was no gap between fantasy and action: and that therefore they *ipso facto* are acting with diminished responsibility. That is, the very fact of their committing the crimes implies that they are not responsible. Isn't that what you are saying?

Cornford: It is not so simple.

Bosanquet: Isn't it precisely as simple? Committing the crime is proof, according to your position, that they are not responsible. How else are we to understand you?

Cornford: I'm not prepared to generalize. In certain cases, where I can explore the psychological background, I may be convinced that committing the crime is, in fact, a sign of lack of responsibility.

Bosanquet: Surely that is making it very easy for everyone? Don't you see that, if we accept your view, if we accept that people don't commit crimes when they are responsible, we can dispense with a good deal of our law?

Cornford: It is not for me to talk about the law. I can only talk as a psychiatrist. I can only talk about specific persons whom I have examined.

Bosanquet kept at him, but Cornford was quite unruffled. He was intellectually too sophisticated not to have gone through this argument, and what lay beneath it, in his undergraduate days. But he was in court, he was determined not to leave his home ground. And further, he had no patience with what he regarded as pseudo-problems. Free will, determinism, the tragic condition, all the rest, if there had been any meaning to them we should have found the answers, he thought, long ago. He was as positive-minded as Martin, but in the opposite sense. We should each of us die, but he liked making people better while they were alive. He was a good doctor as well as a psychiatrist: he was benevolent as well as arrogant, and his world was a singularly sunny one.

Through the morning and afternoon (the cross-examination was going on after the lunch-break) I kept thinking that, in private, he was more variegated than this. He had a touch, as he remarked in his harmonious clinical manner, of the manic-depressive. In the box, however, he was more uniform and consistent than anyone we had heard, reminding me of one of those theologians who set out with sharp goodwill to reconcile anything with anything else, every fact of life being as natural as every other, everything being overwhelmingly and all-embracingly natural: reminding me also of a military spokesman giving a battle commentary on what might have seemed to be a disaster (and which actually was), explaining it away and encouraging us about the prospects to come.

His profiles of all our lives, I thought, would have sounded just as sensible, a little sunnier than those lives had been to live. One could imagine how he would have described mine, or Margaret's, or Sheila's, or Roy Calvert's. But one couldn't imagine it all: he had his own insight, lucid, independent. He would have told us things we didn't recognize or admit in ourselves. He would certainly have been more penetrating, and wiser, about George Passant than I had been. If Sheila had been a patient of his, he would have worked his heart out to reconcile her to her existence. He could not have admitted that to her—and at times to the rest of us, though not to him—it was not tolerable to be reconciled. He would have thought that she was resisting treatment: while she would have gone away, not ready to have her vision blurred, even if it meant living in a nightmare.

When he left the box, it was something like a star going off the stage, to be succeeded by a competent character actor. This was the psychiatrist called on behalf of Kitty Pateman, a dark worried man whose name was Kahn, not so eminent in his profession, nothing like so articulate. In fact, for the rest of the afternoon, he told very much the same story and gave the same opinion. A clear case of abnormality of mind and substantial impairment of responsibility. He gave, to me at least, a strong impression of self-searching and difficult honesty. He did produce one new piece of evidence. At eighteen, a year or two before she met Cora Ross, Kitty had had, without her parents knowing, an affair with a married man. The details were not clear, but Dr. Kahn testified that she had suffered a traumatic shock. In his view, this had been one of the causes which had driven her into her relation with Cora Ross.

THIRTY-ONE

TALK ABOUT
FREEDOM

That was the evening when Martin and I were due for the party at Archibald Rose's house. Driving slowly past the thickening hedges, Martin did not want to talk about the trial. Instead, he was asking me, how much had this bit of the county changed since we were boys? Not much, we thought. It was still surprisingly empty. Now and then a harsh red-brick village interrupted the flow of fields. It was a warm day, unusually so for April, windless and pacifying: looking out into the sunshine, one felt anthropocentrically that the pastures, rises, and hollows were pacified too.

Unlike the house to which Vicky had driven me the previous summer, this one lay half hidden, down beside a wood. When we got inside, there were other dissimilarities, or really perhaps only one: there was nothing like so much money about. Children were running round, Rose's wife, a young woman in her twenties, greeted us, noise beat cheerfully out from what in the nineteenth century might have been used as the morning room. This had once been a dower house, and was still called that: it hadn't been much restored: from the morning room, where the party had already begun, the windows gave onto a rose-garden. It was a room which, like the smell of soap in the morning, wiped away angst, or certainly the lawyers seemed to find it so. They were all there, the two defense counsel and their juniors, Clive Bosanquet, the Clerk of Assize, the judge's clerk, various young men who could have been pupils in chambers. Glancing through the crowd, I didn't notice any of the solicitors. Plates of cold chicken, duck, tongue, ham, stood on the side-table, glasses, bottles of red and white wine. The Roses weren't as rich as Vicky's business friends, but they spread themselves on entertaining. Rose's wife, one child holding onto her hand, was cheerful among all the men. The lawyers were walking about, plates and glasses in hand, munching, drinking, and, above all, talking. Martin and I might have been inhibited, as we drove out, from talking about the trial: not so these. For a good part of that evening, they were talking of nothing else. During the war and after, Martin had spent plenty of time with high civil servants: he was used to their extremes of discretion: with Rose's uncle Hector, for instance, one had to know him, literally for years, before he would volunteer an opinion about a colleague (which, in his case, was then not specially favorable). Martin hadn't seen lawyers relaxing in private during a trial. Ted Benskin, more than ever glinting with grim mimicry, came up and asked what we thought of Cornford's evidence. Bosanquet was standing by. Martin, not certain of the atmosphere, feeling his way, gave a non-committal reply.

"We should all like to know," said Ted Benskin. "I'm damned if I do."

A young man (I took him to be a pupil of Bosanquet's, not long down from the university) said: either we are all responsible for our actions, or else no one is.

"I wish," said Bosanquet, gazing at him like a patient troubled ox, "I wish I were as certain about anything as you are about everything."

"But if you were on that jury," said Archibald Rose, more positive than his leader, "you wouldn't follow the Cornford man—"

Bosanquet said, not eagerly but with weight:

"No. I couldn't do that."

"If you were old Jumbo," said someone, "and summing up, what would you tell them?"

"What will old Jumbo tell them, anyway?"

Someone else said: if we're not responsible for abominable actions, then we're not responsible for good ones. If you explain one set away, then you explain the other. It's the ultimate reduction.

Ted Benskin said:

"Anyway, I've got to put my woman in the box. I wish I could get out of it, but I can't. Clive knows that."

Bosanquet gave a professional smile. If Cora Ross didn't give evidence for herself, the inference was, it was because she might appear too sane.

"It's worse for Jamie here," said Benskin. He pointed to Wilson, who was standing a little apart, looking handsome, hard, distracted. After a while, simply because he looked so miserable, I went into a corner and spoke to him alone. None of them was unaffected: but he was more affected than any. At a first glance in court, I had thought him insensitive. It was one of those impressions, like that which Margaret often produced, which were the opposite of the truth.

"Yes, of course I've got to call her," he was telling me. "And I'm afraid she'll destroy anything the psychiatrists say.

"You've met her, haven't you?" he went on. "I'm afraid she'll seem perfectly lucid. Mind you, I think some of these people are dead wrong," he nodded towards the middle of the room. "I accept one hundred per cent what Adam Cornford said. Don't you?"

"You've talked to her yourself?" I asked.

"Of course," he said, set-faced. "When I'm defending people, I always insist on getting to know them personally."

He added:

"It's not pleasant to be tried for anything. Whoever you are and whatever you have done."

Back among the central crowd, I let Ted Benskin refill my glass, while Martin was listening to some of the tougher lawyers. Freedom. Ultimate freedom. They had picked up the phrase from Adam Cornford. They didn't know, as Martin and I did, how once it had been a slogan in George's underground. But they knew that the two women had used it to excite each other. (I could remember a passage from George's diary. "The high meridian of freedom is on us now. In our nucleus of free people, anyway—and sometimes I think in the world." That was written in 1930, and I had read it two years later. I hadn't imagined, any more than he had, what was to come.)

"It's done a lot of harm, propaganda about freedom," said someone.

"Freedom my arse," said the Clerk of Assize with simpler eloquence.

"Keep your heads, now," said Ted Benskin. "I tell you, my children are happier than we ever were. And I think they're better for it."

"We need a bit of order, though," said Bosanquet.

"You're getting old, Clive."

"Order is important." Bosanquet was as unbudgeable as in court. "This country is getting dirtier and sillier under our eyes."

"Happiness isn't everything," said someone. "Perhaps it isn't the first thing."

"I tell you," said Benskin, "if ever there was a time to keep our heads, this is. By and large, there's been more gain than loss."

Other lawyers rounded on him. How could anyone spend his life in the criminal courts, and believe that? Benskin replied that he did spend his life in the criminal courts: that he proposed to go on doing so, and give them all a great deal of trouble: and that he still believed it.

There were a number of strong personalities round us, clashing like snooker balls: Benskin was ready to go on clashing all night. As he stood there, shorter than the rest of us, with his urchin grin, one of the clerks began to speak of "topping" (he was using the criminals' slang for hanging). The 1957 Act was a nonsense. You couldn't have categories of murder. Why was the murder in this case non-capital, whereas if they had shot the child——?

Mrs. Rose, who by this time had put her family to bed, said with a firm young woman's confidence that she was in favor of capital punishment. Good for you, shouted one of the lawyers. So far as I could tell, there was a majority in support— certainly not Wilson, not a couple of the pupils. Benskin hadn't given an opinion. It was Bosanquet who spoke.

"No," he said, as steady as ever. "I've always been against it. And I still am."

Some rough comments flew about, until, in a patch of quietness, a voice said without inflection:

"Even in a case like this?"

"Yes," said Bosanquet. "In a case like this."

Tempers were getting higher—Benskin, who seemed to have a passion for buttling second only to Arnold Shaw's, was uncorking another bottle—when Archibald Rose mentioned that day's appointments to the bench. It might have been a host's tact: he had been disagreeing with his leader: anyway, whether it was a relief or a let-down, it worked. Two new appointments to the high court. One was (I hadn't noticed it in *The Times* that morning) an old acquaintance of mine called Dawson-Hill. Bosanquet, who might reasonably have expected the job himself, was judicious. Benskin, who mightn't, being years too young, wasn't. "We don't want playboys up there," he said. "He's just got there because he's grand, that's all—"

"But why is he all that grand?" I asked. I was genuinely puzzled. It was one of those English mysteries. Everyone agreed that Dawson-Hill was grand or smart or a social asset, whatever you liked to call it. But it was difficult to see why. His origins were similar to Rose's or Wilson's in this room, perhaps a shade better off: nothing like so lofty as those of Mr. Justice Fane, and no one thought him excessively smart.

"That bloody school," said Benskin, meaning Eton.

"He went to our college," said Martin. "And that's about as grand as the University Arms."

"He must have made a mistake that time," said Benskin with a matey grin.

"Anyway, you can't deny it, any of you, no dinner party in London is complete without our dear D-H."

As he drove down the path, away from the party, Martin remarked:

"To say that was a popular appointment would be mildly overstating the case, wouldn't it?"

Gazing over the wheel into the headlight zone, he wore a pulled-down smile. The back-chat about Dawson-Hill had softened the evening for him. He was a man whose emotional memory was long, sometimes obsessive, at least as much as mine. Often he found it harder for his mood to change. For the past three days he hadn't been able to shrug off what he had been listening to. It had lightened him to be in the company of men who could. Driving on, he was asking me about them, half-amused, half-envious. They were less hard-baked than he expected, most of them, weren't they? Yes, I said, criminal lawyers seemed to have become more imaginative since my time. But the jobs mattered, Martin was smiling, they were pretty good at getting back out of the cold? Archibald Rose had been talking to him seriously about when he should take silk. They were pretty good at getting back onto the snakes-and-ladders, weren't they? Of course they were, I said. I nearly added—but didn't, since I was feeling protective towards my brother, as though we were much younger—that I had heard him written off as a worldly man.

Through the dark countryside, odd lights from the wayside cottages, I was thinking, he must know it all. Political memory lasted about a fortnight. Legal memory lasted about a day after a trial. You had to forget in order to get along. It made men more enduring: it also made them more brutal, or at least more callous. One couldn't remember one's own pain (I had already forgotten, most of the time, about my eye), let alone anyone else's. In order to live with suffering, to keep it in the here-and-now in one's own nerves, one had to do as the contemplatives did, meditating night and day upon the Passion: or behave like a Jewish acquaintance of Martin's and mine, who, before he made a speech about the concentration camps, strained his imagination, sent up his blood-pressure, terrified himself, in confronting what, in his own flesh, it would be truly like.

When the car stopped in front of the Gearys' house, Martin got out with me. It was bright moonlight, still very warm. Martin said: "It's a pleasant night. Do you want to go to bed just yet?" We made our way through the kitchen, out into the garden. Upstairs a light flashed on in the Gearys' bedroom, and Denis yelled down, who's there? I shouted back that it was us. Good, Denis replied: should he come and give us a drink? No, we had had enough. Goodnight then, said Denis thankfully. Lock up behind you and don't get cold.

We sat on a wooden seat at the end of the garden. On the lawn in front of us, there were tree-shadows thrown by the moon. It reminded me of gardens in our childhood, when, though the suburb was poor, there was plenty of greenery about. It reminded me of Aunt Milly's garden, and I said:

"After all, it's the twentieth century."

For a moment, Martin was lost, and then he gave a recognizing smile. It had been a phrase of hers which obliterated all threats, laughed off the prospect of war (I could hear her using it in July 1914, when I was eight years old), and incidentally promised the triumph of all her favorite causes, such as world-wide teetotalism. She had used it indomitably till she died.

After all, it was the twentieth century. We had heard others, who had found their hopes blighted and who had reneged on them, call it (as Austin Davidson did, and most of his friends) this dreadful century. Neither Martin nor I was going to know what our children would call it, when they were the age we had reached now.

Martin lit a cigar. The smell was strong in the still air. After a time he said:

"There was a lot of talk about freedom."

"You mean, among the lawyers? Tonight?"

"Not only there."

Not able to stop himself, he had returned to the two women. Ultimate freedom. The limitless talks. More than most people, certainly more than any of the lawyers or spectators at the trial, Martin and I could recreate those talks. For we had heard them, taken part in them. "What is to tie me down, except myself? It is for me to will what I shall accept. Why should I obey conventions which I didn't make?" It was true that, when we had heard them, those declarations were full of hope. George's great cries had nothing Nietzschean about them. They were innocent when they proclaimed that there was a fundamental "I" which could do anything in its freedom. When you started there, though, Martin said, in an even sensible tone, you could go further. Wasn't that what the man Cornford was getting at with his "escalation?"

"Do you believe," asked Martin, "that—if it hadn't been for all hothouse air we used to know about—those two mightn't have done it?"

He spoke without emotion, rationally. The question was pointed for us both. We were gazing out to the moonlit lawn, like passengers on the boatdeck gazing out to sea. Without looking at him, I spoke, just as carefully. It was impossible to prove. Was there ever any single cause of any action, particularly of action such as this? Yes, they must have been affected by the atmosphere round them, yes, they were more likely to go to the extreme in their sexual tastes. Perhaps it made it easier for them to share their fantasies. But between those fantasies, and what they had done, there was still the unimaginable gap. Of course there were influences in the air. But only people like them, predisposed to commit sadistic horrors anyway, would have been played on to the lethal end. If they had not had these influences, there would have been others.

"Your guess is as good as mine," I said. "But I think that wherever they'd been, they'd have done something horrible."

"Are you letting everyone off?" he said.

"I was telling you, I don't know the answer, and nor does anyone else."

"I grant you that," said Martin.

We were not arguing, our voices were very quiet. He said, in a quite different society, more rigid, more controlled, was there a chance that they would never have killed? He answered his own question. Maybe there might be less of these sexual crimes. Perhaps such a society could reduce the likelihood. "But, if you're right," he said, "no one could answer for those two."

He had turned to me, speaking quite gently. He thought that I might be making excuses for us all: yet they were excuses he wanted to accept. He also knew that I was as uncertain as he was.

All of a sudden, his cigar-tip glowing in the shadow, he gave a curious smile. In an instant, when he spoke again, I realized that he had been thinking of a different society. "I have seen the future. And it works." That had been Steffens's phrase, nearly fifty years before. When Martin repeated it, there was in his tone the experience of all that had happened since. He went on, in the same tone, not harsh, not even cynical: "I have seen freedom. And it rots."

In some moods, he might have said it with intention. But not that night; it was one thought out of many, often contradicting each other, that he couldn't keep out of his own mind and could supect in mine. In fact, he took the edge off his last words almost at once. Anyway, he was saying, unabrasively, as though he too had had his memory shortened, as though he were just content with the calm night, there was something in what Ted Benskin had said, wasn't there? Authority might have disappeared, there wasn't much order about, but our children, like Ted's, seemed happy. Not that there had been much paternal authority in our family; Martin was smiling about our father. "Whereas," he said, "young Charles has to put up with you."

Martin knew Charles very well, in his independence, his secret ambitions, and his pride. They were unusually intimate for uncle and nephew. In some aspects, their temperaments were more like each other than either was like mine.

Martin leaned back, giving out an air of bodily comfort: we seemed to have regressed to a peaceful family night.

"By and by," he said, "I meant to have a word with you about my boy"—he never liked calling Pat by his name of protest.

This wasn't altogether casual, I knew as I said yes. He had been holding it back all week.

"You told me once, it must have been getting on for a year ago, about that nice girl. Vicky," Martin went on.

"What about her?"

"I think someone ought to make her realize that it's all off."

"Are you sure?"

"I shouldn't be saying this," said Martin, "unless I really was sure."

"It's for him to do it," I said, both angry and sad. I wanted to say (the old phrase came back, for which we hadn't found a modern version) that it would break her heart.

"He's genuinely tried, I really am sure of that too. I don't often defend him, you know that." Martin, who did not as a rule deceive himself, spoke as though he believed that was the truth. "But he has genuinely tried. She's been hanging on long after there's been nothing there. It's the old story, how tenacious women can be, once they're in love."

"It's absolutely over for him? He won't go back and play her up again?"

"I guarantee he won't."

"He's not above leaving a thread he likes to twitch. When he's got nothing better to do."

"Not this time," said Martin.

"Why are you so sure?"

"I'm afraid that he's made up his mind. Or someone else had made up his mind for him."

Martin was speaking with kindness of Vicky, more than kindness, the sympathy of one who was fond of women and who might have felt his eyes brighten at the sight of this one. But he was also speaking with obscure satisfaction, as though he had news which he couldn't yet share but which, when he forgot everything else, gave him well-being, and, as he sat there beside me in the garden, something like animal content.

THIRTY-TWO

QUALITY OF A LEADER

Back in court the following morning, we were listening to more psychiatrists, as though this were the normal run of our existence and the family conversation in a garden as unmemorable as a dream. These were the psychiatrists called by the prosecution, and we knew in advance that there would be only two. That was planned as the total evidence in rebuttal, and they were as careful and moderate as the defense doctors, without even the occasional wave of Adam Cornford's panache. In the result, though, through the moderate words, they were each saying an absolute no.

Obviously by prearrangement—as I whispered to Martin, sitting at my side in the box—neither Benskin nor Wilson pressed the prison psychiatrist far. Bosanquet had questioned him about his knowledge of the prisoners: yes, he had had them under observation since they were first arrested. He was a man near to retiring age, who had spent his whole career in the prison service: he had seen more criminals, psychotics, psychopaths, than anyone who had come into court, and yet he still spoke with an air of gentle surprise. Miss Ross and Miss Pateman had shown no detectable signs of mental disorder. Some slight abnormality, perhaps, nothing more. Medically, their encephalograms were normal. He had conducted prolonged interviews with Miss Pateman: Miss Ross had, under examination, not usually been willing to discuss her own history. So far as he could judge, they were intelligent.

Miss Pateman had asked for supplies of books from the prison library. Their behavior was not much different, or not different at all, from other prisoners held on serious charges. Miss Pateman exhibited certain anxiety symptoms, including chronic sleeplessness, and her health had caused some concern. Miss Ross had a tic of obsessive hand-washing, but this she admitted was not new or caused by her being in prison. Neither had at any time been willing to speak of the killing. Occasionally Miss Ross went in for something like talking to herself, monologues about what appeared to be imaginary scenes in which she and Miss Pateman figured alone.

"None of this has made you consider that they are not responsible for their actions?"

"No."

"From all your observations, you would not consider that they acted in a state of diminished responsibility?"

"No. I'm afraid I can't give them that."

"After your long experience, you are positive in your opinion?"

"I am."

It was while Benskin, in his first questions, was asking the doctor to say what he meant by a "slight abnormality of mind" that Martin, plucking my sleeve, pointed to the body of the court. Since the morning before, when the medical evidence had begun, the attendance had fallen off, as in a London theater on a Monday night: the gallery was almost empty that morning, and the lower ranges only half-full: but there (he had not been present at the beginning of the session, he must have entered during the Crown examination) sat George. His great head stood out leonine; he was staring at the witness box with glaucous eyes.

I scribbled on the top of a deposition-sheet *We shall have to sit with him this afternoon.* As Martin read that, he nodded, his brow furrowed, all the previous night's relaxation gone.

Benskin was asking, weren't those opinions subjective, wasn't it difficult or impossible even for an expert to be absolutely certain about some mental conditions? Could anyone in the world be certain about some mental conditions? Weren't there features of the doctor's observations, given in his examination-in-chief, which might be regarded as pointers to deep abnormality? Just for an instant, Benskin (who often suffered from the reverse of *l'esprit de l'escalier,* who thought of the bright remark, made it, and then wished he hadn't) was tempted away from his own strategy. He began to ask when "our expert" had last been in touch with professional trends? Had he read—? Benskin shook himself. The jury wouldn't like it, this was an elderly modest man, the sooner he was out of the box the better. The tactic was to reserve the attack for the heavyweight witness. Disciplining himself, anxious at having to waive a marginal chance, Wilson kept to the same line. He asked a few questions about Miss Pateman's state of health, her record of psychosomatic illness, and then let the doctor go.

The heavyweight witness was a Home Office consultant, brought in as a counterpoise to Adam Cornford. When Bosanquet asked, "Is your name Matthew Gough?" that meant nothing to almost everyone in court, and yet, before he answered the question at all, during the instant while he was clambering up to the box, he had been recognized, as no one else had been recognized in the whole trial. The fact was, he appeared often on television, under the anonymous label of psychiatrist, giving his views—articulately, but with as little fuss as Cornford in court—on crime, delinquency, abortion, homosexuality, drugs, race relations, censorship, and the phenomena relating to Unknown Flying Objects. On the television screen he gave the impression of very strong masculinity. In the witness box this impression became more prepotent still. He was dark-haired, vulture-faced, with a nose that dominated his chin. Despite his peculiar kind of

anonymous fame, which brought him some envy, his professional reputation was high. He wasn't such an academic flyer
as Adam Cornford, but his practice—in a country which
didn't support many private psychiatrists—was at least as
large. He was said to have had a powerful and humane influence upon the Home Office criminologists. I had heard also
that he was—this came as a suprise in his profession—a deeply
religious man.

In the box, his manner was kind, not assertive, but with a
flow of feeling underneath. He had, he answered, spent a
good many hours with each of the two women. He had found
Miss Ross—in this he was odd-man-out from the other doctors
—as communicative as Miss Pateman, sometimes more completely so. It was true that occasionally she put up total "resistance": but his judgment was that this was deliberate, and
could be broken when she wanted. Not that he blamed her,
that was one of her protective shields, such as we all had. To
the puzzlement of many, he differed flatly from the others in
his attitude to Cora Ross; he seemed to find her more interesting, or at least more explicable, than Kitty. Miss Ross's
father had left her mother when she was an infant; not much
was known about him, Miss Ross's memory of him was
minimal and her mother was dead: there was some suggestion that he had been and possibly still was (for no one knew
whether he was alive) mentally unstable. He had been an
obsessive gambler, but that might have been the least of it.
Miss Ross had been left alone in her childhood more than
most of us: it had been an unusually lonely bringing-up.
Perhaps that had conduced both to her immaturity (about
which he agreed with Cornford) and to the sadistic fantasies,
which she had certainly been possessed by since an early age:
but that was common to many of us, so common that the
absence was probably more "abnormal" than the presence.

Without emphasis, Bosanquet led Matthew Gough over
the descriptions Cornford had given. It was a good examina-

tion, designed to show that Gough was as unprejudiced as the other men. Yes, Miss Ross had lived on the fringe of a free-living group. If she had been less timid or inhibited, that might have "liberated" her. Actually it had driven her further into herself. It was hurtful to live in a Venusberg without taking part oneself.

As for her relation with Kitty, he had some doubts about Cornford's analysis. He wouldn't dismiss it altogether: but "guilt" used in that fashion was a technical term. He wasn't easy about this concept of the escalation of guilt. Many homosexual or perverse relations were quite free of it. "Bad sex," in Cornford's sense, was very common: it did not often lead to minor violence, let alone to sadistic killing; it was very dangerous, and unjustified, to try to define a simple causation.

Bosanquet: You would not accept then, Dr. Gough, that this relation in any way diminished their responsibility.

Gough: No.

Bosanquet: Or that any other feature of their personal history did so?

Gough: No.

On Kitty Pateman, he said one puzzling thing (which I half-missed, since just at that time the judge's clerk entered our box, giving me his lordship's compliments, and asking if I would care to lunch with him on the coming Monday). He was speaking about her environment: while Cora had grown up solitary, Kitty had lived her whole childhood and youth in a close family life—as intense, I was thinking, as the fug in that stifling sitting room. That was a good environment, said Gough. Stable, settled, affectionate. This must have been his own interpretation of Kitty's account—or had she misled him? Gough was disposed to believe devotedly in family life, I was thinking. It was then that he surprised me. But even in a stable family, he said, there could be wounds—which only the person wounded might know. Was he being massively fair-minded, or had he picked up a clue?

In the specific case of Miss Pateman, it seemed that she might have had an excessive attachment to her father. But he, Gough, could not regard that as a cause of her later actions. That was over-simplifying. Her relation with Miss Ross, her part in the crime—no one could identify the origins.

Bosanquet:	You discussed the crime with her. Doctor?
Gough:	With each of them. On several occasions.
Bosanquet:	Were they willing to describe it?
Gough:	Up to a point.
Bosanquet:	Will you elaborate that, please?
Gough:	They were prepared to describe in detail, almost hour by hour, how they planned to kidnap the boy. They told me about what happened at the cottage and how they brutalized him. But they wouldn't go beyond the Sunday afternoon. Miss Pateman said they had finished punishing him by then. Neither of them at any time gave any account of how they killed him.
Bosanquet:	Were they at this stage still pretending that they hadn't done so?
Gough:	I think not.
Bosanquet:	Why wouldn't they speak of what they did to him after the Sunday afternoon, then?
Gough:	They each said, several times, that they had forgotten.
Bosanquet:	That is, they were concealing it?
Gough:	Again, I think not. I believe it was genuine amnesia.
Bosanquet:	You really mean, they had *forgotten* killing that child?

Gough: It is quite common for someone to forget the
             act of killing.

In his last question, Bosanquet had, quite untypically, inflected his voice. For once he was at a loss. We realized that he
was getting an answer he didn't expect, and one that the
defense might return to (Benskin was muttering to his
junior). In an instant, Bosanquet had recovered himself:
with steady precision he brought out his roll-call of final
questions, and the doctor's replies fell heavily into the
hush.

"It has been suggested by some of your colleagues," said
Bosanquet, "that a sadistic killing of this kind couldn't be
performed by persons in a state of unimpaired responsibility.
You know about that opinion?"

"Yes. I know it very well."

"How do you regard it?"

"I respect it," said Gough. "But I cannot accept it."

"This kind of planned cruelty and killing is no proof of
impaired responsibility, you say? I should like you to make
that clear."

"In my judgment, it is no proof at all."

"People can perpetrate such a crime in a state of normal
responsibility?"

"I believe so. I wish that I could believe otherwise."

He added those last words almost in an aside, dropping his
voice. Very few people in court heard him, or noticed the
sudden lapse from his manner of authority. Later we were
remarking about what had moved him: did he simply feel
that, if to be cruel one had to be deranged, there would be
that much less evil in the world? And he found that thought
consoling, but had to shove it away?

"And that was true of the actions of Miss Pateman and
Miss Ross?"

"I believe so."

"You are certain?"

"Within the limits of my professional knowledge, I am certain."

"You would not agree that either of them had a real abnormality of mind?"

"We must be careful here. In each of them there is a degree of abnormality. But not enough, in the terms of the Act, to impair substantially their mental responsibility."

"Their responsibility was not impaired? Not substantially inpaired?"

"No."

"That is true of neither of them?"

"Of neither of them."

That was the last answer before the lunchtime break. Hurrying out of court in order to catch up with George, we saw him walking away, not looking back. When I called out, it was some time before he heard or stopped. He didn't greet us, but, as we drew near him, stared at us with a gentle, absent-minded, indifferent smile. He gave the impression that he had not noticed we had been present in the court. Instead of insisting on showing us a place to eat, as he had done with Margaret and me on the first morning, he scarcely seemed to know where he was going. He was quite docile and, when Martin suggested having a sandwich in a snack bar, George answered like a good child, yes, that would be nice.

As the three of us sat on backless chairs at the counter, George in the middle, he did not speak much. When he replied to a question, he did not turn his face, so that I could see only his profile. Trying to stir him, I mentioned that, the previous day, the defense doctors had given strong evidence, precisely contrary to what he had just heard.

"Yes, thank you," said George. "I rather assumed that."

He was just as polite when he replied to Martin, who made some conversation on his other side. I brought out the name of Bosanquet, hoping to hear George curse again. He said:

"He's leading for the prosecution, isn't he?"

After that, he sat, elbows on the counter, munching. One

could not tell whether he was daydreaming or lost in his own thoughts: or sitting there, dead blank.

When we led him back into the courtroom, Martin and I exchanged a glance. It was a glance of relief. There was a larger crowd than in the morning, but still the lower tiers of seats were not full, and we sat, George once more between us, three rows back from the solicitors, gazing straight up into the witness box. Then, the judge settled, the court quiet, Gough took his place. At once Benskin was on his feet, neat and small, wearing a polite subdued smile.

"I put it to you, Doctor," he began, "we agree, do we not, that Miss Ross suffers from a defective personality?"

"To an extent, yes."

"You agree that she has a defect of personality, but as a matter of degree you don't think that it brings her within the terms of the Act?"

"I certainly don't consider that she comes within the terms of the Act."

"But it is a matter of degree?"

"In the last resort, yes."

"I suggest, Doctor," Benskin said, "that any opinion in this matter of degree, about defect of personality or of responsi-bility—in the sense we are discussing them in this case—any opinion is in the long run subjective?"

"I am not certain what you mean."

"I think you should be. I mean, that of a number of per-sons as highly qualified as yourself, some might agree with your opinion—and a proportion, possibly a high proportion, certainly wouldn't. Isn't that true?"

"I have said several times," said Gough, showing no flicker of irritation nor of being drawn, "that I can speak only within the limits of my professional judgment."

"And many others, as highly qualified as yourself, would give a different professional judgment?"

"That would be for them to say."

"You would grant that neither you nor anyone else really has any criterion to go on?"

"I agree that we have no exact scientific criterion. These matters wouldn't cost us so much pain if we had."

"That is, your expert opinion is just one opinion among many? You can't claim any more for it than that?"

"I am giving my own professional judgment."

"I put it to you, Doctor," said Benskin, flicking his gown round him as though it were a cape, "that your judgment shows a certain predisposition. That is, you are more unwilling than many of your colleagues to accept that people can suffer from diminished responsibility?"

"I do not know that you are entitled to say that. I repeat, I have given my professional judgment. I am responsible for that, and for no one else's."

"But cannot a professional judgment betray a certain predisposition, Doctor? Or prejudice, as we might say in less lofty circles?"

The judge tapped his pen on the desk. "I think you would do better to avoid words which might suggest that you are imputing motives, Mr. Benskin. You are asking Dr. Gough about his general attitude or predisposition, and that is permissible."

"I am obliged to your lordship." Benskin gave a sharp smile. "Then I put it to you, Doctor, that you have betrayed a certain predisposition? That you never considered it probable that Miss Ross—or Miss Pateman—were not fully responsible? And you ignored important signs which point the other way?

"Will you be more specific?"

"Oh yes. I was intending to. You said in evidence that Miss Ross, and Miss Pateman also, had actually forgotten the act of killing. You said, I think these were your words, that it was genuine amnesia. To most of us that would appear to indicate—very sharply—an abnormal state of mind. Impaired responsibility maybe. But not to you, Doctor?"

Gough said, in a tone not argumentative but sad:

"I couldn't regard it so."

"Why not?"

"I think I also said this condition is surprisingly common."

"Surprisingly common?"

"That is, among people who have done a killing, it is common for them to have forgotten the act."

"Does that signify nothing about them?"

Gough said:

"It is specially common among people who have killed a child. In my experience, I have not once known any case when they could recall the act."

Benskin had gone too far to draw back. Quietly he said:

"Might not that suggest then a special state of mind, or lack of responsibility, in such cases?"

Gough answered:

"I am afraid not. Not in all such cases. In my experience, that would not be true."

Benskin was pertinacious. He knew he had lost a point, and was covering it up. He was cleverer than the doctor, quicker-witted though not as rooted in his own convictions. I thought later, there were not many better counsel for this type of defense.

Hadn't Doctor Gough glossed over, or explained away, all the other indications of abnormal personality? Their fantasy life: the gap between fantasy and action: Benskin was using Cornford's analysis, jabbing the rival case straight at Gough, trying to make him deny it or get involved in psychiatrists' disputes. Fairly soon Benskin won a point back. Gough hadn't become rattled, he seemed to be a man singularly free from self-regard: but he wasn't so good as Benskin, or as Cornford would have been, in seeing a chess-move ahead. In replying to a question about their fantasy-fugues, Gough let drop the observation: "But of course they are both intelligent."

Benskin did not let an instant pass. His eyes flashed at his junior, and he said:

"Ah, now we have it, perhaps. You are predisposed (there was a stress on the word) to believe that persons of adequate intelligence are automatically responsible for their actions?"

"I didn't say that."

"That is, defects of personality don't really matter, abnormalities of mind don't really matter, if people have a reasonable I.Q.?"

"I repeat, I did not say that."

"Doctor, it was the implication of your remark."

"In that case, I shall have to withdraw it."

"I shall have to ask my lord to make a note of what you actually said. And this gets us in a little deeper, Doctor Gough. I suggested, and you didn't like the suggestion, that you were predisposed to think that Miss Ross and Miss Pateman were fully responsible—perhaps because they were intelligent? No, never mind that. I am now asking you, what sort of persons, in what sort of circumstances, would you ever admit not to be fully responsible? Are there any?"

"I have examined some. And given testimony on their behalf."

"And what they were like? Were they imbecile?"

"One or two were," said Gough without hedging. "By no means all."

"And the rest. They were grossly and obviously inferior mentally to the rest of us, were they?"

"Some were. Not all."

"You will see the force of my questions, Doctor. I am not misrepresenting your position—or predisposition—am I? You are extremely reluctant to admit that persons can be afflicted with a lack of responsibility. And can commit criminal actions in that state. You are reluctant to admit that, aren't you?"

"I have given my testimony in favor of some unfortunate people."

"When they are so pitiable that it doesn't need a doctor to tell us so, isn't that so? But you won't give any weight, as your colleagues do, to a history like Miss Ross's and Miss Pateman's—which isn't as obvious but is, I suggest to you, Doctor, precisely as tragic?"

As he delivered that question, Benskin sat down with a shrug, so as to cut off Gough's reply.

Emotions in the court, provoked and stimulated by Benskin, had risen higher. Mrs. Pateman, who was sitting in the row in front, gave me a flickering frightened glance, so like her daughter's. Whispers were audible all round us, and I could see two of the jury muttering together. As soon as Wilson took his turn to cross-examine, the restlessness became more uncomfortable still: but it seemed to be directed against him, as though the women in the dock had—in the fatigued irritable afternoon—been forgotten. To most spectators, Wilson sounded histrionic, hectoring, and false. When he demanded with an angry frown, a vein swelling in his forehead, whether the doctor had deliberately refrained from mentioning Miss Pateman's adolescent breakdown, it rang out like a brassy put-on performance. The truth was, he was sincere, too sincere. Benskin had enjoyed the dialectic and been in control of himself throughout: but Wilson wasn't, he had become involved, in a fashion that actors would have recognized as living the part. Which almost invariably, by one of the perverse paradoxes, gave an effect of sublime artificiality upon the stage: as it did that day in court. Wilson was totally engaged with Kitty. He felt for her and with her. He believed that she had not had a chance, that all her life she had been fated. So he couldn't repress his anger with Matthew Gough, and almost no one perceived that the anger was real. He even rebuked Gough, Gough of all people, for being flippant. It sounded the most stilted and bogus of rebukes: yet Wilson meant it.

Kitty, who had given up her obsessive note-making since the psychiatric evidence began, listened—often sucking in her lips as though she were thirsty—to her counsel's angry voice. I wondered if she realized that he was struggling desperately for her. I wondered if she was cool enough to speculate on what influence he was having. For myself, I guessed—but my judgment was unstable. I kept foreseeing different ends—that he was doing her neither harm nor good.

That was what I told George as the three of us sat at tea, in the same scented women-shoppers' café as I had visited in January, the day that I first heard the physical facts of the case. The central heating was still on, though it must have been 70° outside: the hot perfumed air pressed on us, as George asked me: "Well. What about it?"

I said, things were back where they were. Bosanquet had wasted almost no time at all in re-examining Matthew Gough: he had merely to repeat his opinion. Diminished responsibility? No. Gough, contradicting Cornford, spoke as scrupulously as Cornford himself had spoken the day before.

Now all the evidence was in—except what the two said when they went into the box themselves.

"That won't make much difference," I said.

"Whatever she says, it can't do her any good," George replied. He lifted his eyes and gazed straight at me.

"What are her chances, then?"

After a moment, I answered:

"Things might go either way."

George shook his head.

"No. That's too optimistic. You're going in for wishful thinking now."

I felt—and it was true of Martin also—nothing but astonishment, astonishment with an edge to it, almost sinister, certainly creepy. We had heard George hopeful all his life, often hopeful beyond the limits of reason: now on that afternoon, the trial coming to its close, we heard him reproaching me.

There was another surprise. His manner—one could have said, his mind and body—had totally changed since lunchtime, only three hours before. Then he had been lolling about in a state of hebetude, getting on for catatonic, as helplessly passive as a good many people become in extreme strain. Now he was talking like an active man. In the hot room the sweat was pouring down his cheeks, his breathing was heavy, beneath his eyes the rims were red: but still he had brought out reserves of fire and energy which no one could have thought existed, seeing him not only that morning but for months past, or even years.

"You're being too optimistic," he said, with something like scorn mixed up with authority. "I can't afford to be."

"George," said Martin, "there's nothing you can do."

"Nonsense!" said George, with an angry shout. "The world isn't coming to an end. Other people have got to go on living. Some of them I've been responsible for. I don't know whether I'm any further use. But I've got to go on living. What in God's name is the point of telling me that there's nothing I can do?"

Martin said he meant that there was nothing George could do for his niece.

Still angry, George interrupted him:

"If they send her to a hospital, then I suppose there's a finite possibility that they'll cure her, and I shall have to be on hand. That's obvious to either of you, I should have thought. But as I've told you—" he was speaking to me as though I were a young protégé again—"that's the optimistic plan. It's over-optimistic, and that's being charitable to you. If they send her to jail—"

I said: "I agree, that may happen."

"Of course it may happen," he said harshly. "Well, in that case, I don't expect to be alive when she comes out."

Was he recognizing his state of health? If so, it was the first time I had heard it.

"So I'm afraid that I should have to regard her as dispensable, so far as I am concerned. She won't be out while I'm alive. There are other people I shall have to think about. And what I ought to do myself. That means a second plan."

Neither Martin nor I could tell whether this was make-believe. He was talking with the decision, buoyed up by the thought of action, such as he used in his days of vigor. He was also talking like the leader which—in his own bizarre and self-destructive fashion—he had always been. When he said that Cora was "dispensable" (just as when he did not so much as mention Kitty Pateman's name, since she was no concern of his), he was showing—paradoxically, so it seemed—a flash, perhaps a final one, like the green flash at sunset, of the quality which made people so loyal to him. For a leader of his kind needed gusto, and he had had far more than most men: needed generosity of spirit, and no one that I knew had lavished himself more: needed a touch of paranoia, to make his followers feel protective: needed something else. And the something else, when I was young, I should have called ruthlessness. That was glossing it over. It was really more like an inner chill. By this time, I had seen a number of men whom others without thought, as it were by instinct, looked upon as leaders. Some in prominent places: one or two, like George, in obscurity and the underground. Of these leaders, a few, not all, attracted loyalty, sometimes fanatical loyalty, as George did: and they were alike in only one thing, that they all possessed this inner chill. It was the others, who were warm inside, more plastic and more involved, who got deserted or betrayed.

THIRTY-THREE

REVENANT

On the Saturday morning in our drawing room, Margaret was asking me about my father. A beam of sunlight edged through the window behind me, irradiated half a picture on the far wall, a patch of fluorescent blue. It was all easy and peace-making. Yet it felt unfamiliar, that I wasn't catching the bus down to the Assize Hall.

I had returned very late the night before, and we hadn't talked much. Yes, I told her now, Martin and I had been to visit the old man (actually, we had gone straight from that tea-time with George). He had complained vaguely that he wasn't "quite A-1": but, when we asked what was the matter, he either put us off or didn't know, saying that "they" were looking after him nicely. "They" appeared to consist of the doctor and a district visitor who came in twice a week. My father spoke of her with enthusiasm. "She goes round all the old people who haven't got anyone to look after them," he said, expressing mild incredulity at the social services. We had told him that it was his own fault that he hadn't someone to look after him, it was his own mulelike obstinacy. But he scented danger, with an old man's cunning, he suspected that we were plotting to drag him away. He wouldn't budge. "I should curl up my toes if anyone shifted me," he said. His morale seemed to be high. Incidentally, he had with fair consistency called Martin and me by each other's names: but he had done that in our childhood, he was no more senile now than when I last saw him.

Margaret gave a faint smile, preoccupied as to whether we ought to leave him there, how far had we the right to interfere.

Just then, Charles, still on holiday, entered in a new dressing-gown, smelling of shaving-soap. Over the last year he had suddenly become careful of his appearance. He said hallo, looking at me with scrutinizing eyes. He didn't remind me of his warning, but I hadn't any doubt that he had searched the papers each day. And his forecasts had proved not so far from the truth. There had been references to my presence at the trial, some just news, a few malicious. An enterprising journalist had done some research on my connection with George Passant. He had even latched onto Gough's casual comment the day before. "Venusberg trial—Lewis Eliot again with boyhood friends."

Not waiting for Charles to be tactful, I asked if he had noticed that.

He nodded.

"Well?" he said.

"One gets a bit tired of it. But still—"

Margaret gave a curse. I didn't tell him, but he certainly knew that it was true for me, that no one I had known, including the hardest political operators, ever quite got used to it. Instead I said (using reflectiveness to deny the here-and-now, the little sting) that this kind of comment, the mass media's treatment of private lives, had become far more reckless in my own lifetime.

Charles was not much impressed. This was the climate which he had grown up in and took for granted.

"Have you done any good?" he asked.

I thought of George at tea the day before.

"Very little," I said. "Probably none at all."

Charles broke into a broad smile. "Anyway, we've got to give you credit for honesty, haven't we?" He teased me, with the repetitive family gibes. Margaret was laughing, relieved that we hadn't reverted to our quarrel. Why did I insist on getting into trouble? Even when I wasn't needed? Fair comment, I said, thinking of George again.

I hadn't seen Charles at all the night before, and he hadn't had a chance to inquire about the trial itself. At last he did so. What was it really like?

I looked at them both. I repeated what I had said to Margaret, just before going to sleep.

"It's unspeakable." Then I added: "No, that's foolish, we've been speaking about it all the week. But not been able to imagine it."

I didn't want to talk to him as I had done to Martin: perhaps I should have been freer if it hadn't been for the sexual heaviness that hung over it all. True, there wasn't much, in verbal terms, that I could tell Charles: he had listened for years to people whose language wasn't restrained, and I was sure the same was true with him and his friends. But together we didn't talk like that. There was a reticence, a father-and-son reticence, on his side as well as mine, when it came to the brute facts, above all the brute facts of this case.

So, I said, it had been appalling to listen to. Like an aeroplane journey that was going wrong: stretches of tedium, then the moments when one didn't want to believe one's ears. I couldn't get it out of my experience, I told him.

"I haven't had as much of it as you have," said Margaret. "But that's true—" She turned to Charles.

Once more, as with Martin, I was remembering Auschwitz. To these two, I did not need to say much more than the name.

A couple of summers before, when the three of us had been traveling in Eastern Europe, I had left Margaret and Charles in Krakow, and had driven off to the camp with an Australian acquaintance. We had walked through the museum, the neat streets, the cells, in silence. It was a scorching August day, under the wide cloudless Central European sky. At last we came to the end, and were walking back to the car. My acquaintance, who hadn't spoken for long enough, said:

"It's a bastard, being a human being."

Often this last week, I'd felt like that, I said to Charles. I was certain that his uncle Martin had as well.

Charles was silent, regarding me with an expression that was grave, detached, and unfamiliar.

After a few moments, I went on:

"Did you know," I said, "that there was a medieval heresy which believed that *this* is hell? That is, what we're living in, here and now. Well, they may have had a point."

Charles gazed at me with the same expression. Almost imperceptibly, he shook his head. Then in a hurry, as though anxious not to argue, trying to climb back upon the plane of banter, he asked me, why was it that unbelievers always knew more about theological doctrine than anyone else? However had I acquired that singular fact? He was being articulate, sharp-witted, smiling, determined not to become serious himself again, nor to let me be so.

Afer tea the following afternoon, when I was in one of the back rooms, Charles called out that there was someone for me on the telephone.

Who was it? He wouldn't say. Soft voice, Charles added— slight accent, north country perhaps.

I went into the hall, picked up the receiver, asked who was there, and heard:

"This is Jack."

"Jack who?"

"The one you've known longest."

"Sorry," I said, unwilling to play guessing games.

"It's Jack Cotery," came the voice, soft, reproachful. "Are you free, Lewis? I do want to see you."

I was extremely busy, I said. All that night. I shouldn't be at home the following day.

"It is important, it really is. I shan't take half an hour."
Jack's tone was unputoffable, wheedling, unashamed, just as
it used to be.

"I don't know when."

"Only half an hour. I promise."

I repeated, I was busy all that night.

"You're alone now, aren't you? I'll just come and go."

He had hung up before I could reply. When I rejoined
Charles, he asked who had been speaking. A figure from the
past, I said. A fairly disreputable figure. What did he want?
"I assume," I said, "that he's trying to borrow money." Why
hadn't I stopped him? Charles inquired, when he discovered
that Jack Cotery was coming round. Irritably I shook my
head, and went off to assemble a tray of drinks, reminded of
how—with pleasure—I had done the same for George that
evening the previous December.

As soon as I heard the doorbell ring, I went and opened
the door myself.

"Hello, Lewis," breathed Jack Cotery confidentially.

I had seen him last about ten years before. He was my own
age to the month: we had been in the same form at school.
But he was more time-ravaged than anyone I knew. As a
young man, his black hair was glossy, his eyes were lustrous,
he had a strong pillar of a neck: he had only to walk along
the street to get appraising glances from women, to the envy
of the rest of us. Now the hair was gone, the face not so much
old as unrecognizably lined, still a clown's face but as though
the clown hadn't put his make-up on. Even his carriage,
which used to have the ease of someone who lived on good
terms with his muscles, had lost its spring. But his glance was
still humorous, giving the impression that he was making fun
of me—and of himself.

I led the way into the study, put him in the chair where
George had sat when he first broke the news.

"Will you have a drink?" I said.

"Now, Lewis." He spoke with reproach. "You ought to know that I never was a drinking man."

In fact, that had been true. "I'm a teetotaller nowadays, actually," said Jack, as though it were a private joke. "Also a vegetarian. It's rather interesting."

"Is it?" I said. I turned to the whisky bottle. "Well, do you mind if I do?"

"So long as you take care of yourself."

Sitting at the desk, glass in front of me, I looked across at his big wide-open eyes.

"Shall we get down to business?" I said. "There isn't much time, I'm afraid—"

"Why are you so anxious to get rid of me, Lewis?"

"I am pretty tied up—"

"No, but you are anxious to get rid of me, aren't you?"

He was laughing, without either rancor or shame. I couldn't keep back some sort of a smile.

"Anyway," I said, "is there anything I can do for you?"

"That isn't the right question, Lewis." Once more, he seemed both earnest and secretly amused.

"What do you mean?"

"The right question is this: is there anything *I* can do for *you?*"

Once I had had some practice in learning when he was being sincere or putting on an act: although, often, he could be doing both at once, taking in himself as well as me. It was a long while since I had met anyone so labile, and I was at a loss.

"I've been following this horrible case, you see," Jack went on. "I'm very sorry you are mixed up in that."

"As a spectator."

"No. Lewis, not quite that. Remember, I knew you a long time ago. I understand why you had to go—"

"Do you?"

"I think I do. Trust your old friend." He put a finger to the side of his nose, in a gesture reminiscent of Azik Schiff talking of millions or of Jack himself, in old days, thinking how to make a quick pound. "You weren't able to forget how George used to shout at us at midnight outside the jail. And we used to walk down the middle of the tramlines, later on at night, when the streets were empty, dreaming about a wonderful future. So when the future came, and it turned out to be this, you thought you had to stand by George. You weren't going to let him sit there alone, were you?"

"That's rather too simple," I said. Also too sentimental, I was thinking: had he always made life sound softer than it was?

"You see, Lewis, you're a kind man." That was more sentimental. I wanted to stop him, but he went on: "I've heard people say all kinds of things about you. Often they hate you, don't they? But they don't realize how kind you are. Or perhaps they do, and it makes them hate you more."

"I wish I could believe you," I said. "But I don't. I strongly suspect that, if I'd never existed, no one would have been a penny the worse."

"Nonsense, man. I'm an absolute failure, aren't I?"

"I don't know what that means."

"I do. I'm no use, if you put me up against the people you live among now. But I can see some things that they wouldn't see if they lived to be a thousand. Perhaps because I've been a failure. I can see one or two things about you. I tell you this. You've lived a more Christian life than most of the Christians I know."

It was my turn to say nonsense, more honestly than he had done. It was an astonishing statement, ludicrous in its own right, and also because Jack, when I knew him, took about as much account of Christianity as he did of Hamiltonian algebra.

"Oddly enough," he said, "that's what I came to tell you. Just that."

It was possible—I was still suspicious, but of course I wanted to believe—that he was not pretending and had come for nothing else. A little later I discovered that he had made a special journey from Manchester—"on the chance of catching you." It would have been more sensible, I said, to have rung up or written. "You know," said Jack, "I always did like a bit of surprise."

Perhaps it had been nothing but an impulse. But he had come to hearten me. Once or twice, when we were young men, he had taken time off from his chicanery or amours, to try to find me a love affair which would make me happier. The tone was the same, he liked bringing me comfort. That afternoon, I might have wished that the comfort was harder and nearer the truth—but none of us gets enough of it, we are grateful for it, whatever its quality, when it comes.

In his soft and modulated voice, Jack was talking, sadly, not nostalgically, about our early days. "No, Lewis, we all did each other harm, I'm sure we did. I was a bad influence on George, I know I was. And he wasn't any good for me. Of course, you didn't see the worst of it. But you suffered from it too, clearly you did."

He said, eyes wide-open, as when he was playing some obscure trick:

"You know, I began to realize something, not so long ago. I thought—look here, I shouldn't like to die, after the life I've lived."

After a moment, I mentioned that, the summer before, I had met his first wife, Olive. He said:

"Would you believe it, I've almost forgotten her."

I knew that he had married again, and asked about it.

"No," said Jack. "I extricated myself, some time ago."

Just for an instant, his remorseful expression had broken, and he gave a smile that I had often seen—shameless, impudent, defiant. Or it might have been an imitation of that smile.

"Have you got anyone now?"

"I've given all that up."

"How long for?"

"Absolutely and completely," said Jack. "For good and all. You see, I've taken to a different sort of life."

He explained that nowadays he spent much of his spare time in church. He explained it with the enthusiasm that once he used to spend on reducing all human aspirations down to the sexual act—and with the same humorous twitch, as though there was someone behind his shoulder laughing at him. How genuine was he? Sometimes one could indulge one's suspiciousness too much. Would there be another twist, was this the end? Of that I couldn't guess, I didn't believe anyone would know the answer until he was dead.

"Let's be honest," said Jack. "I didn't just come to tell you you'd lived a Christian life. There's something else—"

Right at the beginning, I had been counting on a double purpose. Now it came, and the laugh was against me.

"I think you ought to be a Christian—in faith as well as works. I really do."

He asked, had he over-run his time? Could he have a few more minutes? I hadn't expected that afternoon to end with Jack expending all his emotion trying to convert me. The old arguments flicked back and forth. The old theological questions. Then Jack said, you'd find it a strength, Lewis. You'd find it made this hideous business easier to take. Strangely, that was what I had said myself to Superintendent Maxwell. But now, as I replied to Jack, I did not believe it. Faith did not mean that one acquiesced so quietly, did it? Surely it was deeper than that? Believers had to confront these extremist questions: nothing I had read of them suggested that they were any more reconciled. I should have respected them less if they had been.

At last Jack went away. I offered to introduce him to my wife and son, but he reminded me, with a not-quite-saintly grin, how pressed I was for time.

When I joined Charles in the drawing room, he said:

"Well, how much did he want to borrow?"

"As a matter of fact," I said, "the subject didn't crop up."

THIRTY-FOUR

REFLECTIONS OF
AN OLD MAN

Going back to the trial by an early train, I stood outside the Assize Hall, not certain whether the others would arrive. Then Martin's car drew up: he said good-morning as he had done for days past, as though we had been pulled back and couldn't be anywhere else. I had seen politicians meet in the yard like that during a time of crisis, glad that there was someone else who couldn't escape, making a kind of secret enclave for themselves. It was a beautiful morning. Close by, the church clock struck the quarter. A few minutes later, as we were getting ready to go into court, we saw George walking towards us, walking very slowly in the hazy sunshine.

As he came up the slope, he said:

"Anyway, it won't be long now."

I replied:

"Not very long."

"It ought to be over by tomorrow night." George seemed to be entirely preoccupied by the timetable. When I mentioned that, later in the morning, I should have to leave them and sit in the official box, since I was lunching with the judge, he said: "Oh, are you." He wouldn't have been less interested if I had said that I was lunching with the Archbishop of Canterbury. He went on ticking off the last stages of the trial—"I don't see," he said, "how they can keep it going beyond tomorrow."

In the courtroom, more crammed that morning than during the psychiatrists' evidence, Cora Ross went into the box. She stood there, hair shining, shoulders high and square, as she faced Benskin. She had taken on an expression which had something of the nature both of a frown and a superior smile: her eyes did not meet her counsel's but (as I recalled from the conversation in prison) were cast sidelong, this time in the direction of Kitty. It was clear from the beginning that Benskin had one of the most difficult jobs. He didn't want her to appear too balanced or articulate: on the other hand, the jury mustn't have any suspicion that she had been rehearsed in seeming abnormal or was herself deliberately putting it on. There had already been whispers that her outburst in court the previous week was a clever piece of acting. And, of course, he was loaded with an intrinsic difficulty. Even if he had been trying to prove that she was mad, not irresponsible, how did sensible laymen expect mad persons to answer or behave? Had they ever seen anyone within hours of a psychotic suicide? Looking, talking, seeming, perhaps feeling, more like themselves than they would ever have believed?

Benskin was much too shrewd not to have worked this out. In fact, he wasn't going to give her the opportunity to talk much. Not that he need have been so cautious, for she was responding as little, as deadeningly, as she had done to me. She sounded as though she were utterly remote, or perhaps more exactly as though there was nothing going on within her mind. Light, practiced, neutral questions—not friendly, not indulgent, for Benskin had chosen his tone—made no change in her expression: each was answered by the one word, no.

He had begun straightaway upon the killing. Did she now remember any more about it? No. Had she anything to say about it? No. Could she describe the events of the Sunday evening? No.

"You don't deny, Miss Ross, that you were associated with the killing?"

"What's the use?"

But she still had nothing to say of how it happened? No. Or when? No. She had no memory of it? No. Had she ever had blocks of memory before? She didn't know. Did she remember meeting Miss Pateman for the first time? Yes. When? At the ———— Café, in a crowd. (I didn't glance at George: it was one of his favorite rendezvous.) Did she remember setting up house with Miss Pateman? Yes. When? November 17, 1961. The answer came out fast, mechanically. But she had no memory of the boy's death? No.

"I have to press you, Miss Ross. Has it quite vanished?"

Cora gave something like a smile, stormy, contemptuous. Her reply wasn't immediate.

"No," she said.

"You mean, you have some recollection?"

"Something happened."

"Can you say anything more definite?"

"No."

He went on; when she said "something happened," what did that mean? She returned to saying no. It might have been, so people thought afterwards, that she had given away more than she intended: or, as Matthew Gough believed, that there was only a vague sense of tumult, of whirling noise, remaining to her, something like the last conscious memory of a drunken night.

But she didn't deny, Benskin asked, that there had been planning to get the boy out to the cottage? No. The planning had taken place, she hadn't forgotten it? No. Then what had she to say about that?

"When you set out to do something, you do it."

"Someone must have thought about it for quite a time beforehand?"

She answered, head thrown back:

"I thought about it."

"Can you tell us how you discussed it with Miss Pateman?"

"No."

When he repeated some versions of this question, she merely answered no. Here I at least was sure that this was a willed response: she could have told it all if she chose.

"Well. What state of mind were you in, can you tell us that?"

"No."

"Come, Miss Ross, you must realize that you have done terrible things. Do you realize that?"

She stared to one side of him, face fixed, like the figurehead on an old sailing ship.

"If you had heard of anyone else doing such things, you would have thought they were atrocious beyond words. Isn't that so?"

Again she stared past him.

"So can't you tell us anything about your state of mind, say the fortnight before?"

"No."

"You said, a moment ago, you set out to do something. Meaning those atrocious things. Why did you set out—"

She said:

"I suppose you get carried away."

Benskin said:

"Miss Ross, we really want to understand. Can't you give us an idea what you were thinking about when you were making those plans?"

"I thought about the plans."

"But there must have been more you were thinking about?"

"That's as may be."

"Can't you give us an idea?"

"No."

Benskin said:

"Miss Ross, aren't you sorry for what you've done?"

Cora Ross replied, not looking directly at Kitty:

"I'm sorry that I dragged her into it."

Suddenly, as though on impulse, Benskin nodded, sat down, examination over. Some lawyers thought later that he ought to have persevered: to me, sitting in the silent baffled courtroom, his judgment seemed good. On his feet, Bosanquet asked his first question in a voice as always quiet, but not so punctiliously unemotional:

"Miss Ross, you have just told my learned friend that you are sorry to have involved Miss Pateman. Is that all you are sorry for?"

"I'm sorry I dragged her in."

"You know perfectly well that you have done what have just been called atrocious things. Aren't you sorry for that?"

No answer.

"You mustn't pretend, Miss Ross. You must have some remorse. Are you pretending not to understand?"

"You can think what you like."

Bosanquet was, of course, meeting precisely the opposite difficulty to her own counsel's. If he drew dead responses like that last one, or any response which seemed outside human sympathy, then he might, paradoxically, be helping her. Momentarily he had himself been shocked. With professional self-control, he started again, quite calmly.

(Remorse. I was distracted into thinking of genuine remorse. Whenever I had met it, in myself or anyone else, there had always been an element of fear. Fear perhaps of one's own judgment of what one had done: often, far more often, of the judgment of others. I wondered if this woman was one of those, and they existed, who were incapable of fear.)

Carefully, on his new tack, Bosanquet was setting out to domesticate her life. She had lived with her mother until she died? Yes. She had had a normal childhood? She had gone to school like everyone else? She had never been under medical inspection? She had not been in any sort of trouble? She had done satisfactory work at school, she had been good at games? No one treated her as different from anyone else?

"In fact," said Bosanquet, "no one had any reason to consider that you were?"

"I was." For once she had raised her voice.

Bosanquet passed over that answer, repeating that no one treated her differently—?

"I'll answer for myself!" It was an angry shout, like the tirade to the court the week before, mysterious-sounding. She might have been giving out a message—or just stating how, to her own self, she was unique.

With a smooth and placid transition, Bosanquet moved on to her ménage with Miss Pateman. They were living very comfortably when they pooled their resources, weren't they? Their incomes added together came to something like £1,600, didn't they? They paid Miss Pateman's father £200 for their room? It was an eminently practicable and well-thought-out arrangement, their joint establishment, wasn't it?

It was at this stage that I made my way out of court and round to the official box, so that I missed a set of questions and answers. From the court record, when I read it later, Bosanquet was making it clear that their domestic planning was far-sighted and full of common-sense. There were exchanges about insurance policies and savings. Altogether they had been more competent than most young married couples, and as much anticipating that their relation would last forever.

When I slipped into my place in the box, Bosanquet had just finished asking:

"So you managed to live a pleasant leisurely life, didn't you?"

"We did our jobs."

"But you had plenty of leisure outside office hours?"

"I suppose so."

"What did you do with your leisure?"

"The usual things."

"Did you read much?"

"She was the reading one."

As Bosanquet tried to discover what Cora Ross read, the answer seemed to be nothing. Certainly no books, scarcely a newspaper. Music she listened to, for hours on end; all kinds of music, apparently, pop, jazz, classical. Television, often the whole evening through. Films of any kind, but more often on television in their room (they had another set at Rose Cottage) than by going to a cinema. Yes, sometimes they went to a cinema: no special kind of film, they went to see stars that they "liked"—a word which had a sexual aura round it.

Music, the screen. She had been drenched and saturated with sound. No printed words at all: or as little as one could manage with in a literate society. In an earlier age, would she have wanted to learn from books?

"You have everything sensibly organized, Miss Ross," said Bosanquet in his level tone. "Then you thought you might do a little sensible organization about—something else?"

"No."

"Think a moment. What you did to this boy, beginning with a kidnapping, that required a good deal of organization?"

"No."

"It required just as much careful thinking as the way you planned your household accounts?"

"No."

"We know already how you sensibly allocated your combined income. A certain proportion to the drinks bill—"

"She didn't drink."

"No, you were a careful household. But you gave exactly the same sort of attention when you decided to make away with a harmless child?"

Sensible, careful, organized: Bosanquet was reiterating the words, letting no one forget how competent they were. It made an extraordinary picture, just because it was so commonplace: the two of them coming back to their room, Cora allowing herself a couple of evening drinks (a bottle of whisky lasted them a fortnight). It made too extraordinary a picture, for there were many in court, uneasy, disturbed, feeling that their life together, even well before the crime, couldn't have been quite like that. Yet at times it might or must have been.

"You did a great deal of careful planning—when you decided it was a good idea to make away with a harmless child?"

"No."

"Of course you did. You have told your own counsel so. We have all heard how you picked on that child weeks beforehand. You organized the whole operation just as thoughtfully as you did your household, isn't that so?"

"No."

"Do you deny that you planned it?"

She raised her head. "I thought about one or two things."

"You planned it step by step?"

No answer.

"Every inch along the way?"

With a kind of scorn or irritation, she said: "It wasn't like that."

"You planned it very lucidly, Miss Ross. It's not for me to find an answer to why you did so. Were you getting bored with everything else in your life together?"

"No." Her face was convulsed.

"Were you ready for anything with a new thrill?"

"No."

"Well then. What put this abominable idea into your head?"

For some instants it seemed that she was not going to answer. Then, as though she were wilfully getting back into the groove, or as though it were an answer prepared beforehand, she repeated what she had said to Benskin:

"You get carried away."

Bosanquet, looking up at her, said again that it was not for him to find an answer. He returned to the planning, extricating each logistic point, sounding as temperate as though it were a military analysis. By this time—perhaps it was a delayed reaction—Cora had lost her temper. Her monosyllables were shouted, her expression changed from being wild and riven to something like smooth with hate. Then she sank back into sullenness, but her fury was still smoldering. When he finished with her, her eyes for once followed him: face pallid, minatory, deadened.

Benskin half-rose, then thought better of it, and left that impression of her, standing there.

There was not time to begin Kitty's examination before lunch. After the judge's procession had departed, I went out, and found his clerk waiting for me. A car was ready to drive me to the judge's lodgings, in the old County Rooms in the middle of town: he would be following at once with another guest.

In fact, as I walked into his dining room, white-paneled, perhaps later than Georgian but light and lively on the eye, the judge was hallooing cheerfully behind me. "We caught you up, you see," said Mr. Justice Fane.

Do you two know each other? he was saying. Yes, we did, for his other guest was Frederick Hargrave, whom I kept on meeting on the university Court. For an instant I was surprised to see him there, he looked so quiet, unassuming, insignificant beside the judge's bulk: I had to recall that Hargrave (whose grandfather and father had lived in the town like simple Quaker businessmen) was a deputy lieutenant of the county and not unused to entertaining circuit judges.

Still wearing his red gown—he had taken off only his wig—

Mr. Justice Fane stood between us, as tall as I was, weighing two or three stone more, very heavily boned and muscled, offering us drinks. No, that's no use to you, he corrected himself, speaking to Hargrave: his manners were just as cordial and attentive out of court as in. So Hargrave was equipped with ginger-beer, while the judge helped me to a whisky and himself to a substantial gin and tonic.

"It's very good of you both to have luncheon with me today," he said. "I don't like being lonely here, you know."

As we stood up, there was some talk of common acquaintances: but the judge, like the barristers at Rose's house, couldn't keep from living in the trial.

"You haven't listened to much of it, have you?" he said to Hargrave, who replied that he had attended one afternoon.

"It can't have been a pleasant experience for you, Eliot," said the judge.

"Terrible," said Hargrave in a gentler tone.

"I think it's as terrible as anything I've seen," the judge added. In a moment, he went on, his Punchlike nose drawn down:

"I don't know what you think. All this talk of responsibility. We are responsible for our actions, aren't we? I'm just deciding whether to have another gin and tonic. Eliot, if you give me five pounds on condition that I don't have one, I'm perfectly capable of deciding against. That's my responsibility, isn't it? As you don't show any inclination to make the offer, then I shall, with equal responsibility, decide to have another one. And I shall bring it to the table, because it's time we started to eat."

That was a Johnsonian method of dealing with metaphysics, I thought as we sat down, one on each side of the massive old man. The long table stretched away from us, polished wood shining in the airy elegant room.

The judge told us he had ordered a light meal, soup, fish, cheese. He and I were to split a bottle of white burgundy. He was brooding, he was drawn back—as obsessively magnetized as any of us, despite his professional lifetime—to the morning in the court.

"She tried to be loyal, didn't she?" he said to me.

I said yes.

The judge explained to Hargrave who had not been present:

"The Ross girl was loyal to her friend this morning. She tried to take all the blame she could."

"I'm glad to hear that," said Hargrave.

"I don't believe her," said the judge.

"I meant, it shows there's some good in her, after all," Hargrave insisted, at the same time diffident and firm.

"I don't believe that she was so much in charge." The old man was wrapped in his thoughts. Then he looked up, eyes bright, hooded, inquiring.

"Do you know what went through my mind, when I was listening to that young woman in the box? And remember, I've been at this business not quite but almost since you two were born. I couldn't help pitying anyone in her position. You can't help it. But ought you to pity her? Think of what she'd done. She'd helped get hold of that little boy. I expect they promised him a treat. And they took him out there and tortured him. That was bad enough, but there was something else. He must have been frightened as none of us has ever been frightened, just remind yourself what it was like your first days at prep school. You were eight years old and you'd got some brutes pestering you and you didn't see any end to it. Well, that poor child must have gone through that a million times worse. All I hope is that he didn't realize that they meant to kill him. I don't know about you, Eliot, but I can't imagine what he went through. Perhaps it's a mercy not to have enough imagination. So I ask myself, ought you to pity her?"

"I think you ought," said Hargrave.

"Do you?"

"I think we shall all need pity, Judge," Hargrave went on with his surprising firmness, "when it comes to the end."

"Ah, you're a reformer, you believe in redemption. Are you a reformer, Eliot?"

"Of course he is." I had never seen Hargrave so assertive. He spoke across to me: "You're on the side of the poor, you always have been—"

"That's different," I replied. "I'm afraid I'm not a reformer in your sense."

"You don't believe," the judge asked Hargrave, "that any human being is beyond hope, do you?"

"Certainly not."

"You should look at those two. And I tell you, the Ross girl isn't the worst of them. I've got a suspicion that the little one is a fiend out of hell."

That was startling. Not because no one had said it before: the old man knew no more about them than anyone else, he might not be right. But he hadn't said it with loathing, more with a kind of resignation. It was that which shook both Hargrave and me, as we gazed at him, forking away at his sole, looking like a saddened eagle.

In time Hargrave recovered himself.

"You're asking me to believe in evil," he said.

"Don't you?"

(Listening to Hargrave, I wasn't comfortable. Yet he didn't obtrude his faith: was I imagining a strand of complacency which wasn't there?)

"No. We've all seen horrible happenings in our time, we've seen horrible happenings here. But, you know, in the future people are going to do better than we have done. It wouldn't be easy to go on, would it, if one wasn't sure of that?"

The judge didn't wish to argue. Perhaps he too was uncomfortable with faith, or too considerate to disturb it. He may have known that Hargrave had done more practical good than most men, more than Mr. Justice Fane and I could have done in several lifetimes.

"I don't know that I believe in evil," he contented himself by saying. "But I certainly believe in evil people."

He cut himself a very large hunk of the local cheese. He had made a heartier lunch than Hargrave and I put together.

"It'll soon be over now," he said, like an echo of George Passant earlier that morning and sounding for the first time like a tired and aged man. Then he had a businesslike thought. "Unless Clive Bosanquet makes an even longer speech than usual. Clive is a good chap, but he will insist on not leaving any stone unturned. Within these four walls—if in any doubt he thinks it better to turn them back again. And that does take up a remarkable amount of time, you know."

With the comfort of habit, he was mapping out the progress of the trial. His own summing-up wouldn't be over-long, he assured us. Nevertheless, he was tired, and it needed all his friendliness and good manners to prevent him from letting the meal end in silence.

THIRTY-FIVE

THE LIMIT

That afternoon, with Kitty Pateman in the witness box, was for me both the most mystifying and most oppressive of the trial. The courtroom was as packed as it had been on the first two days: the three of us were sitting in the body of the court, with the Pateman family (Mr. Pateman had reappeared that afternoon, and Dick attended for the first time) a few yards away, both men rigidly upright, the back of Mr. Pateman's head running straight down into his collar. Mrs. Pateman turned once, caught my eye, and gave what, strain playing one of its tricks, looked exactly like a furtive but excited smile. A beam of sunlight began to fall directly onto people's faces on the far side of the upper rows; as they fidgeted and tried to shut out the light, nerves were getting sharper, for I was not the only one who felt an inexplicable intensity all through the afternoon.

No one in that court but me had heard the judge's remark about Kitty Pateman. As I sat listening to her, several times it came back to me, but it did nothing but add to the disquiet. For a strange thing was, that as the hours passed and Kitty talked, I couldn't get any nearer forming an opinion about whether that remark had truth in it or not.

There were other strange things. Much of the time I, along with other observers, was certain that she was acting, and Jamie Wilson, without realizing it, was helping her to act. His examination didn't sound, and didn't stay in the memory, like

411

the ordinary questions-and-answers of a trial. It was much more like a conversation in which she was playing the major part, and a part which was quick-tongued, elaborate, and bizarre.

Glance flitting to the jury box, the judge, once to her family, she described what she called her "first breakdown," words hurrying out. Sometimes she could recall it all, sometimes she couldn't: she had told the psychiatrists, but not everything, because she got flustered, and she didn't like to mention that she had heard voices. Yes, voices when she was eighteen that she thought someone was managing to produce in her radio set, tormenting her. Or perhaps taking charge of her, she didn't know at the time; she was frightened, she thought she might be going "round the bend" or else something special was happening to her. She heard the voices over a period of months: sometimes they came just like a telephone message. They told her all sorts of things. They were advising her against her father. He was her enemy. He was keeping her at home, he was planning to keep her at home until her brother had grown up: he wanted her to be a prisoner. They told her to trust "this man" (the man whom Dr. Kahn had mentioned) . She had thought that he was meant to be her escape. But he wasn't, it had been a disaster. The voices told her that he was her enemy, like her father. She was intended for something different, no one was going to imprison her. But then they stopped speaking to her, and she hadn't heard them for years.

The light voice fluted on: I was too intent to get any sense of how others were responding, even Martin—though later I heard a good many opinions, some mutually contradictory, about this part of her evidence. For myself, I had no doubt, on the spot or later, that most of it was a lie. At least the story of her voices was a lie. She was clever enough to have picked up accounts of people's psychotic states: of how some had precisely that kind of aural hallucination, certain that they

were spoken to (in earlier times they would have heard the
messages in the air, nowadays they emanated from machines)
over the wires. She might even have known such a person, for
they weren't uncommon. But I didn't believe that it had
happened to her. She was mimicking the wrong kind of
breakdown. If she were ever going to become deranged—or
ever had been—it would be in a different fashion.

But that wasn't all, it was merely clinical, and only made
her seem more ambiguous and shifting than before. For
when people lied as she was lying, they usually couldn't help
showing some stratum of the truth. She invented stories of
what those voices told her about her father: they said something—though nothing like all—of what she felt for him herself. In the voices, which perhaps as she invented them
seemed both romantic and sinister, and flattered her imagination, you could smell something much more down to earth,
the antiseptic smell of the Pateman house. And you could
hear something not so down to earth, but which emerged
from that same house, and was seething in her imagination—
"something special" was happening to her, she was "intended
for something different."

People afterwards said they hadn't often seen a face change
so much. At times she looked young and pretty, at others
middle-aged. In the box, which gave her height, she had lost
her air of hiding away, and no one thought her insignificant.
She made an impression which separated her from the
lookers-on, and yet didn't repel them, almost as though she
touched a nerve of unreality. Certainly it was an impression
that Clive Bosanquet, as soon as he began to cross-examine,
wanted to dispel.

In his level tone, he asked:

"Miss Pateman, when did you first make plans to kill a
child?"

She looked at him, eyes steadying, and replied without a
pause:

"I don't think I thought anything like that. No, that would give the wrong idea. You see, no one does anything cut-and-dried, you understand—"

Bosanquet was determined to stop her going off on another conversational flight.

"Miss Pateman, there is no doubt that you planned, methodically and over a period of weeks or months, to kill a child. Apparently it needn't have been Eric Mawby, you picked on him at random. I am asking you, when did you first make plans to kidnap and kill a child?"

"Well, kidnapping is one thing that we might have talked about—"

"I asked, Miss Pateman, when did you first make plans to kidnap and kill a child?"

"I was saying, we might have talked about catching hold of one for a little while, you know, we talked about all sorts of things, you know how it is, anyone can make a suggestion—"

"When did this happen?"

"It might have happened at any time, I couldn't tell you exactly."

"It might not have happened at any time, Miss Pateman. When did it happen?"

The judge was regarding her, and spoke as considerately as ever in the trial. "You must try to tell us, if you can."

"Well, if I had to put a date to it, I suppose it would be about the time when I had this second breakdown."

Her counsel had let her introduce "this second breakdown" and then gone no further, as though he and she assumed, and the court also, that she had been living in a haze. But Bosanquet—for once less imperturbable—was having to struggle to clear the haze away. What was this second breakdown? She realized that it had not been adduced in the medical evidence? She had not at any time during this period considered consulting a doctor? She had been working effectively at her job, and living her life as usual in the room at home and out at the cottage?

"You don't know about breakdowns unless you're the one having them, no one could know, not even—" and then she added, with a curious primness—"Miss Ross."

"You were entirely capable of doing everything you usually do?"

"No one who's not had a breakdown can understand how you can go on, just like a machine, you know—"

"You were entirely capable of making very careful detailed plans, everything thought out in advance, to abduct this child and kill him?"

"But that's just what I was saying, you can go on, and you don't know what's happening—"

"You didn't know what was happening when you brutalized this child? And killed him? A child, Miss Pateman, who if you were a year or two older, might have been your own?"

"No, he wasn't, that's got nothing to do with it, it didn't matter who he was."

That reply, like many that she had made, might have been either fluent or incoherent, it was difficult to know which. Just as it was difficult to know whether Bosanquet's thrust of rhetoric, so different from his usual method that it must have been worked out, had touched her. Were the psychiatrists right, how much was she deprived, how much had she wanted to live as other women? How much did those dolls of hers signify? As she lied and weaved her answers in and out, most of us were as undecided as when we heard her first word. Bosanquet brought up the remark—to many the most hideous they had listened to in court—"we wanted to teach him to behave." What did that mean? Wasn't that the beginning of the plan? *Who said it first?*

"Oh, it was just a way of explaining afterwards, I don't think anyone actually said it. I'm sure I didn't, that's not the way you speak to each other, is it, even if you aren't living through a breakdown."

"You found the idea so attractive that you planned everything methodically to abduct the child and then go on to ill-treat him and murder him?"

"No, that's not the way things go, you know how it is, you say lots of things that you don't mean, ever, we used to say, wouldn't it be nice if one could do things, but we didn't mean it."

Her answers were shifting and shimmering like one trans-lucent film drawn across another: underneath them there were marks when a fragment of their day-to-day life ap-peared, and then was obfuscated again. The two of them in that front room at the Patemans': yes, someone had said "it would be nice if we could do things": it might have seemed like an ordinary sexual come-on, voice thick, eyes staring! Who had spoken first? Did that matter? In the witness box, Kitty Pateman was not making the attempt to shield Cora as Cora had done her. She was just intent on seeming crazed. It still had the elaboration, almost the compulsion, of a piece of acting, yet sometimes one felt that through pretending to be crazed, she had hypnotized herself into being so. Had she—or both of them—pretended like that before? In retrospect, when our minds were cooler, one thing struck most of us. She had far more imagination than Cora. But imagination of a kind which one sometimes meets in the sexual life, at the same time vatic and obscene. She might have, and almost certainly had, prophesied to herself a wonderful life through sex, more wonderful than sex could ever give her: and simul-taneously she would never leave a sexual thought alone.

Martin said later that her imagination—or else her nervous force—had its effect on him. Despite the beams of sunlight, the courtroom seemed shut-in as a greenhouse.

But Bosanquet was not a suggestible man. As with Cora, though this was technically the harder job, he wanted to domesticate her answers. He went through a similar routine about their workaday lives. Once or twice she tried a fugue again, but then gave up. Here she couldn't sound unbalanced. Mostly her replies were shrewd and practical. Then he asked her about the books she read. Yes, she read a lot. She produced a list of standard authors of the day. "Sometimes I go a bit deeper." "Who?" "Oh well—" she hesitated, her glance flickered—"people like Camus—"

At that, I should have liked to question her, for I suspected that she was lying again: not this time because of some thought-out purpose, but simply because she wanted to impress. She might even be, I thought, a pathological liar like Jack Cotery in his youth.

For once, Bosanquet was taken aback. He was a good lawyer, but he wasn't well up in contemporary literature. He recovered himself:

"Well, what do you get out of them?"

Again she hesitated. She answered:

"Oh, they go to the limit, don't they, I like them when they go to the limit."

I was now sure that she had been bluffing: somehow she had brought out a remark she had half-read. But it gave Bosanquet an opening. He didn't know about Camus, but he did know that she wanted to show how clever she was. *Hadn't she enjoyed showing how clever she was—when they were planning to capture the child? Hadn't she felt cleverer than anyone else, because she was sure that she could get away with it?* She had said a good deal to her counsel about being "different" and "special"—*wasn't that a way of proving it?*

She was flustered, the current of words deserted her.

"No. It wasn't like that. That was my second breakdown, that's all."

She spoke as though she was astonished and ashamed. She gave the impression that he had hit on the truth which she was trying, at all costs, to conceal. Yet Bosanquet himself, and others of us, knew that wasn't so. Certainly she had enjoyed feeling clever, set apart, someone above this world—but none of us, looking at her, could conceive that that was all.

And yet, of all the questions put to her in the witness box, these were the ones that upset her most. He picked up a phrase of hers—*she had gone to the limit, hadn't she? Wasn't killing a child going to the limit?* That didn't upset her: she got back into her evasive stream. Then he said:

"After it had all happened. Didn't you feel cleverer than anyone else, because you thought you had got away with it?"

Again she couldn't answer. This time she stood as mute as Cora.

"Didn't you talk it over together? You'd brought off something very special, which no one else could have done, didn't you tell yourselves that?"

"No. We never said anything about it."

That, I suspected again, but without being sure, was another lie. It was possible that "going to the limit" had *disappointed* them, grotesque as the thought might be.

Bosanquet left her standing there quietly, not flying off with an excuse which would smear over the picture of the two of them sitting together, congratulating each other on a scheme achieved. At once Wilson set her going again, fugue-fluent, on her breakdowns, first and second, and we listened without taking in the words.

About an hour later—still heavy after the afternoon of Kitty Pateman—I called at the Shaws' new house. During the weekend I had rung up Vicky, asking if I could see her: I wanted to get it over, after my talk with Martin, as much for my sake (since I still detested breaking bad news) as hers. The house was in a street, or actually a cul-de-sac, which I remembered well from my boyhood and which had altered very little since, except that there used to be tramlines running past the open end. On both sides the houses showed extraordinary flights of pre-1914 fancy; most were semi-detached in various styles that various human minds must have thought pretty: one stood by itself, quite small, but decorated with twisted pinnacles, and led into by a porch consisting mainly of stained glass. In the patch of front garden the only vegetation was an enormous monkey-puzzle. When I was a child, I didn't notice how startling the architecture was: I probably thought it was all rather comfortable and enviable, because the people who lived there—it was only half a mile away from our house—were distinctly more prosperous than we were. One of them, I recalled, was a dentist. It looked that afternoon as though the social stratum hadn't changed much, a good deal below that of the Gearys' neighbors, considerably above that of the streets round George's lodgings. The Shaws' house was one of a pair confronting one at the end, unobtrusive by the side of the art nouveau and suburban baroque, but built at the same time, front rooms looking over a yard of garden down the street, perhaps six rooms in all.

When I rang the bell, it was Arnold Shaw who opened the door. After he had greeted me, his first words were:

"This is a long way from the Residence." He wore a taunting smile.

"That's just what I was thinking," I replied.

He led the way into the front room. Vicky jumped up and kissed me, knowing that I had come for a purpose, looking at me as though trying to placate me. Meanwhile her father, oblivious, was pouring me a drink.

"I needn't ask you what you like," he said in his hectoring hospitable tone. There was an array of bottles on the sideboard. However much Arnold had reduced his standard of living, it hadn't affected the liquor.

I gazed round the room, about the same size as our old front room at home. The furniture, though, was some that I recognized from the Residence.

"It's big enough for me," said Arnold Shaw defiantly.

I said, of course.

"Anything else would be too big."

With the enthusiasm of an estate agent, he insisted on describing what he had done to the house. There had been three bedrooms: he had turned one of them into a study for himself. "That's all I need," said Arnold Shaw. They ate in the kitchen. No entertaining. "No point in it," he said. "People don't want to come when you've got out of things."

He hadn't mentioned the trial: to me, at that moment, it was lost in another dimension. Not noticing Vicky, half-forgetting why I was visiting them, I felt eased, back in the curiosities of every day. It was a relief to be wondering how Arnold was really accepting what his resignation meant, now that he was living it. He was protesting too much, he was putting on a show of liberation. I nearly said, all decisions are taken in a mood which will not last: he would have known the reference. And yet, the odd thing was, although he probably put on this show for his own benefit each day of his life, he was also, and quite genuinely, liberated. Or perhaps even triumphant. I had seen several people, including my brother Martin, give up their places, some of them, in the world's eyes, places much higher than Arnold Shaw's. Without exception, they went through times when they cursed themselves, longing for it all back, panoplies and trappings, moral dilemmas, enmities and all: but, again without exception, provided they had made the renunciation out of their own free will, underneath they were content. Free will. For one instant, listening to Arnold, I was taken back to that other dimension. Free will. Arnold had, or thought he had, given up his job at his own free will. He felt one up on fate. It was a similar superiority to that which some men felt, like Austin Davidson, in contemplating suicide: or alternatively in bringing off a feat which no one else could do. Just for once, in the compulsions of this life, one didn't accept one's destiny and decided for oneself.

It didn't sound as exalted as that, with Arnold Shaw grumbling about his pension and discussing the economics of authorship. The university had treated him correctly but not handsomely (that is, they hadn't found him a part-time job) : he was hoping to earn some money by his books. His chief work would be appearing in the autumn, he had the proofs in his study now: it was the history of the chemical departments in German universities, 1814–1860. It was the last word on the subject, said Arnold Shaw. I didn't doubt it. That was the beginning of organized university research as we know it, said Arnold Shaw. I didn't doubt that either. It ought to be compulsory reading for all university administrators everywhere: how many would it sell? Ten thousand? That I had to doubt a little, and he gave me an angry glare.

Forgiving me, he filled my glass again. Then he said, aggressively, jauntily:

"Well, I'd better get back to those proofs. This won't buy aunty a new frock."

As he shut the door and I was still amused by that singular phrase, Vicky had come to the chair beside me.

"Have you got any news?"

She was looking with clear, troubled, hopeful eyes straight into mine.

"I'm afraid I have."

Her face, which had during the past year begun to show the first lines, became clean-washed, like a child's.

"Have you seen him?"

I shook my head.

"Oh well." Her expression was sharp, impatient again, hope flooding. "How do you know?"

"I'm afraid I do know."

"He hasn't told you anything himself?"

"I shouldn't come and say anything to you, should I, unless I was sure?"

"What are you trying to say, anyway?" Her tone was rough with hate—not for him, for me.

"I think you've got to put him out of your mind. For good and all."

No use, she said. She had flushed, but this was not like the night when her father broke the news of his resignation, she was nowhere near tears. She was full of energy, and, with the detective work of jealousy, easy to recognize if one had ever nagged away at it, wanted to track down what my sources of information were. Had I seen him at all? Not for months, I said. Had I been talking to his friends? Did I know them? Young men and young women? The only one of his friends that I knew at all, I said, was my stepson Maurice. He had been home for the vacation, but he hadn't said a word about Pat.

She couldn't accept even now, not in her flesh and bone, that he had deceived her. When she loved, she couldn't help but trust. Even when she didn't love, she found it easier to trust than distrust, in spite of her sensible head. She trusted me that afternoon (even while she was giving me the sacramental treatment of a bearer of bad news) but it was only with her head that she was believing me.

I asked her when she had last heard from him. She had written to him a good many times since Christmas, she said. She didn't tell me, she let me infer, that she hadn't heard from him.

"I can't do any more," she said. "I don't think I can write again."

That didn't seem like pride, more like a resolve. We had all been through it, I told her. It was very hard, but the only way was not to write, not to be in any kind of contact, not even to hear the name.

"No," she said. "I've got to know what's happening to him."

"It's a mistake."

She said:

"I still feel he might need me."

That was the last refuge. She was obstinate as her father: she had no more sense of danger—and she had her own tenderness.

Crossly, for I was handling it badly, I said:

"Look here, I really think you ought to give a second thought to Leonard Getliffe."

I was handling it badly, and that was the most insensitive thing I had done. Nothing I could have said would have made much difference: all the tact in the world, and you can't soften another's disasters. But still, I was handling it specially badly, perhaps because I had come to her from the extremes of death and horror, and, by the side of what I had been listening to, I couldn't, however much I tried, get adjusted to the seriousness of love. Some kinds of vicarious suffering diminished others: unhappy love affairs—in absolute honesty, did one ever sympathize with total seriousness unless one was inside them?—seemed one of the more bearable of sufferings. So that I was, against my will, less patient than I wanted to be. Having met Leonard Getliffe at the Gearys' for a few minutes the week before, which made me think perfunctorily of Vicky, I had merely wished—with about as much sympathy as Lord Lufkin would have felt—that they would get on with it. And now Leonard's name had found itself on my tongue.

She gave a cold smile.

"No," she said.

"I'm pretty sure you under-estimate him."

"Of course I don't. He's a great success—"

"I don't mean in that way. I'm pretty sure you under-estimate him as a man."

She gazed at me in disbelief.

"Once you set him free, I bet you he'd make a damned good husband."

"Not for me," she said.

She added:

"It's no use thinking about him. There's no future in it."

She had blushed, as I had seen her do before when Leonard was mentioned. She still could not understand how she had inspired that kind of passion. Once more she used that bit of old-fashioned slang: there was no future in it. She was utterly astonished at being the one who was loved, not the one doing the loving. She was not only astonished, she was disturbed and curiously angry with Leonard because it was a position she couldn't fit.

Then, as I became more impatient, she tried to prove to me that, of the two, it might be Pat who needed her the more.

THIRTY-SIX

LET-DOWN
OR FRUSTRATION

At the close of Kitty Pateman's evidence, the judge had announced that, on the following morning, the court would begin half an hour early, at ten o'clock, in the hope of finishing the case that day. When the morning came, and we sat there knowing that the verdict was not far away—the two women back in the dock, Kitty not scribbling any more, the triptych of Patemans in front of us—the proceedings were low-keyed and the three final speeches by counsel were all over by noon. It wasn't that they were hurrying, but all they could do, in effect, was repeat the medical arguments for and against. The evidence for mental abnormality wasn't disputed, said Benskin. What had been disputed was how much this abnormality impaired their responsibility: as he had put it to the Crown witness, Dr. Gough, it was a matter of degree: and yet surely, after all the evidence, the impairment wasn't in doubt? Could anyone, said Jamie Wilson, having heard Kitty Pateman's history and *having seen and listened to her in the witness box* (that was the boldest stroke that either he or Benskin made), believe that she was capable of a free choice? That her state of mind allowed her to control what she had done? All that her doctors said showed that this was incredible, and all that she said herself made it more incredible still.

Clive Bosanquet spoke for longer than the other two, but for less than an hour. More than ever, he was meticulously correct. Prosecuting for the Crown, he said, he had the duty to bring home to the jury the attention that they ought to pay to the prisoners' plea: there had not been many cases where such a plea had been thoroughly argued: no one, certainly not the Crown, wished to dismiss that plea if these women were mentally irresponsible. But—and then he examined point by point what Cornford had said, how Matthew Gough had rebutted it, and what "responsibility" had to mean. The unassertive voice went on, not with passion, but with attrition. At one stage he said that it would be possible, or at least theoretically possible, for the jury to admit the plea for one of the women and reject it for the other: but neither defense counsel had wished to argue this, and the prosecution did not admit it: the two were inseparably combined, and what applied to one, as all the technical evidence demonstrated, would apply to the other: it had to be all or nothing. That was all. With a gesture, he got on with the attrition.

All through those speeches, I couldn't listen as I usually did. It was not till I read them later that I appreciated what had actually been said. Odd phrases stuck out, tapped away at circuits in the mind that I couldn't break. Free choice. Who had a free choice? Did any of us? We felt certain that we did. We had to live as if we did. It was an experiential category of our psychic existence. That had been said by a great though remarkably verbose man. It sounded portentous: it meant not more than the old judge declaring robustly that he could decide—it was in his power and no one else's—whether to take a second gin and tonic. It meant no more: it also meant no less. We had to believe that we could choose. Life was ridiculous unless we believed that. Otherwise there was no dignity left—or even no meaning. And yet—we felt certain we could choose, were we just throwing out our chests against the indifferent dark? We had to act as if it were true. As if. *Als/ ob*. That was an old answer. Perhaps it was the best that we could find.

Morality. Morality existed only in action. It arose out of action: was formed and tested in action: expressed itself in action. That was why we mustn't cheapen it by words. That was why the only people I knew—they were very few—who had any insight into the moral life, talked about it almost not at all.

On the stroke of twelve, the judge started to sum up. Suddenly I was listening with acute attention, absent-mindedness swept clean away. I watched the old, healthy, avian face as he turned, with his courteous nod, towards the jury box: I was listening, knowing already what his opinion was.

"Members of the jury, it is now my duty to sum this case up for you." All through the trial his voice had shown, except in one rebuke, none of the cracks or thinning of age, and as he talked to the jurors, so easily and unselfconsciously, it was still unforced and clear: but his accent one had ceased to hear except in old men. It belonged to the Eton of 1900, not cockney-clipped like the upper-class English two generations later, but much fuller, as though he had time to use his tongue and lips. "This, I think, is the seventh day on which you have listened with the utmost patience to the evidence and the speeches. And, at the end of it all, the issue in this case comes down to the point of a pin. It is agreed by everyone, I think, that these two young women have some degree of mental abnormality: is it enough to impair substantially—I have to remind you of that word—their mental responsibility? Are Miss Ross and Miss Pateman not responsible for the deeds, I need not tell you they are terrible deeds, that they have committed? Or, to make the point sharper still, are they not fully responsible, so that we have to make special allowance for them and accept their plea? Which is, you will remember, one of diminished responsibility. Either you will accept that, and bring in a verdict accordingly: which means, you understand, that they will be treated like mental patients who have perpetrated the crime of manslaughter. Or else you will decide that they were responsible for what they have done, and find them guilty of murder. In which case it will be necessary for me to pass the statutory sentence."

Almost from the start of the summing-up, Cora had been yawning. It looked like insolence: I believed that it was her first sign of nerves. The judge went on:

"I do not for one instant pretend that that decision is easy for you. As learned counsel have carefully explained to you, this whole conception of diminished responsibility is relatively new to our law. And you have also been told that it has no really sharp and precise definition in medical or scientific terms. You have actually heard doctors of great distinction, mental doctors or psychiatrists, whatever we like to call them, taking absolutely contrary positions about the degree of responsibility of these two young women. Dr. Cornford and Dr. Kahn have told us—and I am sure that no one here would doubt their absolute professional integrity—they have told us that these women were less than fully responsible, so much less as not really to be answerable for their actions, when they killed the child. On the other hand, Dr. Gough and Dr. Shuttleworth, again with integrity that no one can doubt, have given their judgment, which is that Miss Ross and Miss Pateman were as responsible as any of us, when we perform any deed for good and ill. No, perhaps I have gone a little further than those doctors did. But they were quite positive that these young women's responsibility was not substantially impaired.

"Members of the jury, this is not going to be easy for you. I shall try shortly to give you what little help I can. But I have no more knowledge of these young women's minds than you have. I shall try to remind you what the doctors said, and what Miss Ross and Miss Pateman said themselves. You have listened to it all, and so have I. And it is for you, and you alone, to make the decision.

"But, right at the beginning, I have to tell you two things. I have just said that it is for you, and you alone, to make the decision. I have to repeat it, so that you will never forget it during your deliberations. This issue must not be decided by doctors. I should tell you that, and tell you it time and again, even if the doctors' opinions were not divided. It is not in the nature of our law to have judgment by professional experts. We listen to them with gratitude and respect, but in the end it is you who are the judges. In such a case as this, it would, in my view, be specially wrong for the issue to be decided by doctors. For I am convinced that none of these eminent men would consider stating that they had reached any final certainties about the human mind. Perhaps those certainties never will be reached. Sometimes, for the sake of our common humanity, I find myself hoping that they won't. At any rate, no one can be certain now. It is for you to reach a decision as to whether these young women—as my learned friend Mr. Benskin put it very clearly—are or are not responsible for these criminal actions, in the sense that you are yourselves for what you do. It is your decision. You will have to be guided by your experience of life, your knowledge of human nature, and I must say, by something we sometimes undervalue, by your common sense.

"Now one other thing, before I try to draw your minds back to the evidence. You have had to listen to the story of an abominable crime. When one thinks of the treatment of that young boy before he died, and then of his death, one finds it hard—and here I am speaking for myself, as an aging man— one finds it hard to cling to one's faith in a merciful God.

"But now I have to ask you to do something which you may think impossible. You must do your best, however. I want you to put the nature and details of this crime out of your consideration. You are concerned only with whether these women are, or are not, fully responsible. It would be the same question, and the same problem, if they had committed some quite minor offense, such as stealing half a dozen pairs of stockings or a suitcase. It would be the same problem.

I ask you to approach the decision in that spirit. I know that it will be difficult. I am asking you to banish the natural revulsion and horror that you must have felt. Forgot all those thoughts. Think only of whether these young women were responsible for what they have done."

One would have to be something like clairvoyant, I was thinking, to listen to him now—and then guess right about how he spoke in private. And yet he was relaxed, speaking to the jury, as when he spoke to Hargrave and me in his dining room. It was the habit of a lifetime to be calm and magisterial, to let nothing of himself slip out. Except perhaps a distaste for all the theorists who didn't live in his own solid world. As he went on, underneath the fairness, underneath the amiable manners, he once or twice inflected his voice, just towards the edge of sarcasm, when he discussed the psychiatrists' "explanations." Or did I imagine the inverted commas? He was not a speculative man: in secret, he hadn't much use for intellectual persons. But that had been so all through his career. It was nothing new that day, it didn't affect his judgment, it would have been hard to tell whether he was trying to lead the jury at all.

That was Margaret's impression, as we sat at lunch, the four of us. She had traveled up during the morning, in order to be with us at the end, and had heard nearly all the summing-up, which the judge had still to finish.

"He's not pushing them one way or the other, is he?"

George gazed at her.

"Perhaps he doesn't think it's necessary," he said. He wasn't speaking bitterly: or apathetically: not with much emotion, just as a matter of fact, like one who took the result for granted. He was not looking drawn. The rest of us were showing signs of suspense, but not George. He gave out an air of resolve or even of obscure determination. It was he who took the initiative, telling us it was time to return. "Last sitting," he said in a loud, vigorous, exhorting cry.

In the courtroom, full but not as jam-tight as on the first

day, smelling in the warm afternoon of women's scent, sweat, the odor of anxiety, the judge turned again to the jury box, with a smile that was social, not quite easy or authoritative.

"Members of the jury, thanks to the exertions of the lady who has been taking the shorthand notes, I have been supplied with a transcript of what I said to you this morning, and I see that I have made three very stupid little mistakes." They were, in fact, small mistakes which most of us had either not noticed or discounted as slips of speech, such as transposing the doctors' names: but the judge was flustered, irritated with himself and those he was talking to. Perhaps he had the streak of vanity that one met in men who had not competed much and who weren't used to being at a disadvantage: perhaps he didn't like being reminded that he had reached one of the stages in old age when he could still trust his judgment, but not his memory. At any rate, he wanted to shorten his summing-up, he was distrustful of quoting names, he had to make an effort to assert himself. "Let us get our feet on the ground. We are dealing with reality, and this is certain—" He went on with an adjuration that, I fancied, he might have used before. "You have been dealing with an avalanche of words. This is nobody's fault, of course. It is the only way it could be done. But you are not dealing with things of imagination. You are dealing with actual lives, actual things that really happened." Then he was in command again. He told them that he agreed totally with Bosanquet, and by implication with the other counsel: there was no ground for discriminating between the two. He repeated, slowly and masterfully, that it must be the jury's decision, and not the doctors'. They must detach themselves from their hatred of the crime, and consider as wisely as they could what substantial impairment (he reiterated the words three times) of responsibility meant and what responsibility those two young women bore. At that, he gave his benevolent paternal beck to the jury. "It is in your hands now," he said.

The judge's procession left: the heads of the two women

dipped out of sight. It was about ten to three. Slowly, in jerks and spasms, the courtroom emptied. As soon as we got outside into the hall, Margaret lit a cigarette, as in an interval at the theater. In the rush, we all found ourselves near the refreshment table, where I brushed against Archibald Rose, wig in hand, eating a sausage roll.

"Now we shan't be long," he whispered to me, in a casual detached tone. None of the others had heard that remark: but each of us, certainly George, was behaving as though Rose was right, as though the jury would be returning soon. We talked very little. It was a good many minutes before George said: "Well, I suggest we might as well have a cup of tea." We lingered over it, so weak and milky, like the tea I had tasted in jail. The hall was less crowded, people were edging away. We drank more cups of tea. All of a sudden the delay seized hold of me. I didn't know about the others, but later Margaret and Martin told me it was the same for them.

At half-past four I said: "Let's go for a stroll." George said that he wouldn't bother, found a chair in the now half-deserted hall, sat down and lit a pipe. The others were glad to escape into the free air. Neither of them dissenting, we went away from the Assize Hall, not just round the block, but on into the center of the town, getting on for a mile away. Margaret knew what I was doing: so probably did Martin. I was trying to cheat the time of waiting—so as to get back when it was all over. We had lived through times of waiting before this. I might have recalled that other time with George in this same court: but curiously, so it seemed to me in retrospect, I didn't. Maybe my memory blocked it off. Instead, it was much more like times that each of us had been through: meaningless suspense: bad air trips, making oneself read thirty pages before looking at one's watch: Martin knowing that his son was driving, not told when he might arrive.

"What does all this mean?" Martin said, without any explanation, after we had walked a few hundred yards.

"It must mean that the jury are arguing," I replied.

"I wouldn't have believed it," he said. He had taken it for granted that the defense didn't stand a chance.

"Would you?" Margaret asked me.

"No." I was wondering who might have done. Perhaps the Patemans. Were they hopeful now?

It could be, Martin supposed, that one or two jurors were holding out. None of us had any idea, then or later, what happened in that jury room.

We reached the opulent streets, women coming out of shops, cherishing new hairsets, complexions matte in the clear sunlight. It would take us twenty minutes to walk back, said Martin.

In sight of the Assize Hall, we made out the policemen on the steps. We hurried into the entrance hall: there were a few people round the refreshment-table, others scattered about. George still sitting down. He gave us his open inattentive smile. "Nothing's happened," he said.

During the next hours, we couldn't cheat the time of waiting any more. Except that I had a conversation with a colleague of Edgar Hankins, a bright-eyed, preternaturally youthful-looking man. We had met occasionally at parties, and in the hall he drew me aside. He wanted, he was full of his own invention, to discuss the treatment of criminals sane and not-so-sane. If we assumed that the two young women were sane, which he believed, then he believed equally that they would never do anything of the kind again. In that case, they were no danger to society. So what was the justification for keeping them in jail? It was pure superstition, he was saying. I had always found his kind of brightness boring, and that evening, time stretching out, I found it worse than that. When I returned to Margaret and Martin, they asked what we had been talking about, but I shook my head.

At last—and yet it seemed unexpected—we heard that the jury were coming back. When we went into the courtroom, we

saw it gaping, nearly empty: the time was nearly eight
o'clock: most of the spectators hadn't been able to see the
end. The two women walked up to the dock, Kitty's eyes
darting—with something like a smile—to her family. Cora had
brushed her hair, which shone burnished as the court lights
came on. The jury trampled across the room, making a clat-
ter; it was as though one had not heard the noise of feet
before. As they settled in their box, I saw one of them, a
middle-aged woman with thick arms, gaze intently at Cora
Ross.

The judge took his place and bowed. Then the old routine, in the clerk's rich voice.

"Members of the jury, who will speak as your foreman?"

A grey-haired man said: "I will."

"Mr. Foreman, do you find the prisoner, Cora Helen
Passant Ross, guilty or not guilty of murder in this indict-
ent?"

"Guilty."

The same question, about Katharine Mavis Pateman.

"Guilty."

"And those are the verdicts of you all?"

"Yes, they are."

"Cora Helen Passant Ross, you stand convicted of the fel-
ony of murder. Have you anything to say why you should not
now be given judgment according to law?"

Cora stood erect, shoulders squared, her expression unmoved. "No," she said, in a loud voice. Kitty Pateman followed her with a quieter perfunctory no.

The judge looked at them, and said clearly but without
inflection:

"The sentence is a statutory one, and it is that you, and
each of you, be sentenced to imprisonment for life."

He did not say anything more. He gave them a nod, polite,
almost gentle, dismissing them. They were taken below for
the last time.

Neither in the courtroom, talking to the solicitors and to his junior, nor outside in the hall, when the final ritual was over, would Clive Bosanquet accept congratulations: he had too much emotional taste to do so, in a case like this. He looked, however, modestly satisfied: while Jamie Wilson, speaking to no one, rushed ahead of the others to the robing-room, his face surly with self-reproach. Leaning against the refreshment-table, Benskin chatted with vivacity to other lawyers and gave us a cheerful wave. Of all the functionaries at the trial, the only one I actually spoke to, as we made our way to the entrance hall, was Superintendent Maxwell. He spun his bulk round, came up to me in soft-footed steps, and said, in a quiet high mutter: "Well, they didn't get away with it. Now we've got to keep the other prisoners off them. I don't envy anyone the job."

I didn't hear many comments, among the relics of the crowd. There was none, absolutely none—and there hadn't been during the last minutes in court—of the gloating fulfil-ment which years before I had felt all round me, and in myself, when I heard the death sentence passed. You could call it catharsis, if you liked a prettier name. There was none of that. So far as there was a general mood, it seemed to be almost the opposite, something like anti-climax, let-down, or frustration.

In the tone, firm and yet diffident, in which he always used to issue his invitations, George said to the three of us:

"I should like you to come round to my place for half an hour."

Before any of us replied, my sleeve was being gently tugged and Mrs. Pateman was saying, very timidly: "I wonder if you could have a word with him, sir. It might settle him down. I don't know what's going to happen to him, I'm sure."

She was quite tearless. In fact, she didn't mention her daughter, only her husband, who was standing at the side of the hall, gesticulating as he harangued Dick Pateman. As she

led me towards them, she asked me if I would "humor him a
bit." She said that she didn't know how he would get over
it.

When he saw me, his gaze was fixed and angry. He seemed
possessed by anger, as though that were the only feeling
left.

"I can't have this," he said.

I said that I was sorry for them.

"I can't let it go at this," he said.

I attempted to soothe him. Couldn't they all go and try to
sleep, and then talk to the solicitors tomorrow?

That made him more angry. His eyes stood out, his fists
clenched as though he were going to hit me.

"They're no good to us."

"Well then—"

"I want someone who'll take care of people who are ill. My
daughter's ill, and I insist on having something done about
it."

"That's what we want," said Dick Pateman.

I said she would certainly be under medical supervision—

"I'm not going to be put off by that. I want the best people
to take care of her and make her better."

Again I tried to soothe him.

"No!" he shouted into my face. "I can't leave it like this. I
shall have to talk to you about how I can get things done—"

He was threatening me, he was threatening everyone. And
yet he was crying out for help. The curious thing was, I was
more affected by his appeal than by his wife's. She had known
a good many sorrows: this was another, but she could bear it.
Whatever else came to her, she would go on enduring, and
nothing would break her. But she didn't believe that was
true of her husband and her son. Standing with him, listening to their threats (for Dick joined in), I thought she could
be right. To be in their company was intolerable: in many
ways they were hateful: and yet they were helpless when

there was nothing they could do. Their only response to sorrow, the chill of sorrow, was to fly out into violence. Violence without aim. Shouts, scowls, threats. What could they do? They were impotent. When they were impotent, they were nothing at all.

I told Mr. Pateman that I had no knowledge of the prison service or of prison doctors but that, if he ever wanted to talk to me, he was welcome to. He didn't thank me, but became quieter. Any bit of action was better than none. Getting a promise out of me, however pointless, showed that he was still effective, and was a comfort to him.

THIRTY-SEVEN

FORGETTING

"I should like you to come round to my place for half an hour," George had said, before Mrs. Pateman took me away. When I rejoined the three of them, they were waiting to walk out to Martin's car. As we drove across the town, up past the station, all of us in silence, I was thinking again, yes, that was how George used to invite us—when he was asking us, not to a pub, but to his "place," as though it were a baronial hall. Actually, it consisted of the sitting room and bedroom in which he had lived for nearly forty years. How he managed it, I had never known. George had clung on, with no one to look after him. Not that he needed much.

In the sharp spring night, transistor radios were blaring and people lolled about the pavement, when we drew up outside the door. Inside his sitting room, as he switched on the light, the newspapers and huddle sprang to the eye, and one's nostrils tingled with the dust.

"Now," he said, as, panting, he cleared litter from the old sofa to make a place for Margaret. There were only two chairs. Martin put me in one of them, and himself sat on the sofa-end. "Now," said George. "Is there anything I can get you?"

Margaret glanced at me, looking for a signal. She was tired, after the long nerve-ridden day. She would have liked a drink. But, though she knew George well, she had really no idea about his style of life. Even in her student days, she

438

hadn't seen a room like this. No, she said, he wasn't to bother. If she had asked for a drink, I thought, she would probably have been unlucky. For George, who drank more than anyone round him, had—at least in my experience, in the time I knew him best—scarcely ever drunk at home.

"I can easily make some tea," said George.

"Never mind," said Martin. "We've drunk enough tea for one day."

George looked at the three of us, as if to make sure that the formalities had been properly observed. That gave him pleasure, even now, as it had always done. Then he took the vacant chair at the side of the fireplace, pulled down his waistcoat, and said:

"Well, I thought you ought to be the first to hear."

He was addressing me more than the others, but not personally, rather as a matter of etiquette, because he had known me longest.

He said:

"I'm going away."

"What do you mean?"

"I mean that I shan't put a foot inside this damned town again." He stared past me. "It's quite useless to argue," he went on, though in fact none of us was arguing. "I made my plans as soon as I saw that business of hers"—he meant Cora, but couldn't, or didn't, refer to her by name—"could only come to one end. Incidentally, I thought that you were all deceiving yourselves about that. I never believed that any jury in the country would do anything different."

He said:

"It's horrible, I don't require anyone to tell me it's horrible, but there's no use wasting time over that. I've had to think about my own position. I've got plenty of enemies in this wretched town. I'm perfectly prepared to admit that, according to ordinary standards, I deserve some of the things they want to bring up against me. But I've got enemies because I wouldn't accept their frightful mingy existence and wouldn't let other people accept it either. And all these sunkets want is to make the place too hot to hold me." This didn't have the machinelike clank of paranoia, which one often heard in him. "Well, now the sunkets have something to use against me. They can breathe down my neck until I die. It doesn't matter to them that she hasn't spoken to me for a couple of years. They can smear everything I do. They can control every step I take. By God, it would be like having me in a cage for crowds to stare at."

Martin caught my eye. Neither of us could deny it.

George said:

"That's not the worst of it. If it were just myself, I think I might conceivably stay here and take my medicine. But there is the whole crowd. Everyone who has ever come near to me. You heard what they did to young ——— in the witness box. They'll all be under inspection as long as I am here. Their lives won't be worth living. When I go away, it won't be long before it all calms down again. They'll be all right, as soon as people have forgotten about me."

Again, neither Martin nor I could say that he was wrong. It was Margaret who said:

"That's very generous, George. But are you sure you're really well enough?"

"Well enough for what?"

"Well enough to uproot yourself like that."

George gave her a shifty defiant smile, and said:

"Oh, if I'm not up to the mark, I shall get in touch with some of you."

Had he thought of where he might be going? *Of course,* what did she take him for? For the first time that night, George broke into laughter, loud laughter. For days past— perhaps when he had been absent from the court, and per- haps, I now suspected, for a longer period than that—he had been making logistic plans, like the administrator he might have been. It would take him no time at all to "clear up his effects." He didn't propose to stay in England. He had never traveled much: as a matter of fact, apart from a weekend in Paris and a few days in Ostend, he had not, in sixty-four years, traveled at all. Yet, it was one of his schematic hobbies, he knew the geography, railways, timetables of Europe far better than the rest of us.

"Well, now I've got a bloody good chance to look round," he cried.

He intended to start in Scandinavia, for which he had a hankering, because he had once met a Swede who looked remarkably like himself.

"I'm sorry to nag," said Margaret. "But, before you go, do ask your doctor. You know, you're not very good at taking care of yourself, are you?"

"I shall be all right."

"Or let us find you a doctor in London, won't you?"

"You're not to worry about me."

He answered her with childlike impenetrable obstinacy: nothing was going to stop him now.

Margaret, used to her father and the sight of illness, thought it was kinder to say no more. Then Martin and I, almost at the same instant, mentioned money. Up till then, the grudges, bad luck, resentments of a lifetime had been submerged: all of a sudden, they broke through. *Of course* he was bound to be short of money. After that ineffable firm (Eden & Sharples, and George's curses crashed into the room) had fobbed him off with his miserable pension. Seven hundred and fifty a year; that was all he received for a life's work. When he had saved them from their own contemptible incompetence. If it hadn't been for him, they would have been extinct long ago! Seven hundred and fifty a year. In exactly one year's time, he added, with savage mirthless hilarity, he would get his old-age pension. Then he would have nearly a thousand a year. The glorious reward for all his efforts in this mortal life!

Anyone from outside might have thought that George was

morbidly preoccupied with money, miserly in the fashion of Mr. Pateman. That was dead wrong. No one had minded about it less, or given it away more lavishly. In that storm of protest, it wasn't money that was making him cry out.

But he had his streak of practicality, and I had to answer on those terms.

"Are you going to be able to cope?" I said.

"Can't you work it out for yourselves?"

"You must let us help."

"No. It's rather too late to impose upon my friends."

He had spoken with stiff pride. Then, to soften the snub, he gave his curiously sweet and hesitating smile.

Martin half-began a financial question, and let it drop. There was a silence.

"Well," said George.

None of us spoke.

"Well," said George again, like one of the students before the Court, as though he were seeing us off at a railway station. Martin and I, used to his habits in days past, realized that he was anxious for us to go. Perhaps he had someone else to see that night. As we stood up, George said, amiably but with relief:

"It was very good of you all to come round."

Margaret kissed him. Martin and I (it wasn't our usual way, we might have been saying goodnight in a foreign country) shook him by the hand.

When Martin stopped the car in front of the Gearys' house, the drawing-room lights, curtains undrawn, shone out into the front garden: there were other luminous rectangles in the house-proud road. Denis Geary met us at the door.

"Here you are! It's not so late, after all."

I had rung up from the Assize Hall to say that they weren't to wait supper for us, we couldn't tell when we should be home. Alison Geary was hurrying us into the bright warm room, saying that we couldn't have eaten much. Margaret

replied that she was past eating, but, at her ease as she wasn't
at George's, added that she was pining for a drink. "It's ready
for you," said Denis, pointing to the sideboard. They had
been preparing for us all the evening. Martin, who was ra-
venous, tucked into a plateful of cold beef: we sat, not at the
table, but in easy chairs round the room; outside the French
windows, stars sparkled in the cold clear sky. "That's better,"
said Denis to Margaret, who was now starting on some
bread and cheese. "You all looked a bit peaked when you
came in. We'd been expecting that," said Alison. Margaret
smiled at them, and gave a grateful-sounding sigh.

We hadn't been sitting there for long before we told the
Gearys about George's decision. Is he really going? Alison
wanted to know. Yes, we said, we were certain that
he meant it. Margaret added that he wasn't fit to go off alone,
his physical state was worse than any of us imagined. Denis
looked at her; "I'll see if I can check on that," he said.

"I don't think he'll thank you for it," I told him.

"I tried," Margaret said.

George was going, we said to Denis. He didn't intend to
listen to anything that got in his way. I thought—but Margaret believed he could be deceiving himself—that he knew
he wasn't a good life.

"So we can't stop him, you think?" said Denis, frowning,
chafing to be practical. Then he added gently, having seen,
more continuously than we had, the whole course of George's
existence:

"Perhaps it's all for the best."

Soon afterwards he said:

"Anyway, this town isn't going to be quite the same without him."

He said it without any expression on his elder statesman's
face. It might have been a platitude. None of us was feeling
genial, no one smiled. But Denis, though he was a very kind
man, was not without a touch of irony.

He refilled our glasses. He looked across at his wife, as

though they were colloguing. Then, in exactly the same tone, firm and sympathetic, in which he had greeted me on the first night of the trial, he spoke to the three of us:

"Now then. You've got to put all this behind you."

For an instant, no one answered.

"All of it," Denis went on. "The whole hideous business you've been listening to. You've got to forget it. You've got to forget it."

Very quietly, speaking to an old friend whom he respected, Martin said:

"I absolutely disagree."

All of a sudden, in the bright comfortable room, we were back in the argument—no, it wasn't an argument, it was at once too much at random and too convergent for that, we agreed more than we disagreed, the dialectic existed only below the words—which I had been having with Margaret for a long time past and with Martin on those nights together during the trial.

It was wrong to forget. We had forgotten too much. This was the beginning of illusions. Most of all (this was Martin, speaking straight to Denis Geary) of the liberal illusions.

False hope was no good. False hope, that you hold onto by forgetting things.

The only hope worth having was built on everything you knew, the facts you didn't like as well as the facts you did. That was a difficult hope. For the social condition, it was the only hope that would give us all a chance. For oneself—

Was anyone tough enough to look at himself, as he really was, without sentimentality or mercy, all the time?

For an instant I thought, though I didn't report it, of something that had happened to me during the trial. When Kitty Pateman was being cross-examined, when we all might have expected to forget our own egos, I found myself shutting my eyes, flooded with shame. It was entirely trivial. I had suddenly remembered—I had no idea what trigger set it off—

an incident when I was about eighteen. My aunt Milly had just been making a teetotal pronouncement, her picture was in the local paper, and I was talking to some friends. One of them suspected that she was a connection of mine: I swore blind that I had never seen her in my life.

It wasn't the memory itself that rocked me, now that it returned in the Gearys' sitting room. Who hasn't stood stock-still in the street, blinking away some petty shame which has just jabbed back to mind? No, what shook one was the sheer perseverance and invading-power of one's self-regard. Whenever we made attempts to loose ourselves, that confined us. And yet, in brutal terms, it also saved us to survive.

Reason. Why had so much of our time reneged on it? Wasn't that our characteristic folly, treachery, or crime?

Reason was very weak as compared with instinct. Instinct was closer to the aboriginal sea out of which we had all climbed. Reason was a precarious structure. But, if we didn't use it to understand instinct, then there was no health in us at all.

Margaret said she had been brought up among people who believed it was easy to be civilized and rational. She had hated it. It made life too hygienic and too thin. But still, she had come to think even that was better than glorifying un-reason.

Put reason to sleep, and all the stronger forces were let loose.We had seen that happen in our own lifetimes. In the world: and close to us. We knew, we couldn't get out of knowing, that it meant a chance of hell.

Glorifying unreason. Wanting to let the instinctual forces loose. Martin said anyone who did that either hadn't much of those forces within himself, or else wanted to use others' for his own purpose. And that was true of private leaders like George as much as public ones.

(Were others thinking, as I did, of those two women? Was it true of one of them?)

Midnight had passed. Margaret and Alison were trying to look after each other. Margaret knew that the Gearys were not, like the rest of us, buoyed up by the energy of strain. We were feeling tireless, as one does in the crisis of a love affair, ready to talk all night. The Gearys had had nothing to make them tireless: Margaret said it was time to go to bed. But Alison had a sense that we were getting a curious kind of nepenthe, even when we were speaking as harshly as we could. We weren't being considerate: at times we should have said that we didn't mind reawaking our own distress or anyone else's: and yet, it seemed that we were producing the opposite effect. It was like being made hypocrites by accident. Whatever we said, however hard our voices sounded, just by being together we were creating an island of peace.

No, said Alison, he (Denis) didn't have to go to school tomorrow. She would make us a pot of tea. To herself, she thought it was good for us to go on sitting there.

We shied off tea, which had been offered to us enough that day. Then Denis ordered us to have another drink. Martin refused, saying he had to drive his car back to Cambridge before the morning. Margaret settled down in her chair, wakeful, but all of us quiet by now.

Denis said: "We can only do little things, can't we? But we must go on doing them. At any rate, I must. There's no option. I shall have to go on doing the things that come to hand."

Martin nodded. They spoke about old acquaintances, whom they had known when they were in the same form together. Denis broke off:

"Look here, I'm the Martha of this party. Much more than she is." He put his hand over his wife's. "There's a certain amount of debris to be cleared up. You'd better remind me what I ought to do." A call on George before he left—he was ticking off: "those Patemans": inquiries about the prisons. That all?

Then, leaning forward, he surprised us—it came out without any lead at all—by asking what was the name of that old man, who, living in riches, said he felt like a beggar holding out his hand for another day of life. Was that going to happen to us all? When did it begin to happen? He was in his early fifties, but, half-smiling, he wanted an answer. I was the oldest there, but I shook my head.

"I've got an uncomfortable idea," said Denis, "that someday it is going to happen to me."

V
THE FLOW RETURNING

THIRTY-EIGHT

THE COST
OF MR. PATEMAN

You've got to forget it, Denis Geary had said, that night in his house after the trial. But, for at least a couple of prosaic reasons, it wouldn't have been easy, even if we had been different people: one of those reasons was the result of some activities of Denis himself. He had duly paid his call on George Passant, who had mentioned that, once he left the country—which he did within a week—there was no one to visit Cora. Perhaps it might be arranged for me to do so? It was the most off-hand of legacies. I did not hear a word from George direct, although he had passed on a *poste restante* address.

I got in touch with Holloway prison, and was told that Cora was totally uninterested: she was, by her own choice, living in solitary confinement, and would scarcely speak to the doctors or prison officers. A few weeks later, I had a telephone call from the governor. "Now she says that she wouldn't mind seeing you some day. It won't be pleasant for you, but I expect you must be prepared for that."

It was a bright afternoon late in May as I drove through the low indistinguishable North London streets, which after living in the town so long I had never seen: betting shops, little shabby cafés with chalk-scrawls on blackboards outside, two-storey terrace after two-storey terrace, these porticoed houses, oddly prosperous, in sight of the pastiche castle itself. In a public garden the candles stood bright on the flowering chestnuts, but when I got out of the car in front of the jail, the air blew bitterly cold from the arctic, the late spring cold that we were getting used to.

As I was signing my name in the visitors' book, I should have been glad to get as used to prisons, hospitals, any institutions where the claustral dread seized hold of me: even now, I couldn't get rid of that meaningless anxiety. The corridors, the stone, the smells: the sight of other visitors taken passively off. By a mistake of my own, I was led to the wrong reception room, something like a café, plastic-topped tables with trolleys pushing between them. It was a general visiting day, the tables were already full, I was wondering if I could have picked out prisoners from the relations who came to see them. Some wearing their remand dresses, blue and pink, as Cora had done in the local jail. As I waited, standing in the corner, I noticed one woman chain-smoking, with a packet of cigarettes in front of her. It looked as though she was determined to get through it before the hour was up.

In a few minutes one of the staff had found me.

"Oh no," she said, with a commanding smile, like a hospital nurse's, "we couldn't let her in here. It wouldn't be safe."

With anyone inside for her kind of crime, she was explaining, the other prisoners would try to "do" her. It was as Maxwell had said. Cora was making a rational choice in opting for solitary. It showed that she had thought out how to preserve her own life.

"It's a headache for us," said the deputy. "And it's going to be a headache as long as she's here."

Each time they took her out for exercise, it meant a security operation; to the same extent, but in exact reverse, as if she were a prisoner about whom plans were being made for an escape. As for herself, she gave no trouble. She didn't grumble, her cell was immaculate. Apart from what they had on paper, the prison staff knew nothing more about her.

The deputy, whose name was Mrs. Bryden, took me to

another block and opened the door of a very small room, perhaps ten feet by six: inside were a table and two chairs, the backs of both chairs almost touching the walls, which were papered but had no decorations of any kind. On the table, curiously dominant, the only other object in the room, stood a single ashtray. "You've an hour to yourself," said Mrs. Bryden. "Two officers will be waiting in the corridor outside to take her back."

The door opened again, and, one of those officers on either side of her, Cora stood in the doorway. She was wearing one of her own dresses, one which she had worn on the first day of the trial. She nodded as Mrs. Bryden greeted her and said goodbye to me.

As the two of us sat there alone, I offered her a cigarette, grateful right at the beginning—as in a hospital visit—for anything which got some seconds ticked away.

I had to break the silence.

"You know George has gone away?" My voice sounded loud and brusque.

Again she nodded.

While I was thinking of another opening, she said:

"I liked George."

"He'll come back sometime."

"Will he?" she said, without reaction.

Another interval. My tongue wouldn't work any better— maybe worse—than when I saw her before the trial.

"What's it like in here?"

Her glance met mine, slid viscously away, pale-eyed in the heavy handsome face. She gave a contemptuous shrug.

"What do you think it's like?" she said. Then her tone became a violent mutter:

"There's the soap."

"What?"

"The soap. It's diabolical. Every morning when I go to wash, it makes me want to throw up."

I listened to a long, unyielding, gravelly complaint about

the soap. It sounded as though she had a sensitive nose. Against my will, I felt a kind of sympathy.

"Why don't you tell them?"

"They wouldn't care."

She gave up complaining, and sank into muteness again. Inventing one or two questions, I got nothing but nods. Calmly she asked:

"Will they let me see her?"

"I don't know." I did know: but it wasn't for me to tell her, or at least I rationalized it so.

Another patch of muteness. Again calmly, she said:

"What's the position about letting us out?"

I said surely her solicitors had told her already. She said yes, and then, with implacable repetitive calm and obstinacy, asked the question once more.

Well, it spun the time out to explain. The sentence, as she knew, I said, was a statutory one: but, as she also knew, it didn't mean what it said. In some years, no one could tell quite when, the authorities would be reviewing their cases: if there was thought to be no danger, then they might be released.

"How long?"

"In some cases, it's quite a short time."

"They won't do that for us. People will be watching what happens to us."

That was more realistic than anything I had heard from her before. Raising her voice, she asked: "I want to know, how long do you think they'll keep us in?"

I thought it was a time to speak straight. "If they're sure there's no danger, my guess would be something like ten years."

"What are you talking about, danger?"

"They'll need to be sure you won't do anything of the same kind again."

She gave a short despising laugh.

"They needn't worry themselves. We shan't do anything like that again."

For an instant I recalled that colleague of Hankins's, too clever by half, making bright remarks before the verdict. Then, more sharply, Mrs. Pateman talking of her daughter.

"We shan't do anything like that again," said Cora.

She added:

"Why should we?"

I couldn't reply. Not through horror (which at that moment, and in fact through that interview I didn't feel): through something like loneliness, or even a sense of mystification that led into nothing. It was a relief to ask her commonplace questions—after all, if my guess was right, when she came out she'd still be a young woman, wouldn't she? Not much over thirty, perhaps? What did she intend to do?

"I haven't got as far as that," she said.

But she had. It came out—she wasn't unwilling to let it—that she had been making plans. The plans were down to earth. They would go and live somewhere else, in a large town, perhaps London. They would change their names. They might try to change their appearance, certainly they would dye their hair. They wouldn't have much difficulty, if the labor market hadn't altered, in getting jobs. They would have to cover up for not having employment cards, but still they'd manage. In all she said, there was no vestige of a sign that she was thinking of reshaping her life—no more than George ever had, though about that I had once believed otherwise. She had no thought of finding another way to live. I was listening for it, but there was none at all. All she foresaw, or wanted to foresee, was picking up where she had left off.

Throughout she had been using the word "we." It was "we" who were going to find another place to settle in. Was that going to happen in ten years' time? How would she endure it, if it didn't happen? It was difficult to have any prevision of what Kitty would be like. She might be imagining a different kind of life. If she were capable of that, when the time came she would throw Cora away as though she didn't recognize her face.

The hour wore on. I was trying, when she dropped her chin, to catch a glance at my wristwatch below the table.

"I don't know how to pass the time," she said. She hadn't observed me: she was saying it—not as a complaint, but as a matter of fact—about herself. What did she do all day? I couldn't make out. Sometimes "they" let her listen to the radio.

"It's all right for her," she said, once more as a matter of fact, without envy. "She'll be doing a lot of reading."

She repeated:

"I don't know how to pass the time. She'll be learning things."

She seemed to be thinking of tomorrow and the next day, not of the stretch of years.

My time, not hers, was nearly up. I said that I should have to go. As though she were imitating the judge after he had sentenced them, she gave me a dismissive nod.

Meanwhile, I had been having another reminder, which, except by disconnecting the telephone, I could not escape. I had told Mr. Pateman—in his frenetic state, when his wife led me to him—that he was at liberty to talk to me. He took me at my word. When we had returned to London, on the first evening, the telephone rang. A personal call: would I accept it, and reverse the charges? Mr. Pateman's grinding voice: "I can't let it go at this." His daughter was ill. They hadn't listened to what the doctors said. They were behaving like rats in mazes. Something must be done about his daughter. Something must be done about people in her condition. What about all the authorities "high up": when could I get them moving? Patiently that first night, I said that neither I nor any other private citizen could do anything at all: this was a matter of law—"I can't be expected to be satisfied with that." When should I be coming to the town again, so that he could explain his "point of view?" Not for some time, I had no engagement there: in any case, I said, I knew very well how he felt. No, he had to explain exactly.

The conversation was not conclusive. Three or four times a week the call came through: reverse the charges? The same voice, the same statements, often identically the same words. Rats in mazes. Authorities high up. His point of view. He wasn't rude, he wasn't even angry, he just went grinding on. Once he had found words which contented him, he felt no need to change them.

It was no use Margaret answering the telephone, and saying that I was out. He was ready to ring up again at midnight, 1 A.M., or very early the following morning. We thought of refusing to accept the calls: but that we couldn't bring ourselves to do. Whatever his wife had feared, whether it was that he might become clinically deranged, seemed not to be happening to him now. In hectoring me, in grating on with this ritual, he had found an activity which obsessed and satisfied him. He might even have lost contact with what the object of it was. Over the telephone I couldn't see—and didn't want to see—his face. I suspected that he was beginning to look as when I had first seen him, the dislocation going, the confidence of *folie de grandeur* flooding back.

Yet each night we became fretted as we waited for the telephone to ring. And, there was no denying it, we found ourselves showing a streak of miserliness, as though we were being infected from the other end of the line. It was ridiculous. Margaret had never counted shillings in her life. We spent more on cigarettes in a week than those reverse charges could possible amount to. Nevertheless, with the experience of the trial only a few weeks behind us, we scrutinized our telephone bill with indignation, calculating what was the cost of Mr. Pateman.

THIRTY-NINE

A YOUNG MAN ON
HIS OWN

A few days after my visit to the prison, Charles and I were sitting under a weeping willow on the river-bank. It was a fine afternoon, and I had gone down to his school to settle what he should do during the next academic year. Not that there was much to settle, for he had made up his mind months before. He had cleared off all the examinations, and it was time to go. The only issue remaining was not when, but where. He wouldn't be seventeen for a good many months, and he had to fill in three terms before he went to the university. He was taking the chance to start off on his travels, and it was some of those plans that we had been discussing.

"You might even write a letter occasionally," I said.

He grinned.

It would have seemed strange in my time, I said, to be going off on one's own at his age. In fact, among my friends, it would have been not only strange, but unimaginable. Of course, we didn't have the money—

"Do we really grow up faster, do you think?"

"In some ways, yes, you do."

I added:

"But, for what it's worth, I wanted to get married before I was twenty."

"Who to?"

"My first wife."

458

"You didn't marry her for six—or was it seven—years after-wards, did you?"

"No."

"If it had happened when you were twenty—what would it have been like?"

"It couldn't have been worse than it turned out."

Charles gave a grim sagalike smile, similar to his uncle's. But I was thinking that, though he knew the facts of my life with extreme accuracy, he didn't know how torn about I'd been. He wouldn't have believed that I had gone through that long-drawn-out and crippling love. He saw me as bal-anced and calm, a comparatively sensible aging man. Some-times I was amused. I permitted myself to say:

"You haven't got the monopoly of temperament in this family, you know."

It was easy to talk to him, as to Martin, on the plane of sarcasm. As we sat there, I mentioned the telephonic activi-ties of Mr. Pateman. "You've brought it on yourself," said Charles, operating on the same plane. An acquaintance of his sculled by, and Charles gave an amiable wave—rather like, since he was leaving so soon, Robin Hood gazing on the exploits of the budding archers. When the swell had passed, the river was mirror-calm, the willow leaves meeting their reflections in the water. It was something like an afternoon with C.L. Dodgson, I said to Charles, and went on to tell him that I had talked to Cora Ross in Holloway.

"Haven't you packed all that up by now?"

"Not quite." I added, sometimes it seemed that I never should.

He leaned forward, confronting me.

"I think you're wrong."

"What do you mean, I'm wrong?"

"This is an incident. If it hadn't been for sheer blind chance, it wouldn't have been an incident that mattered to you. All along, you've given it a significance that it doesn't possess." He was speaking lucidly, articulately, but with force and something like antagonism.

"I could have found other incidents, you know. Which would have affected me in the same fashion."

"That's because you are looking for them," said Charles. "Do you remember, that weekend I was at home, you were breathing hell-fire and damnation about Auschwitz? I disagreed with you then. You noticed that, did you? And I still disagree with you."

"Auschwitz happened."

"Many other things have happened. Remember, Auschwitz happened years before I was born. I'm bound to be interested in what's happening now—"

"That's fair enough."

"Of course there are awful things. Here and now. But I want to find them out for myself."

"Retracing all our mistakes in the process."

"That's *not* fair enough." He said it politely, but as though he had been thinking it out alone and his mind had hardened. "I don't think I'm easily taken in. My generation isn't, you know. We've had to learn a fair amount."

"It's curious how you talk about 'your generation,'" I said. "We never did."

He wasn't distracted. "Perhaps that's because we know that we have a difficult job to do. You don't deny that, do you?"

I said that would be the last thing I should do.

He was referring to his friends by name. As a group, they were abler, very much abler, than those I had known as a boy. Some of them would take the world as they found it: become academics, conventional politicians, civil servants: that was easy enough, they had no problem there. But one or two, like himself, were not so content. Then what do you do? "We should like to find something useful. Perhaps I ought to lower my sights, but I don't feel inclined to, until I've had a shot. And I don't think it would be very different, even if I hadn't got you on my back—"

He threw in that remark quite gently. I said that he could forget me.

He said, still gently but with a flick of sarcasm, that he would do his best to. That was the object of the exercise.

No, not really the object, just the first condition, he corrected himself. He wanted to throw in his weight where it would be useful: and he wanted to be sure it was his weight and no one else's.

It had the ring of a youth's ambition, at the same time arrogant and idealistic, mixed up with dreams of happiness. Some of it sounded as though it had been talked out with friends. Most of it, I thought, was solitary. He seemed spontaneous and easy-natured, but he kept his secrets.

He said that he had no more use for "doctrines of individual salvation" than I had. (I wondered where they had picked up that expression?) Any of those doctrines was dangerous, he said: they nearly always meant that, either actively or passively, one wished harm onto the world. Of course, he wanted for himself anything that came. What did he want? He was imagining something, but kept it to himself. He returned to saying that, whatever he found to do, it was going to be hard enough: so he couldn't afford to carry any excess luggage with him.

"I want everything as open-ended as it can be, isn't that right?" he said. "I don't want to set limits yet awhile. Limits about people, I mean. So that's why I can't take this trouble of yours as tragically as you do. Do you mind that?"

All I could answer was to shake my head. I was sure by now that he had come to this meeting resolved to make his declaration: once he had got it over, he was in high spirits. Cheerfully he stretched himself, sucking a stem of grass. It was almost time, he said, for us to move off into the town for tea. "Tea's not much good to you, is it?" he said. "Well, afterwards we'll go to a hotel and I'll stand you a Scotch. Just to celebrate the fact that this is the last time you'll have to come down to this establishment—" he spread out a hand towards the river, the fields, the distant towers across the meadows.

I asked whether he would miss it all: but I guessed the answer, for here we were very much alike.

"Who knows?" he said.

Yes, I knew, the places, the times one was nostalgic for were not the obvious ones, not even the happy ones.

"Anyway," he went on, "I can always send them home thoughts from abroad."

A moment later he said.

"It will be good to be on the move."

Then, before we stirred ourselves, he inquired about how we should be getting on at home. Maurice would presumably still be round: he was close to his mother, and that was fine. "He's very sweet," said Charles, who, like others of what he called his generation, wasn't ashamed of what mine would have considered saccharine expressions. He was fond of his half-brother, and sometimes, I thought, envied him, just because he seemed so untainted by the world. What would happen to him? "I wish," said Charles, "that he could get through his damned examinations." Was there nothing we could do?

Charles was busy about others' concerns, joyful, vigorous, since in independence he was setting off on his own. It would be good to be on the move, he had said. I wasn't resenting the rapacity and self-absorption of his youth, perhaps one couldn't in a son when the organic links were strong, when one had known in every cell of one's body what that state was like. I should worry about his remaining alive, I myself was dead. It was strange, though—not unpleasant, a kind of affirmation, but still strange—to see him sitting there, as much on his own as I was now or had ever been.

FORTY

DEATH OF
AN OLD MAN

As Margaret and I sat over our breakfast, the telephone
rang. Good God, I said, was it Mr. Pateman again?—not so
amused as Charles had been, hearing of this new addition to
our timetable. Margaret answered, and as she stood there
nodded ill-temperedly to me: it was a trunk call, from the
usual place. Then her expression altered, and she replied in a
grave and gentle tone. Yes, she would fetch me. For an instant she put a hand on mine, saying that it was about my
father.

"This is Mr. Sperry here."

"Yes?"

"I'm afraid I've got bad news for you, I'm very sorry, I'm
sure. Old Mr. Eliot—"

"Yes?"

"Early this morning. He passed away."

Again I said yes.

"I was with him when he went."

Mr. Sperry was asking me about the funeral. "I'm doing
what I can," he said. I replied that I would arrive at the
house by lunchtime. Mr. Sperry, sounding more than ever
apologetic, said that he had a piece of business then. Could I
wait till half-past three or four? "It doesn't matter to him
now, does it? He was a fine old gentleman. I'm doing what I
can."

Returning to the breakfast table, I repeated all this to

Margaret. She knew that she would be desolated by her own father's death: she was tentative about commiserating with me about the death of mine. Somehow, even to her, it seemed like an act of nature. He was very old, she said: it sounded like a good way to die. It was a pity, though, that instead of having only his lodger with him, there was none of us. "I'm not sure that he even wanted that," I said.

We found ourselves discussing what he would have wanted in the way of funerals. It was so long since I had talked to him seriously—I had talked to him seriously so seldom, even when I was a child—that I had no idea. I suspected that he wouldn't have cared a damn. I forgot then, though later I remembered, that once he had expressed a surprisingly positive distaste for funerals in general, and his own in particular. He was rueful that if he died before his wife (he had outlived her by over forty years) she would insist on "making a fuss." But I forgot that.

Neither Margaret nor I felt any of that singular necrophilic confidence with which one heard persons express certainty about what a dead relative would have "liked." I had once stood with a party at Diana Skidmore's having drinks round her husband's grave, carefully placed near a summerhouse on his own estate. Diana had been positive that there was nothing he would have liked more than to have his friends enjoy themselves close by: she was equally positive that he would, curiously enough, have strongly disliked golf balls infringing the air-space over the grave.

Margaret and I had no such clear idea. My father must have a funeral. In church? Again we didn't know. As one of his few gestures of marital independence, he had always refused to attend church with my mother, who was devout. I was pretty sure that he believed in nothing at all. Yet, for the sake of his choir practices, he had frequented church halls, church rooms, all his life. When I rang up Martin to tell him the news, I asked his opinion. Rather to my surprise, for Martin was a doctrinaire unbeliever, he thought that maybe we ought to have a service in the parish church. Quite why, he didn't or couldn't explain. Perhaps some strain of family piety, perhaps a memory of our mother, perhaps something more atavistic than that. Anyway, wherever his impulse came from, I was relieved, because I had it too.

This was a Wednesday, still mid-June. Martin's family would all travel the next day, and so would Margaret and Charles. The funeral had better be on Friday, if I could arrange it. That was what I had to tell Mr. Sperry, as we sat in Aunt Milly's old "front room" that afternoon—the room where, with indignant competence, she laid down the battle-plans for the teetotal campaigns. But I couldn't tell Mr. Sperry about the funeral at once, for he had a good deal to tell me.

It was a dank close day, and when he opened the door he was in his shirt-sleeves. As though he wouldn't have considered it proper to speak of "the old gentleman" dressed like that, he immediately put his jacket on. The Venetian blinds in the front room were lowered, a crepuscular light filtered through, Mr. Sperry gazed at me with an expression that was sad and at the same time excited by the occasion.

"I'm very sorry, I'm sure," he said, repeating his greeting at the door. I thanked him.

"Of course, it has to come to us all in the end, doesn't it? He had a long innings, you've got to remember that."

Yes, I said.

"Mind you, he's been a bit poorly since the winter. But I didn't expect him to go like this, and I wonder if the doctor really did, though he says it might have happened any time."

From his first words he had been speaking in a hushed whisper, the tone in which my mother always spoke of death. In the same whisper, he went on:

"There was someone, though, who knew his time had come."

He said: "The old gentleman did. Himself."

"When?"

"Last night."

He paused. Then, more hushed: "I was just getting in from a job, I had been looking after Mrs. Buckley's drainpipe, it must have been getting on for half-past six, and I heard him call out, Mr. Sperry, Mr. Sperry. He had a good strong voice right up to the end. Of course I went in, he was lying on his sofa, it was made up to sleep in, you know; he said, Mr. Sperry, I wonder if you'd mind staying with me tonight. I said, yes, Mr. Eliot, of course I will if you want me to. I said, is there anything the matter? He said, yes, stay with me please, I think I'm going to die tonight. That's what he said. So I said, do you mind if I go and get a bit to eat. He said, yes, you have your supper, and I went and had a bit of salmon, and came back as soon as I could. He said, I wonder if you'd mind holding my hand. So I stayed there all night. I kept asking him, do you want anything else, but he wouldn't say."

I asked, was he in pain.

"He didn't say much after I got back, he didn't seem to want to. Sometimes he gave a kind of shout. I didn't think he was going, but he did. I wish I'd sent for the doctor sooner, Mrs. Sperry and me, we blame ourselves for that. His breathing began to make a noise, then the sun came up. I'm sorry to say—"

I said, "You did all that anyone could do."

"It was full light before he went. The doctor got here a few minutes after."

He added:

"I got her"—Mr. Sperry didn't explain who that was—"to lay him out this morning. He didn't look very nice before, and I didn't think you'd want to see him like that."

He said:

"I never heard anyone say a bad word about him."

That was a formal epitaph, such as I used to hear in my

childhood in that road. But Mr. Sperry, as well as keeping his sense of propriety about a death, had also been totally efficient. The death certificate had been signed: the undertaker would be calling to see me later that evening. At last I had the opportunity to tell Mr. Sperry that we wanted a church service. Mr. Sperry was ready to cope with that. It meant that I ought to go round to the vicar's and fix a time, before the undertaker came. All the old gentleman's "bits of things" had been sifted through and collected in his room. So far as Mr. Sperry knew or could discover, he had not left a will.

"Why should he?" I asked. Yet, in fact, he owned the house: it was dilapidated now, not worth much, a thousand at most. Anyway, whatever arrangement Mr. Sperry had with him (I later found that Mr. Sperry was paying £2.2.6 a week). that must go on. Mr. Sperry would not have brought up the subject—certainly not until after the funeral—but he was relieved.

He said:

"Now you'd like to see him, I'm sure."

He took me into the hall, opened the door of my father's room, touched my sleeve, and left me alone. As I crossed the threshold into the half-dark, I had a sense, sudden, dominating, of *déjà vu*. I could just make out the short body lying on the sofa: then, though all the superstitious nerves held my fingers back, I switched on the light, and looked at him. Strangely, he appeared much more formidable than in life. His head had always been disproportionately larger than the rest of him: as it lay there above the sheets, it loomed strong and heavy, the clowning all gone now that the spectacles were off and the mild eyes closed. His moustache had been brushed and didn't droop any more. It might have been the face of a stranger—no, of someone bearing a family resemblance, a distant relative whom I hadn't often seen.

Standing by the bed, I stayed and looked at him. It took an effort to move away, as I went to inspect the other side of the room, where Mr. Sperry had neatly stacked my father's "bits of things." There were a couple of old suits: a bowler hat: a few shirts and pairs of long woolen pants: another nightshirt, as well as the one his body was dressed in. An umbrella, one or two other odds and ends. No papers or letters of any kind that I could see (he must have destroyed all our letters as soon as he read them). A couple of library books to be returned, but otherwise not a single book of his own. The two clocks—but they had not been moved, one still stood on the mantelpiece, presentation plaque gleaming, the other in the corner. That was all. He hadn't liked possessions: but still, not many men had lived till nearly ninety and accumulated less.

I went back and looked at him. All of a sudden, I realized why I had had that overmastering sense of *déjà vu. It wasn't a freak, it was really something I had already seen. For it was in that room that, for the first time in my life, at the age of eight, I had seen a corpse. My grandfather, when he retired, had lived in this house with Aunt Milly, and he had died here (it was early in 1914). I had come along on an errand for my mother. I couldn't find Aunt Milly, and I ran through the house searching for her and rushed into this room. Just as when I entered today, it was half-dark, chinks of light round the edges of the blinds: there lay my grandfather in his coffin. Before, afraid, I ran away, I saw, or thought I saw, the grey spade beard, the stern and massive face. He had been a man of powerful nature, and perhaps my father's comic acts, which lasted all his life, had started in self-defense. And yet in death—if I had really seen my grandfather as I imagined— they looked very much the same.*

When I put the room into darkness again, and rejoined Mr. Sperry, he asked me:

"How did you like him?"

"Thank you," I replied.

Satisfied, he gave me the vicar's address. They couldn't

afford to live in the vicarage nowadays, said Mr. Sperry. That
didn't surprise me: the church had been built after I was
born, the living had always been a poor one. The vicar I
remembered must have been a man of private means: he and
his wife had lived in some state, by the standards of the
parish, and he shocked my mother, not only by his high-
church propensities (he's getting higher every week, she used
to whisper, as though the altitude of clergymen was something illimitable) but also by rumors of private goings-on
which at the time I did not begin to understand. Parties!
Champagne, so the servants reported! Women present when
his wife was away! My mother darkly suspected him of having
what she called an "intrigue" with one of the teachers at the
little dame-school which she sent me to. My mother was
shrewd, but she had a romantic imagination, and that was
one of the mysteries in which she was never certain of the
truth.

There was nothing of all that about the present incum-
bent. He was living in a small house near the police station,
and politely he asked me into a front room similar to Mr.
Sperry's. He was a youngish red-haired man with a smile that
switched on and off, and a Tyneside accent.

I told him my name, and said that my father had died. At
once, both with kindness and with the practice of one used to
commiserating in the anonymous streets with persons he did
not know, he gave me his sympathy. "It's one of the great
losses, when your parents go. Even when you're not so young
yourself. There's a gap that no one's going to fill." He was
looking at me with soft brown eyes. "But you've got to look
at it this way. It's sad for you, but it isn't for him, you know.
He's just gone from a nasty day like this—" he pointed to the
grey cloud-dark street— "and moved into a beautiful one.
That's what it means for him. If you think of him, there's
nothing to be sad about."

I didn't want to answer. The vicar was kind and full of

faith. Young Charles, I was thinking, might have called him sweet.

I went on to say that, if it could be managed, we should like the funeral in two days' time, on Friday. "Excuse me, sir," said the vicar, "but could you say, have you any connection with this parish?"

That took me aback. Without thinking, I hadn't been prepared for it. My mother, hanging onto the last thread of status after my father's bankruptcy: her stall at the bazaar, her place at the mothers' meeting: she had felt herself, and made others feel her, a figure in that church until she died. Yet that was long ago. He had never heard of her, or of any of us. When I mentioned my name, it had meant nothing at all.

Of course, he said (both of us embarrassed, as I began lamely to produce the family credentials), he would be glad to take the funeral. Was there anything special that I required? A musical service? An organist? Once more that day I found myself thinking, as simply as my mother would have done, of what the old man might have "liked." He had loved music: yes, we would have an organist. In that case, said the vicar, the service couldn't happen till early evening on Friday, when the "lady who plays the organ for us" got out of work. They couldn't afford a regular organist nowadays, he said: the church was poorer than it had been when I lived here, not many people attended, there were no well-to-do members of his congregation. The only one in my time (at least he seemed well-to-do to us) would have been the local doctor. "The present doctors don't come to church," said the vicar, with his switched-on acceptant smile.

As I left his house, it was like walking home when I was a child. The church might have become poorer, but the houses —though many of them were the same houses—looked more prosperous: in front of several of them, cars were standing, which, when my mother and I walked that quarter of a mile from church, we never saw. One of my father's neighbors was trimming the patch of grass between his front wall and the road. Others glanced at me from their windows: they must have known my father, at least by sight, but not me.

As soon as I got back to Mr. Sperry, he asked me, in his obsessive considerate fashion, what I would care to do until the undertaker came. Without knowing why, I said that perhaps I could sit in the garden for a few minutes. At once Mr. Sperry let me out, past the barren plum tree which Charles had seen from his grandfather's window, through the paved yard, down the steps into the garden. There, from a little shed, Mr. Sperry brought out a deck-chair, and said that he would call me when the undertaker arrived. For the second time, not exactly timidly but like one to whom physical contact didn't come easy, he touched my arm.

I knew the geography of that garden as well as that of ours at home, which in fact I could see over a couple of low walls, not more than thirty yards away: the apple-trees had been cut down, under whose shade I used to sit reading on summer nights like this. Aunt Milly's garden had always been better kept than ours, thanks to the devotion of her husband. It was this one I had been reminding Martin of, when we returned to the Gearys' after that lawyers' dinner in the middle of the trial. It occurred to me that, since I ceased to be poor, I hadn't had a garden of my own to sit in: that was a luxury (the thought might have pleased my mother) which I had enjoyed only in our bankrupt house.

In the moist air, the smells of the night stocks and roses were so dense that they seemed palpable. For, though Aunt Milly's husband had been a conscientious gardener, Mr. Sperry was a master: which, now I had watched him in action, didn't surprise me. But I couldn't remember seeing a garden of this size so rich. Phlox, lupins, delphiniums, pinks on the border, rambler-roses on the wall: a syringa-bush close to the bed of stocks. The scents hung all round me, like the scents of childhood.

From my chair, looking up at the house, I could see the French windows of my father's room. They stood dark-faced, the curtains drawn since that morning. It was up the steps to those French windows that I had led Charles, over a year before. I should not go up that way again.

FORTY-ONE

ANOTHER FUNERAL

Sunlight shining on the lacquer, the empty hearse stood outside the church. Martin's car, and the one that I had hired, were drawn up in line. We had arrived early, and had been waiting on the pavement, near the iron palings which guarded a yew tree and the 1908 red brick. Irene and her daughter were wearing black dresses, and Margaret was in grey: Martin, Pat, Charles, and I had all put on black ties. The Sperrys, though, who had just walked slowly along the road from what used to be my father's house, were in full mourning, or at least in clothes such as I remembered at funerals in this church, he in a black suit with an additional, and almost indistinguishable armband, she in jet from her hat to her shoes. As they passed us, they said a few soft words.

One or two other people were approaching, perhaps members of his old choir, who had sent a wreath. The solitary cracked bell began to toll, and I took Margaret, our feet scuffling on the gravel (was that sensation familiar to Martin too?) towards the church door. The pitchpine. The smell of wax and hassocks. The varnished chairs. In my mother's heyday, we used to stop at a row immediately behind the churchwarden's, which she had appropriated for her own. But we couldn't now, since the church, small as it was, was full of empty space. There were the undertaker and his four bearers. The Sperrys. The seven of the family, walking up the aisle.

473

Three others. I didn't know, but it might have been about the size of the congregation on Sunday mornings nowadays. With the organ playing, we moved up to the second row: there, all of us except Margaret having been drilled in anglican customs, we pulled out the hassocks and went down on our knees. It was a long time since I had been to any kind of service, longer still to a church funeral. On its trestle behind the altar-rails, the coffin rested, wreath-covered, brass-handled, short, unobtrusive.

While the organ went on playing, I glanced at the hymn board, record of last Sunday's evensong, and began mechanically—as though the boyhood habit hadn't been interrupted by a week, organ music booming on lulled but uncomprehending ears—juggling with the numbers in my head. Once that game had made the time go faster, helping on the benediction.

The vestry door had opened and shut: the vicar was standing in front of the altar. His voice was as strong as the Clerk of Assize's at the trial, without effort filling the empty church.

I am the resurrection and the life, saith the Lord: he that believeth in me, though he were dead, yet shall he live: and whosoever liveth and believeth in me shall never die.

At one time I knew those words by heart. I couldn't have told whether I was listening now.

We brought nothing into this world, and it is certain we can carry nothing out. The Lord gave, and the Lord hath taken away: blessed be the name of the Lord.

I couldn't have told whether I was listening now. Even at Sheila's funeral, my first wife's, though I was ill with misery, I couldn't concentrate, I was dissociated from the beautiful clerical voice—and yes, from the coffin resting there. Yet this time I half-heard, *It is certain we can carry nothing out.* Just for an instant, I had a thought about my father. I wondered if the same had come to Martin, whom I had told about his possessions. No one had had much less to carry out.

For a thousand years in thy sight are but as yesterday: seeing that is past as a watch in the night.

In the morning it is green, and groweth up: but in the evening it is cut down, dried and withered.

For when thou art angry, all our days are gone: we bring our years to an end, as it were a tale that is told.

The days of our age are three-score years and ten: and though men be so strong, that they come to fourscore years: yet is their strength then but labor and sorrow, so soon passeth it away, and we are gone.

That was being said over my father in his late eighties. It must have been said also at the funeral of Eric Mawby, aged eight.

First Corinthians Fifteen. By this time I was scarcely trying to listen, or even to follow the words in my prayer book. At school I had studied Corinthians for an examination, and I couldn't keep my mind from drifting to my father's forebears, who had listened to that passage, there was no escaping it, generation after generation for hundreds of years.

The last enemy that shall be destroyed is death.

Not my grandfather. That deep Victorian agnostic had never been inside a church after he left school at the age of ten. Yet—one couldn't trust a child's memory, I might be romanticizing him, but I didn't think so—he was pious as well as agnostic, he had a library of nineteenth-century religious controversy, and then decided, just as Martin might have done, that he didn't believe where he couldn't believe. He would have made a good nineteenth-century Russian. I was sure, and here I did trust my memory, that he was a clever man. He would have got on with his grandchildren and with Charles.

What advantageth it me, if the dead rise not? Let us eat and drink, for tomorrow we die.

But his father and grandfather: they hadn't had the education he had hacked out for himself. He believed, he told me when I was five and could read quite well, that that was more than they could do. So far as he knew, his grandfather could only make his mark. Yet, he insisted, they were strong intelligent men. He was bitter about them, and the muteness from which they came. Small craftsmen one generation: then back to agricultural laborers (not peasants, for England had had no peasants for long enough), no history, no change, further back than the church registers went. There was none of the social moving, the ups and downs, that had happened on my mother's side. The Eliot families must have gone to the funeral services in the village churches, and listened to this Pauline eloquence for at least a dozen generations. Some of that gene-pool was in us. Gone stoically, most of them, I thought. As with us, phrases stuck in their memories. As with me as a child, the rabbinical argumentation washed over them.

Death is swallowed up in victory. O death, where is thy sting? O grave, where is thy victory? The sting of death is sin: and the strength of sin is the law.

How old was I when I first became puzzled by that last gnomic phrase? We had all listened to it, the whole line of us, life after life, so many lives, lost and untraceable now.

The vicar led the way out of church: following him, the bearers' shoulders were firm under the coffin. Margaret and I walked behind, then Martin and Irene, then the grandchildren. As the coffin was slid into the hearse, windows so clear that there might have been no glass there, the undertaker stood by, rubicund, content that all was in order, holding his top hat in a black gloved hand. "Easy on," muttered one of the bearers at the last shove.

Slowly the little procession of cars drove down the side street into the main road. On the pavement people passed casually along, but one old man stopped in his walk and took off his hat. The parish church, being so new, had never had a graveyard: and in fact all the parish graveyards in the town had been full for years. My mother had been buried in the big municipal cemetery, and it was there, along the sunny bus route, cars rushing towards us and the suburbs, that we were driving. But my mother, as she had died young, had not arranged to reserve a grave beside her: and that was a matter to which my father would not have given a thought. So his coffin was carried to the opposite side of the great cemetery, new headstones glaring in the sun, flower vases twinkling, angels, crosses, such a profusion of the signs of death that it gave an extra anonymity to death itself: as in one of the wartime collective graves, where all that one took in was that the victims of a siege were buried here.

In a far corner, a neat rectangle had been marked out, and below the edge of turf one could see the fresh brown earth. Wreaths away, coffin lowered (again one of the bearers muttered), and we stood round.

There were no prayer books to follow now. Rich voice in the hot evening.

Man that is born of a woman hath but a short time to live, and is full of misery.

In the midst of life we are in death.

I had noticed which of the bearers was holding bits of earth in hand. At the end of the appeal he was waiting to hear *Suffer us not, at our last hours, for any pains of death, to fall from them.* Promptly he stepped forward and, with a couple of flicks, threw down the earth upon the coffin.

Opposite to me, across the grave, Charles's mouth suddenly tightened. He had not heard that final sound before.

For as much as it hath pleased Almighty God of his great mercy to take unto himself the soul of our dear brother Herbert Edward here departed: we therefore commit his body to the ground; earth to earth, ashes to ashes, dust to dust, in sure and certain hope of the Resurrection to eternal life . . . the voice went on, it was soon all over, the collect and the bless-ing.

We were very near one entrance to the cemetery, and be-fore long were standing there, shaking hands. Our voices, which had been so subdued as we waited for the bell to toll and on the road to the cemetery, suddenly became loud. I heard Martin's, usually quiet, sound hearty as he thanked the vicar. I shook hands with the undertaker and the bearers, one of whom kept rubbing his hand on his trousers, as though he couldn't get rid of the last particle of earth. Margaret was telling the Sperrys, once again, how grateful we were for their kindness.

Thanks given and regiven, we stood about, not knowing what to do. No one wanted to make a move. Pat's face, more labile than any of ours, was suiting itself to sadness, just as it did to a party. Charles, tall by his cousin's side, politely an-swered questions from Mr. Sperry. The truth was, we were at a loss. I had made a mistake, or forgotten something. After funerals such as this, my mother and her friends had always departed to a meal, spending on it often much more than they could afford. Singular meals, so far as I remembered— ham, chicken (bought for this special occasion) , blancmanges, jellies, cakes. Port wine. When I was Charles's age, that seemed to me as naïve as it would to him. Yet maybe it was wise. It made an end. As we stood about at the ceme-tery gate, this was no sort of end.

Glancing round with bright apprehensive eyes (the same treacle-brown eyes that one could see in her son and daughter), Irene said:

"Well, perhaps we ought to be thinking of—" her voice trailed off.

Martin, once more over-hearty, was saying to the Sperrys: "Now are you all right for transport? Are you sure you're all right? Or else I can get you home—" The vicar and the un-dertaker assured him that they had room for the Sperrys.

More thanks. At last that party moved towards the hearse, and we to our own cars. My niece said to me, through the hair which obscured half her face: "That's over, isn't it, Uncle Lewis?" She might have said it by way of comfort. Charles, who was walking with her, flashed me a hard and searching look, as though I had mismanaged things.

FORTY-TWO

A BIT OF NEWS

We were all staying at the hotel which Martin had used during the trial. There were too many of us to go to friends: and in fact, we shouldn't have chosen to. Without a word passed between us, Martin and I hadn't wanted to see a person we knew on this last family occasion in the town. Let it be as obscure as the old occasions. The local paper had printed a one-inch paragraph about our father's death, and that was all.

As our party was walking past the reception desk towards the lifts, Martin hung behind.

"Get down before the rest, for a few minutes," he said to me, very quietly.

"Where?"

"Oh, the old bar."

It was the bar, aquarium-lit, in which he had spoken to me with pain and ruthlessness in the middle of the trial. I was down a little before him, and when he entered and we looked at each other, I hadn't forgotten and knew that nor had he. This time the bar was emptier: it was later, the pre-dinner drinkers had sifted away. Just one single acquaintance called out to Martin: "You here again?" Here again, Martin, affably, impersonally, called back.

The alcove, where we had talked before, was vacant. We sat ourselves there, and I asked him what he would drink. No, he said, the drinks were on him. As he carried them to our table, I watched his face, set, controlled: yet somehow, as I had seen once or twice in his life, it was illuminated from within, like one of the turnip heads in which we used to place candles when we were boys.

"I have a bit of news," he said.

"Yes."

"Pat is going to get married."

"Is he, by God?"

Then I asked, who to: but I thought I knew.

"Muriel. Roy Calvert's Muriel."

Martin was so happy that I had to be happy for him. I said, using our own cipher, well, Pat might have done worse.

"He might have done worse," said Martin, all cautiousness gone.

It would have seemed strange thirty years before, I said, to think of his son marrying Roy Calvert's daughter. Actually (though I didn't bring it back to mind) he and Roy had never been more than acquaintances. If Roy were alive now, he would have been fifty-three.

"It's hard to imagine him like that, isn't it?" said Martin.

"Anyway, you're obviously glad."

"I'm very glad."

The engagement would be announced the following Monday, he said. He didn't want any mention of it at dinner that night.

"Why ever not?"

He shook his head.

"Whatever could be more natural?" I meant, an old man dies, his grandson gets married: after all that we had said, and felt, in this alcove a few weeks before, we were back in the flow of things. It mightn't be very grand: there was the splendid, of which we had seen a little, there was the hideous, of which we had seen enough: yet this was neither, it was what we lived in, in order to endure.

"I don't think Irene would like it," he said.

Well, I said, he knew his wife better than I did. But didn't he remember her at the Christmas Eve party, shouting out birth, copulation, children, death, as though that was the biography of us all?

"At that party," Martin broke in, "you knew what we were in for? About the trial?"

"I had an idea."

"I only realized later that you must have done."

He went back to talking of Irene.

"She's more conventional than I am, you know."

That sounded strange, after the life she had led. But he was certain. She wouldn't consider it proper to celebrate an engagement on the day that we had buried our father.

"Also," he added, "I don't think she's too happy about the marriage, anyway."

In that case, I said, she was pretty hard to please. The girl was attractive: she was said to be clever, not surprising for Roy's daughter: she had a small fortune of her own. They wouldn't have to support Pat any further, presumably. Martin, with a brotherly grin, said he had thought of that.

"To be perfectly honest," I said, "I'm surprised you didn't get more obstruction from the other side."

"The young woman," said Martin, "made up her mind."

He added:

"But still, Irene doesn't really like it." He shrugged. "That doesn't count. It's going to happen soon."

"When?"

"Very soon. In about a month."

"What's the hurry?"

Martin smiled. After a moment, he said, off-hand:

"Oh, the good old-fashioned reason." His smile spread, masculine, lubricious, paternal. He gazed across the table: "In any case, it's time there was another generation."

He explained, he explained with elaborate detail, that they had been planning to marry weeks before she became preg-

nant—they were already planning it when we sat in the
Gearys' garden and he warned me about Vicky (whose name
had not been mentioned in our alcove that night), and some
time before that. All the while Pat had been in some sort of
conflict with his father, and still so intimate that Martin
knew it all. Again I thought, it takes two to make a possessive
love. Pat might be one of the more undesirable of sons, but he
wanted his father. Whereas, if Martin had had Charles for a
son, he would have been spared most of the suffering, and
found that the son had slipped away.

That night in the Gearys' garden, Martin had—in the
midst of all that had gone wrong—been sustained by a kind of
content. Talking to me in the alcove, the night after the funeral, he felt more than content, he felt sheer simple joy.

"It will be the making of him," he repeated. No one could
have thought Martin a simple man. What he had been saying
to me, over the past weeks, wasn't simple: it wasn't comfortable, it didn't leave him much, or me either. He meant it, he
continued to believe it, it was what he had to say. Yet that
night he was full of joy, because of one of the simplest of all
things.